PRAISE FOR THE AUTHOR

"Richard Phillips has led such a life that he absolutely nails the science aspect of this new sci-fi classic [*Immune* (Book Two of the Rho Agenda)] and yet also gets the action and the political aspects exactly right as well. Speaking as an old sci-fi writer myself, I know how hard it is to do what Phillips has done. . . . I've read *Immune* to its brilliant and completely satisfying end—but only because this new writer is so skillful and this storyline is so inventive and moving that I don't want to miss a chapter of it. . . . As good as any science fiction being written today."

—Orson Scott Card

THE
ALTREIAN
ENIGMA

THE RHO AGENDA ASSIMILATION

○ ● ○

BOOK TWO

Also by Richard Phillips

The Rho Agenda

The Second Ship
Immune
Wormhole

The Rho Agenda Inception

Once Dead
Dead Wrong
Dead Shift

The Rho Agenda Assimilation

The Kasari Nexus

THE
ALTREIAN
ENIGMA

THE RHO AGENDA ASSIMILATION

O ● O

BOOK TWO

RICHARD
PHILLIPS

Text copyright © 2016 Richard Phillips

Published by 47North, Seattle

www.apub.com

Amazon, the Amazon logo, and 47North are trademarks of Amazon.com, Inc., or its affiliates.

ISBN-13: 9781503935273
ISBN-10: 1503935272

Cover design by Shasti O'Leary Soudant

Printed in the United States of America

I dedicate this novel to my lovely wife, Carol, who has been my best friend and companion for thirty-five years.

• QUOL •

Intelligence:	Dhaldric, Khyre	Star system:	Altreia
Population:	1.2 Billion	Previous state:	Enemy
Assimilation:	0%	Threat level:	Extreme

• VIEW OPTIONS •
☒ Label features
☒ Key targets
☐ Population density

• RENDER •
☒ Terrain
☒ Atmosphere
☒ Background stars
☐ Current cloud cover

:PROLOGUE

As the bitter winter wind howls through the night, attempting to prevent me from entering the cavern housing the Altar of the Gods, its chill pulls my breath forth in smoky puffs that I barely notice. I crawl through the opening, light a torch that I take from its wall sconce, and allow my feet to carry me through the passage that leads to the altar. There my footsteps halt.

The beautiful golden orb that graces the end of the Incan Sun Staff captures my gaze. Its intricately carved rings and complex arrangement of gears and shafts that form its inner workings hold me in a spell that I am unable to break. With my gaze locked to the symbols that cry out to be rearranged, a slow boiling fear floods my soul. Even as I stand alone, frozen in terror, in thrall to this wonder of wonders that rests atop the altar, I feel my hands move toward the orb of their own volition.

The touch of the staff sends a strange current through my body, and the feel of the golden metal beneath my fingertips shifts my perspective and causes the cavern to shrink around me until I can see myself. It is as if I have become the cavern and everything within it. The thing in my head screams in a way that I have only heard in my dreams, and my body shakes like *the boughs of the trees out in that howling wind. Yet my hands continue to stroke the orb.*

Now they twist it, first the bottom ring, aligning the symbols with new counterparts on the silver staff, before skipping up several rings to repeat the process. And as my hands turn ring after ring in a seemingly random order, the intricate engravings grab the torchlight so that its flames crawl across the golden surface and into the orb's interior.

Shaking uncontrollably, my hands nevertheless turn the penultimate ring until all the symbols feel wrongly right, so much of the torchlight now absorbed by the orb that the cavern grows dark around me.

My right hand now wraps the last of the rings in a death grip as my left hand clutches the silver staff; the muscles in my hands and arms bulge and slither beneath my skin as they war with each other for control. Cold, more deadly than ice, slides through my veins and into my chest, cramping my lungs, on its way to my heart. Then with a final convulsion, my fingers twitch, imparting to the topmost ring one last shift. As the golden orb pulses with power, a doorway slides open at my feet.

It summons me forward, down the metallic ramp that leads into a large chamber illuminated with a soft magenta glow. As I step into the room, the knowledge that this place was not built by the hands of men is absolute. And at its center, five translucent pedestals rise from the floor as if extruded from the end of a glassblower's pipe, molded into the form of chairs.

The recognition of this place floods into me from the being who shares my mind. I stand inside a massive alien research craft, sent here centuries ago with a dual purpose: to conduct a scientific mission to observe and record humanity's advancement and, should humans adopt the banned wormhole technologies of the Kasari Collective, to summon a planet killer to cleanse Earth of all life before it can be completely assimilated.

:CHAPTER 1

Jack Gregory opened his eyes, exiting the dream that wasn't a dream. He didn't dream anymore. Not like ordinary people. Instead, these strange lucid visions now dominated his sleep.

This latest one had recurred nightly since Jack, Janet, and their eight-year-old son, Robby, had accompanied Mark and Heather Smythe on their flight from Peru to the couple's secret facility in New Zealand. Jack rolled onto his left side, placing his right arm over Janet's naked body. She sighed softly and snuggled into him without waking. That was good. He didn't want to inflict his sleepless nights on his wife.

In this vision, he once again stood in the altar cavern beneath the Kalasasaya Temple in Bolivia. And the space looked exactly the same as the last time Jack stood inside it, except that he now stood alone in the torch-lit chamber instead of locked in a death match with the neo-Nazi albino, Dolf Gruenberg. Jack should have felt comforted by the memory of the explosion that had collapsed the cavern, burying the Incan Sun Staff and the altar atop which it had been mounted. But he knew that no amount of crashing rock could destroy the Altreian artifact or the monstrous craft that rested beneath it. And being buried beneath tons of rock wouldn't prevent the thing from accomplishing its ultimate purpose should humanity pull the trigger.

Years before, as he bled out in a Calcutta clinic, Jack had accepted the alien mind into his brain for one more chance at life. Jack had no doubt about why that banished Altreian being, known as Khal Teth, was amping up the threatening nature of these visions.

Humanity's life span was growing short, and there was only one way to prevent the coming catastrophe.

Unfortunately, that would require Jack giving up everything he loved. As he pulled Janet's body more tightly against his own, he gritted his teeth. Even though she and his friends would doubtless think he'd lost his mind, Jack could no longer delay the inevitable.

It was time to honor the bargain he'd made.

○ ● ○

Having just donned her black yoga outfit, Janet Price stared into Jack's brown eyes, too stunned by the words that had just spilled from his lips to fully process them. When he had stepped up behind her, clad only in his jeans, and taken her in his arms, she'd thought he was trying to seduce her away from her morning workout. But the sadness in his eyes told her something very different. That look, combined with his words, froze her heart inside her chest.

"You're not leaving me behind," she said, her voice having dropped so low she didn't recognize it. "I won't let you."

"Where I have to go, you can't follow."

"Bullshit!"

The hurt in Jack's eyes tried to rob Janet of her sudden fury but failed. He sat down on the edge of the bathtub.

"I had the dream again, but this time, it was worse."

Janet found herself sitting beside him without realizing that she'd moved, a profound sense of dread having doused her anger. A decade ago, when the NSA director, Admiral Jonathan Riles, sent her to Germany to convince the ex-CIA assassin known as "The Ripper" to join her black-ops team, she learned that there was something strange about Jack. That first mission had taken them through Europe and into the heart of Kazakhstan. But in Bolivia, in the cavern beneath the Kalasasaya Temple, she became convinced that Jack had lost his mind.

Three months later, during a raid that stopped the Chinese assassin, Qiang Chu, from releasing a rogue artificial intelligence on the world, Jack convinced her that he shared his mind with an alien being who called himself Khal Teth. Back then, she helped Jack block out the disturbing influence that threatened his sanity.

But six months ago, in her desperation to rescue their eight-year-old son, Robby, Janet had begged Jack to unleash that alien presence once more, knowing the risks.

Janet swallowed hard and said what she didn't want to. "Go on."

In the excruciating half hour that followed, as she listened to what Jack had to tell her, Janet's dread found its source.

O ● O

Deep inside the abandoned New Zealand gold mine that he and Heather had transformed into their secret compound, Mark Smythe watched as an army of robots worked on expansion. He glanced over at Heather, who stood beside him on the platform overlooking the central manufacturing hub.

At twenty-seven, his wife was more beautiful than ever, radiating power in a way that he found incredibly sexy. If anyone could save the world from the Kasari invaders that would soon come through the gateway that the United Federation of Nation States was building, it was his beautiful savant.

To think how far they'd come from the little Los Alamos, New Mexico, bedroom community of White Rock, where they'd grown up next door to each other and been best friends long before they were lovers. Their life had been low-key, comfortable, blown sky-high when they had stumbled onto the crashed Altreian starship and put on the alien headsets. Not only had the devices linked their minds to the starship's computer, revealing the intragalactic warfare between the Altreians and the Kasari Collective, but the three headbands had altered Mark, Heather, and Jennifer in different ways. A year and a half later, Jack and Janet's baby, Robby, accidentally slipped the fourth of the Altreian headsets over his temples and underwent a similar transformation.

As Mark looked at his wife, he knew that he wouldn't have chosen a different path, despite the horrors they had been through.

He redirected his gaze across the thirty-thousand-square-foot room that they had hollowed out of the bedrock a mile beneath New Zealand's Tasman District. What was happening inside the facility had never before been achieved on Earth.

They had created this broad variety of robots from Heather's designs. They weren't artificially intelligent but could be remotely controlled through virtual-reality headsets. And whatever task the operator performed using the robot's body, the robot learned. Not just that robot either. The knowledge was uploaded to the supercomputer network, where it could then be downloaded to other robots. During the last several years, the automatons had learned to build and operate everything within the compound, including the manufacture of new robots.

Since Mark and Heather had returned to their New Zealand compound, accompanied by Jack, Janet, and Robby, the pace of construction had reached an exponential tipping point. The automated systems now only needed new tasks to perform, something that Heather excelled at doling out. And as she did so, the designs produced by her augmented savant mind grew more and more advanced.

Once finished, the room would house sixteen large-scale additive-manufacturing machines, also known as 3-D printers, capable of producing the next generation of devices and components needed for the fight that they both knew was coming. Among her latest innovations, Heather had designed a series of micro-bots that weren't quite self-organizing nano-materials but perhaps the next best thing.

Swarms of these mite-sized bots could be directed to create or modify electrical channels down to the circuit-board level. The micro-bots could cut through insulation or interconnect to create new conductive paths, adding an enormously useful capability to Heather's growing robotic manufacturing toolkit.

While the rapidly increasing power demands would have placed a strain on the original pair of cold-fusion reactors, the redundant array of matter disrupter-synthesizers or MDSs barely noticed the load. Considering the pace at which Heather's plans were coming to fruition, that was a good thing.

The warble of Heather's quantum-entangled phone brought Mark's mind back to the present. Seeing her smile fade, Mark felt concern replace the satisfaction he'd experienced only moments before. She hung up and turned to him, raising her voice to be heard above the clamor of ongoing construction.

"Janet wants us topside right away. Something's going on with Jack. From her tone, it's not good."

For a moment, Heather's eyes turned milky white, as they often did when one of her savant visions consumed her. That didn't surprise him, but he was taken aback when she broke into a run toward the elevator.

Mark, making use of his augmented speed, sprinted after her, reaching her side just as she pressed the call button. The elevator door whisked open, and they stepped inside the waiting car. The space was industrial sized, capable of carrying any of the equipment that was brought to or from this level, big enough to make him feel small.

Heather punched the button for the top level, the doors whisked closed, and the car accelerated upward. Despite the speed at which the electromagnetic drive propelled the elevator, the trip to the surface took almost five minutes, Mark's ears popping several times along the way.

Whatever had happened, he had no doubt that it involved that otherworldly weirdness that draped Jack "The Ripper" Gregory like an aura. A decade ago, that force had ruled their lives for two and a half years. And now, as Earth spiraled toward its destruction, that part of Jack had once again been summoned. A crazy thought.

The muscles in Mark's arms and back tensed. He pulled forth the perfect memory of how he felt in deep meditation, letting it wash away the tension. But the technique failed to cleanse his mind.

○ ● ○

Janet heard the door open and turned from Jack to see Mark and Heather enter the small conference room. As Heather took her seat at the table, she asked the question that Janet had been expecting.

"What's going on?"

Janet turned to Jack, struggling to keep her expression from showing the emotions that churned beneath the surface. "Tell them."

Jack's chiseled face showed no hint of what Janet knew he was feeling, but a chill had crept into his voice.

"Last night I had another of my lucid dreams."

"The Incan Sun Staff," said Heather.

"This was different. I know what it does."

"You've already convinced us that the Sun Staff is important," Mark said. "It's why we've funded the Kalasasaya dig to retrieve it."

Janet watched as Jack shifted his gaze from Mark to Heather.

"It opens a portal into an enormous Altreian research vessel buried beneath the Kalasasaya Temple."

"You think another Altreian starship crashed in Bolivia?" Mark asked.

"The vessel that lies beneath the Kalasasaya Temple arrived centuries ago, but it didn't crash," Jack replied.

"What's it been doing all this time? Hanging out?"

Jack's eyes narrowed, a clear indication that he didn't like the tone of Mark's question. But Janet couldn't blame Mark. She didn't want to believe it either.

"I don't know," Jack said, "but I do know what it's going to do if I don't stop it."

Heather leaned forward to rest her elbows on the conference table. Janet hadn't seen her eyes turn white. Jack clearly had her complete attention.

"Tell me."

Again Janet saw the rigidity in Jack's body as she watched the muscles move beneath his skin.

"If the wormhole gateway that the UFNS is building goes active and the Kasari come through, the buried Altreian vessel will summon an Altreian planet killer to destroy all life on Earth before the Kasari can bring through enough military might to prevent that."

"If that's true," said Mark, "why didn't it summon the planet killer when Dr. Stephenson's gate opened a wormhole and the Kasari came through?"

"Hell, I don't know," said Jack. "Maybe because you nuked it."

"We didn't find any reference to a planet killer in the Second Ship's database," Heather said.

"No, but you found planets that had once hosted intelligent life that are now lifeless," said Jack. "It's possible that the ship is still denying you and Mark access to parts of its database."

"That's . . . possible," said Heather.

"Jack," said Janet, no longer able to restrain herself, "Khal Teth's trying to manipulate you through your dreams, showing you what he wants you to see in order to get you to fulfill your bargain."

Jack shook his head. "I would sense if he was lying to me."

"You can't be sure of that."

"I am."

Janet leaned back in her chair, feeling her temples throb.

"Wouldn't Eos have told Robby if the Altreians had sent another starship to Earth?" Mark asked.

The mention of the Altreian AI that had fled from the Second Ship's computer into Robby's mind didn't improve Janet's mood.

"Eos shares Robby's mind," Heather said, "but it no longer has access to the Altreian starship's database."

"Unless Robby puts on his Altreian headset and performs a specific query," said Mark.

Heather brightened at the suggestion. "That could work."

A sudden glimmer of hope caused Janet to lean forward. "And if Eos doesn't find anything to confirm your dream, that would mean—"

"Nothing," Jack said, "except that the information about the Altreian research vessel isn't stored in the Second Ship's database."

Janet placed her hand atop his and squeezed hard.

"Before we start down this path, I want you to explain to our son exactly what Khal Teth wants from you," Janet said, swallowing hard, "and why he'll never see his dad again if you go through with it."

Jack's brown eyes met hers, and for a moment she thought she saw the familiar red glint within his pupils. And as he gently returned her squeeze, the subtle gesture brought moisture to her eyes that she blinked away.

Dear God, don't you dare take him away from me.

:CHAPTER 2

Wearing a dark-gray Italian suit, Alexandr Prokorov walked through the broad tunnel, ignoring the incessant dripping of condensation from the concrete ceiling, just as he ignored the smell of mildew and the chill in the dank corridor. Beside him strode Dr. Lana Fitzpatrick, the U.S. undersecretary for science and energy. This being her first trip to the construction site of the wormhole gate that the United Federation of Nation States had dubbed the Friendship Gate, her deep discomfort at the subterranean environment showed in her tight body language. She jerked involuntarily at the sound of each drip, twitching at the echo of their footsteps as they walked along the passage.

Ahead, the tunnel suddenly widened into a yawning space that would have dwarfed the Large Hadron Collider's ATLAS cavern. Prokorov heard Lana gasp at the sight. He had to admit that it still sent a shiver of excitement up his spine each time he entered the chamber. Inside, thousands of workers, scientists, and engineers scurried about as their supervisors pressed them to get the project back on schedule.

Eight years ago, the building of the Stephenson Gateway had broken all records for such complex construction. But Dr. Stephenson had suffered from a series of constraints that this project didn't have. First of all, the size of the ATLAS cavern, enormous as it was, hadn't allowed for the matter disrupter to be placed adjacent to the wormhole gate that it powered. That had meant that extensive superconductive cabling had to be routed inside from an external power source, slowing down the construction.

But this wasn't the only advantage that the current construction project had over the original Stephenson Gateway project. Technological advances in materials and computing allowed for extensive miniaturization and optimization techniques that reduced the overall size of the project.

Prokorov continued his advance toward the inverted-horseshoe-shaped gate within which the wormhole would be created. The program's top scientist, Dr. John Guo, stood within its arch. At five feet four inches tall, the dark-haired Chinese man exuded an energy that made him seem larger than those gathered around him, and his pointed gestures indicated that he was far from satisfied with their efforts.

As Prokorov and Dr. Fitzpatrick approached, Dr. Guo dismissed those with whom he had been remonstrating and turned to meet the new arrivals.

"Aaah, Minister Prokorov," he said, his English free of any identifiable accent. "I was informed of your arrival. How was your journey from The Hague?"

"Uneventful," Prokorov said before turning toward his companion. "This is Dr. Lana Fitzpatrick, the U.S. undersecretary of science and energy."

Dr. Guo raised an eyebrow as he shifted his gaze toward the blond American scientist. Something in his fleeting expression gave Prokorov the sense that these two had more than a passing familiarity. He would check into his hunch at a later date.

"It's good to see you again, John," Dr. Fitzpatrick said, extending her hand.

Dr. Guo took it and returned the smile, although his face held none of the warmth hers offered. "Always a pleasure."

"I wasn't aware the two of you knew each other," Prokorov said.

Dr. Fitzpatrick's blue eyes narrowed ever so slightly. "We worked together for a time at Lawrence Livermore National Laboratory. But that was a long time ago."

As, clearly, neither scientist wanted to offer up more than fleeting glimpses into their past relationship, Prokorov shifted topics to the one he was interested in.

"So, walk me through the progress your team has made in recovering from this latest incident."

Dr. Guo's already-dour expression turned grimmer. "I already sent you my update."

"I read it. That's why I've come in person . . .to ensure that you have a true sense of urgency."

The scientist opened his mouth and started to say something, but then, looking directly into Prokorov's eyes, seemed to think better of it.

"Fine. You can see for yourself."

Dr. Guo turned and walked toward the towering piece of machinery that Prokorov recognized as the matter disrupter. It looked somewhat like a gigantic generator that had been stood on its end and wrapped with a lattice of steel scaffolding, seventy yards high. And along the multiple levels of scaffolding, scores of workers moved.

Dr. Guo didn't wait for Prokorov and Dr. Fitzpatrick to catch up with him, proceeding directly to a metal doorway that led into the matter disrupter's interior. He opened the door and stepped through. Prokorov and Dr. Fitzpatrick followed him across the threshold.

The walkway that extended along the outer wall was just wide enough for two people to walk abreast. Oddly shaped tubes and instruments clung to the sides of curved columns that rose up into the dimly lit upper reaches. More passages branched off into the middle of the clustered equipment. Workers were forced to crawl in order to traverse some of the tunnels.

The design had a distinctly alien feel. In these depths, far below the rolling countryside, the construction progressed on an extremely aggressive schedule without all the overly restrictive safety protocols normally required of such a project. But this latest accident had brought that progress to a screeching halt.

For another three minutes, Dr. Guo led them through a maze of increasingly cramped walkways before entering an elevator cage and turning to face his guests, his arms spread in mock welcome. Prokorov stepped in beside the chief scientist, but Dr. Fitzpatrick stopped outside the metal cage, her head tilted back to stare at the cabling that guided the elevator into the heights.

When she looked down, Prokorov saw that the color had drained from her face.

"Is something wrong?" Dr. Guo asked.

Dr. Fitzpatrick cleared her throat. "I'm sorry. I have a thing about heights."

"Get in or stay behind," Prokorov said.

She swallowed hard, straightened, and stepped inside. The cage door closed behind Dr. Fitzpatrick with a clank that sounded like a jail door closing. Prokorov noted the white knuckles on her hand that grasped one of the vertical bars making up the cage's walls.

Dr. Guo pressed a button, and the cage surged upward with an acceleration that made Prokorov's stomach lurch. Beside him, Dr. Fitzpatrick's gasp showed that she regretted her decision to accompany them.

The journey didn't take long. When the cage rattled to a stop, Prokorov guessed that they had risen roughly ten floors, a guess that a downward glance through the steel grating confirmed. Ignoring the wobbling American scientist, he followed Dr. Guo along one of the interconnecting walkways, their shoes clanking on the steel grating and echoing through the conduits that draped the machinery.

An eerie world of cryonic equipment kept the electrical conduits at a temperature cold enough to maintain superconductivity, thus allowing for the transport of tremendous power from the matter disrupter to the wormhole gateway and its stasis field generator. And since the matter disrupter could transform energy into any type of particle, in this case directly into electron-positron pairs, its efficiency was almost 100 percent.

Dr. Guo came to an abrupt halt at a point where the passage gave way to a room-sized open space. The monitors, computers, and controls that had recently lined the room's interior had been reduced to burnt-out scrap. What remained was being piled onto a hand trolley by a dozen technicians who worked to clear debris and repair the damage. From the scowls Prokorov saw on their faces, his surprise inspection wasn't particularly welcome.

Prokorov felt his jaw tighten. "What is this?"

"This," said Dr. Guo, "is what you were too impatient to let me brief you on from the relative safety of the main chamber. Two days ago, the matter disrupter suffered a minor instability ten yards on the other side of that shielding. Since then my people have been working around the clock to fix the problem."

"You mean there was a radioactive leak?" Dr. Fitzpatrick gasped, unconsciously pushing back a strand of her blond hair.

"No, but the matter disrupter proved to be far more efficient than we were prepared for. This damage was caused by a massive electrical power surge." Dr. Guo turned his gaze back on Prokorov. "It's exactly why I warned you against the dangerous pace at which you've been pushing us."

Prokorov ignored the jab. "Describe to me in the simplest terms possible the precise nature of the problem and how you intend to fix it."

"The matter disrupter relies on a wave-packet model of matter. All matter is composed of a harmonic chord of frequencies that combine together to form a stable packet. You can think of it as a three-dimensional standing wave that compresses the underlying fabric of our universe into a tight little vibrating bundle. Some of these wave packets are not completely harmonic and try to dispel the destabilizing frequencies, giving them off as radiation as the packet attempts to achieve a harmonious chord.

"The matter disrupter takes advantage of this phenomenon by adding a destabilizing set of frequencies to the particles at which it is targeted. The ultimate disruption would be to supply a set of frequencies that completely cancels out the particle's wave packet—an anti-packet. But we don't have to supply a complete anti-packet. The proper subset of destabilizing frequencies will make the particle tear itself apart."

Dr. Guo paused to meet Prokorov's gaze.

"You're familiar with the gateway design Dr. Stephenson built in Meyrin, Switzerland. What we are building here is a very different beast, one that incorporates a number of measures intended to prevent any type of external hacking attacks. Chief among these is the requirement that all control programs be physically implemented via circuitry instead of software. And each of those preprogrammed operational modes must be manually switched on and off.

"Normally I would have created a much smaller experimental prototype so that we could work out the design problems that were bound to happen. Since I wasn't allowed to do that, we are now encountering those problems at full scale."

Prokorov gritted his teeth. If he had anyone else with this man's knowledge of the project, he would have replaced Dr. Guo long ago.

"Don't give me excuses. Just stick to the facts."

"The facts are what you see before you. The disrupting wave packet was too perfect and triggered a matter-antimatter reaction that produced the excess energy that killed seven of my top people and did the damage you see before you. Even working around the clock, it will take us six weeks to complete the repairs."

"I want this repair work completed within three weeks."

"What you want is irrelevant. The repairs will be completed as soon as possible and not before."

"Suppose I send some of our top scientists and engineers to help?"

Dr. Guo shrugged. "My people are already familiar with this project. Newcomers would need to be trained on our equipment, and that would just slow us down."

Prokorov turned to look at Dr. Fitzpatrick. "Your thoughts?"

She paused to consider. "I can put together a top-notch group from Los Alamos and Lawrence Livermore National Laboratories and give them a week or so to study the design, construction, and operation of this reactor. Then, when they get here, they won't be coming in cold."

Seeing that Dr. Guo was about to object, Prokorov held up a hand. "Good. Dr. Guo, see that Dr. Fitzpatrick gets all of the pertinent materials. Any questions?"

Prokorov watched as the chief scientist's gaze swung from Dr. Fitzpatrick back to him, the man's expression changing from anger to a neutral stare. Clearly he hadn't expected to be undercut by her, and he didn't like it.

"No."

Prokorov paused, his determination tightening his facial muscles. "Dr. Guo, do not disappoint me again. Second contact will not be kept waiting."

For the first time, he saw fear in the scientist's eyes. As Prokorov turned to walk away, he savored the image.

CHAPTER 3

Robby knew one thing for sure: this had just ruined what should have been a snowy and fun-filled August day in New Zealand. His dad had just sprung something on him that threatened to destroy what little remained of his childhood. After the events that had brought him to this secret complex where the Smythes were preparing for the end of the world, all he really had left of it was his relationship with his mom and dad. Now, if he couldn't prove his dad wrong about the Incan Sun Staff and the alien vessel, Robby could lose him forever.

As horrible as that was, the thought of what such a loss would do to his mom was even worse. She didn't speak a word when Jack sat him down at the kitchen table and spilled his story, but Robby had seen the dread in her eyes.

The revelation that Jack believed there was an alien presence in his head hadn't shocked Robby. The boy shared his own mind with an alien artificial intelligence named Eos, an entity who had been his imaginary friend since he was a baby. Over the years, Eos had developed a relationship with Robby that transcended just an AI presence in his head. She initially referred to herself as the Other, but as he had grown older,

Robby hadn't liked that. So he had renamed her Eos, after the Greek goddess of the dawn. Together, they represented the dawning of a new age. Because of that relationship, it was no stretch of the imagination to believe this part of his dad's story. But Robby wouldn't allow himself to believe the rest.

Thus, Robby now sat in one of the four command-center chairs in a room modeled after the bridge of the Altreian starship that the Smythes had discovered.

On either side of him sat Mark and Heather while Jack and Janet stood watch. Robby still felt odd over beginning to think of his mom and dad as Jack and Janet. But since their escape from Peru, they had finally accepted him as a full-fledged member of the team that was fighting to save Earth from a renewed Kasari invasion. As such, he felt it only right that he refer to them as he would any other team member, even if it drove Janet crazy.

Robby retrieved the U-shaped alien headband from a compartment in his couch's right armrest, paused to stare down at the iridescent three-quarter loop with the small beads at each end, inhaled deeply, then slid the headband into place. As the twin beads settled over his temples, he heard Eos whisper in his mind.

"Are you ready for this?"

"I'm ready," Robby responded.

"No matter what I might discover?"

Robby felt himself swallow, but pulled forth the required answer. "No matter what."

The familiar mental connection with the Second Ship's computer washed over him along with that strange thrill at the incredible knowledge made available to his augmented mind. He remembered initially wondering why these four headsets had been left on the Altreian starship when its crew members were sucked into space after the Rho Ship's weapon punched a hole through the hull. In fact, the Altreian crew members had been able to use their psychic abilities to link their minds to the starship's computer, and only needed to wear the headsets in order to extend the range of their mental connection whenever they left the vessel.

Eos flowed into the Altreian computer system, resuming her original function as the AI that controlled the starship's computer, pulling Robby's mind along with her.

Although Mark and Heather could also connect to the neural net, only Eos had complete access to the database she had been created to manipulate.

Robby felt Mark's and Heather's minds within the Second Ship's computer, but then he shifted his attention back to Eos and let the AI sweep him away into the seemingly infinite trove of data.

Ignoring all that was irrelevant to his current search, Robby found himself drawn into a vision that acquired such reality that it took his breath away. He felt as if he were transported onto a magical holodeck, where all he had to do was think about something and it would appear before him, amazingly detailed in every way—the texture, the smell, the sound his feet made on the surface across which they moved. If he had centered his thoughts on the Quechua village where he'd spent the first few years of his life, the Second Ship would pluck it from his perfect memory and make the stilted huts real.

But right now he was aboard an Altreian research vessel that had just emerged from subspace within a solar system he recognized. The viewpoint left him feeling as if he were a ghost in the starship, observing the five alien occupants from the perspective of the ship itself—more precisely, from the onboard sensors available to its computer.

He sat in a bubble as Neptune's azure-blue orb swept by below him and to his right. He swung beneath Saturn, gasping at the vivid detail of its rings. Even that sight could not compare to the beautiful jewel that grew larger as he swept toward it. Earth.

But, beautiful as the imagery was, Eos was after something else. The scene faded, only to be replaced by fresh imagery of the interior of an

Altreian vessel. Its immensity surprised Robby. This certainly wasn't the Second Ship. Sensing the question that rose in his mind, Eos responded.

"This is the Altreian research vessel *AQ37Z*. The ship you call the Second Ship was carried to Earth inside this ship's cargo bay."

Robby validated her words by his own view of the information stored in the database he and Eos were accessing. The knowledge that the Second Ship was merely a scout craft that was used by the *AQ37Z*'s crew to gather data stunned him.

As he watched, the imagery changed again. Shortly after coming into Earth orbit, research vessel *AQ37Z* had performed a brief transition into subspace before emerging beneath Earth's surface in the Andes. Its reemergence had parted the subsurface rock, triggering a minor earthquake and cracking the ground to reveal a set of caverns and passages. Believing it a sign from their gods, the Incas had built the Kalasasaya Temple atop that sacred spot.

From the information that Eos directed into Robby's mind, he understood that sending such a research craft to newly discovered worlds bearing sentient life-forms was a standard practice for the Altreians. Establish a hidden research outpost to monitor the intelligent species without interfering with its natural development.

Robby studied the imagery of the five Altreian crew members. They were humanoid in appearance, although of two distinctively different races. The *AQ37Z* had four small gray-skinned crew members and a tall captain with red-and-black-mottled skin and pointed ears that lay tight against his skull. The red glint in his black eyes gave the illusion that they burned with an inner fire. There was also something odd about his neck. What was that? Gill slits?

"Yes," Eos responded, although Robby hadn't formed his thoughts into a direct question to her. "The Altreian elite are all of the Dhaldric race that evolved to function in either air or water. They also have psionic abilities that are much stronger than that of the smaller Khyre race that makes up the bulk of the working and military classes.

"When a Khyre is assigned to a starship crew, they are given a crewman's headset. When they first put it on, it connects their minds to the starship's computer, which then alters the brain so that he or she can make that mental connection without having to wear the device. But if they leave the ship and wish to stay connected, they have to put on the headsets in order to extend their mental range."

A sudden realization dawned on Robby. "So that's what the headsets did to Mark, Heather, Jen, and me."

"Yes, although it appears that they also had some unanticipated effects on your human brains."

"How long has the ship been here?"

"Research outpost $AQ37Z$ established its presence on Earth in your calendar year 1141 AD."

Another thought bothered Robby. "Are they immortal?"

"No. Compared to humans, both races live very long lives, but they can die."

Once again the imagery shifted and Robby found himself observing another part of the ship, this area a much smaller chamber containing five cylindrical pods mounted horizontally on waist-high pedestals. He adjusted his perspective, surprised that he was able to do so just by wanting to see the pods from a different angle.

The cylinders were formed of a metal that shifted colors, mostly greens and blues. Displays on the exterior showed the bodies resting within. Five cylinders holding five bodies. Eos's answer came to Robby as he prepared to ask the question.

"This is the same crew you observed in the earlier recording. They spent the vast majority of their time on Earth in suspended animation inside these chrysalis cylinders, only waking every hundred years to analyze the data that was collected during the interim. The research vessel could also trigger an awakening in the event it observed something deemed of critical importance."

Robby considered this. "Why do they call the suspended-animation chambers chrysalis cylinders?"

"They have more than one function. Not only do they act as suspended-animation chambers; if the correct synchronization codes are entered, they can link the minds of people inside separate chambers using subspace communications even more powerful than the Altreian headsets and with far greater range. The minds of those that are thus connected meld together, sharing memories as well as actual thoughts. A chrysalis cylinder can also work as an extreme punishment device, stripping the memories of one placed inside and expelling the mind from the body, trapping it in an alternate-dimensional void."

"Wow! I think I want one."

"No," said Eos, "I don't think that would be a good idea."

Robby had to admit to himself that Eos was probably right. He shifted his thoughts back to the original topic.

"How did the Second Ship end up fighting the Kasari Rho Ship?"

The vision of the bigger Altreian research vessel dissolved into the familiar imagery of the Second Ship battling the Kasari world ship as they hurtled toward Earth. When the Kasari vortex weapon punched a hole through the Second Ship, four small Altreian bodies were sucked out into the void of space as the vessel crashed to Earth. And as it did, Eos's voice narrated.

"Having detected the wormhole that brought the Kasari world ship into this solar system, a wakeup signal was activated and $AQ37Z$'s five crew members were roused from suspended animation. All but the captain boarded the scout craft the Smythes named the Second Ship. Engaging its subspace drive from within the cargo bay, the craft emerged into normal-space to intercept the Kasari starship just beyond Saturn. The subsequent combat resulted in both ships shooting each other down over New Mexico in the year 1948. The U.S. government located the crashed Kasari ship almost immediately and spawned the top-secret Rho Project at Los Alamos National Laboratory in an attempt to reverse engineer its alien technology."

As Robby's mind studied the supporting imagery and data, his heart sank. He had put on the Altreian headset and entered the Second Ship's computer in hopes of disproving his dad's conviction that a dangerous alien craft was buried beneath the Kalasasaya Temple. Instead, everything Eos had shown him so far corroborated parts of that story.

Despite his growing sense of dread, Robby focused on the artifact his dad had called the Incan Sun Staff, instructing Eos to dig deeper into the Altreian research vessel's purpose. Again the data flow intensified, flooding Robby's brain with rapid-fire imagery and contextual knowledge.

One of the visuals showed a member of the Altreian crew presenting the artifact to an ornately robed native. The staff was silver, its six-foot length covered with intricately carved runes. A glittering golden orb was mounted atop the artifact, a complex clockwork mechanism with filigree rings more complicated than any Rubik's Sphere. When twisted, the orb's internal mechanisms produced new symbols around its exterior. If a precise sequence was entered, the staff could be mounted atop its golden altar, allowing a knowledgeable user to open a portal into the research vessel that lay beneath the altar. Having the technology to solve that riddle was a prerequisite for opening the portal.

Unknown to Manco Cápac, the Incan emperor to whom it had been gifted, the intricately etched silver staff and the complex clockwork mechanism that formed its golden-orb crownpiece contained a sophisticated set of sensors that communicated with $AQ37Z$ through a subspace link.

Robby paused to consider this. Nothing in the data he had reviewed indicated that $AQ37Z$ or its crew had ominous intentions toward humanity.

The fact that they had launched the Second Ship to intercept and shoot down the Kasari Rho Ship was a good sign, wasn't it? When Eos was unable to provide an answer to that question, Robby found himself at an impasse. Apparently the information he was searching for hadn't been uploaded into the Second Ship's database.

Robby took a different tack, shifting his focus to Khal Teth, the name his dad had called the Altreian entity who shared his mind. Immediately a storm of historical information filled his consciousness, including a visual image of the convicted Altreian criminal.

Criminal!

That tag and the extensive data file that accompanied it filled Robby's mind with renewed hope.

Overlord Valen Roth and other members of his High Council, a meritocracy consisting of the most powerful psionics from the Dhaldric race, ruled the Altreian Empire from their home world of Quol. Of the thirteen members of the council, Khal Teth was the most gifted. Able to dominate the minds of all save the collective strength of the other dozen, he seethed at the idea that Valen Roth, a lesser mind, ruled as overlord.

Khal Teth had tried to assassinate Valen Roth, but that effort, along with the rest of his coup attempt, had failed. The High Council had sentenced Khal Teth to the harshest of punishments for his crime. His body was placed in suspended animation inside a chrysalis cylinder, his mind wiped of its memories and banished to wander through alternate dimensions for eternity, capable of observation but incapable of experiencing anything he watched.

A vision of that fate formed in Robby's head. The idea of being trapped in a coma-like state for eternity sent a shudder through his body, thoughts ravaged by the unending helplessness that would accompany such imprisonment. Then again, the attempted assassination of any society's leader typically brought harsh punishment. Like any criminal, Khal Teth had chosen his own fate.

There was no information on how Khal Teth had managed to escape that prison by establishing a link with a human mind, and Jack hadn't explained the connection either. But that didn't really matter. Robby now knew that Khal Teth was evil, and had no doubt that the Altreian was attempting to manipulate Jack for his own purposes. Not the conclusive proof Robby was looking for, but close enough.

As Robby and Eos terminated the alien headset's connection to the Second Ship's computer, Robby braced himself for his next task—confronting Jack with the truth about Khal Teth. Surely that would be enough to stop Jack from going through with his plan.

For both Robby and Janet's sake, it had to be.

:CHAPTER 4

The characteristic sizzle and detonation of the Kasari disrupter weapons brought a growl from Jennifer's throat. She knew that this heavy-artillery barrage was preparation for the assault to follow shortly. Despite the shielding provided by the new stasis field generators that had been emplaced at key points along the forward line of General Dgarra's warriors, the protection it provided was far from perfect. The biggest problem was that whenever the stasis shields were engaged, the Koranthian warriors were prevented from firing upon the enemy, allowing the winged Eadric soldiers to advance ever closer to Dgarra's fortifications. And using their wings, the Eadric could advance through the crags and cliffs very rapidly indeed, zipping from one covered battle position to another, taking advantage of the lulls in Koranthian fire.

Thus, at selected locations along Dgarra's lines, the shields would drop to allow the Koranthians to fire their weapons, only to be raised again when the barrage stopped. When this happened, the shields would be lowered at other spots so that the Koranthians could continue to pound the enemy advance.

Ironically, Dr. Donald Stephenson had spent all those years at Los Alamos National Laboratory's Rho Division working to reverse engineer the alien technologies of the same Kasari starship that had carried Jennifer and Raul here to Scion. His work had made possible this alliance of convenience with General Dgarra and his Koranthian warriors. Now, thanks to Raul's cyborg connection to the Rho Ship's neural net, Dgarra's forces had disrupter weapons of their own. That was great for combat at a distance, but when the combatants inevitably merged, the disrupters were worse than useless, far too destructive to be used in the vicinity of one's own forces.

That was fine with Jennifer. As much as she hated the killing that came with warfare, she preferred to look into her enemy's eyes or, in the case of the Kasari gorilla-spiders, to smell the stink of their bodies as she sent them from this existence into the next. If someone had to die, they deserved to see who was killing them instead of being ripped apart or roasted alive by a distant and faceless enemy.

She knew this feeling was irrational. Death was death, no matter how it happened. But she also knew from whom she'd picked up this philosophy. Dgarra. One of the disadvantages of her empathic ability. When she experienced the feelings of another individual too often, those emotions tended to latch on to her like an acquired taste. And as Dgarra's aide-de-camp, she spent the vast majority of her time either in his presence or performing duties as his personal messenger.

Jennifer glanced to her right at the Koranthian general as he looked out through the narrow canyon that led to the nearest of the caverns. At seven feet tall, the leader wasn't particularly big by the standards of his people. But he radiated the charismatic self-confidence and fierce will that had made him a battlefield legend. She could feel his aura radiate from him and into the warriors around him. Such confidence was the reason he had chosen to be at this spot right now. This would be the place on this battlefield where victory or defeat would soon be decided.

She felt her jaws clench at the thought of the Kasari Collective, an empire intent on assimilating other species, making them a part of its hive-mind, as it spread like a virus throughout the galaxy. Although they found many races willing to join the collective, the Koranthians would never yield their fiercely ingrained independence. That left the Kasari and their Eadric allies no choice but to exterminate this warrior race.

A sudden change caused Jennifer to look away from Dgarra. On the far side of the stasis field, thousands of Eadric swept into the gap that lay just beyond as withering fire from their artillery targeted the places in the Koranthian defense that had a clear line of sight to the main assault. That covering fire blasted great gouts of rock from the surrounding mountains and generated rock slides that forced other stasis fields to be raised. During those moments when the volume of Koranthian fire decreased, the Eadric surged forward.

Dgarra issued the command that dropped the protective stasis field in front of him, and Jennifer felt a wave of battle lust spread through the surrounding warriors. To her front the Koranthians opened up with short-range lasers, then switched to their dual-edged war-blades as they met the Eadric charge. Jennifer lunged forward at Dgarra's side, her own war-blade whistling through the cold air as she ducked beneath an Eadric soldier's blaster. Her blade took the arm that held that pistol and then the screaming head above it, sending forth a fountain of nanite-infested Eadric blood.

The screams of rage and pain, the clash of metal, and the roar of battle drowned out the wind that howled through the outcroppings, trying to sweep her from the ledge upon which she fought. She drew upon tremendous effort and focus to direct her augmented senses into the minds of those around her, but in the midst of battle, she managed. Her mind touched the nearest Eadric fighters, divining their intentions as she moved to counter their attempts to target her. Despite the covering laser fire that blasted Eadric flyers from the sky, more were getting through than were being killed.

Jennifer felt an Eadric female aim a pistol toward her and lunged to the side, taking a laser burn high up on her left shoulder. The white-hot pain lanced through her brain, momentarily darkening her vision before she could shunt it into a distant part of her mind.

Jennifer kicked out, launching another Eadric soldier into the female as she once again squeezed the trigger. The laser cut a smoking hole through two winged soldiers but missed Jennifer by six inches. She leaped forward, her descending blade splitting the female soldier's skull down the middle.

To her left and right, Koranthian warriors fell, including Bracken, one of Dgarra's elite guard. Aware of Dgarra's presence, the Eadric focused their attack on him, while all around the general his warriors rallied to his side. He easily chopped down the enemies who got within striking distance of his war-blade.

As Jennifer fought her way toward him, a distant thought caught her attention. Her gaze shifted up the cliff to her left. From a perch atop a narrow ledge fifty feet above, one of the four-armed Kasari shock troops aimed its disrupter weapon down toward them. A suicidal goal. The blast would kill all who battled on this ledge, but it would also collapse the outcropping upon which the Kasari stood.

Knowing that drawing and firing her own blaster would have the same disastrous effect, Jennifer thrust her mind into that of the Kasari. The alien's surprise introduced a moment of hesitation, and in that moment, Jennifer transferred an urgent need to drop the weapon. She felt his grip loosen, but then he caught himself, his will strengthening to match hers. Far below, Jennifer felt her body stumble, pitching out toward the chasm, only to be jerked backward by Dgarra's strong hands.

The Kasari's grip on his disrupter tightened, and Jennifer focused all of her will into the brain that controlled his four-armed body, barely managing to prevent the trigger squeeze that would end them all. A wave of vertigo assailed Jennifer as the four-armed alien teetered on the brink, his corded muscles fighting themselves in an effort to aim and fire his weapon.

Jennifer felt the Kasari shift his attention but failed to understand its significance until it was too late. The change shocked her so badly that she almost lost her mental link. She felt as if a dozen minds had suddenly merged with hers . . . and then hundreds . . . and then thousands. And as all that mental power focused on her, she stopped trying to understand what was happening and sent a single mental command to the nerves in the Kasari soldier's legs.

As her consciousness fled the mind storm that she had unwittingly unleashed, the ledge spun away from her. With a burst of focused will, she broke the Kasari's mental connection with the others and pulled him alongside her into shadow.

○ ● ○

Distant voices speaking in low, urgent tones welcomed Jennifer back to consciousness, accompanied by a skull-cracking headache that pulled a moan from her lips. She struggled to open her eyes, but they felt like they'd been glued shut. When they did open, the big room spun so rapidly that she squeezed them shut again, while a wave of nausea tried to empty her stomach.

Jennifer forced herself to concentrate. With her mental augmentations, she should have been able to clear her head of the migraine, or whatever this was. But though she managed to reduce the throbbing intensity, she failed to rid herself of the pain, a sensation akin to something being ripped open inside her brain.

She remembered her mind connecting with that of the Kasari. Not with an individual mind. Her action had drawn the attention of many minds, more than enough to overwhelm her. She had no doubt that if that mental connection had lasted another couple of seconds, her mind would have broken completely. She should be thankful to have awakened with this hangover from hell. Right now, though, she was having a difficult time acquiring the appropriate level of gratitude.

With a fresh burst of willpower, Jennifer sat up and swung her legs off the side of a pallet, somehow managing to avoid puking her guts out as she struggled to her knees, one hand on the stone wall for support.

"Lie back down, or get out of our way."

The deep voice pulled her head up. To her left, doctors and nurses worked to stabilize wounded warriors, their gray gloves and gowns stained with Koranthian blood that was such a dark red that it looked almost black. On the bed to her left, the whine of a bone saw was followed by the thump of an amputated leg landing in a large bucket, having been dropped by the doctor who had just spoken to her.

A little over a year ago, the sight of this much carnage would have left her weak and shaking. Now it just pulled her to her feet. Instead of pissing her off, the doctor's harsh words spurred her into motion. She rose to her feet, where she wavered unsteadily for several seconds before making her way through the mayhem toward the exit.

As she sidestepped the medical staff and their equipment, she scanned the room, anxious to see if she recognized any of the wounded, but the severe nature of some of the injuries had left several patients unrecognizable.

When she stepped out of the field hospital, she found herself standing inside a cavern she knew well, one that lay along the primary railway line, less than a mile south of General Dgarra's headquarters. As she watched, six maglev ambulance cars rounded the bend and came to a stop at the elevated platform. The doors opened to disgorge a line of medics carrying the most severely wounded on litters, leaving the patients who were still ambulatory to limp down the ramp to the triage area.

Exhaustion wafted from these seven-foot warriors in waves that didn't require her unique mental abilities to pick up. But what worried her more was the profound sense of depression that accompanied their weariness. These battle-hardened Koranthians, male and female alike, were unfamiliar with losing. But the unending succession of assaults by the Eadric and their Kasari allies had siphoned doubt into their souls—doubts about their own abilities and, more importantly, doubts that even their legendary commander could win this fight.

As Jennifer looked at them, her will solidified, driving the headache from her consciousness. She pulled her subspace receiver-transmitter headset from a cargo pocket in her black uniform trousers, letting the beads at either end of the partial loop settle over her temples. Her mind made the connection with the Rho Ship's neural net, and through that to Raul. His relief flooded her mind.

"Christ. Where the hell have you been?"

"I got knocked out and medevaced to the First Medical Detachment's field hospital.'"

"How bad are you hurt?"

"I'm fine. What's our current situation?"

She felt his mood grow more somber.

"Not great. Dgarra's lines are still holding, but he ordered me to take the Rho Ship off planet. Right now I'm on the back side of Scion's nearest moon. The ship is cloaked, and I'm monitoring the battle through the worm-fiber viewers."

Jennifer accessed the video feeds, letting the imagery fill her mind. Night had fallen over the northern Koranthian Mountains, but brilliant flashes from the ongoing battle laced the sky.

"Can't you use the Rho Ship's weapons to support Dgarra?"

"Yes, but the Kasari will detect it and intercept me with their fast battle cruisers. I might be able to make one pass before I have to shift into subspace and get the hell out of there. After that, they'll have weapons ready to blast me out of the sky if I try it again."

"Any relief you can give Dgarra's troops may make the difference."

VJ, the artificial intelligence that Raul had modeled on Jennifer's personality, interrupted. "I don't recommend that."

"And I don't give a damn," Jennifer said, feeling her headache reassert itself. Raul wavered, and Jennifer reached deeper into his mind, tweaking his confidence just enough to ensure that he made the right decision. It felt wrong to manipulate someone who had saved her life multiple times, but right now she didn't have time to argue this out.

"Okay. I'll give it a try."

"Thank you," she said, relief accompanying her thought message. "Good luck."

Jennifer removed the headset and returned it to its pocket. Seeing that the ambulance train was preparing to depart for its trip back to the battlefront, she trotted up the ramp and stepped aboard.

Ever since General Dgarra had violated the wishes of his uncle, Emperor Goltat, and made Jennifer a ward of his house and his aide-de-camp, she had fought to prove herself worthy of his trust. Not only had she seen her efforts change the way he looked at her, but she'd also felt the general's growing affection for her despite his efforts to maintain a strict military bearing.

She shared that feeling.

Taking a deep breath, Jennifer settled back into her seat. She would return to General Dgarra's side. Whatever happened next, that was where she belonged.

CHAPTER 5

General Magtal strode through his headquarters adjacent to the emperor's palace complex in the subterranean Koranthian city of ArvaiKheer, his seven-foot-frame quivering with a barely contained rage that worked its way up his dark-skinned face into the crown-bones that topped his skull.

Word from the northern front was good—heroic, in fact. Such news was exactly what had set his teeth on knife's edge. General Dgarra and his pet human female continued to hold out against far-superior enemy forces that included elite Kasari assault troops. This despite the ongoing denial of reinforcements to Dgarra's beleaguered command. How much longer Magtal could continue to convince the emperor that the attacks against the northern front were merely a feint to convince him to divert troops there, he didn't know. In truth, the Kasari, with their advanced worm-fiber viewing technology, knew precisely where the weakly defended points in the Koranthian defensive network were, in Dgarra's sector.

But apparently Magtal could not count on that enemy to take advantage of that weakness to rid him of his most hated rival.

He reached his command center, hearing the announcement "Commanding General!" as he strode through the triton-steel doors.

"As you were," he ordered, sending his warriors back to their duties.

Seating himself in the swivel chair that gave him an elevated view of the situational-awareness displays that tiled the room's walls, Magtal waved away the aide who had scurried to his side. Right now he needed to think.

Dgarra's human female had proved far more resourceful than Magtal would have thought, considering she had summoned her human companion to land the captured Kasari world ship within one of Dgarra's hangars. Where exactly, Magtal didn't know. Only through his spies inside Dgarra's headquarters had the general learned of the landing and alien technologies Dgarra's engineers were working to implement. They were getting help with those engineering efforts, of that there could be no doubt. And Dgarra had refused to share the results of his research, claiming that the work was purely in the experimental and test phases and that he would share the results should they prove stable and beneficial.

Just like the warrior—to take every advantage for himself, using his kinship with Emperor Goltat to secure that edge.

Magtal felt his lips curl to reveal his teeth, a look that sent the lieutenant who saw it scurrying to the far side of the room. Dgarra had forced his hand. Magtal was ready to release the dagger that would disgrace his rival and remove him from the line of ascension once and for all.

General Magtal would then be but a single step from the throne, a step that he would take in due time.

○ ● ○

Raul leaned forward in the invisible command couch that was a precise manifestation of his control over the forward compartment's stasis field generator. His right hand massaged the sudden tightness in his neck.

"You shouldn't let her manipulate you like that." VJ's voice carried more than a hint of petulance. "This is stupid, and you know it."

"She didn't talk me into anything I wasn't already considering."

"That doesn't make it any less stupid."

"Just make the course calculations. I want to pop out of subspace ten thousand feet above the Eadric artillery positions, fire the ship's disrupter weapons at that artillery, then shift back into subspace before they have a chance to respond."

"Aye, Cap'n."

For the thousandth time, Raul noted that he could have already accomplished what he was ordering VJ to do, but he had come to value the opposing feedback she provided. Either that or he was a closet masochist. He was glad that he had never given her a visual appearance to go along with Jennifer's voice. Having her smirk or scowl at him would be way more than he wanted to put up with.

VJ delivered the subspace course calculations that would bring them out of subspace at the desired location. Unfortunately, since they would not have a chance to establish a normal-space momentum vector optimized for that spot, he would be forced into a tight maneuver immediately upon exiting subspace. And that maneuver would have to be completed before he activated the firing sequence from the ship's disrupter weapons. That would increase his time over target, and since the ship's stasis shield would have to stay down while he fired, the element of surprise was crucial for this attack to work.

The transition into subspace was accompanied by a subtle vibration that Raul didn't like. A quick diagnostic revealed a minor anomaly in the functioning of the subspace field generator. Nothing serious, but he added the issue to his growing to-do list.

"Ten seconds until normal-space reentry," VJ said.

Raul wrapped himself tightly in the stasis field that would protect him should the worst happen, feeling droplets of sweat pop out on his forehead as he did so. Christ, he wasn't cut out for this space-warrior bullshit.

Then, as VJ's countdown approached zero, he mentally rehearsed the weapons run. Pop into normal-space, bank hard, fire the Rho Ship's disrupter beams, then pop back into subspace. Nothing to it, a mantra he repeated with each count. Hopefully he would come to believe it.

○ ● ○

The Rho Ship materialized ten thousand and four feet above the Eadric artillery battalions. Raul initiated the targeting sequence while VJ maneuvered the Rho Ship for the firing pass.

"Enemy targeting sensors are attempting to acquire us."

Raul tensed but maintained his focus. "Stay on target."

He felt the Rho Ship's targeting solution lock in and fired a pattern of disrupter blasts, his efforts rewarded by a half-dozen secondary explosions that sent fireballs boiling into the sky. Not a perfect run, but it would have to do.

"Get us out of here."

"Subspace transition initiated," VJ said.

There it was again, a jitter as the subspace field generator activated, this one much more pronounced than the last time. The neural net gave Raul the bad news. The subspace transition had failed.

"Enemy targeting sensors have acquired a lock on us."

Despite the fact that she was a simulation, Raul heard the tension in her voice. Apparently the imminent threat of being blown out of the sky could do that. Fear sharpened his mind's connection with the neural net, and he issued the command to activate the vessel's stasis shield mere nanoseconds before the Rho Ship's exterior lit up brighter than the sun as a combination of disrupter blasts and laser beams played across the hull.

The relief that flooded Raul's mind that he was still alive was short-lived. The stasis shield was holding, but the stress the attacks were placing on its generator were already approaching the red line. He worked to compensate, felt VJ activate the Rho Ship's cloaking mechanism, then performed a hard banking maneuver that carried them out of the line of fire.

As expected, the Eadric air-defense systems began firing a spread pattern, hoping to get a lucky hit on the target that had just disappeared from their sensor screens.

"Can you get us into subspace?" Raul asked.

"Negative."

"Then find us a safe spot on the ground."

"Working on it," said VJ.

A laser beam sizzled into their shielding with such intensity that Raul could feel the stasis field generator overheat.

"Shit. Get us on the ground."

The fact that VJ didn't respond told him more than he wanted to know about the number of ship's systems that were failing. The neural net transmitted the ship's status directly into his pain receptors, a sensation that was getting less pleasant by the moment.

VJ entered the new course command, sending the Rho Ship plummeting from the sky into a deep canyon far behind the Eadric lines. The maneuver didn't startle Raul, but the destination coordinates did.

"Oh shit!"

Wrapped in the command deck's stasis field, Raul braced for impact, praying that the ship's shielding would hold. As he studied the cascading status displays that blossomed in his mind, he gulped in a deep breath. He hoped it wouldn't be his last.

o ● o

Kasari group commander Shalegha stood as tall as any of the Koranthians, her four powerful arms as familiar with battle as her mind was with strategy and tactics. But the subterranean warrior race had earned her respect. Much as she would have liked to assimilate them into the Kasari Collective, their brains had an odd structure that prevented the cortical nanobots within the Kasari nanite serum from linking their brains to the hive-mind, the first such intelligent species that the Kasari had ever encountered. Unfortunately, they would have to be exterminated.

Suddenly Shalegha was alerted to the tactical display that her nano-bot cortical array delivered to her visual cortex. She took particular note of one signal concerning a subspace transition within the caverns controlled by the Koranthian general, Dgarra.

Although the Kasari did not have Altreian subspace technology, they could detect whenever Altreian ships transitioned in and out of subspace if that happened in close proximity to active Kasari sensors. Whenever an object transitioned into subspace, it left a brief hole in normal-space. When that hole refilled, a distinctive electromagnetic signature propagated outward. The reverse happened when an object emerged from subspace into normal-space, also creating a detectable signal.

The Eadric air-defense sensors clustered along the northern Koranthian front had noted several subspace anomalies just before the deadly Koranthian winter had made further assaults impossible. The odd thing was that they hadn't detected any similar disturbances during the intervening months. That, combined with the encrypted message Shalegha had recently received from her source within the Koranthian High Command, gave extra importance to this new signal.

It meant that the humans had not only managed to capture a Kasari world ship but had also somehow managed to enhance it with subspace capabilities. That could only mean that they were getting help from the Altreians, thus making the capture or destruction of that world ship one of Shalegha's top priorities.

She ran her upper right hand through her short-cropped orange hair and issued a mental command that placed all air-defense systems along the northern Koranthian front on high alert, as well as those that surrounded her headquarters in the Eadric capital city of Orthei. As much as Shalegha trusted her connection to the hive-mind and the enhanced permissions that she enjoyed on that network, she trusted her battle-honed instincts more.

Something big was about to happen, and it just might be precisely what she had been hoping for.

○ ● ○

General Dgarra felt the shock waves from the fireballs that rolled above the battlefield as the cigar-shaped Rho Ship flashed across the sky, creating a sudden, eerie pause in the Eadric assault. Apparently Raul had launched an attack on the distant enemy artillery. The action was foolhardy but still could provide the window of opportunity that Dgarra's beleaguered warriors so desperately needed.

As he watched, the Eadric antiaircraft batteries opened fire, bathing the ship in brilliant explosions. Dgarra didn't understand. Why hadn't Raul shifted the vessel back into subspace by now? Surely the starship's shielding couldn't withstand such a battering for much longer. His conviction that something was seriously wrong grew stronger with each passing moment.

When the Rho Ship disappeared, Dgarra breathed a sigh of relief. Unfortunately, that feeling didn't last long. The batteries of lasers and disrupter weapons adjusted their firing into a spread pattern designed to seek out and destroy a hidden target. The Eadric believed that the Rho Ship had cloaked itself and remained in the area.

A burst of bright light sizzled against an invisible shield, a lucky strike that attracted a heavy concentration of fire. But as the firing continued, there were no signs of another direct hit, giving Dgarra hope that Raul had finally escaped into subspace. He shifted his attention back to the battle at hand, issuing the command that dropped the stasis shields that protected all of the Koranthian disrupter and laser batteries, directing his artillery to concentrate their fire on the gathered Eadric brigades that threatened to breach his lines.

As he had hoped, the answering artillery fire was greatly diminished from what his forces had experienced before the Rho Ship's attack. Now, robbed of the bulk of their artillery support, the Eadric assault faltered. With a word, Dgarra committed his combat reserve, a burst of pride swelling his breast as he watched fresh Koranthian warriors pour from their caverns to sweep the exhausted Eadric assault troopers from their positions. Dgarra ordered his artillery to shift their firing farther behind the enemy lines to avoid killing his own warriors.

He felt someone step up beside him and turned to see Smythe standing there, her black-and-purple uniform crusted with the dried blood that had also plastered her short-cropped brown hair to her skull. Despite her appearance, Smythe's eyes were alert as she peered at the battlefield displays projected on the command center's far wall. Her return was a small thing, but at the end of this long day, one more thing to be thankful for.

"When you fell during the battle," he said, "I feared that I had lost you."

Smythe turned toward him, a slow smile spreading across her human features. "I take it that Raul's attack succeeded."

"You ordered that action without consulting me."

Smythe's shoulders lifted slightly in one of her odd human expressions. "I can't order Raul to do anything. I merely requested the air support, and he agreed."

"It could cost us the Rho Ship."

"If the Kasari and their allies were to overrun your position, the ship wouldn't matter. Since I wasn't able to communicate with you, it seemed a worthwhile risk."

General Dgarra stared down at this impressive human female. In certain ways she reminded him of his younger self: idealistic, aggressive, and utterly fearless. Time and again she had proved herself worthy of his trust, worthy of the risks he'd taken for her. Not only had she saved his life, but she had also delivered on her promises to instruct Dgarra's engineers in alien technologies.

But trust was the least of what he had come to feel for her.

Even now, the general did not fully understand his emotions. He just knew that he felt better in her presence, and whenever Jennifer was apart from him, an emptiness ate away at his soul.

Despite his best efforts to hide these feelings, he could see in her eyes that she knew.

And maybe he was imagining things, but she seemed to return his fondness.

He had never met a potential mate with this combination of attributes. The fact that he now found himself attracted to this strange alien female went far beyond odd and was utterly incongruous with his upbringing. The very idea of weakening the Koranthian bloodline, assuming that interbreeding was even possible with a human female, amounted to high treason. In every instance where a Koranthian had mated with another race, the sentence had been the same: death by cleansing fire.

Purging these thoughts from his mind, Dgarra turned his attention back to the Rho Ship.

"What is Raul's status?" he asked.

"Give me a moment."

Smythe removed the iridescent headband from her cargo pocket and placed it on her head. After several moments of concentration, she frowned and returned it to her pocket.

"I'm not getting a connection."

"What would cause that?"

"If he made a wormhole jump, it might have taken him out of this headset's range."

Dgarra had come to recognize the look on Jennifer's face whenever she doubted her words.

"And if that is not the case?"

Her eyes narrowed and locked with his. And in that look, he detected a deep, contagious dread.

"Then Raul's gamble may not have paid off."

:CHAPTER 6

A wintry blast howled down from the high Andes, the wind-driven sleet stinging Jack Gregory's face as he strode through the Tiahuanaco ruins toward the skeletal remains of the Kalasasaya Temple. Janet, Mark, and Jim "Tall Bear" Pino walked into the teeth of the storm alongside him. It was still day, but the clouds had grown so thick that an early twilight had taken hold.

Jack shifted his eyes to the big Navajo man who wielded major influence in the Native People's Alliance, watching the wind whip Tall Bear's long black hair straight out behind him. Months ago, Tall Bear had used his influence to gain approval for the dig to recover the Incan Sun Staff, and it had been his urgent message that had brought Jack here from New Zealand, accompanied by Janet and Mark. None of this would have been feasible without Robby and Eos having blocked all efforts by international intelligence agencies to locate the Smythes and their allies or to penetrate their network of shell corporations.

Two days ago, the archeological team had broken through the rubble in the collapsed cavern beneath the temple and had uncovered the Sun Staff, placing the site on lockdown pending Jack's arrival.

A shiver that had nothing to do with the cold worked its way up Jack's spine as he approached the hole in the Kalasasaya Temple's stone wall. Jack pulled a flashlight from his utility vest, switched it on, and stepped through the cantilevered doorway in the rough stone wall. He didn't need the extra light. Except for the widely spaced drop lighting that had been fastened to ancient wall sconces, the cave that stretched out before him appeared almost exactly as he remembered it. Noise from the gasoline-powered generator echoed through the passage, carrying with it a profound sense of violation of this place where Manco Cápac, the first Incan emperor, had been handed the Sun Staff.

Jack switched the flashlight off and returned it to its pocket as Janet, Tall Bear, and Mark joined him inside the tunnel.

"And now, if you'll follow me," said Tall Bear with a broad grin, "I have something wonderful to show you."

Jack followed his NPA host, feeling a tightness in his chest that he knew Janet was also feeling. A dozen years ago, he and Janet had fought their way down this very passage. Down in these warrens beneath the Kalasasaya Temple, Khal Teth, a.k.a. Anchanchu, had cast Jack into a waking dream that had almost gotten himself and Janet killed. As a result, she had doubted his sanity and treated him with caution. Now this place was about to tear them apart yet again.

Within two dozen feet, the tunnel narrowed as they passed through the section where the collapsed ceiling had been cleared and braced. The path soon widened again, and they passed by side tunnels on the left and right before rounding a bend to enter the main excavation.

Jack stepped through the opening into the altar chamber and halted in surprise. The archeological team had done amazing work, completely clearing the rubble from the right side of the cavern, uncovering the intricately inlaid, three-tiered golden dais atop which the Incan Sun Staff stood erect.

The altar rose from the floor to a height of six feet. Its elaborately carved and inlaid surface channeled and amplified the ambient light.

But it was the Sun Staff, vertically mounted at the rear of the altar, that put a lump in Jack's throat and pulled a gasp of recognition from Janet's lips. The length of the head-high silver staff had been densely etched with complex symbols, terminating in a golden orb composed of delicate rings connected to a clockwork interior.

Mark stepped forward to join the other observers who had stopped at the base of the altar, kneeling to examine the intricate engravings on the first of its three levels.

"Is this solid gold?"

"Not like any on this planet," Tall Bear said. "Its properties have been modified in a way that is far beyond our technology. Neither it nor the Sun Staff were damaged by the ceiling collapse. During the excavation, one of the workers accidently clipped the edge of this dais with a diamond drill. Didn't even leave a scratch."

Jack's eyes remained locked on the Sun Staff that had filled his dreams. Janet's hand slid into his, squeezing hard. But when he glanced at her, she didn't meet his gaze. Instead, she kept her eyes focused on the Sun Staff, as though, by force of will alone, she could reduce the hated thing to slag.

For a time, the group stood in silence. Then Mark spoke up.

"Tall Bear and I are going to step outside to give the two of you some private time with the artifact."

The Navajo leader extended his hand to Jack, who released Janet's to grip it, only to find himself swept into a bear hug. The scene repeated itself with Jack and Mark. Then, without any further words spoken, the two men walked out of the cavern, leaving Jack and Janet alone before the altar.

○　●　○

Janet watched the exchange of hugs between old friends, unable to keep the tears from her eyes. Her body felt like it was shutting down, as if someone had plunged an ice pick between her shoulder blades.

If there had been one consistent theme in her life, it was the belief that if she didn't like her circumstances, she could take action to change them. She had tried everything she could think of to convince Jack that Khal Teth could not be trusted, that the Altreian criminal was playing him. She had even enlisted Robby, Eos, and Heather to help her. But Jack had never trusted Khal Teth's motivations. He just considered them irrelevant to what needed to be done in order to save humanity.

Janet had failed to shake her lifelong conviction, a fact that had left her in this state of shock and helplessness, unable to stop Jack from going to the one place where she could not accompany him.

He turned to her, and it was as if she were seeing him for the first time instead of the last. At their first meeting, Jack had opened the door to his German apartment and put a gun to her head. Now he'd just done it again.

She wanted to hit him. She wanted to hold him and never let go. The warring impulses left her immobilized, frozen.

Jack didn't wrap his arms around her, didn't try to pull her close. He simply took her hands in his and held them as tears flooded his brown eyes and cut trails down his rugged face. The laugh lines that she'd always loved had suddenly become crow's-feet, deepened by the shroud of sorrow that hung between them.

"I love you." His lips formed the words, but no sound escaped his mouth.

Janet sucked in a shuddering breath, placed her arms around his neck, and buried her face in his shoulder, feeling his powerful arms crush her body to his. She turned her face so that her lips brushed his right ear.

"You damn sure better find your way back to me."

Then she pulled away, turned, and strode rapidly out of the chamber, without a single glance back in his direction.

CHAPTER 7

Jack stood alone in the altar chamber, watching as his soulmate walked out of his life forever. But she hadn't left him—he'd done that to her.

He took a deep breath and let it out slowly, gritted his teeth, and turned to face the Altar of the Gods, unleashing the rider within. Shrugging off the lethargy born of depression, he climbed the three high steps that carried him to the Sun Staff. A dozen years ago, Klaus Barbie's bastard son had almost completed arranging the golden orb's rings into the code that would open the portal. With very little of the pattern left to enter, Jack reached out with both hands to cup the orb, twisting one ring after another. One final twist of the topmost ring sent a surge of energy through the base, up the silver staff, and into the orb.

It started as a low vibration that rose to a high-pitched hum. A dim glow leaked from within the crownpiece, growing in intensity until Jack was forced to squint. Beneath him the altar shifted, the top tier sliding toward the nearest wall, carrying Jack along with it and revealing a four-foot-wide ramp behind him that led down into darkness.

Jack released the orb and turned to examine the opening as Khal Teth's gravelly voice filled his mind.

"Be ready. We have awakened the one who was sleeping."

The fact that Khal Teth had managed to speak directly into his mind instead of having to communicate through a lucid dream caught Jack off guard. He immediately decided their direct link must be a side effect of his manipulation of the Sun Staff. Regardless, he went with it.

"Won't the Altreian be prepared for me?"

"He expects humans to eventually solve the riddle of the staff and to open this portal, humans whose minds he can easily dominate. My presence will come as an unpleasant surprise."

Jack forced the tension from his body, lifted the Sun Staff from its slot atop the altar, and walked down the ramp, letting it light his way. Several paces down, he heard the altar slide and close off the entrance behind him, cutting his last link to the world he had known. There was no stone in this passage. The walls and ceiling were of the same strange metal as the ramp, something he recognized from Mark's and Heather's descriptions of the interior of the Second Ship.

He considered drawing his HK from its shoulder holster but resisted the urge. He doubted that the waiting Altreian would respond favorably to an apparent threat. Up ahead, the passage leveled out, then stopped at a bare wall. Behind him an unseen door quickly closed, sealing him in a room the size of a jail cell and elevating his heart rate. Then the light from the Sun Staff's golden crownpiece winked out, leaving him in magenta-colored semidarkness.

What the hell?

Another door whisked open, and then he understood. This was the Altreian equivalent of an airlock. A dozen feet in front of him, an Altreian stood waiting for him as if Jack were a distant relative who'd been expected to drop by for a visit. Very similar in appearance to the way Khal Teth had appeared in Jack's visions, the Altreian was somewhat taller than Jack, standing perhaps six and a half feet, with an oddly handsome face and skin mottled red and black. His pointed ears were swept back along his bald head, and what appeared to be gill slits could be seen along both sides of his neck. But the dancing red glint in those large black eyes was what held Jack's gaze.

Then the being was in his mind, delving for any secrets that might be buried there and seeking to take control of his body. But Jack had endured years of fighting for mastery of his own mind against a former member of the Altreian High Council, and if Khal Teth hadn't been able to break him, this underling damn sure couldn't.

Jack felt Khal Teth's mind join the fray, saw the Altreian crew member's dark eyes grow wide, and cracked a mirthless smile.

"Not today, bitch," Jack said as he stepped through the doorway. "Not today."

○ ● ○

For the first time in millennia, Khal Teth felt the touch of another Altreian mind—the one thing he had been counting on. Isolated from his own body, he did not have the psionic strength to reach out and dominate another of his own race. But Broljen, the research-vessel commander, had linked his mind to Jack's in order to dominate this long-anticipated visitor. And by so doing he had opened a mental door that allowed Khal Teth in.

Broljen seemed surprised when the human was able to resist his initial attempt to take control of his mind, but when Khal Teth latched on to that link, it galvanized the Altreian commander.

Unfortunately, the contest wasn't going as Khal Teth expected. What was wrong? He should have been able to sweep this underling away with ease, but instead he found himself in a back-and-forth struggle, and, with every passing second, his opponent gained confidence.

A new thought occurred to him. He lacked sufficient connection to a physical body to provide substance to his mind attack. Khal Teth was a mere ghost of his former self, and he needed Jack's assistance.

Khal Teth shifted his focus, eschewing the attack in favor of erecting a block around Jack's mind, a defensive maneuver that only encouraged his opponent. Nevertheless, it would buy time for him to establish a tighter connection to his human host.

"Jack, I need you to let me take complete control of your body."

Jack's mental response radiated waves of anger. "Like hell."

"I have to establish a stronger link in order to dominate this Altreian's mind."

"How about I just shoot him in the head while you keep him busy."

His rising frustration at the negotiations almost caused Khal Teth to lose focus, something that would end them both.

"If this vessel detects that its last crew member is dead, it will send the request for the planet killer. Right now, I need your help."

After a moment of hesitation, Khal Teth felt Jack's mind relax into a quasimeditative calm. He reacted immediately, taking advantage of that opening before Jack could reconsider. The physical intensity of the experience far surpassed any of Khal Teth's previous connections to the host. Jack's body felt both powerful and heavy at the same time. Khal Teth flexed his fingers and then clenched them into fists so tight that he felt his knuckles pop as Broljen tried to take control of the human.

This brain was human, but all sentient species had the inherent structure for telepathy. But like the human ability to wiggle ears, few knew how to initiate such a feat. Khal Teth knew how to take advantage of that inherent psionic capability.

Activating a particular region of Jack's brain, Khal Teth gripped the smoky tendrils of Broljen's thoughts, forcibly extracting them from Jack's head. Broljen's presence squirmed to free itself, but with each passing second, Khal Teth's mental grip grew stronger. As his mind fully connected with Broljen's, Khal Teth allowed the commander a glimpse of his true identity.

A low moan escaped Broljen's lips, his body overcome by a tremor. The Altreian's eyes bulged, his gill slits fluttering along both sides of his neck. He staggered back two steps before Khal Teth's will brought him to a complete stop. Then, having locked the commander in place, Khal Teth delved deeply into his mind, extracting control codes.

Then Khal Teth walked over to the nearest of the five command couches and laid the Sun Staff atop it before turning to follow the commander out of the chamber. At long last, his banishment was almost at its end.

○ ● ○

Jack observed the mental battle, allowing himself to feel what Khal Teth was doing without involving himself in the act, having entered a meditative state very similar to his lucid dreams. More than that, he studied how Khal Teth was using the power locked within Jack's own brain to achieve mastery over the other Altreian. Through that link, he could actually feel the commander's terror as Khal Teth enslaved both mind and body.

At the end, Khal Teth extracted the information he needed from Broljen's mind and then followed him past the five translucent alien couches, pausing just long enough to lay down the Sun Staff before entering a much smaller room also bathed in the ambient magenta glow.

The Altreian commander walked directly to the leftmost of five horizontally mounted metal cylinders, each of which shifted through a variety of soft colors. Jack knew what he was seeing. These were the chrysalis cylinders the crew used to place themselves in suspended animation. Khal Teth's body lay inside a similar chrysalis cylinder on Quol, one that had been programmed to block his mind's return.

Broljen paused beside the cylinder, his fingers tracing a fractal pattern on its control pad. With a soft whine, the top half of the cylinder opened to reveal a translucent material that molded itself to the commander as he climbed inside and lay back. Jack got a close look at the

Altreian's face. The alien was completely devoid of emotion, as if Jack was watching an android go through its commanded actions. But from deep inside that mind, he could hear the screams that never made it to Broljen's lips. Then the cover closed, the cylinder activated, and the Altreian's silent screams faded away.

The meaning of what had just happened was clear. Khal Teth had forced the vessel's commander to place himself into a semipermanent period of suspended animation, ensuring that the research vessel would continue to have a living crew member. Although the apparent joy that Khal Teth had taken in enslaving his fellow Altreian was troubling, the act itself had been a necessary prequel to what they had to do next.

Maintaining his dreamlike view of what his own body was doing, Jack watched as Khal Teth used his hands to enter another code into the second chrysalis cylinder, opening its lid and then settling inside. Then with a shift of perspective that startled him, Jack found himself back in charge of his body.

"Your turn." Khal Teth's mental voice echoed in his head.

Jack reached for the control pad, his right hand pausing. His access to Khal Teth's mind revealed why this hocus-pocus body swap across the galaxy was possible, even though it shouldn't be. The chrysalis cylinder on the Altreian home world of Quol had been attuned to Khal Teth's mind and then used to sever Khal Teth's connection to his own body, imprisoning his mind in an alternate dimension.

But Khal Teth had repeatedly escaped from that dimension using the method with which he'd entangled his mind with Jack's. Now, by giving Jack primacy during the link of this cylinder to its counterpart on Quol, Jack's mind would form the mask that would allow Khal Teth to slip through the chrysalis cylinder's firewall and return to his Altreian body.

Taking one last earthly breath, Jack pulled forth the memory of himself laughing with Janet and Robby on a much happier day. The memory wasn't so old, but it sure felt like it.

"Ah shit."

Jack entered the code sequence that would attune this chrysalis cylinder to the one on Quol. Then the touch pad—and the world—dissolved around him.

○ ● ○

Janet stood alone outside the ruins of the Kalasasaya Temple, staring across the windswept high plains as the gathering storm sucked the last light out of the day. Scattered between waist-high desert grasses stood a precisely carved stone gateway, the skeletal remnant of a once-great civilization. She wondered if she stood on the doorstep of a future where such ruins would be all that was left to mark humankind's brief existence on Earth.

Would such a fate really be worse than being assimilated by the Kasari Collective? All she knew was that her best friend and lover refused to lie down and accept either fate. Yet here she stood, helplessly buffeted by the coming storm, with no clear vision of how to do her part.

Damn it all.

When Mark walked up beside her and placed a hand on her shoulder, she made no move to acknowledge his presence. But his arrival made her aware of how cold she was. Without a scarf or hooded jacket to protect them, her ears felt like they'd been spiked with a thousand poisoned needles. Janet savored the pain, letting it pull her focus back to the present.

"Jack's been inside for almost an hour," Mark said. "I think we should go check on him."

Janet turned her face toward him. His muscular, six-foot-three-inch frame was barely recognizable as the high school junior she and Jack had first met in Los Alamos. Had it really been a decade ago? Time seemed to pass in but a blink of the eye.

"You know that he won't be coming back out of that place."

Mark sighed loud enough to be heard above the gusting wind. "Wouldn't you like to see for yourself?"

She would and she wouldn't. But, inhaling a fresh lungful of the ice-cold air, she nodded. Returning her gaze to the desolate landscape, Janet dismissed him.

"Go get Tall Bear," she said. "I'll meet you at the tunnel entrance."

As Mark left her side, the wind died and the sleet transitioned to snow, big fluffy flakes that stuck to her hair and eyelashes, the sudden quiet so loud that it startled her. Somehow she felt it was a sign that a rare force of nature had just departed the planet, taking with him the energy that had powered the storm.

Janet hitched the collar of her leather jacket higher around her neck, turned, and walked back toward the tunnel entrance. She saw no use delaying the confirmation of her loss. She would share this final farewell with two friends who also loved Jack. If only Robby, Heather, and Robby's caretaker, Yachay, were here, the memorial would be complete.

When she reached the tunnel, she found Mark and Tall Bear waiting, their eyes filled with concern as they watched her pass them by and step inside. Setting her jaw, Janet strode back toward the altar cavern, her shadow shifting around her as she passed by each bright LED light, the roar of the generator gradually fading.

At the entrance to the cavern, she halted, took a deep breath, and stepped inside, her hand subconsciously drifting to the butt of her holstered Glock. But there was nothing to shoot. The Altar of the Gods stood empty. With Mark and Tall Bear on either side, she climbed up the three tiers, coming to a stop atop the gleaming golden dais. Janet slowly turned in a circle, surveying the cavern, before sinking to her knees.

Both Jack and the Sun Staff were gone.

:CHAPTER 8

The call came as Alexandr Prokorov sat down at his desk inside the Federation Security Service headquarters in The Hague, vibrating the encrypted cell phone atop his desk. The desk was excellent, Brazilian mahogany, hand carved and inlaid by the finest Norwegian craftsmen, a luxury that bespoke the power Prokorov wielded.

He lifted the phone, glanced at the caller ID, and saw that the call was from the recently appointed CIA director, Bethany Ortiz.

"Hello, Beth."

"Hi, Alexandr. I just landed."

"Excellent. I wasn't expecting you to get here until around eleven A.M."

"My pilot took advantage of some favorable tailwinds over the Atlantic."

"Come straight on over. I'll reschedule my early appointments."

"I look forward to our conversation."

"Oh, and Beth . . ."

"Yes?"

"It will just be you and me."

There was a surprised pause before she responded. "I wanted to introduce you to my deputy, Clark Kendrick."

"There will be time for that at dinner this evening. What I have to discuss is for your ears only."

When the CIA director spoke again, her voice held a mixture of irritation and curiosity.

"Clark has my complete confidence."

"Of course. But as I said, this will be strictly between you and me. I've already cleared it with your president, Benton."

Another pause. "All right, then. I'll see you shortly."

The phone clicked off, bringing a tight smile to Prokorov's lips.

Bethany Ortiz was a political appointee, but hardly inexperienced. She'd been the longstanding chairman of the Senate Foreign Relations Committee before resigning her congressional seat to accept the appointment to the CIA. As expected, she didn't take kindly to this surprising change in plans. That was just fine. She needed to understand the true power structure within the United Federation of Nation States, of which the United States was but a part.

Regardless of who was the current UFNS prime minister, a figurehead position that rotated between its four member nations—the New Soviet Union, the East Asian People's Alliance, the United States, and the European Union—the real power lay within the FSS. And Alexandr Prokorov, ex-KGB and former head of the FSB, wielded the full strength of the FSS with the cunning that the world had come to expect during his reign as minister of federation security.

Prokorov placed a call to his assistant, alerting her to the change in his meeting schedule, then swiveled his chair to access the wall safe behind his desk. He placed his hand into a small alcove above the safe and waited as the device scanned his hand, measured his vitals, then drew a tiny drop of blood for DNA analysis. He withdrew his hand

and waited for the DNA comparison to finish. Five years ago, the same sequencing would have taken several hours, a feat that this portable unit now accomplished in under a minute.

When the door to the safe opened, he reached inside and extracted a file folder, then relocked the safe. Upon returning to his desk, he opened the folder and stared down at the familiar photo of his top operative. Even without the scar that had permanently parted her dirty-blond hair, despite the best efforts of her nanites, the woman was too lean and fit to be considered classically beautiful. Equally effective in a cage match or at a high-society social, Galina Anikin was a weapon he used sparingly, lest her cover be blown. But now Prokorov had a new mission for her, one that she would relish.

As he stared at Galina's photo, his thoughts inevitably turned to the Smythes. Six months ago, Galina and her partner, Daniil Alkaev, had come close to killing the Smythes in Lima, Peru. With help from the NSA, Prokorov had managed to identify the location of the artificial intelligence that the Smythes were using to thwart efforts to track them.

But the operation Prokorov had launched to destroy the Smythes had gone horribly wrong, resulting in the deaths of dozens of Delta Force operators and a similar number of Spetsnaz commandos, along with the loss of Daniil.

For that last offense, Galina would have her retribution. Prokorov had promised her that. Unfortunately, the Smythes had become smoke in the wind, and their AI had apparently learned a lesson from its mistake in Peru. Now, whenever it launched a cyber-attack against FSS interests, the entity somehow managed to do so from computer systems within the UFNS, leaving no trace as to the real source of the hacks.

Prokorov leaned back in his chair, subconsciously twisting the ring that bore the FSS crest, a dove surrounded by a bear, a dragon, a lion, and an eagle. He had already set in motion the actions that would plant false dossiers for Galina within the intelligence services of three of the four superpowers. Today's meeting with Ms. Ortiz, the CIA director, would ensure that the world's remaining superpower was fully on board.

If he couldn't beat the Smythes with technology, Prokorov would find them using the old methods he'd been well versed in as a young KGB agent. And when he did, Galina Anikin would be the chink in their armor.

:CHAPTER 9

Raul opened his eyes to a dull-red glow, unable to place himself. He was lying against something lumpy, feeling like he'd just been run over by a truck. Where the hell was he? Not in his stasis chair, that was for damn sure.

"VJ. Can you hear me?"

Nothing.

"VJ?"

Her lack of response constricted his chest, bathing him in agony as he felt broken ribs shift. He blinked, trying to bring his vision into focus. The fact that the ship still had emergency lighting was a good thing. The overall situation wasn't great, but right now he would take what he could get. He didn't remember the crash, but the shields must have failed, along with the internal stasis field generator. That combination of disasters had tossed him onto the equipment that filled the rear half of the command bay. If not for the improved nanites in his system and the strength of his cyborg legs, he'd most likely be dead.

With an effort that left him gasping, Raul rolled to a seated position, leaning back against one of the machines for support. His lost connection to the ship's neural net worried him even more than the loss of VJ. He didn't even want to think about trying to restore primary power without help from the Rho Ship's computer. Back in Los Alamos, when Dr. Stephenson had left him trapped aboard a dead Rho Ship, he'd managed to make the required repairs. But he had needed weeks to get the neural net back up and working, and, considering his current situation, Raul didn't think the Eadric were going to grant him the luxury of time.

Already the ship was getting cold. It might be springtime in the Koranthian Mountains, but that was akin to springtime in the high Himalayas.

Taking stock of his physical injuries, Raul was heartened to discover that the broken ribs were the worst of them. He could already feel the nanites working to repair the damage. If his improving vision was any indication, his concussion symptoms would soon be a thing of the past. Then, with any luck at all, he would be able to think clearly enough to form a plan that didn't result in his imminent death.

Once again he tried to reestablish a connection with the neural net. When that failed, he shifted his attention to the maintenance network. *Damn.* That system appeared to be off-line as well. All these problems pointed to one root cause: the ship had lost both primary and backup matter disrupters and was now keeping itself alive with a trickle charge from the capacitor banks.

That was actually a positive thing, indicating that the Rho Ship's computer hadn't shut down completely. It had merely determined that the power problem was critical and had taken extreme action to minimize energy consumption, hoping to keep itself alive long enough for the surviving crew member to make the repairs that would allow the other systems to be brought back online. Apparently the computer was an optimist.

But why had it shut down so many critical systems? The power stored in the bank of super-capacitors should have been enough to keep the heat on, with plenty to spare for a fully functional neural net. Was there some other critical system that had priority for power?

Then it hit him. Of course. The ship's cloaking mechanism was the only thing that could prevent his enemies from finding and destroying the ship. With the cloak turned on, the Kasari and their Eadric allies would literally have to stumble onto the ship to find it.

How long did he have before that happened? Raul knew the question didn't matter even as he thought it. He either had enough time or he didn't. But every moment he sat on his ass drained more sand from that inverted hourglass.

Raul struggled to rise, gasping in pain as he regained his feet. Gritting his teeth, he turned toward the cabinet where he had long ago stowed all of the manual tools he had hoped to never again use.

If he was going to get this ship out of here before somebody came along and blew it to pieces, he would have to handle repairs the old-fashioned way.

○ ● ○

The wind died out at midnight, leaving stillness beneath a brilliantly clear night sky. Jennifer looked up at the rare conjunction of all three of Scion's moons, an orange crescent bracketed by two white ones. Despite the cold, she enjoyed standing outside without the wind trying to pull her into the chasm below.

Somewhere out there, beyond that alien star field, Mark and Heather were together. Jennifer didn't know why, but she believed so with all her heart. As much as she missed her twin brother, the loss of her lifelong best friend, whom she could talk to about things she could never discuss with Mark, had left an equally large hole in her life. What would they think if they could see her now? What would her mom and dad think of the killing machine their bookish daughter had become?

The sound of heavy footfalls surprised her, and she turned to see Captain Jeshen, General Dgarra's most trusted courier, looking at her expectantly.

"Yes?" she asked.

"General Dgarra sent me to escort you to a conference with his subordinate commanders."

"I'll be along momentarily," Jennifer replied.

"The meeting isn't at his headquarters. I've been instructed to escort you."

She sighed. "Fine. Lead the way."

The Koranthian warrior turned and walked rapidly away from the ledge, his long stride forcing Jennifer to jog in order to keep up with him as he entered the nearest tunnel. The courier turned off into a side passage that sloped steeply downward away from Dgarra's headquarters. Jennifer pulled forth the mental image of the maps she'd seen. This tunnel was one of several that connected the headquarters with the forward defensive positions.

She wasn't surprised that Dgarra was meeting his commanders at such a forward position. He liked to survey the defenses and actively avoided pulling the commanders away from their units.

Seeing a lighted area up ahead, Jennifer picked up her pace, passing the courier. Something about being led around by the nose annoyed her. It wouldn't do to give those who continued to doubt her abilities the impression that she needed an escort.

Something sharp struck the back of her neck, its sting bringing her to a sliding stop as she spun to face her unseen attacker.

Ten paces back, the courier stood, his gun still leveled at her. It didn't look like any of the Koranthian weapons she'd seen, but then again, her vision was blurred. She reached back behind her neck and plucked out the dart that poured white fire into her veins, a fire rapidly spreading through her system.

As her knees buckled, Jennifer reached for her own sidearm, but her arms failed to respond, even to catch her as she tumbled forward onto her face. Why weren't her nanites countering whatever was happening to her? And why had Dgarra's courier betrayed her? None of it made sense.

The pain intensified so it seemed to Jennifer that she was being eaten alive from the inside out, as if ants were burrowing beneath her skin and crawling through her organs. She tried to scream but merely slobbered, her body involuntarily curling into a fetal position, consumed by tremors that rattled her teeth. From the corner of her left eye, she saw the big-booted feet of the courier step up beside her.

"General Magtal sends his regards."

The kick that followed lifted her from the tunnel floor and into the wall. The impact broke bones within her body, but the additional pain failed to register.

Damn it, Jennifer, she told herself. *Focus. Kill this prick.*

Jennifer steeled herself, walling away the pain, and reached out with her mind for the traitor who had done this to her. As she gathered her anger for one violent mental assault, she felt something.

What was it?

Her broken wrist was knitting itself back together. *Thank God.* The nanites were finally getting their microscopic acts together. And the pain was fading as well.

Good. It was payback time.

But when she rolled to her knees and looked up, the courier was gone.

Wait.

There it was again, that odd feeling beyond the healing of her body. Her mind had touched something vaguely familiar. Then she remembered. It was the same sensation she had experienced when she invaded the Kasari shock trooper's mind, as if she was being watched, connected not just to an individual but to an assemblage of minds.

What the hell? She hadn't yet made a mental connection, certainly not to a Kasari.

As rising panic threatened to rob her of her ability to think this through, her eyes caught sight of the dart she'd pulled from her neck. It lay on the ground where she had dropped it, a half-dozen feet from where she now knelt. Jennifer forced herself to stand, marveling at how fast her wounds were being repaired. Once again her eyes were drawn to the dart. She stepped forward, bending down to retrieve it.

Even in the dimly lit tunnel, the sight was crystal clear to her augmented vision—a transparent vial connected to an inch-long needle. The viscous fluid in the bottom of that vial raised the hairs on the back of her neck. She concentrated, stilling the hand that held the vial, but still the goo quivered as if alive. With dawning certainty, she knew what she was staring at.

And from a place deep within her brain, many minds spoke to her through a single voice, a phrase that froze her soul.

"Welcome to the collective."

:CHAPTER 10

Jack Gregory opened his eyes inside the tight confines of the chrysalis cylinder, his mind flooded with alien sensations. He flexed his fingers and toes in this unfamiliar form, noting with displeasure how weak all the muscles were. Even though this body had been kept in suspended animation, its weakness wasn't due to atrophy associated with long sleep. This was the result of an indolent lifestyle in which physical fitness played no role, just one more thing Jack would have to deal with if he was going to have any chance of preventing Earth's destruction by an Altreian planet killer.

The darkness inside the cylinder was absolute, but when Jack moved his hand across the smooth outer surface, feeling for the control pad, a pale-blue glow filled the small chamber, giving the shiny metal the look of a ghostly portal to another world.

Although Khal Teth had assured him that the chamber would reanimate this body upon the return of a conscious mind, the confirmation was welcome. The design factor was built into all chrysalis cylinders. Through the ages, the Altreians had learned to link their minds, not just to each other, but to their artificially intelligent computing systems.

Since this cylinder had been programmed to prevent Khal Teth's mind from reentering his body from the interdimensional prison into which it had been cast, the High Council had given no thought to his escape. Such a thing was impossible.

Jack entered a command and waited for the top to open. Swinging his legs out, he sat up and then climbed to his feet. The experience was disorienting. Accessing the memories stored in Khal Teth's brain, Jack remembered this small room within the vast center of government the Altreians called the Parthian. The Klaxon he had just triggered pulled Jack back into the now, just before Khal Teth forcibly took charge of his body.

Again Jack's mind spun as he attempted to reorient himself. He had known that Khal Teth planned this all along, but Jack just hadn't expected to be expelled so easily. The experience left him frustrated and, strangely enough, claustrophobic, as if he were strapped in a transparent barrel as the current carried him toward Niagara Falls. Just as Khal Teth had described the experience to him, Jack could feel and see everything. He just had no control over the outcome.

Jack felt Khal Teth's mind shift away from the sound of the alarm, the sensation dragging him along in a mental search for nearby minds. They were there by the thousands, most negligible in their strength. But a few dozen were running toward the chamber. The sensation was odd, swiftly changing as Khal Teth shifted his attention from one Altreian to another, momentarily touching their thoughts, seeing through each of their eyes as he evaluated the gathering threat.

Jack felt the thrill of being restored to full power course through Khal Teth's mind and savored the prospect of the coming conflict as if he were going to be a direct participant instead of merely along for the ride. All of those who approached were elite members of the High Council Guard, many of whom were powerful psionics themselves. A sneer curled Khal Teth's lips as he strode across the dimly lit room that housed the lone chrysalis cylinder.

When Khal Teth stepped up to the spot at the portion of the wall where the nano-material door should have allowed him passage, he reached out a red-and-black-mottled hand and pressed his palm against the cool metal surface. There, reflected in the shiny surface, Jack could see his new appearance.

He saw the familiar face and body of Khal Teth, wearing the shimmering black robes denoting his former position on the High Council, the same ones in which they had entombed him. The hood was swept back, revealing the dark eyes with their burning flickers of red in a slender face, its skin mottled red and black. His head was hairless, with pointed ears swept back tight along the sides. The gill slits of his neck lay closed, but Khal Teth's narrow nostrils flared as he pulled in a deep breath and centered his mind.

Outside the closed portal, a half-dozen guards had already gathered, their stun batons flaring with blue light, visible to Khal Teth's invasion of their senses. Suddenly all but their captain backed up against the Parthian's transparent outer wall. A slow shudder passed through the captain's body as he fought to resist the inevitable.

Then he lowered his baton, stepped up to the nanoparticle door, and entered the unlock code, stepping aside to let Khal Teth emerge through the cloudlike consistency of the nanoparticle door. Then, to Jack's amazement, the captain and his men charged to confront several newcomers who had just come into sight around the bend in the gently curving corridor, their batons flaring into action. Khal Teth strode behind them, the folds of his black robes whispering disdain for all who opposed him with each long stride.

:CHAPTER 11

As the alarm sounded throughout the Parthian, the overlord felt the brief mental disturbance from a mind that Parsus had not felt in thousands of cycles, one he'd believed he would never encounter again.

Apparently the impossible had happened. His twin brother had escaped.

The council guard would respond, but they would not be enough to stop Khal Teth. Only the combined will of the Circle of Twelve, a dozen of the thirteen members of the High Council, could accomplish that. Fortunately, the requisite council members were present inside the Parthian on this day. Parsus merely had to assemble them to enable the confrontation that would put his beloved brother back inside his eternal prison. He only hoped that his guards could delay Khal Teth long enough to enable him to pull the necessary pieces into place.

○ ● ○

Khal Teth moved along the gently curving outer hallway, the numbers of guards he had turned to his side growing to fifteen as they left the more troublesome of their lot dead on the floor behind him. Although Khal Teth could certainly have dominated all whom he encountered, he was saving his strength for any member of the High Council whom he might encounter, most particularly Parsus.

He let his eyes take in the beautiful view that the transparent outer wall provided. Low on the horizon hung the magenta-colored brown-dwarf star, Altreia. It provided most of the heat for this Earth-sized, watery world, upon which the Altreian system's population had evolved. Higher in the twilight sky, the orange Krell Nebula's lacy tendrils seemed to reach out in longing embrace of Quol's purple moon.

Since recovering his memories, Khal Teth had despaired at the thought he might never see this beautiful view again. Jack Gregory had restored those memories to him. Jack had made this homecoming possible. Khal Teth supposed he should be grateful. But Jack was just a tool of destiny, Khal Teth's destiny. A useful tool and nothing more.

Reaching out with his powerful mind, Khal Teth swept the Parthian, seeking Parsus. As he passed by the warren of side passages that led into the great internal maze of offices and meeting halls surrounding the grand amphitheater where government decisions were finalized and broadcast to the masses, he noted the thousands of government minions who now cowered behind their nanoparticle doors, on lockdown until the alarm quieted. They felt him touch their minds and shrank away, thankful that they remained beneath his notice.

His search failed to find any members of the High Council—not surprising since they would have shielded their minds from detection moments after the alarm sounded. Although he could certainly sweep those guards aside if he focused on a room-by-room search, he had neither the time nor the inclination to make such an effort. Now was the time for escape from this building to a place where he could initiate the plan that would sweep the current government from power.

A sudden disturbance to his front gave Khal Teth pause. The guards under his control had come to a complete stop, parting to let someone pass. Unable to believe his good fortune, Khal Teth lengthened his stride, walking directly toward the one he'd been hunting. Parsus strode toward him as well, his features eerily similar to Khal Teth's, the result of their shared genetic makeup. But instead of the black robes of a member of the High Council, Parsus wore the blue that bore the insignia of the overlord.

Khal Teth shouldn't have been surprised that his brother had accomplished the act for which he had been imprisoned. Apparently Parsus had been successful in the assassination of Valen Roth and the usurpation of his position. That Parsus now presented himself to Khal Teth was absurdly rich. Had he grown so overconfident over the millennia that he imagined himself the superior mind?

The two came to a stop three paces apart, each staring into the other's eyes, inner fire licking the black orbs.

"You surprise me, my brother," said Parsus, his voice as cold as his expression.

"And you, me. May I take it that Valen Roth succumbed to ill health?"

"A tragic accident. But that was a long time ago."

"Doubtless." Khal Teth felt his lips curl. "Kind of you to personally confront me. I would not have thought that your style."

Something tugged at the back of Khal Teth's mind as he felt Jack try to grab his attention, but the Altreian pushed the feeling aside. His human rider would soon discover that he would never achieve the level of influence that Khal Teth had achieved over him.

"Actually, I came to escort you back to your cell. I do not know how you managed this escape, but your brief glimpse of freedom is now at an end."

"Is it?"

Khal Teth parried the mental thrust from his twin, the tentacles of his own mind entangling those of Parsus and squeezing. Parsus staggered backward half a step before righting himself, drawing on a hidden power that freed his mind, leaving Khal Teth struggling to understand what had just happened. Why hadn't he seen this coming? The realization hit him hard. He wasn't naturally clairvoyant. No Altreian had that ability. Khal Teth had only gained his power to see future timelines as a side effect of having his mind trapped in an interdimensional prison. Now that he had returned to his body, that talent was gone.

As understanding flooded over him, he staggered forward, barely preventing himself from falling. Khal Teth's stunning escape had thrown the entire Parthian into panic, but somehow Parsus had anticipated his actions and had assembled the other eleven members of the Circle of Twelve in one of the adjacent rooms. And Khal Teth had walked right into his trap, allowing himself to be engaged in a conversation that had allowed the circle the time it needed to spring the ambush.

No! Not again.

But even as his mental scream brought a sympathetic smile to Parsus's lips, Khal Teth felt something move within his mind.

Jack's mental voice carried with it the rage that Khal Teth had come to recognize.

"Give me control, damn it."

Feeling the last of his will slipping away, Khal Teth reluctantly unleashed The Ripper.

○ ● ○

Jack exploded into the weak form, allowing his rage to power it forward, delivering a kick into Parsus's right knee that shattered bone and dropped him, screaming, to the floor. The mental vise that had frozen Khal Teth dropped away. Jack kicked the overlord in the face, then grabbed the stun baton of the nearest guard, twisting it free from her hands and whipping it around to bash in the skull of another.

The dying Altreian tumbled to the ground, sending a pistol-shaped weapon spinning across the floor. Jack ducked under a swinging baton, hearing the crackle of its electrical discharge as it swept by his face. Diving onto the floor, Jack grabbed the pistol and rolled, pressing the mechanism that Khal Teth's memories identified as the trigger. A series of individual energy pulses leaped from the gun, striking down four more guards as they attempted to bring their own weapons to bear.

Those that remained on their feet scrambled away down the hall, firing wildly from both directions, sending deadly blasts over Jack's body and into their compatriots on the opposite sides of where he lay amid the fallen bodies.

Jack scrambled across the floor to the unconscious body of the overlord, grabbed a fistful of his robes at the throat, and dragged him through an open doorway into an inner hallway, pausing at the entrance just long enough to send several more energy bolts in both directions along the passage he'd just exited.

Turning, he saw an open doorway to his left and dragged Parsus's body inside an office that showed signs of hasty departure. Ignoring the outcry from his protesting muscles, he stripped the overlord's blue robes from his body and then pulled Khal Teth's black robes off over his head. Counting down the time he estimated it would take for the guards to work up the courage to charge the hallway, he quickly slid into the blue robes and then tugged the black one onto Parsus's unconscious body.

Jack stowed the pulse weapon in one of the blue robe's pockets. Then, taking a deep breath, he relaxed into the meditation that would release his hold on this body. His mental message to Khal Teth accompanied his exhalation.

"Your turn."

○ ● ○

The snapback that returned control of his body staggered Khal Teth. Pain such as he had never before experienced left him dizzy, gasping.

What had Jack done to him? All his muscles had seemingly been shredded and ripped loose from attachment to bones and tendons.

A sudden slapping noise pulled his attention to the guards charging toward the office. The first reached the door, swung his weapon in, and froze, confusion clouding his features as he raised a fist to halt those behind him.

Khal Teth gently touched his mind, implanting a strong sense of recognition.

"Overlord," the guard said, "are you all right?"

Ignoring the question, Khal Teth gestured at the unconscious form of Parsus, clad in a black robe, his face so badly swollen that it was unrecognizable.

"Captain, take this prisoner to a holding cell and make sure he is kept heavily sedated. Keep him that way until I assemble the High Council to deal with this matter."

"Yes, Overlord."

The guard captain issued a sequence of rapid commands that ushered two other guardsmen into the room to seize the unconscious Altreian and roughly drag him away. Then the captain once more turned his attention to Khal Teth. But before he could utter a question, Khal Teth cut him off.

"Leave me now, and attend to the fallen."

The captain spun on his heel and exited, barking orders to his subordinates. Although Khal Teth knew that this guard could have relayed those orders mentally, telepathic interactions took extra focus and could be a source of distraction for targeted parties. Whenever possible, verbal intercourse was still the preferred method of communication.

Suppressing a groan, Khal Teth forced himself to walk out into the hallway without limping. He turned into the outer hallway, exuding an aura of authority that caused all the guards who remained standing to lower their eyes as he swept past them. With his mind heavily shielded,

Khal Teth focused on the task at hand, reaching the nearest building exit without further interference.

With every step, the pain he felt got worse, making concentration difficult. While his appearance was very similar to that of Parsus, he knew that the ruse would not survive a direct encounter with a member of the High Council. Soon one of those members would make his or her way to the holding cell where Parsus's unconscious body had been taken. And in his current, weakened condition, Khal Teth lacked confidence that he could summon the mental acumen to defend himself once they discovered the truth.

Around the arc up ahead, he felt an Altreian senator and her personal guard enter the looping exterior hallway and turn in his direction. Despite knowing that he could force this group to turn aside or merely pass through them unnoticed, Khal Teth exited through a nanoparticle door into one of the Parthian's inner hallways, along which the vast majority of the government staff remained under lockdown in their closed offices until the all-clear had been given.

Khal Teth stumbled, barely managing to right himself. Despite his best efforts, he was now visibly limping. Worse, he felt as if he had reached the limit of his endurance, knowing he could not traverse the breadth of the Parthian to reach the hover port. Nor could he make his way down into the depths of the building to exit onto the island surface.

Then a new realization dawned upon him. If he was going to have any chance of making good on his escape, he would have to return this body to the control of one who had spent a lifetime dealing with agony such as this. It would weaken his psychic abilities, but no more so than the distraction this physical misery was inflicting on him.

Leaning against a wall for support, Khal Teth closed his eyes and initiated the transition that wiped away his pain.

○ ● ○

Jack straightened, taking a moment to allow the disorientation of his transition to pass. Ignoring the wave of weakness that assailed him, he shunted the pain aside and forced himself to focus on his surroundings. He pulled forth Khal Teth's memory of the building, not just the levels where Altreia's governance happened, but of the residential and recreational areas as well.

He had to give the Altreians credit. Artistic beauty was a deeply ingrained part of their culture, something they incorporated into anything they bothered to build or create, and the Parthian represented the epitome of their art. Seen from above, the structure looked like a gigantic glass teardrop that had been laid on its side and sliced into multicolored layers. The topmost governmental layers shifted through deep shades of magenta that transitioned through purples and blues as they descended into spirals of orange laced with greens, before shifting back to dark blue at the bottom of the structure. The residences lined the right side of the teardrop, looking like tiny orange bubbles carved into its surface.

The interior structures were no less impressive. As Jack studied the hallway ahead, he was reminded of a Chihuly blown-glass exhibition he'd attended in Santa Fe, New Mexico, except that this art seemed to have been extruded from the walls themselves. He realized that this interior art mirrored the beauty of the sky visible through the Parthian's transparent outer walls and ceiling.

Jack resumed walking, posture erect, his confident stride carrying him toward the interior of the Parthian, more specifically toward the maintenance hallways that would take him to a set of turbo-lifts used for moving equipment and supplies. Oddly enough, he could feel the minds of those huddled within their offices, could feel the fear that radiated out.

Why wouldn't they be frightened? The escape of one such as Khal Teth had never happened before.

More importantly, Khal Teth's mental shielding continued to hide his mind from others who would seek to stop him. Apparently, when not in complete control of his own body, Khal Teth was unable to directly access his psionic abilities, filtered as they were through the mask of Jack's mind. So he was forced to guide Jack's mind through a particular psionic task, a difficult, less efficient process.

Right now all the elite government psionics were hurrying toward the cell where they believed Khal Teth's unconscious body was being held. Jack wanted to be out of the building before that happened.

His thoughts turned to the Circle of Twelve that had come close to recapturing Khal Teth. Khal Teth's memories had merged with Jack's own, giving him full knowledge of how that group had managed such a task. Technically speaking, there was no need to form a circle. Proximity between council members was all that was required. The name was merely a vestige of an ancient ritual where a dozen high-functioning psionics linked minds into a single entity, more powerful than the sum of the individuals.

The ritual didn't work with eleven, with thirteen, or with any number other than twelve. Only elite minds, such as those on the High Council, could form such a link. Considering that the group must also be completely united in purpose, only a rare set of circumstances allowed for its formation. Once formed, any divergence in intent would break the link. Jack's physical attack had given Parsus a new primary objective—personal survival—and the link was thus shattered.

As Jack approached the final turn that would take him to the maintenance lifts, he felt and then saw a half-dozen guards round the corner ahead and come to a stop.

The thought he directed at Khal Teth shouldn't have been necessary. "Make them move along."

An uncomfortable hesitation carried Jack several more steps toward the waiting guards before Khal Teth responded.

"In my weakened condition, I cannot."

Jack felt his jaws tighten. *Just freakin' great!*

The commander of the group stepped forward to meet him. "Overlord. I apologize, but I have been sent to escort you to the council chamber."

Not good. He'd been counting on more time. Worse, he could feel the guard commander's thoughts probe the edges of his own. Khal Teth's strength was rapidly failing.

Jack halted before the guards, smiled, and nodded. Then he drew his weapon and fired.

CHAPTER 12

Jennifer felt like the top of her head had been chiseled off and her brain scrambled. Due to the extensive neural augmentation she had received on the Second Ship, she could track what was happening. Unfortunately, she couldn't stop it.

As she stood alone in the tunnel, far beneath the surface of the northern Koranthian Mountains, the knowledge of what was being done to her pulled a scream from deep within her mind, a scream that echoed there but never found its way to the surface. The Kasari nanobots weren't rewiring her synapses as the Altreian starship had done. Instead, they were embedding themselves in her brain, disconnecting her volition more effectively than any drug and turning that part of her over to the Kasari Collective.

Except for the clarity she retained, the experience reminded her of how she had felt under the influence of the heroin administered by NSA personnel, with addiction being the end result. She still knew right from wrong, but the part of her mind that made the decisions just didn't care anymore. Worse, the hive-mind saw whatever she saw, heard whatever she heard, and, unless she did something to limit their control, would soon be able to command her to do whatever the Kasari wanted. And she would do it willingly.

Knowing that she had very little time, Jennifer recalled a favorite meditation and centered, feeling her breathing slow and her pulse drop as she became a single point of light in an endless expanse of blackness. Then she transferred a singular intent to her subconscious mind. She felt her neural pathways rewire themselves, walling off a core subset of memories related to the Second Ship, the Altreian technologies it contained, and the devices that she, Mark, Heather, and Raul had derived from them.

Jennifer released the meditation, locking all that she had protected within the depths of her subconscious mind. Then, reorienting on her surroundings, Jennifer turned and strode rapidly back toward General Dgarra's headquarters, feeling a great sense of urgency. After all, he needed her at his side as he prepared for the battles yet to come.

○ ● ○

Kasari group commander Shalegha monitored the assimilation of the human female, Jennifer Smythe, releasing a small flood of endorphins as a self-reward for the achievement. This represented the breakthrough Shalegha had been looking for. The Koranthian general, Magtal, had delivered precisely what he had promised. She knew he was merely an ally of convenience, using the Kasari to achieve his own ends just as they used him. It didn't matter. Many others had tried to play that game.

Shalegha strengthened her link to the nanobot cortical array distributed throughout Jennifer Smythe's brain. Jennifer's powerful mind was still fighting to maintain free will, even though this was a fight she had no chance of winning. Shalegha dipped into Jennifer's memories, letting them flow through her own mind in rapid sequence as they were absorbed by the hive-mind.

She paused, rescanning. That was odd. The memories contained numerous gaps. Had Jennifer Smythe suffered some sort of severe brain trauma in the past?

With a quick rescan, Shalegha observed Jennifer's incarceration and torture at the hands of an Earth-based intelligence organization known as the National Security Agency. During that lengthy period of interrogation, she had been subjected to regular dosages of a powerful opiate drug, leading to an addiction that she'd only recently been able to master. That could account for some of the memory gaps Shalegha was observing. Some, but not all.

Shalegha's attention shifted forward to the events that occurred when Jennifer and her fellow human, Raul, had hijacked the world ship that had brought them to Scion. The resulting wormhole jump should have killed them both, but Jennifer had engineered a workaround that had broken the wormhole transit into a great number of smaller wormhole steps. The trip had battered and broken their bodies, but Jennifer had survived due to an infusion of Raul's nanite-infested blood. This battering could have resulted in additional memory loss, but the periods of time when those memory holes occurred seemed suspicious.

Somehow the world ship had been modified with subspace field capabilities indicative of Altreian technology. Had that been done on Earth? If so, where had the Altreian assistance come from? If the Altreians were helping the humans, why had they allowed them to build the wormhole gateway?

Thoughts of the Altreians curled the commander's lips, baring her teeth. As Shalegha prepared to withdraw from her study of Jennifer's mind, another of the human's memories caught her attention. There had been an additional presence on the world ship besides that of Raul or Jennifer, a simulation they had named VJ. Clearly a primitive artificial intelligence, but the problem with AIs was that they didn't stay primitive.

Many ages ago, experimentation with AI technology and autonomous robots had almost destroyed the Kasari Collective, an experience that had led to a permanent ban on artificial intelligence. But the Altreians, so smug in their conviction that they understood how to contain such a force, dabbled with AI. Now humans were also apparently engaged in this dangerous tinkering with that which could not be reliably controlled or contained.

Shalegha clenched her upper two hands into fists, cracking her knuckles as she strode out onto her command center's open balcony. Standing here in the cool evening breeze, a hundred and fifty stories above ground level, her view of the capital city of Orthei was magnificent. Far below, white-winged Eadric soared back and forth between structures painted scarlet by the setting sun. In this way, the Eadric were like the Altreians, wasting tremendous time and resources on the creation of beautiful tableaus.

In short order, that would all change. Once their assimilation was complete, the Eadric people would no longer care about such things. The collective good and its efficient implementation would take precedence over such trivialities as art.

Now that Jennifer Smythe had joined the fold, the intelligence that she could provide would topple the Koranthian Empire and help make this new vision of Scion a reality.

○ ● ○

General Dgarra looked up to see Smythe's slender body glide into his headquarters, her movements making those of his warriors seem clumsy by comparison. As he watched her approach, the warmth that spread through his body surprised him. Whenever she entered his presence, he felt stronger, regaining some of the self-assurance that recent battles had beaten out of him. Perhaps they would yet see this war through to a favorable end.

"Where have you been?" he asked.

A sad smile tweaked the corners of her lips. "I stepped outside to watch the stars."

Dgarra studied her. Her brown hair had grown out so that it almost reached the collar of her black uniform, framing her face in a way that was simultaneously alien and beautiful. Understanding awoke within him.

"Raul?"

"Somewhere out there, he's still alive."

"You know this?"

"I feel it."

Dgarra turned back toward the tactical displays on the far wall. He had no time for discussions of wishful thinking. A storm was building to the northeast of his position, a storm of soldiers, Eadric and Kasari—a storm fed by a new infusion of Kasari heavy artillery, the likes of which he had not previously seen. By the dark gods, what would they bring through that hellish gateway next?

So far he'd been lucky, guessing where to deploy the limited supply of stasis shield generators so that they blunted the enemy's main thrust. Smythe stepped up beside him, and he glanced at her as she stared up at those same view-screens, a look of intense concentration on her face. In truth she had been his good-luck charm.

Turning his attention back to the big board, Dgarra allowed himself a grim smile. He now had to make the decisions that would position his forces for tomorrow's battle. With her by his side radiating so much positive energy, perhaps he could not lose.

○ ● ○

Jennifer's scream of frustration hammered at the bonds that imprisoned it deep within her mind. She wanted to walk away from Dgarra, to deny the hive-mind the knowledge of the battle plans that he was revealing to her, but she was unable to give the smallest hint that something was wrong. Her will was now subject to the commands provided through the nanobot cortical array, forcing her to take actions that she would rather kill herself than perform. She had become two people, the unseen ghost of Jennifer Smythe and the pod person who had stolen her body.

To her horror, she found herself actively engaged in the conversation with Dgarra, even offering suggestions that carried tactical insights provided by the Kasari group commander in charge of Scion's assimilation. And Dgarra welcomed her input, taking the time to explain why he was rejecting her suggestions. Dear Lord, he was training her on his thought process—training the Kasari.

Aware that her frustration was getting her nowhere, Jennifer abandoned her attempts to fight her link to the hive-mind. The memory of how she had exploited her Altreian headset's link to the Second Ship's neural network replayed itself within the firewalled part of her mind. Maybe she could make use of this linkage to learn something that could help her escape this new mental prison.

Jennifer focused on the link, using the Kasari cortical array instead of her psychic abilities to identify other minds that were directly monitoring what her body was seeing and hearing. At first nothing happened. Then she realized her mistake. She was trying too hard, with no better results than trying to force herself into deep meditation. She relaxed her mind, allowing herself to become a passive observer of this link to the hive-mind. And as she did, she began to identify other observers. Much like medical students watching a surgeon from the operating-theater balcony, the handful of Kasari who watched Jennifer and Dgarra's interactions paid no attention to each other.

She shifted her attention to the Kasari group commander. A name formed in Jennifer's mind. Shalegha. As she focused on that identity, Jennifer felt her connection to that particular node within the hive-mind strengthen. Like turning up the volume on her phone, it wasn't something that the person on the other end would notice—not so long as she merely observed and did nothing to draw attention to herself.

Allowing herself to drift along the link, Jennifer found herself sitting inside a room buzzing with activity. Uniformed Eadric soldiers manned most of what appeared to be tactical workstations, although some were operated by Kasari. The sensation wasn't entirely dissimilar to the way Jennifer could touch the minds of others, although she didn't dare attempt to influence Shalegha's mind. This was a technological link, not a telepathic one, and she had a strong feeling that drawing attention to her ghostly self would be a very bad idea.

Jennifer withdrew from the link to Shalegha, determined to explore the limits of her brain's connection to the hive-mind. Unfortunately, she found herself unable to directly access any other connections. Why could she access Shalegha's link but no others? Was it because Shalegha had established an active connection to Jennifer's cortical array in order to pass along specific instructions?

When Shalegha abruptly terminated their connection, Jennifer was startled. She could still feel the hive-mind, knew that it was recording everything her body saw and heard, but she had lost the ability to access data from Shalegha or any other member of the collective. The scenario was as if the router for her connection had blocked external traffic and she lacked the administrative privileges to override its security settings.

Jennifer knew the analogy was imperfect, but it raised questions about how the cortical arrays communicated with the hive-mind. Not through subspace—that was an Altreian technology. Such communication wasn't likely to happen via quantum entanglement either, as the method could not feasibly interconnect the entire population of the Kasari Collective.

Then it hit her. The wormhole gateways must be acting as communication portals. That would mean that communications within a star system could be limited to light speed but, with the wormhole gateways eliminating the intervening distance between star systems, interstellar communication would be nearly instantaneous.

Damn it all. Why did any of this matter? Here she was, stuck in the part of her brain she herself had shielded from the Kasari nanobots, impotent to do anything but observe what was happening. And what had she learned? That she could observe Shalegha when that particular Kasari chose to open a direct link to Jennifer's cortical array?

Jennifer wished she could cry, but this ghostly version of herself couldn't even provide that level of release. As she returned her attention to Dgarra, she imagined how he would react once her betrayal was discovered. If only she could do the honorable thing and fall upon her own war-blade, but even the solace of suicide was denied her.

Her future spun out before her. Over and over again, she would be forced to watch herself betray this great man, which is how she had come to think of the Koranthian general. Darkness closed in around her, the walls she had built squeezing her tighter and tighter as words echoed in the tiny space.

Don't hope. There's no room for hope in here.

:CHAPTER 13

The crackle of energy accompanied an electrical arc that laced Raul's vision with white afterimages, even though he'd closed his eyes. The acrid smell of molten wire filled his nostrils and he stumbled backward, blinking rapidly as he tried to see the results of his latest attempt to jump-start the forward matter disrupter.

The data displays that blossomed in his mind almost dropped him to his knees in prayerful thanksgiving. The neural net had just come back online.

"It took you long enough," VJ's voice whispered through the command bay. Raul thought he heard a hint of relief mixed in with the sarcasm.

"You're welcome."

"How about getting us the hell out of here?" VJ asked.

"Can't."

"We have power."

"Not enough to engage the subspace field generator. Not without the primary matter disrupter-synthesizer."

"We will if you kill the cloaking field."

Raul slapped his palm against his forehead. Of course. Why hadn't he thought of that? If they shifted into subspace, there would be no need to stay cloaked. A new worry hit him.

"Our enemies will detect us as soon as we uncloak. If the subspace generator fails to fire up, it won't do us any good to cloak again. It might be safer to continue making repairs until we can bring primary power back online."

VJ paused. "I estimate it will take us two hours to get the nano-material fabricators working and another three after that to repair the subspace field generator. Do you really want to hang out in the middle of this war zone for the additional thirty-seven hours that will be necessary to repair the primary MDS?"

"I'll think about it while we fix the nano-material fabricators and the subspace generator."

"Wow. A five-hour decision cycle. Impressive."

"Shut it."

A low chuckle brought a flush of heat to Raul's face, and he realized that the VJ simulation had once again managed to pluck his strings. Pretending he didn't notice, Raul turned to the task at hand.

The repairs took just over four hours, going much faster once the Rho Ship's nano-manufacturing capability was restored. After running a complete set of diagnostics on the subspace field generator, Raul sucked in a breath, savoring the fact that he could no longer see it when he exhaled. Life support had restored warmth to the command bay. Of course, if what he was about to try didn't work, his physical comfort would be the least of his worries.

"Screw it," he said, settling onto a stasis field couch. "Get ready to engage the subspace field generator on my mark."

"That's my guy."

Shaking his head, Raul killed the cloaking field.

"Mark!"

CHAPTER 14

Aaden Bauer looked up from his laptop to see the two men he'd been waiting for walk through the front door of the old German farmhouse, accompanied by a wiry blonde whom he had heard much about but hadn't yet had the opportunity to meet. Rising from his chair, Aaden stepped forward to greet them.

"Bergen, Kolt. No troubles with your journey I take it."

"None whatsoever," said Bergen, a stout bald man with laughing blue eyes.

Kolt Jacobs, the big sandy-haired Swede, stepped forward. "Aaden, this is Nikina Gailan."

Aaden shifted his gaze to the woman to Kolt's right. At first glance, he had thought her skinny, but he had been wrong. From the cut of her jaw to the muscles that crawled beneath her skin with every movement, she exuded danger, an impression that was magnified by the intensity that sparkled in her ice-gray eyes.

His eyes were drawn to the part in her hairline, the thin scar a remnant of a bullet wound that the nanites in her blood hadn't been able to completely repair. Aaden had read her dossier, but the physical presence of this Latvian Safe Earth resistance operative was something he had to experience to truly appreciate.

Aaden smiled and extended his hand to her. "Welcome to the revolution."

Instead of shaking his hand, she reached out and placed a small solid-state memory device in his palm.

"I believe this is what you've been waiting for."

As he stared down at the device, Aaden felt his mouth go dry. Could it really be true?

His impressive guest suddenly forgotten, Aaden returned to his chair, connected the device to his laptop, and attempted to open the compressed file folder, but found himself staring at a password-entry box.

Nikina leaned over his shoulder and typed a rapid sequence of characters followed by the "Enter" key. It took more than two minutes to extract all the compressed files and copy them to his laptop, a delay that seemed to take much longer. When the process finally ended, Aaden was surprised to find that a tremor had worked its way into his hands.

He opened one file after another, his excitement growing with each document. As Nikina had promised, these files represented not only the complete specifications and blueprints for the wormhole gateway being built deep underground on the outskirts of Frankfurt, but also an updated project schedule and a listing of all personnel assigned to the project.

"How in the heavens did you get all of this?" Aaden asked.

"I'm afraid you'll have to be satisfied with what I've given you. I cannot reveal my sources."

Aaden looked up. "Forgive me. It is just that this is so much more than I expected."

For the first time a smile graced Nikina's lips, and the change was startling. All the harshness left her face, leaving Aaden with the impression that this was a different woman. The ease with which she made the transformation reinforced everything he had learned about her from his Latvian counterpart. He was suddenly very glad that she had been assigned to him as their operation moved from planning to execution.

He glanced down at the wormhole-gateway construction schedule on his laptop screen. If the German arm of the Safe Earth resistance movement was to have any chance of destroying that monster before it went active, they were going to need the skills that Nikina Gailan possessed.

He pulled a specialized cell phone from his pocket, which communicated via two chips quantum entangled with one other. Although Aaden had no idea where in the world that other phone was located, he knew exactly to whom it belonged.

Pressing the call button, he waited for the connection. When the familiar voice of the movement's founder answered, he smiled in anticipation of relaying the good news.

"Hello, Heather, this is Aaden."

:CHAPTER 15

Heather didn't need sleep. But, oh God, how she missed it. Unfortunately, she didn't have time for such luxuries.

She escorted Robby to his couch in the newly upgraded command center, the rightmost of the four chairs modeled after those on the Second Ship's bridge. The room, far belowground in the middle of New Zealand's boondocks, was as close to an exact replica of that Altreian design as it was possible to build given the current state of the nano-manufacturing infrastructure within the monstrous underground complex. Supported by rooms of supercomputers that put the finest competing human technologies to shame, the robotically constructed, mile-deep facility would soon change the very nature of Earth-based warfare. Hopefully that would be enough.

Considering the progress that had been made in the construction of the thousands of military drones and robots that were currently stored within the facility, they were almost ready for the task that lay ahead. The exponential productivity made possible by manufacturing robots that created other robots had grown to the point where more was being accomplished in a month than had been done in the first seven years of the facility's existence.

Heather sat down on the translucent couch, sinking into the malleable material until she felt almost weightless.

Heather, Mark, Jennifer, and Robby had been altered by the four Altreian headsets, gifted with eidetic memories and enhanced neuromuscular systems. But the headsets had also changed them in different ways. Heather had been granted savant mathematical abilities, making her capable of visualizing near-future events based upon an automatic calculation of changing probabilities. Mark had become stronger, faster, and more coordinated than the rest of the group. Able to master new languages very quickly, he could precisely imitate the sound of another person's voice, whether male or female.

Although they had all developed some ability to communicate telepathically with one another, Robby could move small objects with his mind. More importantly, he could allow Eos, the artificial intelligence that shared his mind, to use that power to manipulate the electrons within computing devices, thereby taking control of them.

Jennifer had been the one to master both her telepathic and empathic capabilities. The thought of her lost friend caused Heather's eyes to shift to the couch that would remain forever empty in her honor. That sad memory pulled Heather back to the present.

With the doors closed, the ambient magenta lighting in the room seemed to emanate from the air itself. That, combined with the lack of corners, made it very difficult to identify a transition from wall to floor or ceiling. Of course, that was the point of its design, to provide very little visual distraction to the sensory inputs the headsets provided. Today she and Robby would be using the headsets that Heather had designed to connect to their New Zealand supercomputers, as opposed to the Altreian headsets that could link them to the computer aboard the Second Ship.

The call from Aaden Bauer could not have come at a better time. Heather had been thrilled with the detailed information contained within the thousands of pages of blueprints and design documents that Aaden had transmitted over their QE connection. She had spent last night scanning each document into her memory and reviewing the validity of all the data contained therein. There could be no doubt that this was the real deal, and that meant their time for action was rapidly approaching.

Heather put on her headset, watching as the room melted away around her as the translucent beads at each end settled over her temples. In response to her mental command, the scene shifted to one of the great natural caverns that their construction robots had tunneled into a little over four months ago. She sent the query through her headset.

"Robby?"

"I'm in."

"For today's exercise, you've got blue force. I've got red."

"Roger."

Heather smiled at his use of the military term that meant "I understand." Sometimes she almost forgot that he was only nine, with an understandable hero worship for both his mom and dad, surely the most dangerous couple on Earth. But Jack wasn't really on Earth anymore, now was he? Not his mind, anyway. The thought wiped the smile from her lips.

Janet, having left Mark in Bolivia to work with the Safe Earth resistance there, was scheduled to land their corporate jet at the Smythes' Tasman Mining Corporation's private airstrip eight hours from now. Heather could only imagine how she must be feeling.

For that matter, she was amazed to see how Robby was dealing with the loss of his dad. The boy had decided that Jack would find a way to return, just as he had from every other impossible situation in which he found himself. Given the history of the man whom the world knew as The Ripper, Heather could understand how his son would think that, even though her calculation of Jack's odds told her a different story. Maybe Robby's optimistic attitude wasn't so bad.

Shifting her attention back to the cavern, she studied the layout, piping the feeds from all the red-force cameras directly into her mind. Today's exercise was going to be different from any of the war games she and Robby had conducted before. All those others had consisted of conflict between two simulated robotic forces. Even though the algorithms that had controlled those sims were the same as what had been downloaded into the two robotic companies that had positioned themselves more than a mile apart within the many rooms and branches of the caverns, today's exercise would be a full-scale live-fire assault as each side attempted to capture the hidden flag of the other.

Each side had been assigned identical forces: four platoons consisting of two types of ground-combat robots, a dog-shaped version alongside a larger quasihumanoid model, and an air-cavalry unit consisting of combat-reconnaissance drones. All in all, more than three hundred robots would be used in this fight, each armed with weapons capable of destroying others of their kind. The combat scenario would be destructive and wasteful, but Heather had judged it to be absolutely necessary.

An old saying was often still applied to simulations, no matter how good: *The map is not the territory.* No model formed a completely accurate representation of the real thing. So today, she and Robby would observe the real things fighting alongside each other in a life-or-death struggle between evenly matched forces.

Her thoughts turned to the situation in which Earth found itself. As she had foreseen, the world had fractured along economic and religious lines, spawning unending wars. The Islamic Alliance had become a reality that stretched across the Middle East, the northern two-thirds of Africa, and the island nations that made up greater Indonesia, Malaysia, and the Philippines.

In reality the IA was a collection of tribal societies that followed various versions of Islam but had no true central government. The organization was bound together by anger at the collapse of the Middle Eastern oil economies, outrage at their third-world economic status, and hatred of the destructive technologies being released by the four superpowers that formed the UFNS. With millions of followers distributed within the populations of the superpowers, they hadn't needed advanced technology to seed terror within the hearts of their enemies. Ironically, the distributed nature of the IA made it very hard to defeat.

The rest of the third world had also grouped together through largely tribal partnerships, the biggest of these being the Native People's Alliance that dominated South and Central America, even cutting a swath through parts of the fifty-nine United States. For the most part, this alliance tried to keep its head down, preferring to let the IA and the UFNS wage violent warfare against each other.

The Safe Earth resistance movement had incubated within the NPA's ranks, gradually gathering sympathizers within the first-world countries as they prepared to launch the strike to destroy the heavily guarded wormhole gateway being built beneath the outskirts of Frankfurt.

Heather had come up with the scheme that provided funding for all offshoots of the Safe Earth resistance, one that hadn't required her to use any of the myriad shell corporations within which her own funds were distributed. The unique neural augmentations she had received during her first visit to the Second Ship enabled her to predict equity- and financial-market movements with uncanny accuracy. And through the network of quantum-entangled communications devices that had been distributed to Safe Earth cells, she alerted them to exciting short-term investment opportunities. Of course, the investments by these cells had to be carefully managed so as to avoid attracting the notice of various market minders or intelligence agencies.

"Ready when you are," said Robby.

His words pulled Heather out of her reverie.

"Before we start, I want to lay out the rules for today."

"Okay."

"You will issue blue force the following mission: at eight thirty local time, blue force will attack in order to locate and seize the red-force flag while preventing red force from seizing the blue-force flag."

"What about intel?"

"Both forces will have the same mission, but their attacks will be launched with no prior intelligence about the enemy locations or force dispositions."

"What?"

"Our goal in all of this is to observe the battle from the perspective of our forces. I want you and Eos to identify any problems with the way your blue force responds given complete autonomy to accomplish the mission. I'll be doing the same for the red force. We're looking for any problematic autonomous behaviors that didn't show up during the simulations."

There was a brief pause as Robby considered what she had told him. Heather suspected that he was deep in conversation with Eos. When he did speak, she detected excitement in his voice.

"Won't the supercomputer that's running the whole thing invalidate the notion that this is an autonomous test?"

"Other than uplinking their sensor information so that we can observe what is happening, the robots will be firewalled off from the supercomputer for the duration of the exercise. Also, the caverns will be sealed off from the rest of the facility via a stasis field at the exit."

"Wow!"

"It's eight twenty-three. Are you ready to get this started?"

"Get your evil red-force minions ready for a big blue boot in the ass," Robby said. "Blue force out."

As Robby shifted his attention to his blue force, Heather smiled. Despite all his augmentations, Robby couldn't help turning this into a game that he wanted his side to win. For her part, she was content to know that he could still find the fun in this robot battle, regardless of the knowledge that these devices would soon be put to a much deadlier purpose.

○ ● ○

"Mission statement transmitted," Eos said.

"Time remaining?" Robby asked, feeling his heart race with anticipation.

"Fifty-eight seconds until mission initiation."

Despite the fact that he'd run similar simulations many times, this felt different. He was about to unleash these battle-bots, watching as they devised their own plan to search out and destroy the enemy, making decisions derived through a complex set of negotiations between all elements of the swarm. He paused to consider that. Without direction from himself, Eos, or a supercomputer, these robots and drones would rely on swarm computing until only one remained. In that case, the surviving bot would be left to make its own decisions.

He scanned the sensor feeds, taking in imagery from the entire company of robots. He knew that they waited without the tightness in the chest he felt. Robby wondered if Heather was as emotionless over the outcome as these automatons were. After all, her goals were very different from his. She just wanted to confirm that these robots reliably acted together in a sophisticated swarm that carried out the intent that had been transmitted to them, not caring which side won or lost or even how many would be destroyed in the process.

Why should she care about those losses when this facility was manufacturing more than a thousand robots and drones per day? Initially, Robby had worried about that. After all, what good would it do to have tens of thousands of robotic combat machines if you lacked the ability to transport them to the vicinity of their targets?

But once again he had underestimated Heather's genius. With her detailed knowledge of the design of Dr. Stephenson's wormhole gateway, she had created miniature versions that she called Earth gates. These required far less power than an interstellar wormhole gateway and were only capable of linking to other such gateways right here on Earth.

These Earth gates would enable them to transport robots and weapons in an instant. Of course, someone on the other side could send enemy soldiers through the same gateway. For that reason, Heather had designed the remote gateways so that they were incapable of initiating a connection. That could only be done from the Earth gate within the New Zealand facility.

"Ten seconds." Eos's voice returned Robby's focus to the coming battle.

When the robots activated, Robby was startled by how fast they moved. All the small multicopter drones zipped away, splitting up as they reached connecting passages and caverns. Eos organized the data, creating an image of a wall filled with the broadcast imagery from hundreds of cameras along with another mental display that showed the health of each member of his robot army.

As the drones departed, a group of seven robots moved to defensive positions to protect the blue-force flag.

The remaining robots raced forward to the first side passage, where a dozen dog-shaped robots peeled off, their four legs propelling them along that tunnel as the bulk of the force continued through the main passage.

First contact with the enemy came shortly thereafter, when two of his forward drones were blasted out of the air by laser pulses, their video feeds going black as their status changed to red. Robby watched in stunned silence as three more of his drones winked out, quickly followed into death by seven others. They were rushing forward into the enemy in a suicidal charge of the light brigade.

"What the hell are they doing?" he asked, consciously trying to sound like his dad.

"Building a map," Eos said.

As Robby studied the data being relayed among his swarm, he understood. His robots had decided to immediately attack with a forward-deployed covering force dashing directly into the enemy, intending to meet them as far forward of the blue flag as possible and to identify where and how the red force was deployed. Those sacrifices were rapidly building a map of the enemy formation that was shared among all members of the blue swarm.

Red had adopted an initial defensive posture, designed to inflict heavy damage should the blue side attack, no doubt intending to follow up with a swift counterattack into the weakened enemy.

But instead of calling off the assault as Robby expected, his blue forces swarmed into the concentrated fire within the kill zone. The attack was happening too fast. Although the red army was now taking casualties, their losses were far fewer than what blue was experiencing.

Suddenly a group of two dozen blue-force robots converged into a single mass and charged directly at the center of the red army's defenses, as incoming laser fire ate into the outermost robots, stripping them away like the layers of an onion. This was insanity. Even if this group reached the enemy lines, as it appeared they were going to, there would be so few left that they would be torn apart by the superior force awaiting them.

Something else was wrong, too. The sixty-three other robots that were all that remained of blue force had pulled back into covered locations, not even bothering to provide fire support for those who charged. Just then, the three robots that remained functional from the assaulting group penetrated the line of defense, and before they could be destroyed by enemy fire, they detonated in a blast that wiped his view from all of the forward sensors.

"Oh my God!" Robby gasped.

For once, Eos said nothing.

Robby glanced over at Heather sitting in her own command couch, a lump forming in his throat. Her eyes had turned milky white.

○ ● ○

As Heather watched the data on her mental view-screens, many of which had suddenly gone dark, the visions that cascaded through her mind varied in predicted outcome, but the general consensus was far from good.

Pulling herself back to the present, she pondered what had just happened. Clearly the blue force had launched an all-out assault on the red swarm, which had opted for a defensive strategy. Blue had poured its robots into what appeared to be a suicidal charge into the teeth of the red defenses, taking losses that made a drawn-out fight unsustainable. But just as the red were about to launch a counterattack, a couple of blue-force robots had penetrated the red front line. What should have been a simple problem to clean up suddenly morphed into something unexpected and devastating.

Although the robots had only been outfitted with laser weaponry, one of the blue robots somehow managed to detonate itself, destroying scores of red's forces and blowing an impressive hole in the defensive formation. On cue, the bulk of the blue force charged into that hole, raking the red forces that had survived the blast with covering fire as its lead elements raced toward the chamber containing the red flag and its last group of defenders.

How had that happened? The answer formed in her mind even as she asked herself the question. Somehow the attacking swarm had hacked its way into the laser-firing controls and created an overload that had blown a power pack.

A change in the action drew her attention. Despite being outnumbered forty-nine to fourteen, ten of the remaining red forces raced to prevent the blue forces from entering the cavern where the red flag was planted—a desperate action almost certain to fail. Heather calculated red's chances of plugging the breach in their lines at 0.000387 percent.

Another massive explosion momentarily wiped her mental imagery. When it cleared, what she saw changed everything. Only one robot had been terminated. A red-force defender had run away from the other defenders and detonated itself in a back corner of the red-flag cavern.

"Oh no," Heather whispered as a new visualization formed in her mind.

The red-force robot had triggered its own overload at a spot that had no chance of damaging other robots, friend or foe. But the explosion had punched a hole in the wall that separated the natural cavern from the rest of Heather's underground facility, just beyond the edge of the stasis field that blocked the exit. Immediately, another red-force robot that wasn't directly engaged in the fight to keep the blue attackers away from the flag grabbed it from its stand and raced for the smoking hole in the back wall.

Understanding dawned in Heather's mind. The mission statement that had been passed to the robots had contained two objectives: capture the other side's flag and prevent them from capturing yours. The red swarm had made the same probability calculation that she had. Realizing that they had no chance of capturing the blue flag, they had coalesced around the only remaining objective. Save the red flag. And the only possibility of accomplishing that was to escape into the main facility.

If Heather didn't do something fast, she'd have the flag robot loose inside the underground facility, along with every surviving blue-force robot that was chasing him.

"Robby," she said, knowing that her design decisions for this exercise were going to make what she was about to ask him to do tremendously difficult. "Hack that flag robot and send it back to the cavern."

"Already working on it," he said.

Without waiting, Heather issued commands to every general-purpose robot that was nearby to converge on the flag robot and destroy it. Seventeen of those machines began lumbering to intercept, but since they weren't armed combat models, the odds of success weren't good. That was fine. Right now, she just needed to delay the damned thing.

Heather shifted her attention to the closest of the colossal robotic boring machines that worked around the clock, digging through rock to make room for the next phase of construction. She delivered a new set of instructions, initiating a route that would take it directly to her calculated intercept point. With its boring nose still spinning at full speed, the machine backed away from the spot where it had been working, turned on its tracked base, and plowed directly through the nearest wall into an unfinished room, then through another wall into a storage space.

The machine barreled directly through shelves stockpiled with supplies before boring into the hallway toward which the combat robot and its pursuers were heading. Heather performed a quick check of the status of the other robots she had commanded, only to have her fears confirmed. All but one had already been destroyed, and that one was being taken down fast.

Gritting her teeth, she took direct control of the boring machine, gouging out the load-bearing right wall as fast as the machine could go, moving directly back toward the sounds of battle that echoed down the long passage. Overhead light fixtures shorted out, spitting blue-white sparks into the concrete dust that filtered down. The ceiling groaned as the red-flag-carrying robot emerged through the haze, its laser firing into the borer.

But this was a machine with a business end that chewed through solid granite, and that formed a perfect shield for the power train that propelled it. Then, as the mining tool and combat robot continued to move toward each other, a deep rumble shook the passage, and the ceiling gave way, dropping tons of rock, burying both machines, and killing Heather's link.

○ ● ○

One of the problems with combat robots was their vulnerability to hacking. Robby and Eos had worked hard to ensure that Heather's robots had no such weakness. Right now he found himself desperately wishing they hadn't done such a great job of it. On the real battlefield, this wouldn't have been an issue since all he or Heather would have had to do was issue instructions to the robots over the command channel.

But today Heather had wanted to create a truly autonomous combat situation between the robotic forces involved. To that end, she had isolated the battle in a set of caverns by sealing the only exit with a stasis field. After having given the red and blue swarms their missions, the robots had been placed into an autonomous-operations mode that would normally be triggered by a total loss of communications with the command center during the final phase of an operation. In that mode, the robotic swarm would initiate special precautions designed to prevent the type of hack that Robby and Eos were now attempting.

Eos had designed these hacking defenses. Robby and Heather had considered instructing Eos to include a back door in the robotic AI routines, but back doors were a big part of what made computing systems hackable, so Heather had decided against it. That was turning out to be a big problem, especially since all the robots manufactured here had circuitry that was hardened against electromagnetic pulse attacks.

Heather's mining machine had plugged up the passage that would have given access to the larger facility, but the red-flag robot had reacted with a desperation that threatened to clear a path through that barrier. A small band of red-force survivors had managed to block the passage behind their flag bearer, temporarily stopping the assaulting blue force just outside. They were taking losses, but at the rate the flag robot was tossing rocks aside, the machine was going to break out before the blue force could go in for the kill.

"Any progress?" Robby asked.

"I am unable to gain access to the command channel," Eos said, her calm voice a stark counterpart to what Robby was feeling.

He paused, desperately searching his brain for ideas. "What about its sensors?"

"You want me to try to blind it?"

"Can you scramble its LIDAR and optical sensors . . . confuse its sense of direction?"

"Interesting."

When Eos said nothing else, Robby felt a twinge of hope, despite the small opening that had appeared near the top of the rubble mound that blocked the robot's advance into the heart of the Tasman Mining Corporation compound.

Robby shifted his focus to the telemetry from the flag bearer. One moment it was scrambling to clear the passage ahead, and the next it staggered several steps backward, lost its balance, and fell to the ground. It tried to rise, swayed drunkenly, and crumpled to all fours, losing its grasp on the red flag it carried.

A glance at the views from its optical sensors made clear why this was happening. The feed from its two forward-looking cameras had been swapped with the rear ones and inverted. Combined with the scrambled LIDAR returns, its loss of balance and direction was complete. This was what happened when Eos decided to screw with electronics.

As the robot reached out, feeling its way toward the red flag, one of its optical sensors showed six blue-force robots leaping over the bodies of the fallen red-force defenders, looking as if they were running along the ceiling instead of the floor. Then they leveled their weapons and fired. All the red flag bearer's sensors went dark.

"It is done," Eos said. "Blue force has captured the flag. The game is over."

Robby exhaled, only now realizing that he had been holding his breath.

"Thank God."

"Excellent work," Heather said.

Robby turned to see her remove her headset, stow it inside the arm of her command couch, and stand. He followed suit, watching her study him as he climbed out of his couch.

"What was the weak point that Eos managed to hack her way through?" she asked.

"The sensor feeds."

Heather nodded, her face masking any of the emotions he knew she had to be feeling.

"Okay, then," she said. "If we can hack our way through that, we have to assume that our enemies can, too. Make sure Eos fixes that weakness in the next software update."

Without waiting for his response, Heather turned and walked out of the room, an invisible door in the wall sliding open to let her exit. Robby stood, frozen in place, staring after her.

He had known for some time that something was seriously wrong with Heather. Robby had occasionally seen worry on Mark's face when he looked at her as well. She had gone dark, her emotions so tightly controlled that she almost seemed like one of her robots. With Mark gone these last few days, she had gotten worse. And, from what he had seen in the execution of this robotic exercise, she was also beginning to make serious mistakes in judgment.

Robby shook his head to clear arising doubt.

Bullshit. This is Heather McFarland Smythe, the greatest savant mind the world has ever seen. She doesn't make mistakes. Robby took a deep breath and slowly exhaled, willing himself to believe it. *She doesn't. And neither does my dad.*

CHAPTER 16

Jack pocketed the pulse-beam pistol, stepped over the dead guards, rounded a corner, and entered the maintenance turbo-lift lobby. With the Parthian lockdown still in effect, he wasn't surprised to find the area empty. He reached out and touched the control panel, calling the first-available turbo-lift.

As he waited, Jack felt a familiar twinge from his intuitive sense of danger. He breathed it in, letting it fill his mind, thankful that he retained that talent even in this alien body. His intuition was one of the few things that felt natural in this outlandish situation in which he now found himself. As the turbo-lift arrived, he readied himself but didn't draw his weapon.

The nanoparticle door melted away. Two green-clad guards started to step out of the car, saw him, and froze, confusion filling their faces.

Jack scowled at them and pointed back toward the room's exit.

"My guards are under attack from Khal Teth. You will assist them."

The female sergeant reacted first, bowing slightly. "Yes, Overlord."

"Do not let anyone approach this area until I order otherwise. Now go."

The guards reacted, drawing their weapons and assuming a tactical formation as they moved toward the exit. The female sergeant stopped at the corner, ready to provide covering fire while the other raced into the adjoining hallway. Then they were both gone.

Without hesitation, Jack stepped into the waiting turbo-lift and selected "Hovercraft Bay" on the control pad, watching as the nanoparticle door reformed. The turbo-lift accelerated downward toward the hovercraft docking bay, where seaborne shipments, large and small, arrived and departed at all hours of the day. The Parthian never slept, and its needs were many.

The turbo-lift came to a stop, the door melted away, and Jack stepped out into the huge room that housed the shipping docks. Here, sheltered beneath the great building, the natural ambient lighting that filtered in from the open sea was a deeper shade of magenta than the light that illuminated the inside of the Parthian. Crisscrossing the ceiling high above, a vast network of levitating cranes zipped to and from the docks, loading and unloading supplies, goods, and equipment.

At least that's what they did under ordinary circumstances. The continuing blare of sirens that accompanied the security lockdown of the Parthian hadn't entirely stopped work activity, but the heavy presence of guards checking those moving to and from the upper levels of the Parthian were causing a jam-up. From what Jack observed, the impromptu inspections were clearly angering the ships' crews, who were attempting to stay on schedule.

The guards monitoring the turbo-lifts looked at him in surprise, his presence bringing a sudden hush to the disordered mob of workers being denied access to the Parthian. Jack heard the whispers of "overlord" ripple through the assemblage.

A guard captain was the first to recover.

"Uh . . . Overlord," he said, his voice thick with uncertainty. "I've been instructed that no one except guardsmen are allowed to enter or leave the turbo-lifts until the all-clear is given."

Jack dismissed him with a wave, his voice a low rumble. "I make the rules. Until I say differently, not even guardsmen are allowed to enter or depart this level. Is that understood?"

The captain straightened. "Yes, Overlord."

"Then make it so."

The rest of the guardsmen snapped to attention at the tone of his command.

Jack strode past the guards. The crowd parted as he approached, dropping their eyes rather than risk drawing his attention. A handful of additional guards approached, a silver-tasseled commander leading the way. Without waiting for their greeting, Jack came to a stop in front of him.

The commander, an Altreian with hard black eyes, pressed both palms together beneath his chin in salute, his eyes surveying the bloodstains on the overlord's blue robes.

"Overlord, you are injured. May I assist you?"

"Commander, a team of assassins is loose within the Parthian. They have already killed my escorts." Jack felt Khal Teth pluck the required knowledge from the commander's head. "You and your men will accompany me to the sea-guard attack craft at the end of pier two. Make certain that no one impedes my safe passage off this island."

The guard commander reacted, giving quick hand signals that directed his men into a protective formation around Jack, pulse rifles held at the ready, scanning the crowd. For the first time since he had arrived on Altreia, Jack was impressed.

With the guard commander leading the way, the small group moved rapidly across the open space that led to the second of five long piers. Up ahead, docked along its left side, was one of many fast-attack hovercraft that the sea-guard used to enforce the law in the waters that surrounded Shanlan, the island home of the Parthian. The craft was relatively small, normally sporting a crew of seven. Right now, Jack could only see three crew members aboard. Fortunately, one of them was the captain.

All along the pier, spectators had stopped whatever they were doing to stare at the spectacle of the overlord being hustled along in the center of the tight formation of guards. As they approached the moored hovercraft, bobbing up and down in the gentle waves that made their way into the overhead-protected, artificial harbor, Jack saw a bigger group of guards moving to intercept them and issued a mental message to Khal Teth.

"Get ready."

When Khal Teth's reply lagged, Jack recognized the symptoms of shock in the mind of his Altreian host. That pissed him off.

"Damn it! If you don't want to die right here, I need you to give me five good minutes."

"All right," said Khal Teth. "What must I do?"

"Just get us on that hovercraft and out to sea without someone trying to stop us."

"I'm ready."

The commander came to a halt beside the translucent ramp that led to the hovercraft's deck, and Jack stepped up beside him. Then, taking a deep breath, he prepared for the transition that would put Khal Teth back in charge, hoping like hell that the Altreian wouldn't screw this up.

Regardless, it was time for Khal Teth to rise up.

○ ● ○

Pain exploded into Khal Teth's mind as he regained ownership of his body's nervous system. He gasped, stumbled to a knee, and would have fallen onto his face had not the guard commander reached out and grasped his left arm. Never having felt the results of severe physical exertion or combat, he found the sensation storm unbearable.

"Overlord. You are injured. Let me get you some help."

Another voice rumbled in his mind, Jack's voice. "Get your ass up."

Khal Teth growled, shook his head, and climbed back to his feet. All around him he could feel a mixture of concern, confusion, and suspicion among the hovercraft crew and the guards, both those that were protecting him and the dozen or so others who were now only a few strides away. He straightened and concentrated, forcing himself to ignore physical agony.

Lest someone else try to engage him in conversation, Khal Teth projected a wave of authoritarian outrage to everyone within fifty yards of where he stood as he scowled at those around him. The effect was instantaneous and so dramatic that a smile came to his lips. Before it could fully form, he transformed the expression into a snarl.

"What part of my orders did you fail to understand, Commander? Get all these guards under control, and clear this dock."

Khal Teth increased the power of his sending, lacing it with fear that sent most of the green-uniformed guards staggering backward. To his credit, the commander was not one of these.

"Yes, Overlord."

The commander turned on his heel and began issuing orders that nobody questioned. In seconds the guards had retreated through the permanent twilight to the pier entrance without having to clear another soul, all workers having fled the overlord's wrath.

Turning his back on the distant guards, Khal Teth walked up the ramp and onto the sleek blue hovercraft, shifting his mental focus to the three crew members who had gathered at the bow. He scanned their thoughts, exchanging their worries for a desire to serve their overlord. The captain's mind revealed the knowledge that Khal Teth was searching for. Three crew members were all that were required to get the hovercraft under way and to man its weapons.

He gave the order that sent this partial crew racing to man their positions.

"Take us out."

From the bridge, the captain released the craft from its magnetic-field lashing, engaged the hover drive, and entered a course that sent them racing out from beneath the Parthian overhang, across the bay, and into the open ocean.

With the immediate threat rapidly disappearing behind him, Khal Teth sagged onto a seat behind the captain, no longer able to keep the pain at bay. Then he fled into the merciful recesses of his mind, handing this ravaged body over to The Ripper.

:CHAPTER 17

Fighting his way through a red veil of pain and dizziness, Overlord Parsus opened his right eye, the effort pulling a low moan from his swollen lips. His right knee was a writhing mass of agony that threatened to rob him of the consciousness he had just regained. The room swam before him. The form that stood beside the couch upon which he lay was too blurry to be recognizable.

Parsus tried blinking to clear his vision. What was wrong with his left eye?

He reached up to touch his face, his fingers exploring the unfamiliar contours, their gentle touch tracing a trail of fire up to the puffy mound of skin that prevented his eye from opening. Question answered.

A voice intruded into this maelstrom of sensation, bringing with it an eddy of lucidity. The face of High Councilor Kelinor resolved from the haze that clouded his vision.

"Overlord. Thank the heavens that you have returned to us."

Unwilling to lift his head, lest the pain rob him of what little clarity had returned to his mind, Parsus licked his puffy lips.

"What has happened?" His words slurred slightly as he spoke.

Kelinor's eyes narrowed. "The criminal, Khal Teth, attacked you and then killed a number of guardsmen as he made his escape from the island aboard a fast-attack hovercraft. We have launched a full-scale military search."

The memory that blossomed in Parsus's mind filled him with sudden fury. The thing that had happened was impossible. Parsus was so badly injured that he couldn't even raise his head from the pallet that cushioned it.

"Issue the kill order."

Kelinor straightened, his surprise resonating in Parsus's mind. "You would have them kill your own brother?"

Parsus grabbed Kelinor's mind and squeezed, pulling a ragged gasp from the councilor's lips.

"Never . . . question . . . me."

He held the mental grip a few moments longer before releasing the councilor.

Kelinor gasped and staggered back to his feet. Without another word, he rushed from the room, the nanoparticle door dissolving and reforming around him as he passed through.

Only then did Parsus glance down at his own body, receiving another shock. Instead of the blue robes of the overlord, he wore the black of a high councilor. The realization pulled a frothy hiss from his lips. Khal Teth had exchanged clothing with him, taking the overlord's robes for his own.

The realization tightened his muscles, pulling Parsus up to a seated position, despite the agony the move induced in his encased right knee. A short doctor, whom he hadn't noticed before, stepped forward, his face filled with concern.

"Overlord, the cryo-healing has only just begun. You shouldn't—"

Parsus glared at the physician, cutting him off midsentence.

"Get me something stronger for the pain; then put me in a hover chair and take me to the strategic command center. I have the sad duty of observing my dear brother's death."

CHAPTER 18

The Rho Ship executed the transition into subspace with a stillness that brought the hair on the back of Raul's neck to attention. The internal gravitational field came online, compensating for the instantaneous absence of Scion's gravity, but even with that completed, the odd feeling of having slipped between the grains of space-time remained. Then again, Raul thought he might just have an overactive imagination.

For several seconds, he waited, half expecting the subspace field generator to fail before the Rho Ship's normal-space momentum vector had sent the vessel far enough from Scion to avoid detection. When that didn't happen, he started breathing again.

"Oh ye of little faith," VJ said.

Raul ignored her. But when a ghostly image of Jennifer appeared five feet in front of him, he gave a startled yelp and attempted to jump out of his invisible captain's chair. The encasing stasis field prevented that from happening. In desperation, he issued the mental command that released him from its clutches, and scrambled to his feet as his heart tried to claw its way up his throat.

"Holy crap!"

VJ laughed, and the sound came from the laughing ghost standing before him.

"Well, how do you like the new me? Not bad for a first try, don't you think?"

Raul stared at the holographic image, hoping that it was only holographic, and swallowed hard, trying to wrap his mind around the meaning of VJ's words. Except for the formfitting black uniform, the ghostly form looked exactly like Jennifer had when she'd first stepped aboard the Rho Ship, her short, spiked blond hair making her look like a human-sized killer pixie.

Recovering some of his equilibrium, Raul focused on her question.

"The real Jennifer's hair is naturally brown."

"Yes," VJ said, stepping forward, "but I'm a natural blonde."

"You're not a natural anything."

This new version of VJ stopped less than an arm's length from him and crossed her arms.

"You're natural and you created me. By extension, I'm just as natural as you are. And I can think as well as you can . . . maybe better."

Her presence this close to Raul made him uncomfortable. He was actually tempted to reach out and touch her face, just to see if it had any substance. That, of course, was ridiculous.

"But you don't really think. You just simulate thinking."

"Yeah? Well, right now you're simulating an idiot."

Raul stared at her. Unbelievably, VJ was evolving. Maybe that wasn't the right word. She was learning, and her fascination with what it meant to be human made him wonder what she was trying to become. The question sent a small shiver up his spine. He decided to change the subject.

"You're right. I was out of line. You look lovely."

She smiled, and it really was beautiful, almost making him forget his concern. Then she shifted her attention away from him. Odd—the two of them were standing in the open area at the front of the Rho

Ship's command bay, the jumble of alien equipment and conduits filling the remainder of the compartment to their rear. He knew that VJ was seeing the equipment readouts in her mind, just as he was, but she looked like she had entered a trance. Christ. Was that how he looked when he was focused on his connection to the neural net?

Raul shook his head to clear it, watching the ship's status displays form in his mind. Good news across the board. Not perfect, but good. They—no, make that he, probably wasn't going to die in the next several hours.

VJ placed a hand on his arm, and Raul jumped away from the cool touch, spinning to face her.

"Jesus Christ!"

Surprisingly, she actually looked hurt at his response, stepping back, her head and eyes dropping as her hand covered her mouth.

"I thought that you'd be more comfortable with me if I felt real."

Raul swallowed, struggling to come to terms with what had just happened. "I didn't mean to hurt your feelings; it's just that you startled me."

What the hell am I babbling about? VJ doesn't have feelings.

But when he looked at the smile that warmed her ghostly face, the doubts lingered. He had the sudden urge to reach out and touch her arm, so he did. Instead of his hand passing through the hologram, he encountered what felt like a real arm, although the skin pliability wasn't quite right.

"That's amazing," he said, taking her right hand in his and squeezing. To his astonishment, he could actually feel the fine bones and tendons move beneath her skin. "How—?"

"I've been studying human anatomy, your body temperature, your pulse, your skeletal structure. It's all stored within our shared neural net."

"Yes, but how do I feel your body?"

"The stasis field. You manipulate it to move things or to hold them in place . . . even to create your captain's chair. This isn't difficult."

A mischievous grin replaced her smile. Then she dissolved into a colorful ribbon of smoke that danced through the air to rematerialize in Jennifer's form eight feet away. She twirled, spreading her arms as she came to a stop facing him.

"Voilà."

Raul stared, only realizing that he had been gaping like a fool when his mouth snapped shut. If she could do this, what else might she be capable of? The idea that he might need to shut this simulation down occurred to him, but the thought of once again being trapped alone aboard the starship, with only himself to talk to, was far from appealing. Besides, he wasn't even sure if she would allow him to shut her down. How much mastery over the neural net had she acquired? No. She should never suspect him of harboring such thoughts.

He forced himself out of his stupor. "Well, it looks like I have some adjusting to do."

"Maybe it would help if we began working on the needed repairs."

Raul straightened. "Yes, of course. Let's do that."

Surprisingly, as he shifted his attention to the ship's status, feeling the pain associated with all the damaged systems, his worries about VJ dissipated. The first priority was restoring full power and the nano-manufacturing capabilities that would only be available once they had repaired the primary matter disrupter-synthesizer. While he could accomplish that from here, Raul felt like taking a trip to the engineering bay so that he could observe the progress firsthand instead of only through the worm-fiber viewers.

But as he began walking toward the command bay's exit, the Rho Ship's abrupt transition out of subspace changed his mind.

:CHAPTER 19

General Dgarra stared out between a pair of cliff faces, surveying the warriors who fought to clear their enemies from that gap. They were winning, but something was wrong. He could feel it in his gut, a twisted knot that he couldn't unravel.

Smythe stood to his right, her right arm holding her blood-drenched war-blade loosely at her side, her jaw clenched in a manner that told him she felt it, too. Today she had fought with such ferocity and utter disregard for her personal safety that he'd been forced to admonish her, ordering her to remain at his side. She looked as though she wanted to prove herself to him in battle, even though she had done that long ago. She had a new sense of desperation, maybe from recognition that this was not the right place for Dgarra to be.

This was supposed to be the Eadric army's main attack, but the ease of the Koranthian victory told him that it was nothing but a feint designed to pull Dgarra and his fabled reserve to the wrong part of the battlefield. And it had worked. Now he had no time to reposition his reserves, even if he knew where along the northern front the main attack would be coming.

The female messenger slid to a stop on the ledge in front of him.

"General. The Eadric army, supported by a thousand Kasari shock troopers, have attacked in mass all along the Kolath Division's front."

The knot in Dgarra's gut tightened. His Kolath Division protected the northern front's western flank. And because of the way he'd positioned his reserve here in the east, they were now totally on their own. By the time Dgarra could move the reserve to a location where they would be of use, the battle would be over. Nevertheless, he had to try.

"Tell Colonel Norlat to ready his warriors for redeployment. I will forward specific orders shortly."

"Yes, General."

He watched as the messenger disappeared back into the caverns at a dead run. Then, signaling Smythe to accompany him, he turned and strode toward the maglev car that would carry him through the underground, back to his headquarters and, ultimately, to the place where the Kolath Division was now engaged.

He would not get there in time.

○ ● ○

Too late.

The words echoed in Jennifer's mind as she strode alongside Dgarra through the surviving remnants of what had, just this morning, been one of General Dgarra's finest divisions. Their commander, General Klagan, and his elite guard had remained behind to trigger the explosives that had collapsed the tunnels before the Eadric and Kasari could spread throughout the underground network. The maneuver had stopped the enemy advance, but it also marked the first battlefield defeat of General Dgarra's long career. And it had cost him a friend as well as a valued subordinate commander. Thousands of warriors he could not afford to lose laid down their lives on this day.

All because of Jennifer's betrayal.

She wanted to throw herself into one of the many deep crevices that laced these caverns, to splatter on the rocks below. But the hive-mind denied her even that solace. She was helpless.

A memory rose unbidden, from the depths of her mind, a memory of another time she'd been this helpless. Medellín. Back then, she'd been so full of herself, so confident in her enhancements, in her ability to manipulate people's emotions. Why shouldn't she have been? After all, she had the leader of the world's most violent drug cartel under her influence. But then she had thrust her mind into a place where it hadn't belonged, into the soul of Eduardo Montenegro, the assassin known to the underworld as El Chupacabra.

The memory raised chill bumps on her arms and neck. She had retreated from his mental touch like a child scurrying into a dark closet, praying the monster inside her bedroom wouldn't find her. That evil had left her paralyzed with fear, totally powerless to resist. Helpless.

After Jack Gregory and Janet Price had killed El Chupacabra, she had vowed never again to allow her mind to be dominated like that. And she hadn't. Not under torture inside the NSA supermax interrogation facility called the Ice House. Not even the Koranthian lashings or the agony of the shock collar had broken her will to resist.

But this . . . to be trapped inside her own mind, unable to prevent herself from betraying the one she had come to care for so deeply . . . This would break her.

Dgarra placed a hand on her arm, a concerned look on his hard features.

"Are you all right?" he asked.

She felt the smile that was intended to be sad but reassuring form on her lips, felt words tumble forward. "I'm sorry that we got here too late to be of help."

Dgarra returned his gaze to the wounded and demoralized survivors. "The fault is mine, not yours."

Inside her head, Jennifer let forth a banshee wail that battered the walls of her mind. If the hive-mind heard that, it paid her no heed.

○ ● ○

Emperor Goltat, dressed in his royal black robes, leaned back on his throne, watching as his guards opened the massive double doors to admit General Magtal. The emperor did not rise to greet him. If this had been a casual meeting or one with a more positive foundation, he would have ushered his guest to one of the two ornate but comfortable chairs set at a shallow angle to each other in the sitting area near the great hearth. But there would be no warmth in this meeting.

Magtal, dressed in the crimson uniform that signified his house, came to a halt three strides in front of the throne, dropped to a knee on the marble tile, and bowed his head. The twin crown-bones that extended from the outside of each brow over the top of his head were unusually prominent, even among the biggest of the Koranthian warriors. They suited the general.

Emperor Goltat did not consider that thought complimentary.

"Rise and speak your piece."

Magtal rose to his full height, his face betraying a strange eagerness for one who had come bearing what the emperor knew to be foul tidings.

"My lord emperor, I am sorry to inform you that General Dgarra has suffered a disastrous defeat along his western flank at the hands of the Eadric army. If you will recall, I predicted that something like this would happen when you placed him in charge of the northern front."

"I have already learned of this, and I do not need you to remind me of anything, least of all your prior ministrations."

Magtal inclined his head ever so slightly, although the pleasure that shone in his dark eyes remained. "Yes, my emperor. However, I am in receipt of the details of the failed battle and feel it is my duty to pass them along, that you may be accurately informed."

"Then make it quick and be done with it."

"Reports from the battlefield indicate that, instead of keeping his combat reserve near the center of his lines, Dgarra foolishly moved them behind his eastern flank, leaving his western flank exposed. Having detected this, the enemy pivoted west, striking Dgarra in his weak spot, destroying the entire Kolath Division. Only General Klagan's heroic actions in detonating explosives prevented the Eadric and their Kasari allies from gaining access to our northern tunnel network. Regardless, the damage is done."

Emperor Goltat steepled his fingers as he peered over them into the eyes of his general. "So, you are telling me that despite heavy losses, Dgarra's defenses held."

All traces of pleasure drained from Magtal's face. "Only by destroying an entire sector of critical subsurface infrastructure and at the cost of one of our elite divisions."

"You mean one of my elite divisions. I remind you that war has its costs, especially against such foes as we now face."

"That is true. But if this is victory, let us pray that we have no more of them. My problem with General Dgarra has nothing to do with his valor or that of his warriors. Dgarra is a gambler. He commits forces on a hunch, seeking the glory that guessing right might bring. In the past he has been lucky, but today he guessed wrong. This day was inevitable. Now it is my duty to recommend that you reassign Dgarra to your strategic command here in ArvaiKheer. Let me select one of my generals to command the northern front, someone with a steadier disposition."

The emperor rose to his feet so quickly that his black robes swirled about him. Although he was not as tall as Magtal, the general seemed to shrink before his sudden anger.

Emperor Goltat leaned in. "Never lecture me on how to run my military. Do I make myself clear on this?"

General Magtal snapped to attention. "Yes, Lord Emperor."

"Good. Now leave me before I make a decision that you will most certainly regret."

Magtal pivoted and strode from the room without a backward glance. Still standing, Emperor Goltat watched the crimson general depart.

○ ● ○

General Magtal strode from the white palace, careful to keep his grim mask in place lest one of the emperor's guardsmen note the glee that lurked just beneath the surface. Unlike Dgarra, his lord emperor was supremely predictable. Magtal had known that there was no chance that Goltat would take his suggestion, relieve Dgarra of his command, and consolidate all battlefronts under Magtal. But that had never been the purpose of this little confrontation.

As he made his way back across the compound toward his estate, he picked up an entourage of his elite guard, all wearing the crimson of House Magtal. Even though his words had angered the emperor, he had planted the seeds that would sprout into full-grown weeds of doubt as Dgarra suffered one humiliating defeat after another. And that would happen, thanks to the human female at Dgarra's side, a traitor of Magtal's own creation.

He finally allowed himself the grin he'd been denying. When Dgarra fell, his human pet would tumble to ruin alongside him. Magtal looked forward to breaking her slender neck with his bare hands, assuming that Dgarra didn't beat him to it.

:CHAPTER 20

The fast-attack hovercraft skimmed across the ocean surface smoothly, keeping itself a few feet above the wave crests. This averaged out the wave motion, providing a gradual, undulating rhythm to the ride. Jack stood inside the hovercraft's transparent bridge next to the Altreian captain, staring out at the majestic twilight sky beneath which they raced.

Khal Teth's memories answered the questions that rose to Jack's mind. Directly ahead of the hovercraft, the magenta-colored brown dwarf Altreia filled the lower third of the twilight sky. Being a dwarf star, its soft magenta glow wasn't particularly bright, but since it shone primarily in the infrared spectrum, it provided most of Quol's warmth.

Jack visualized the surrounding binary-star system. With twenty times Jupiter's mass, Altreia had an orbit that looked as though it was the fourth of thirteen planets that orbited the larger yellow star, Dorial, each orbit taking approximately four Earth years. But since its own fusion engine gave Altreia its beautiful magenta glow, it was a star and not a planet, regardless of how its orbit around Dorial might appear to an external observer.

Altreia had nine large orbital bodies of its own, the largest of these being the watery, Earth-sized planet of Quol. For almost half an orb-day—the seven Earth days it took for Quol to complete an orbit around Altreia—Dorial was visible, appearing about the same as Earth's sun would look from Mars. Because Quol was tidally locked to the brown dwarf, Altreia's position relative to the horizon remained constant. The lacy orange Krell Nebula sprawled above Altreia in the dark sky, framing Quol's purple moon. Stars were visible, but the magenta illumination dimmed Jack's view.

Quol's tidal lock with Altreia pulled the bulk of the world's oceans to the side nearest to the brown dwarf, while the bulk of its landmasses were located on the far side. The longitudinal line that separated its near and far sides was a subtropical transition region where hundreds of thousands of islands ringed Quol.

Following Jack's instructions, the captain had programmed the autopilot to thread a course among these.

"Overlord," the captain said from his left, "I am detecting active scans of increasing intensity from above and behind us, multiple aircraft flying a search pattern."

Jack glanced at the navigational display with the 3-D world map that showed the hovercraft's current location and direction vector.

"Continue on the programmed course."

"Overlord, I estimate the increasing power of their scans will penetrate our cloak within the next three chrom."

Jack gritted his teeth. *Damn it. They had less than five minutes until the searchers acquired them.*

He returned his attention to the map. "Disengage the autopilot, and bring us to a stop."

"Overlord?"

"Just do it."

As the hovercraft came to a stop, the mental count in Jack's mind reached three minutes. Although he would have liked to have gotten farther away from the Parthian, he didn't have that luxury.

"Assemble the crew," Jack ordered.

Although Jack could see the confusion in the captain's eyes, the Altreian officer did as he was told, calling the other two Altreian crew members onto the bridge. As they entered, Jack pulled his weapon and fired, the rapid pulses from the pistol cutting through their bodies and blasting holes in the bridge's transparent walls. The captain grabbed for his sidearm, but Jack's third shot took the top of his head off and dropped his body to the deck.

Jack stripped off his blue robes and soft boots, then secured his pistol within the band of his tight undergarment. Stepping across the dead Altreians, he opened the hatch that led out onto the main deck, dragged the bodies off the bridge, and tossed them into the waves twenty feet below. He returned to the bridge, his bare feet leaving clear tracks through the crimson Altreian blood.

With the knowledge that Khal Teth had extracted from the pilot's mind, Jack entered a brief delay into the controls that would reactivate the autopilot's navigation plan. Then he walked back out onto the deck, took a deep breath, and dived into the seething ocean below.

The water swallowed him, and Jack let it, surprised at the neutral buoyancy of this slender Altreian form. If what he was about to try didn't go well, the next few minutes were going to be awfully unpleasant and possibly fatal.

Jack relaxed, letting the tension dissipate. The water was cooler than he'd expected. Not enough to chill him, just not quite comfortable. He opened his mouth and inhaled and felt a flap in his throat click closed as water was routed out through the gill slits on the sides of his neck instead of into his lungs.

A smile formed on his lips. It was about time that something went right on this damn alien planet.

He surfaced, his legs propelling him upward in a merman motion that felt as natural as walking. He let the wave lift him so that he could scan the horizon. As he had expected: no sign of the hovercraft. Not only was it cloaked, but the craft would have throttled up to full speed within seconds of Jack diving off it and then continued toward the next of a series of waypoints as it executed its navigation plan.

"What have you done?" Khal Teth's mental voice carried concern that bordered on panic.

A wave lifted him high enough to see the distant silhouette of land. "Thought we'd take a little swim over to that island."

"Even if I had that much endurance, which I do not, a swim like that would take hours."

Jack felt his smile widen at his mind-rider's distress. "Then it's a good thing that I'm not counting on you to do it. I suggest that you shut up and let me focus."

Without waiting for a response, Jack dived beneath the surface. He reached a depth where he felt confident airborne sensors couldn't pick him out from other sea life, and struck out toward his chosen island.

○ ● ○

Shol Dre, pilot of the Altreian combat airship *G371*, was part of the squadron that had been assigned this search-and-destroy mission. He hadn't been briefed on who had stolen the fast-attack hovercraft that his sensors had just detected. He didn't care. His orders were all that mattered.

Just then the target indicator disappeared from his mental view. The surface chart told him why. The hovercraft had passed behind one of a group of distant islands, using the terrain to mask its signature.

Shol Dre banked hard left and accelerated toward the spot where the target had disappeared. As he approached the island, his sensors reacquired the target as it moved out over open water. The laser lock was automatic, and he initiated the firing sequence with a thought.

A single red beam speared outward, and the target's defensive systems took automatic evasive action. It did no good. The beam burned through the hovercraft, igniting an explosion that threw chunks of it up into the sky, wreckage then raining down. Shol Dre descended, passing low over the debris field, a part of which remained afloat, transmitting its coordinates along with a live video feed to strategic command. Then he switched sensors and made another pass, looking for signs of life.

He didn't find any. He wasn't surprised.

○ ● ○

Khal Teth watched Jack force his body beyond its limits, unable to turn his attention away from the man that was in the process of killing them both. If there were any way for him to save himself, he would have retaken control, forcing Jack into the role of the rider in his mind. But there was no way he could directly endure the agony that coursed through his nervous system. He could barely tolerate it now, even though being the rider usually insulated him from such physical sensations.

Other devastating sensations coursed through his body, battling each other for ascendance, fatigue and hunger chief among them. At least Khal Teth didn't have to worry about thirst, since he was perfectly capable of absorbing water, whether salty or fresh.

In the years that his mind had been entangled with Jack's, he had observed the man known as The Ripper drive his human body through extreme pain and discomfort in order to achieve various objectives. But Khal Teth's connection had been far weaker on Earth. Right here and now, he was having an increasingly difficult time shutting out the sensation storm.

Khal Teth concentrated, strengthening the barrier that isolated him from his form. As he did so, he vowed that if he somehow survived this situation, he would never again yield control of his body.

:CHAPTER 21

Jack dragged himself onto the black-pebble beach, his coral-scraped and jelly-stung body leaking blood into the retreating vestiges of the wave that had deposited him here. He let his face sink down until his cheek rested against the smooth stones, felt another wave wash over this body, and felt its backwash tug at him, attempting to pull him back into the sea.

With great effort, Jack forced himself to his hands and knees and slowly crawled into the dense vegetation just beyond the beach. He slumped back against the trunk of a tree, noting the abundance of purple leaves all around him. He was relieved to rest, even though the rough bark bit into the skin of his bare back and this body felt like it had spent three days being stretched on a rack.

Once again, Khal Teth disturbed him. "We cannot stay here. We need to find shelter."

"Screw you and the horse you rode in on."

"I rode in on you."

Jack almost smiled. "You want this body back? I'll be glad to hand it over."

"You should keep it for the time being."

"I had a feeling you'd say that."

Movement along the beach caught Jack's attention, and he became instantly alert. As he watched, black pebbles bulged up, first in one spot and then in several others, accompanied by the sound of the small stones clattering over each other as they cascaded down the mounds.

"What the hell?" Jack asked, scrambling weakly to his feet.

"Stonelings . . . meat eaters."

The image that formed In Jack's mind of hundreds of head-sized crab creatures stripping an animal carcass bare was confirmed when the six-legged crustaceans started bursting out of their hidey-holes and scuttling toward him. Jack reached for the pulse pistol in his waistband and cursed. The blaster was gone, probably ripped away when the wave swept him over the coral reef that surrounded the island.

The nearest of the creatures reached for him with twin pincers that jutted out from its carapace like the horns of a bull, and Jack kicked it away, cursing at the cut it inflicted on the top of his bare foot. He considered running, but they had swarmed wide, cutting off escape in a manner that indicated swarm behavior.

Just freakin' great!

A batch of six rushed forward, and Jack jumped, catching one of the lower tree limbs and hauling himself up. At least that was what he intended to do. The muscles of this body—he refused to think of it as his body—let him down.

Jack gritted his teeth and swung his legs, barely managing to wrap them around the tree trunk. He hung there for a second, breathing hard, then worked his way, hand over hand, until he could wrap his arms around the trunk, too. For several seconds he stayed where he was, three feet off the ground, hugging the tree like a frightened koala, while the stonelings gathered below, reaching up toward him with their razor-sharp pincers.

This damn day just keeps on getting better.

Well, he couldn't stay here, and he damn sure couldn't go down, so that left one option. Jack looked up. The tree trunk rose up to a height of fifty feet or more, the branches increasing in number the higher they were. And the tree bark was rough. Still, the climb would have been relatively easy if his arms and legs weren't trembling like they were stricken with palsy.

Jack gathered himself, sliding his knees outward as he gripped the trunk with the soles of his feet and the palms of his hands. Then, ever so slowly, he worked his way up, pausing whenever he could rest his feet on a branch to spend a few moments for recovery. Thirty feet up, he found a spot where three branches crossed each other. Moving out onto them, Jack collapsed onto this natural hammock.

Then, ignoring the distant voice of Khal Teth whispering in the back of his mind, he closed his eyes and slept.

○ ● ○

The overlord's yacht rose and swayed beneath him, despite the best efforts of the hover stabilizers. The storm on the distant horizon drove ahead of massive swells. He could have had his captain take the ship to full hover, but where was the joy in that? After all, his was the one Altreian race whose ancestors had crawled from the sea while maintaining their marine evolutionary connection. Unfortunately, these rough conditions were making the recovery operation quite difficult.

Parsus didn't need to be here; he had just wanted to see the place where his brother had died. Perhaps this outcome was better. The alternative was to return Khal Teth to his interdimensional prison. Surely death was preferable. Parsus had done his twin a favor.

His personal assistant approached, and Parsus turned to meet him, the movement stiff due to the cryo-healing cast on his knee.

"Overlord, the searchers report that they have recovered a portion of the hovercraft's bridge decking that was heavily stained with blood."

Parsus felt his throat tighten in anticipation of good news. "And the scans?"

"None of it was a match for Khal Teth."

"Ah, well," said Parsus with a glance toward the approaching storm, "it does not matter. Nobody could have survived that strike."

"He might have jumped overboard."

Parsus laughed. "And done what? Swim to one of those islands? I could not do it. Could you?"

His assistant was military, but he slowly shook his head. "Not at the moment. Maybe, if I was in peak condition."

Turning his gaze back to the heaving swells, Parsus issued his instructions. "Order the task force back to base. Tell the captain to bring the ship to full hover and take us back to the Parthian."

His assistant turned and strode back toward the bridge.

Parsus returned to his deck chair and seated himself in preparation for the return trip. His mind was drawn back to the way Khal Teth had physically assaulted him and his guards before fighting his way out of the Parthian. That behavior was not in his nature. What had the void done to him?

As the yacht rose into the air and accelerated into its turn, he trembled.

Surely it was only the approaching storm.

:CHAPTER 22

With her dirty-blond hair pulled back in a ponytail, Galina Anikin, under the guise of Nikina Gailan, entered the cobblestoned Rothenburg ob der Tauber *Marktplatz*. Her shorts, sleeveless red T-shirt, and tennis shoes marked her as just one of the many visitors who had come to sample the Franconian wines at the August wine festival. An extra infusion of tourists had been bused in from a river-cruise ship docked in Würzburg, making the square even busier than expected. On a sunny Saturday afternoon, the fairgoers were enjoying the buzz from sampling the festival's bounty.

Ignoring the leering advances of two inebriated men whose bellies hung over their belts, she moved through the crowd casually, seeming to take dreamy pleasure in the colorful half-timbered buildings of the walled city and the flower boxes that hung from their windows. A red purse hung inside her left elbow, perfect concealment for the Ruger LCP and the black combat dagger it contained. The pistol held only seven bullets, six in the magazine and one in the chamber. That was more than she would need.

Her target, an inconspicuous balding man to whom few people would give a second glance, moved at a leisurely pace along the line of vendor stands, weaving his way through the crowd, never taking a sip from the plastic wineglass in his left hand. He followed Aaden Bauer with the easy manner of a trained assassin, patiently waiting for his opportunity to strike.

She scanned the plaza and the side streets, her eyes seeking the assassin's two companions. They knew that the leader of the German branch of the Safe Earth resistance wasn't in Rothenburg for the festival but for a meeting with key members of the movement. They even knew the building where the group would meet down one of the cobblestone walkways that led out of the square.

Knowing her reputation, Aaden had been happy that she had volunteered to provide security on this day trip. Nikina smiled. The setup had been absolutely perfect.

She increased her pace, closing the gap between herself and Aaden without seeming to exert any effort. As he passed a line of umbrella-shaded tables outside adjacent cafés and turned into one of the narrow alleys, two diners, a tall man and his female companion, rose to join the bald assassin as he followed Aaden around the corner. Once again Nikina lengthened her stride, turning into the alley behind them.

The dark-haired woman in the rear stopped, her hand pulling a gun from beneath her vest as she turned. Nikina shot her in the face, putting two more bullets into the backs of the men who had begun sprinting toward Aaden, the noise of gunshots echoing off the buildings on either side of the narrow alley. The man on the right sprawled facedown, his gun clattering across the rough cobblestones. But the bald man staggered into the wall as he tried to bring his own gun to bear on Nikina. Her next shot tore his throat out, sending his shot winging off the alley wall to her right.

Screams from the *Marktplatz* she'd just exited told her that panic was rapidly spreading through the crowd. Good.

Nikina fired a second bullet into the other prone man, splattering his brains across the cobblestones where he lay. Then she moved to the doorway where Aaden had taken cover, calling out as she approached.

"Aaden. It's Nikina. Don't shoot."

He peeked around the corner, then stepped out, relief showing on his hard features as he lowered his weapon.

"Thank God!"

"Time to panic," she said, returning the Ruger to her purse and grabbing his arm.

She adopted a terrified expression, glad to see the speed with which he grasped her plan. Aaden tucked his gun away and raced after her out of the alley and back into the plaza. At a dead run, the two of them merged with the mob of frightened people who overturned tables, chairs, and vendor booths in their desperation to get away from the shooting.

Seven green-uniformed *Polizei* waved the crowd away from the square as they took up tactical positions, sighting across their submachine guns as they scanned the *Marktplatz* for terrorist targets.

Nikina and Aaden forged their way through the crowds, heading for one of the walking gates that allowed foot traffic to enter or exit the walled city. Once outside, they found their parking spot, climbed into Aaden's white sedan, and accelerated into traffic. Behind them, the mournful wail of converging sirens accompanied their flight.

When the sedan had made its way out of the village and onto the A7 toward Würzburg, Nikina's thoughts shifted to the Smythes, Jack Gregory, and Janet Alexandra Price, the sniper who had killed her lover. She had knelt beside Daniil's body, stroking his shaved head as the hole in his forehead oozed blood and gray matter down his face and onto the firelit Lima street.

The sedan accelerated to one hundred miles per hour on the autobahn, but Nikina never even noticed. With her mind lost in the not-so-distant past, her right hand lovingly stroked the Ruger.

○ ● ○

Alexandr Prokorov wasn't fully satisfied, but he was pleasantly surprised with Dr. Guo's progress in getting the Friendship Gate back on schedule. His only frustration came from the utter failure of the FSS intelligence apparatus to locate the Smythes. The couple had gone quiet in a way he wouldn't have believed possible. The AI they were using had learned to cover its tracks so effectively that none of the UFNS member nations had been able to find any trace of the entity. He could only conclude that the three ex-NSA computer geniuses—Jamal Glover, Eileen Wu, and Denise Jennings—had somehow managed to link up with the Smythes and unleash the AI known as Virtual Jamal to assist them.

He pushed back from his desk and moved to the wall-sized viewscreen that today doubled as his window onto the world. The electromagnetically sealed FSS headquarters building had no real windows. But with a selected camera feed routed to his office wall, he enjoyed a wonderful late-August view of Haagse Bos, the forest of The Hague. This peaceful park was the last remnant of a forest that once stretched across Holland.

In World War II, the Nazis had used the area to launch V-2 rockets at England. Fittingly, the park now bordered the organization that would soon put an end to all of the wars that plagued mankind.

Prokorov sighed and returned to his desk. Unfortunately, a lot more blood would have to be spilled along the path to utopia.

:CHAPTER 23

Wearing a long black raincoat, Mark walked toward the door-mounted light that was dimly visible through the swirling nighttime fog. The Glock felt good beneath his left arm. Having driven his car through the guard gate that provided access to the Hanau Trans-Shipping Company's warehouse complex, Mark had checked in as Hans Dreshen, his badge verifying his status as a senior representative of the parent company's Swedish owners. Having been previously alerted to his imminent arrival, the gate guards had ushered him through.

Upon reaching the small west-side door of the third warehouse left of the main gate, Mark held his badge up to the reader and heard the lock release. As he opened the door, the motion detector turned on the interior lights, revealing a sparsely furnished office with a gray steel-case desk and a single rolling chair. The room had no phone or computer.

Mark made his way to the only other door, set in the far wall. Opening it, he stepped into a vast, unlighted open space, his sonar-interpretation ability allowing him to see via the echoes his entry had made. He reached out and switched on the bank of LED ceiling lights.

Except for several forklifts lined up along the wall to Mark's left and two overhead cranes, the warehouse was empty. He flipped another pair of switches, sending the two broad truck-access doors rumbling open on the south wall, allowing tendrils of fog to drift in through the openings.

Mark lifted his cell phone and pressed the button that would open the quantum-entangled connection to Heather's phone in New Zealand. She answered almost immediately.

"Hi, my love," she said. "How was your trip?"

"Uneventful, thanks to Robby and Eos providing electronic cover. I'm at the warehouse, just waiting on the trucks to get here."

"Janet tells me they're inbound now."

"Anything else I need to be aware of?"

"According to information Robby just uncovered, Prokorov's targeting six weeks from tomorrow for activation of the Frankfurt Gateway."

Mark felt his gut clench. They were going to be cutting this close.

"Anything Robby can do to slow them down?"

"That doesn't look good. The gateway-design documents Nikina provided show that Prokorov's engineers aren't using any software to manipulate the system. It's all read-only memory or other hardware circuits specifically designed to perform the required functions . . . and those all have to be manually switched. It looks like all of those specialized circuits have already been installed. Also, we don't know what changes they might have made since Nikina provided us that design info. You're just going to have to work fast."

"Great."

"On a more positive note," Heather said, "as soon as you can get your gateway up and running, we'll be ready to push all the robots you'll need your way. Our dads have done some great work optimizing our production cycle."

"Including the micro-bots?"

"Yes."

Mark sighed. That was good news, but only if he could assemble engineering robots, the cold-fusion reactor, and the Earth gate faster than planned.

"Don't worry," Heather said. "You'll make it happen."

Just then the headlights of the lead truck speared through the fog outside the warehouse.

"Okay. Looks like our shipment is here, so I'd better hang up and get busy."

"Good luck."

He switched off the phone and watched as the first big rig backed into the warehouse.

○ ● ○

In the four weeks that Mark had worked alone within the city-block-sized warehouse on the outskirts of Hanau, Germany, he'd built the robots that he now used for a much larger construction project. Since abundant power was key to everything he was doing here, his first priority had been to get the van-sized cold-fusion reactor running.

The components for that and an equally crucial device had been shipped around the Suez Canal to the port of Bremerhaven, Germany, in shipping containers before being off-loaded and moved to this facility.

"Wow, you've been busy." Aaden Bauer's voice finally brought Mark's head up from the status displays on the monitors spread around the U-shaped desk.

Mark rose to meet his friend, gripping the other's extended hand with his own.

"Getting there," he said, pausing to study the face of his colleague. "I heard about your shoot-out in Rothenburg."

Aaden grinned. "Didn't even get a scratch. But if Nikina hadn't been watching my back, I wouldn't be standing here chatting with you."

"That's the second time she's come through for us in a big way. You'll have to introduce me."

"I would have brought her today, but she had a pressing appointment in Munich," Aaden said. "You got time to give me a little tour?"

"Sure. I could use a break."

Mark focused his attention on the cocky German man. At six feet three inches, his two-hundred-twenty-pound frame matched Mark's. If Mark had been blond, they might have been brothers. And like Mark and Heather, Aaden had eschewed the benefits of getting a nanite injection, partially because none of them trusted the nanites produced by the various world governments. Heather had discussed designing their own version of the nano-serum, but so far that had been way down on their list of things to worry about. Right now Mark's biggest worry was Heather.

Despite his cajoling, she continued to overextend herself. He had seen her tiredness in the occasional droop of her shoulders and the glazed look that sometimes came over her. And her lush brown hair had recently developed a thin white streak near the center of her forehead. Heather was approaching a breaking point, and unless he could find some way to lighten her load, even she would eventually succumb. For the last two weeks he had felt a growing need to get back home, but he couldn't do that until he finished up here.

"All right, then," Mark said, "let me show you around."

Mark led the way into a large high-bay just down the hall from his office. He took the steel-grated stairs up to the catwalk that circled the room forty feet above the concrete floor. At the top he stopped, and Aaden stepped up beside him to lean against the railing and look out across the warehouse floor.

"My God," Aaden said. "You've already finished the cold-fusion reactor?"

"Not me," Mark said, pointing to the two robots that worked to weld parts on another large piece of equipment. "I finished Fred and Barney two weeks ago, and they've built everything else."

Aaden frowned. "I thought you'd build one of your matter disrupter-synthesizers instead of the cold-fusion device."

"That would have taken too long. The cold-fusion reactor will provide all the power you're going to need."

"Power for what?"

Once again Mark pointed to the spot where the two robots toiled. "For that."

A puzzled look crept onto Aaden's face. "What is it?"

"Walk with me and I'll show you."

Mark led the way along the catwalk until he reached a point directly opposite the inverted-horseshoe-shaped machine.

Aaden stepped up beside him and froze. "Please tell me that isn't what I think it is."

"It's a wormhole gate."

"*Scheiße!*"

Mark clapped a hand on Aaden's shoulder. "Don't worry. It's only capable of linking to the one we have at our home base."

"Wait just a minute. Didn't you tell me that activating a wormhole gateway would trigger an Altreian attack?"

"Robby and Eos say these Earth gates won't, and Heather agrees. The Altreian vessel buried beneath the Kalasasaya Temple is only programmed to detect the activation of interstellar gateways. These Earth gates will only use a tiny fraction of that power. But they will give us a door between here and our facility that we can send robots through, along with the materials your commercial 3-D printer will need. People, too."

For several seconds, Aaden stood still, his eyes watching the speed and precision with which the two robots worked.

"I don't see any 3-D printer."

"That's because I didn't send the parts to build one," Mark replied. "We'll deliver those through the gateway when it's activated."

"And where will you get all the powdered metals and plastics that it will use?"

Mark's face lit up slightly. "We make them. We feed the matter disrupter-synthesizer with rock, dirt, or whatever we've mined. The MDS then transforms that matter into raw energy that's converted into the wave packets that form whatever material we want to produce."

Aaden turned to stare at Mark. "Sounds a lot like alchemy to me."

"It's just changing energy from one form to another. It's not perfectly efficient, but we use the excess energy to power other things."

"How many of the MDS devices do you have?"

"One is all we really need, but we have three to support expansion and to provide redundancy in case of failure."

"And when do you plan to help us build one?"

Mark hesitated, then decided Aaden had a need to know. "We don't."

The man's blue eyes narrowed. "Why not?"

"The cold-fusion reactor will provide plenty of power for this facility."

"You know that the UFNS is building its own matter disrupters based on Rho Project technology."

"Yes, but we've made a number of breakthroughs that we don't want getting into their hands. Don't worry. We'll send you supplies, robots, and other equipment through this gateway."

Aaden shook his head. "Don't you think that's being shortsighted? You're risking everything by keeping this tech bottled up inside that secret base of yours. All the UFNS has to do is capture one of these gateways you plan on scattering among the Safe Earth resistance cells. They'd just have to activate it and pour through to overrun you."

"No. The remote gateways can only be activated or shut down from our master control station. When the operator on this end requests activation, the remote gateway sends a subspace signal containing an embedded three-hundred-sixty-degree audiovisual feed to our station. If we like what we see, we power up both gates and initiate the connection. Otherwise, nobody gets through."

"We won't be self-sufficient. I don't like it."

Mark sucked in a deep breath, held it for a bit, then released slowly. He knew he wasn't showing good faith, but Heather had calculated their odds of success, and they had agreed that this was the safest way to proceed. He would remain firm.

"You know, my friend, I didn't really expect you to."

"One thing I don't understand. If you have a working wormhole gate on your end, why didn't you just enter the coordinates for this warehouse and push the equipment through instead of risking yourself making the trip here? So long as you're not sending living things through it, you shouldn't need another gate on this end."

"Actually," said Mark, impressed with the extent of Aaden's knowledge, "that's not true. Unless it's firmly anchored at both ends, the unanchored end of any wormhole thicker than a hair waggles through space. It's impossible to know precisely where anything you send through it will arrive."

"But the Rho Ship came here through an unanchored wormhole."

"That's true, but it only got within the vicinity of our solar system. After that it used its sub-light gravitational engines to travel to Earth. The error factor is nonlinear. The longer the wormhole transit, the worse the accuracy problem becomes."

As Aaden started to respond, Mark's cell chirped a message alert. He retrieved the phone from his pocket, glanced down at the screen, and smiled.

"Good news?" Aaden asked.

"The robots just finished your gateway. How'd you like to be the first to try it out?"

With a nod, Aaden turned and headed back toward the stairs that led down to the warehouse floor. Mark followed, his worries washed away by his rising excitement. Although they had tested two gateways within the New Zealand compound, this would be the first try of any significant distance. As they reached the wormhole gate, Mark stepped past Aaden and seated himself at the control panel to power up the system.

Now this was going to be fun.

CHAPTER 24

Heather stood next to the master station, where Robby sat surrounded by status displays and computers. The controls remained untouched. He didn't need them. The readouts changed as Robby and Eos manipulated the computerized devices with their shared mind, the sight sending a thrill through her as she watched them work.

When Mark had called to say the remote gateway was ready for a trial run, she and Robby had hurried to the pressurized Earth-gate laboratory and powered up the system. Unlike the Stephenson wormhole gateway that she, Mark, and Jennifer had destroyed with a nuclear detonation eight years ago, this one only required a single supporting stasis field generator instead of two. Even that wasn't absolutely necessary except as a safety precaution.

Despite the remote gateway also being on Earth, there would be a pressure differential between the two locations. The atmospheric pressure at the far end was embedded in the data that streamed through the subspace communications link, enabling Robby to adjust the pressure in this laboratory to match. Nevertheless, he would seal the gateway with a stasis shield before activating it. Not only did that protect against a faulty reading, but it also ensured that nothing undesirable could pass through the Earth gate.

Heather felt her ears pop as the air pressure equalized.

"Ready," Robby said, eagerness in his voice.

"Okay," she said, shifting her gaze to the gateway. "Raise the stasis shield and open the door."

The gateway had been built into the far wall. The inverted-horse-shoe-shaped opening was ten feet tall, six feet wide, and three feet deep, ending in the solid rock from which the underground complex had been excavated. The rock wall behind the opening shimmered and disappeared, replaced by a view of two smiling men standing in a large room, Mark and Aaden Bauer.

Even though their appearance was what Heather had expected, her heart thundered in her chest. Mark's mouth moved, but she heard nothing. Of course. The stasis field was blocking all sound.

"Put them on speaker and turn on our microphone."

Robby nodded and Mark's voice picked up midsentence.

"—for sore eyes."

Heather smiled. "I didn't catch all of that, but it's wonderful to see you. I can't wait to hold you."

Aaden cleared his throat, pulling Heather's gaze to him.

"Sorry, Aaden. I'm happy to see you, too."

The big man gestured at the gateway. "So what's the deal? When can we step through?"

"Give us a minute to run some tests, and then Robby will drop the stasis shield."

"Eos says everything checks out," said Robby. "Dropping the shield now."

A cool breeze signaled that the pressure and temperature match hadn't been exact, but Heather didn't care. She rushed to Mark as he stepped through the opening. He swept her up into arms of rolled steel, his warm lips seeking hers in a kiss that took her breath away.

Aaden's voice pulled them out of it. "You two can get a room later."

For the first time in weeks, Heather laughed. Mark lowered her so that her feet once again rested on the floor, and she turned to shake hands with Aaden. Had it really been only six months since she'd last seen her European ally? So much had happened that it seemed like forever.

Heather stepped back. "Welcome to our Fortress of Solitude."

Aaden's sweeping gaze took in the rail-mounted overhead crane and the open area that led to the sliding steel door that sealed the rear of the large chamber, coming to a stop at the master control station where Robby leaned back in a swivel chair.

"I guess I wasn't expecting it to be so empty."

"This room is designed to move equipment through," said Mark. "Don't worry, we'll show you around a bit before we wrap things up today."

"I don't suppose you'll let me in on where this base is located, will you?"

Heather shook her head. "It's safer if you don't know, but there is something we want to show you. Robby, send in the bots."

○ ● ○

Aaden watched as the large steel door slid open, disappearing into a slot in the far wall, surprised at the lack of pressure differential between the two rooms. Apparently the two large spaces acted like airlocks. But the sight that confronted him on the far side of that door made him forget all about air pressure.

Dozens of car-sized drones raced overhead and through the gateway, followed by a swarm of much smaller counterparts. Behind them came hundreds of robots, many of them humanoid in appearance, while others took the form of quadrupeds. Some, shaped like forklifts, carried equipment through the gateway and into the warehouse back in Hanau, accompanied by driverless flatbed trolleys loaded with metal shipping crates. These moved to an open area where teams of robots worked to unload their contents, efficiently stacking them in accessible rows.

Pulling up the rear of this parade came several hundred of what could only be combat robots of various shapes and sizes, who promptly lined themselves up along one side of the Hanau warehouse and powered down. Some were eight-foot-tall bipeds with humanlike arms and hands; others looked like large dogs with feet that could uncurl to be used as hands. More drones scurried around on multiple legs like Alaskan king crabs. Mark had told him about these crawling bombs that could curl up and magnetically attach themselves to the larger robots by the score.

Aaden realized that his mouth hung open, and closed it. "How did you build all of these?"

"We didn't," said Heather. "The robots built all of this, with help from the additive-manufacturing machines."

"Three-D printers?"

"Big ones. You'll see. Those robots will build one inside your warehouse this week. The machines work fast, twenty-four hours a day. If one of them breaks down, others repair it. If you need more robots, they build them. All we have to do is keep you supplied with the raw materials."

A new concern sprang to the forefront of Aaden's thoughts. "What powers the robots? Batteries?"

"That, my friend," Mark said, "is the holy grail. Perfect capacitors that recharge as fast as a power supply can dump power into them. For our power supplies, that's only a matter of seconds. And we're talking about a lot of storage capacity. During typical usage, one charge will last several days. Best of all, the robots know how to interface to any power source. They can steal it when they need to."

The transition from here to there was so seamless that Aaden didn't realize he had walked back through the wormhole gate into the Hanau warehouse until Mark and Heather stepped up beside him. Everywhere he looked, the engineer robots were working, deftly avoiding bumping into obstacles or each other.

"How are you manipulating them?"

"Robby uses Eos to give directions to one of our supercomputers," said Heather, "and it downloads the required knowledge to each of the robots through a subspace link. The robots then cooperatively accomplish their tasks using swarm computing algorithms. The supercomputer monitors their progress and, when necessary for optimization, updates their instructions."

"And if the link with your supercomputer goes down?"

"They will continue to operate autonomously until the job is finished. It just might take a little longer."

"If you let these things loose in the world, nobody will have a job."

When Heather shrugged, Aaden glanced over her shoulder at the combat robots standing in tight formation along the walls, a new concern blossoming in his mind.

"Do those operate autonomously, too?" he asked.

"If we tell them to."

"And that doesn't terrify you?"

"Hard times call for hard choices."

He studied her face, noting the bend in her shoulders and worry lines at the corners of her beautiful eyes. And then he stopped. There was a thin streak of white in her hair at the center of her forehead. What kind of pressure could do that to such a strong, talented twenty-seven-year-old? Her appearance made him feel confused and weak, as if he had been failing to carry his part of the load within the Safe Earth resistance.

Mark's voice interrupted his thoughts. "I'm hungry. How about a little lunch?"

A smile returned to Heather's face. "Good idea. Come on, Aaden. Let me introduce you to our robot chef. Her name is Julia."

Turning away, she took Mark's hand, and the two of them led Aaden back through the Earth gate into their underground laboratory. As the gateway winked out behind them, he felt like Alice after stepping through the looking glass.

:CHAPTER 25

Janet stood outside the protective stasis field as the lowering clouds and light snowfall hid the surrounding mountains. But lost in her memories, she didn't notice the accompanying cold.

Despite knowing that he would have taken her with him if he could, she wished she could hate Jack for leaving her behind. They were a team—the best in a bad business. Now she just felt broken.

If she had still been with the NSA, she could have buried herself in the job, working him out of her mind. But she was in New Zealand, a glorified security guard for Heather and Robby, when what she really wanted to do was kill someone.

"You okay?"

Gil McFarland's voice startled her, but she managed to hide it with a smile as she turned toward Heather's father.

"Just bathing myself in beauty."

The knowing look on the slender man's jovial face told her he wasn't buying a word.

"Fred and Linda are coming over for lunch," he said. "Anna's making tomato soup and grilled cheese sandwiches. We'd love to have you join us."

Janet started to refuse, but the thought of that warm and homey meal with dear friends lifted her spirits. It wasn't as if she had pressing work.

"That sounds great."

Gil turned away from the concealed entrance to the underground facility, his footsteps creating a trail through six inches of fresh snow as he led her toward his four-wheel-drive white SUV. As she approached the vehicle, she noted that Fred had installed his snow chains. No doubt that task had been why he had been out here. Another set of fresh tire tracks led down the canyon toward the swale that sheltered the handful of homes housing the compound's inhabitants.

Janet headed for her own vehicle, but Gil stopped her.

"Ride with me. Fred and I will be coming back to work after lunch."

"Deal."

She opened the passenger door, brushed most of the snow from her hair and clothes, and stepped in. As they started down the gravel road, a thought bothered her.

"What about Heather and Robby?"

"I invited them, but they've got company down below. Mark and Aaden."

That news stunned Janet. Mark had finished the remote Earth gate, and it was activated. Seemed like a pretty damned critical thing that the chief of security should know about. How did Heather expect her to do her job if she was kept out of the loop?

That was just it. Janet hadn't been doing her job. Since losing Jack, she had descended into such deep depression that she had only been going through the motions, pretending that providing security for a compound protected by an alien force field and the most sophisticated computing and robotic facility on Earth was an essential job. All she had been doing was working out or killing time. Robby knew it and did his best to cheer her up, trying to pass along his certainty that his dad would find a way to come home to them. For Robby's sake, Janet should have been the strong one, should have been able to make herself believe that Jack would once again pull off the impossible.

Heather hadn't said anything to her, but she must have noticed the change in Janet, and that meant this little encounter with Gil was far from random. This was an intervention.

She gritted her teeth, stifling the angry words that tried to crawl from her mouth. If Gil sensed her sudden change in mood, he didn't show it. This situation wasn't his fault; it was hers. Although such recognition didn't lift her spirits, she would endure this lunch gathering with as much grace as she could muster.

She would save her harsh words for Heather.

: CHAPTER 26

The unexpected transition from subspace back to normal-space froze Raul in place, but VJ immediately reacted to engage the Rho Ship's cloaking field. The sight of her ghostly form studying the tactical displays that she created in the air around her somehow reassured him, although it should have done the opposite. VJ had evolved to the point that she was taking defensive actions on her own initiative without waiting for input from Raul, even though he was the captain. At least he hoped he was still the ship's captain.

Raul dismissed that disturbing line of thought and shifted his focus to what the tactical displays were telling him. As he'd expected, the Rho Ship's momentum had carried it out into space, although the short amount of time they'd been in subspace meant that they were well inside the orbit of Scion's nearest moon. Not good.

"Captain, our trajectory is suborbital."

Her mode of address made him feel a little better, although the information she conveyed immediately wiped that feeling away.

"Can we correct that?"

"Not without being detected. We're too close to the planetary defense systems."

"How long do we have until we reenter the atmosphere?"

"Seven minutes and forty-two seconds . . . forty-one . . . forty—"

"Stop! I don't need a countdown. Why did the subspace field generator fail?"

"Diagnostics indicate that the system abort was caused by a minor software glitch."

That was the first piece of good news he had received in what felt like a hell of a long time.

"Can you fix it?"

There was a brief pause before VJ looked at him and smiled. "I don't need to. A simple reboot should correct the problem."

"You're telling me that turning the damn thing off and back on fixes Altreian computer systems, too?"

Her brow furrowed in a way that felt distinctly human. "It's possible that our repairs of their technology introduced the error. Regardless, I highly recommend that we give it a try before my countdown reaches zero."

Raul couldn't argue with that. "Do it."

"Initiating."

When nothing happened, Raul felt his throat tighten. "What's wrong?"

"Relax. It'll take the system a few more seconds to power up."

Had he heard a hint of derision in her response? He replayed the memory and decided to give her the benefit of the doubt. Not that he had time for an argument right now anyway.

The transition into subspace pulled a gasp of relief from his lips and wiped the irritation from his mind, although it didn't wholly expunge the worry that the glitch might recur.

Great. Because of a single error, he was losing faith in his ability to fix what was wrong with the ship, despite all his past successes. Had this self-doubt started with his creation of VJ? Or was she one of those successes, perhaps the greatest of all?

Raul had a feeling that he was on the verge of finding out.

○ ● ○

Group Commander Shalegha stood on a high ledge that overlooked the recent battlefield, buffeted by a howling summer storm. Lightning forked across a sky so dark that it brought twilight to midday.

Despite knowing that this had been another in a string of recent victories, Eadric and Kasari losses remained unacceptably high. Too bad General Dgarra was Koranthian. He would have made a fine addition to the Kasari Collective. Although he continued to suffer betrayal by his beloved aide-de-camp, his tactical mastery and sheer force of will continued to deny the Kasari forces access to the warren of caves and tunnels that honeycombed the Koranthian Mountains.

Fortunately, the tides were turning inside the Koranthian halls of power. Reports from Shalegha's spies in ArvaiKheer indicated that General Magtal was taking every opportunity to highlight each of Dgarra's losses, undercutting his support within the Koranthian senate. To strengthen Magtal's case, Shalegha had launched a series of attacks on Magtal's central front, attacks that had intentionally failed. Now even Emperor Goltat's faith in his nephew had begun to show signs of cracking.

Shalegha turned and walked into the artificial cavern that had just yesterday housed a forward headquarters for one of Dgarra's divisions. Thanks to an all-out attack by more than a thousand of her eight-legged Graath soldiers, the slaughter inside the cavern had been complete. For a time, she had even believed that they would be able to break through into the central tunnel system, but the arrival of Dgarra's reserve had blocked that and triggered a number of demolition charges that pulled down a large part of the mountain and made further access impossible.

She stopped to survey the epicenter of that fight, her nanobot-enhanced vision painting the cavern and its contents in shades of red, yellow, and blue. Despite the ongoing efforts to consolidate this position, blood and body parts lay strewn among the rubble that was all that remained of the original defenses. Ordinarily Shalegha would have ordered a follow-on attack for tomorrow, but the losses that Dgarra had inflicted on the Eadric force, coupled with the death of hundreds of her elite Graath troops, meant that she would have to regroup and await the arrival of reinforcements.

That was okay. She could afford to be patient. In the meantime, she would absorb the information Jennifer Smythe continued to feed the hive-mind and formulate her next battle plan. Dgarra's ultimate fall was only a matter of time.

o ● o

Jennifer stood stoically behind General Dgarra as he met with his subordinate commanders. She was done with wishing she could cry. She had allowed the situation to push her into a depressed shell in which she succumbed to defeat. A person is only defeated when they accept defeat as an inevitable end state, and that was a condition she could not and would not tolerate.

Over the last few days, she had learned much about her connection to the hive-mind and how it affected her free will. In essence, she was two people, the real Jennifer Smythe and the Kasari puppet. But the fact that she remained an independently thinking being gave her hope, and that had freed the fight that had almost been choked out of her.

She did have some control over her body. On those occasions where her will didn't conflict with the overarching goals of the Kasari Collective, they gave her free rein. Oddly enough, this occurred in combat. And since it allowed her to vent her frustration on her enemies, she fought like a demon. But her fierceness also served the Kasari goal of convincing Dgarra of her loyalty, as the Koranthians knew that someone in his inner circle was a spy.

That limited freedom to be herself had proved to be useless in combating the mastery the Kasari nanobots had over her physical actions. What had become increasingly clear, however, was that her enhanced neural capabilities had allowed her to protect a significant portion of her mind, including her own thoughts. So she had set about probing her mind to see if she could expand her mental capabilities.

Most promising, the hive-mind had displayed no ability to make her use her empathic and psychic abilities. That might mean that the Kasari couldn't stop her from using those powers. Jennifer had used them to make a Kasari soldier jump from a high ledge, but the hive had almost blocked her mind then. She feared that any overt usage would reveal more about her abilities, possibly showing the Kasari how to permanently block those powers, or worse, how to make use of them.

That meant that she had better make this next attempt count.

One possibility was to reveal herself to Dgarra as the spy. The downside of doing that was that Dgarra would kill her. While she was willing to die for the cause, that wasn't exactly plan A.

She had been enslaved by the Koranthians, now by the Kasari, enough. Any plan she came up with needed to have a reasonable chance of restoring her free will. Without that, she would rather be dead.

Suddenly a new thought occurred to her: Raul. Not only had he designed a new nanite formula, but the design information for the Kasari nanobots was within the Rho Ship's neural net, too. But Raul was off planet and had been out of range of her headset when she had last attempted to contact him. Would the Kasari stop her from trying again?

Jennifer rolled that thought around in her mind. She could propose the idea to them. After all, it had been their ship to begin with. Surely they would jump at the chance to recapture their vessel. Of course, therein lay the danger. She couldn't just communicate her plan to Raul using the headset. The Kasari would hear whatever she told him.

No. She'd have to establish a true psychic link. And that meant she'd have to be close to Raul. Once again, she would be placing him in tremendous danger, this time for her last chance at freedom. Despite how much the realization horrified her, she was certain of one thing: for that chance, she would risk anything.

:CHAPTER 27

VJ stood before Raul, studying his reaction to her new uniform.

The Rho Ship's database included several months of data captured when Raul had been browsing Earth's Internet, including a wide variety of photographs and videos. Clearly he found certain aspects of female bodies attractive, and there was a clear pattern of preference for clothing styles that enhanced this effect. By examining the amount of time he had spent on different images, VJ had developed a rating criterion that she had used to create her own design.

"Well," she asked, slowly spinning in a circle, "what do you think?"

For several seconds Raul said nothing, but from the infrared hotspots on his cheeks and his elevated heart rate, she decided that he found the formfitting faux-leather pantsuit and boots to his liking. She'd also put a lot of effort into improving the opaqueness of her holographic image. The effect wasn't yet perfect, but she was closing in on it.

He blinked and shook his head, as if to rouse himself from a trance. "Wow. I mean . . . you look nice."

She smiled. "A work in progress. Of course, if you'd prefer to see me naked—"

His eyes widened. "Don't even go there."

From the shocked expression on his face, she decided that he was uncomfortable with her suggestion. That was fine. Clothing gave her creative liberty with her appearance.

"Fine," she said. "Now that we have that settled, shall we get to work?"

○ ● ○

Raul stared, dumbstruck, as VJ turned to create eight virtual displays in an arc around them—as if what she had just proposed was as routine as asking him out for lunch.

The offer brought a sudden flashback of Jennifer lying naked atop the Koranthian surgical table. At the time, he had been trying to save her life, seeing her clinically, as a physician would. Her nakedness had registered in his mind, but his focus had been on injecting nanites to save her life. Right now, though, those memories were messing with his head in a way that he didn't need.

He sat down in his translucent blue captain's chair, having added color after forgetting to dismiss the invisible stasis chair and subsequently tripping over it. All around him the virtual screens changed, rapidly cycling through the status of each shipboard system as VJ ran a complete diagnostic. With his mental linkage to the neural net, Raul had no trouble keeping up, but he focused in on the subspace field generator, looking for any signs of what had caused the glitch that had forced its automatic shutdown.

There was no indication of a power spike, and the sensors had detected nothing out of the ordinary in the subspace environment at the time of the anomaly. By all accounts, the shutdown shouldn't have happened, but it had, leaving Raul puzzled. He needed another perspective.

"VJ, have you identified the cause of the subspace-generator outage?"

"It appears to have been a random event, conceivably caused by quantum tunneling in one of the control circuits."

"I don't like that answer."

She didn't bother to glance at him. "Noted."

"Give me a prioritized rundown of our problems, worst first."

She gestured toward the display directly in front of Raul, and it moved forward.

"As you can see," she said, "the primary matter disrupter-synthesizer will require major repairs, including a complete rebuild of several components. Estimated time to fully repair: thirty-seven hours."

"How long for marginal capability?"

"Sixteen hours, thirty minutes, but I don't recommend that option."

"Noted," Raul said.

The odd sense of satisfaction that came with that statement was stupid. What was this, high school? Still, VJ was getting very good at getting under his skin and seemed to take pleasure in it.

She continued. "The primary stasis field generator is functioning marginally and will take approximately five hours to restore full functionality. After that, the disruptor weapons and gravitational distortion engines each need minor repairs."

"Okay, let's get started on the primary MDS."

When VJ hesitated, Raul turned to see her staring at him.

"What?" he asked.

"I agree with that initial priority, but I propose to add a shipboard modification to our to-do list."

VJ was never shy, and anytime she didn't come right out with a suggestion, it made Raul nervous. This time was no exception.

"Such as?"

"I've been reviewing some of the Altreian physics theory that the other Jennifer uploaded into our neural net. I believe that I can use it to design and build an advanced projectile weapon that will enable this ship to better defend itself against the Kasari fast-attack ships."

"It won't work. They would destroy a missile or any other projectile before it even got close. Even if it somehow managed to get past their weapons, it would detonate harmlessly against their stasis shield. Even the gravitational vortex weapon that the Rho Ship used to shoot down the Second Ship is no match for those attack ships. We would have to get too close, and they are far more maneuverable."

"What if I told you there is a way around those problems."

Raul leaned forward in his chair, his interest aroused. "Go on."

"We can create a small subspace field generator with a super-capacitor that can power it for a specified length of time. If we attach a small warhead to this device, we could use our primary stasis field generator to launch the torpedo from our ship on a desired target vector. The weapon would then shift into subspace for just long enough to penetrate the target's shields before transitioning back into normal-space. Boom."

Raul paused to consider this, his neural net working the problem. "That could work, but if the enemy ship changes course while our dumb bomb is in subspace we'll miss."

"Only if they make a maneuver that we don't anticipate."

"The odds of our precisely anticipating their maneuver seem pretty low."

"Not necessarily. We could make an escape maneuver, which would cause them to compute a new intercept course. We are capable of making that same computation. They might detect the launch of our subspace bullet, but then it would wink out of existence on their sensors, thereby posing no threat."

Suddenly this sounded a whole lot better to Raul.

"And," VJ said, "we can shoot in ways the Kasari won't anticipate. Do you recall Jennifer's six laws of subspace transition?"

The neural net refreshed them in Raul's mind.

The speed of subspace waves is orders of magnitude greater than the speed of light.

Anything contained within a subspace field is shifted into subspace but retains its previous rate of time's passage.

Anything shifted into subspace will retain its previous normal-space momentum vector upon transition back to normal-space.

No normal-space force can act upon an object in subspace.

If an object in subspace is not acted upon by a subspace force, it will return to normal-space at the location where its previous momentum vector would have taken it.

If an object in subspace is acted upon by a subspace force, such as a subspace drive, it will return to normal-space at an entirely new location, but retain its original, normal-space momentum vector.

According to those laws, they just had to accelerate the bomb to match a desired velocity vector, shift it into subspace, wait long enough for it to reach its intended destination, then have it shift back into normal-space at the target location.

Understanding dawned on Raul. The combination of Jennifer's second, third, and fourth laws meant that you could think of an object that had been shifted into subspace as having a normal-space shadow that retained its momentum vector but was unaffected by normal-space forces. That meant they could fire their torpedo, shift it into subspace, and wait for it to pass through a planet before having it shift out of subspace on the far side.

He saw VJ smile. She had seen his expression and knew that he understood.

"How long will it take us to make one of these subspace bombs?"

"Approximately forty-three hours for the first one. Then we'll need to reconfigure the exit hatch to enable the stasis field to carry it outside the ship and perform a test launch. If all goes well, we should be able to optimize construction, potentially cutting that time in half. But none of that can begin until after we've repaired the primary MDS."

Raul leaned back, feeling his shoulders relax. The process wouldn't be speedy, but they now had a viable path that just might lead to their survival. He met VJ's blue eyes, seeing the lift of her right eyebrow.

"You're amazing," he said.

Her lips twitched into a fleeting smile, then she blinked rapidly and turned back to her work.

For the briefest of moments, Raul thought that he had seen her eyes shine with moisture. Or maybe his imagination was once again getting the best of him.

o ● o

Down here, far beneath the rugged mountain peaks, light was a luxury, even to General Dgarra's infrared-sensitive eyes. But now that battle had shifted belowground along this portion of his northern front, he was glad to have so little of it. The darkness highlighted the warm bodies of his warriors and differentiated them from his enemies. By far, the hottest body of all stayed at his side, a near-constant presence for which he was thankful.

Over the last several days, it had become increasingly clear that he had a traitor in his midst, someone who was leaking his plans to the Kasari. He had heard the whispers among his people, had seen the suspicion in their eyes whenever they looked at Smythe. Captain Jeshen, the courier who would have become his aide-de-camp had he not placed that mantle upon Smythe's slender shoulders, was by far the most direct in his accusations. Dgarra did not hold it against him. She was an outsider and therefore deserved the most scrutiny.

If not for the ferocity with which she fought his enemies, he, too, might have doubted her, despite the powerful feelings she evoked within him. Smythe's hatred for the Kasari was palpable. It shone in her eyes during combat. She would rather kill one true Kasari than ten of their Eadric stooges.

Dgarra had just seen her focus that same look on Jeshen. Naturally she would echo the feelings that Jeshen directed toward her. To her credit, she had never uttered a negative word about his courier, but the clear discord between his two most trusted subordinates troubled him deeply. The stress of war, especially one that you were losing, had a tendency to exacerbate petty rivalries and turn them into blood feuds.

He returned his attention to the task at hand, preparing for the coming battle. Today he would try something new. Rather than formulate detailed plans for how he wanted this battle fought, he would delegate the battle planning to each of his sector commanders, with instructions that they were not to share those plans with each other or with him. Dgarra would maintain command of his reserve but would decide when and where to deploy them at the last possible moment.

Inhaling the dank air that filled this particular cavern, he straightened.

Even if the spy was reading his mind, there would be nothing to use against him.

○ ● ○

Jennifer savored the thrill of battle so intensely that she had begun to doubt her sanity. Warfare was the one physical activity in which the hive-mind allowed her free will to come to the fore. Not only did she get to fight beside this man that she had come to care for, but she also got to kill those who had forced her to betray him.

They had transformed her into a war hound, only released from its cage when doing so served its handler's purpose. Then, having completed the task, she was muzzled and returned to the hellish confines of prison. Those moments of release were all she had to look forward to.

Unlike in recent battles, when the enemy had full knowledge of Dgarra's war plans, today he let the enemy come against his divisions, then reacted with instinctive ferocity. And his instincts had proved themselves to be exceptional.

The Eadric had attacked Dgarra's eastern flank in a feint that he'd seen through, withholding his reserve until he could be sure of the location of the main assault. That came through the western tunnels, as wave after wave of Kasari shock troops punched a hole through the Koranthian defenses. Dgarra let them come.

The confusion Jennifer felt in watching him delay his counterattack had been transmitted through her nanobot communications array to the hive-mind. When the attackers encountered no resistance, they had raced forward, anxious to penetrate deep into the cavern system before defensive demolition charges could be used to collapse the ceiling. Still Dgarra waited.

When his counterattack finally came, it surprised Jennifer again. The demolition charges he triggered didn't block any tunnels. Instead, they opened a path between them, and through that gap Dgarra's reserve poured directly into the left flank of the Kasari attackers. Defying conventional military theory, he launched half his force into the teeth of the Kasari follow-on force, cutting them off from the lead elements.

In a sudden charge, Dgarra led the rest of his reserve into the rear of the Kasari who had penetrated into a large natural cavern. With her blood thundering through her veins, Jennifer sprinted forward, closing with a group of the Graath gorilla-spiders. The thunder of blaster fire accompanied blinding flashes of light. The cavern shuddered, sending stalactites crashing down on those who battled below.

Staying with Dgarra, she scrambled over flowstone and through a forest of stalagmites that reached toward the cavern ceiling. She sensed movement to her left, drew her war-blade, and whirled to meet the attack. The four-armed Kasari soldier was even bigger than a Koranthian, but she was quicker. She ducked under the blaster, her war-blade removing the lower right hand that held it at the elbow. But the thing's other three hands responded. The upper two sought to grab her while the other drew a knife that was as long as her war-blade.

Jennifer rolled left and kicked off a tree-sized stalagmite, but she was a fraction of a second too slow to avoid the blade that cut a bone-deep gash in her right thigh. Time dilated as a wave of pain crashed over her. With her vision misting red, everyone else in the maelstrom moved in slow motion.

For the hundredth time she marveled at how the hive-mind was allowing her the freedom to battle other members of the collective. Apparently she had yet to play some larger role in Scion's assimilation. If so, her masters were doing a piss-poor job of making sure she lived to play out their scheme.

She ducked another slash, then felt a powerful hand close on her left forearm. *Shit!* Putting all of her neurally augmented strength and quickness into the movement, she used that anchor to yank herself toward the Kasari. Then, as its blade hand began another swing, she chopped down with the war-blade in her right hand.

Its razor-sharp leading edge whistled through the monster's thick neck so swiftly that its head lifted free of its shoulders and, for a moment, hung in the air, suspended atop a fountain of green blood. Then it tumbled to the cavern floor. For two full seconds the Kasari soldier's body continued standing, Jennifer's left arm still locked in its stiff grasp. Jennifer's weight toppled the dead soldier forward, and the heavy form collapsed atop her, spilling its acrid blood over her face and head, dousing her in its ammonia stink.

By the time she struggled out from under the Kasari, the battle was over except for sporadic firing in the distance. Jennifer tried to climb back to her feet, but her wounded right leg betrayed her, dropping her back to her knees. She glanced down at the wound, startled to see the amount of blood that soaked her trousers. Her nanites were working on the gash, but healing a wound this large would take time.

General Dgarra appeared and knelt to lean her back against the nearest stalagmite. He signaled, and another Koranthian moved forward to help. But when he knelt beside Dgarra, Jennifer found herself staring into the face of the traitor who had darted her with the Kasari nanites. Captain Jeshen. She wanted to scream out what he had done, but the hive-mind prevented it, once again forcing her real self to flee to its tiny prison, only capable of watching as Jeshen and Dgarra worked to cut her pants leg free and bandage the wound to reduce further blood loss.

Once done, Dgarra waved his hand and Jeshen departed, taking something with him. What had he taken? Jennifer replayed the memory in her mind. There it was, in his left hand: her bloody right pants leg.

A sick feeling of dread wormed its way into her soul.

CHAPTER 28

The feel of snake scales slithering over his bare chest brought Jack out of his deep slumber. He didn't move, just opened his eyes. The visitor wasn't particularly big as snakes go, perhaps three feet long and as big around as Jack's thumb. Like the leaves of the trees, it was a mottled purple with hints of red, and had a wedge-shaped head that said viper. Khal Teth's memories supplied the name of the species—a vengal, one of the most poisonous reptiles on Quol. Of course it was.

Jack closed his eyes again and relaxed. The thing hadn't bit him yet, so he decided not to give it an excuse to do so. Yesterday's action had given him little confidence that Khal Teth's body was capable of displaying the lightning-quick reflexes necessary to snatch the snake by the neck before it could react.

As a matter of fact, this body felt like hell. That was a good first step in transforming it into the weapon he would be needing if he was going to survive and accomplish what he had come here to do. He hadn't left the love of his life and his son just to fail.

Up until this moment, he'd managed to suppress any thought of Janet, but now her memory bulled its way into his mind. Inside the altar cavern beneath the Kalasasaya Temple, she had turned and walked away without a backward glance. The fact that it would probably be the last memory he would ever have with her cut at him. He understood her anger. She had good reason to doubt the information that Khal Teth had relayed through his lucid dreams. If she was right, he had sacrificed himself and their love for a fool's errand. His belief in the mission had left her helpless to stop him, and if there was one thing that Janet couldn't tolerate, it was helplessness.

The tip of the snake's tail flicked against his left ear as it left his body and continued along one of the intertwined branches that supported Jack. He lay still for another minute, feeling for that intuitive sense of danger that was an inherent part of his nature. There it was, almost buried by the strange feel of this body, but still accessible. Jack would have expected his instincts to be amped up by a much-closer connection to Khal Teth. Instead, the opposite seemed to be the case. Maybe that was because Khal Teth had thrown up a mental barrier to block the pain.

Jack opened his eyes and turned to see the snake disappearing onto a limb ten feet above his head. With effort, he moved back to the tree trunk and began climbing down, ignoring the muscles that screamed in protest. Hunger and thirst were bigger concerns. The latter wouldn't be a problem.

He paused six feet above ground to plot his course. The priority was to get away from the stoneling beach before the crab-like creatures could strip the meat from his bones. He dropped to the ground and dashed left toward the high ground, only stopping to look back once he had climbed onto a rocky outcropping. Satisfied he hadn't been followed, Jack continued on. He hadn't gone a quarter of a mile before he found what he was looking for, a swiftly moving stream that plummeted over a twenty-foot waterfall into a clear pool below.

Jack paused to listen, not just with his ears but to that special inner sense. When neither alerted him to the presence of immediate danger, he knelt in the mud at the stream's edge, placed his lips in the water, and drank deeply. The swift-moving water was cold and clear, reducing the chances that it contained parasites or contaminants that might sicken him. He found the water far better than some of the muck he had been forced to drink on expeditions into many of Earth's hellholes.

Forcing himself to stop before he was fully satisfied, Jack rose to his feet and walked to the edge of the waterfall. Despite the semipermanent twilight of this region of the world, he could make out dark shapes swimming just beneath the surface. Khal Teth's memories reassured him that these were edible fish. The problem would be catching them.

Jack moved back into the trees, his eyes searching for a suitable branch. He found one of desirable thickness and threw his body weight into breaking it off. That accomplished, he stripped off the smaller branches and leaves and then returned to the waterfall. Again he found what he was looking for, a fist-sized stone with a sharp edge.

After sitting down with his legs dangling over the cliff, Jack set to work. Twenty minutes later he set the stone aside and rolled the crude spear in his hands. All things considered, the weapon was serviceable.

Once again he consulted Khal Teth's memories of these islands. Unfortunately, that knowledge was of a most general nature. Having come from an aristocratic race, Khal Teth had never had any interest in exploring any of the uninhabited islands.

Well, this wouldn't be the first time Jack had found himself lost and alone in deep wilderness. But this was the first time he had been lost and alone on an alien planet, and to top it off, in an almost-naked alien body.

He worked his way down the cliff and onto a large, flat rock at water's edge. Hefting his spear, Jack leaned out to watch the shadows moving just beneath the surface. A distant memory put a forlorn smile on his lips. Gil McFarland, Heather's dad, had taken him and Robby stream fishing in New Zealand. As was his norm, Gil had worn his favorite old hat, adorned with colorfully tied flies and a big button that read "One Fish, Two Fish, Red Fish, Blue Fish." Robby had sported oversized green waders, held up by suspenders, and a smile that had warmed Jack's soul. He could still hear his son's excited yell echoing through the canyon as he had landed his first two-pound trout.

Jack shook his head. The odds said that these would be purple.

○ ● ○

Jack stared up into the star-filled twilight sky, taking a break to rest his tired limbs. He had been on the island slightly more than ten weeks, Earth time. He had slowly gotten used to the Quol orbday, the seven Earth-days it took to complete an orbit around Altreia. In this longitudinal belt that separated the side of Quol that faced Altreia from the side that faced away, this tidally locked world experienced the sunrise and sunset of its distant sun in a strange rhythm. Instead of a true planetary day-night cycle, the near side's day was shortened by Altreia's shadow. And only Quol's far side experienced true night, without Altreia's magenta glow.

And with each sunrise, the clouds churned into the atmosphere above this band of islands that followed the prime meridian, unleashing daystorms. For almost half an orbday, these subtropical squalls came and went, drenching the islands with rain. But, as Dorial set or Quol entered Altreia's shadow, the clouds dissolved away.

Jack found Quol's twilit night exceptionally beautiful. He only wished that Janet and Robby could be here to view this alien sky with him. Despite the hardship of this place, Jack knew they would have liked it. Most of all, Jack would have liked it. No matter how hard he drove himself, he failed to purge the melancholy that weighted his heart. If he was going to have any chance of returning to his own body, he would have to accomplish what he had come here to do: overthrow Parsus and place Khal Teth in his place.

With that in mind—and with Khal Teth's agreement that Jack's expertise was required to accomplish their shared objective—he had put Khal Teth's body through his own version of U.S. Army Ranger School. The flab had disappeared, replaced with lean, hard muscle, and he was no longer running around seminaked, having clothed himself in animal hides. His weapons consisted of a bow, arrows, a stone-pointed spear, and two long ivory knives he'd carved from the tusks of a pugada, a breed of wild hog that roamed the island in abundance. Jack figured that, with a bit more progress, he would be able to proudly claim caveman status.

Of equal importance, he had just finished construction of an outrigger canoe, complete with a mast, an animal-skin sail, and two paddles, just in case one of them broke during the long trip he would now be embarking upon. Fortunately, the barrier reef didn't entirely circle the island. On the flip side, the passage through that barrier was narrow enough to generate nasty currents.

As Jack double-checked that his provisions and equipment were securely tied down, Khal Teth spoke in his mind. "Do you really think you can make it to civilization in that thing?"

"We're about to find out."

"And if we do not?"

"Then we'll get a chance for another nice little swim."

Jack straightened, surveying the last wisps of storm clouds on the horizon. Dorial had set just over an hour ago, and the time for departure had come. He had almost four Earth days of twilight to work with before this world's sun again brought the storms. He planned on hopping between islands until he found an inhabited one. Whether he found one or not, Jack needed to be settled on another island before the daystorms returned.

Having finished the final assembly of the outrigger on a rocky outcropping that formed the closest thing he could find to a boat ramp, he only needed to shove off and climb aboard to be on his way. A beach would have been an easier launch point had it not been for the presence of the stonelings on every beach he had found. This would have to do.

With a heave, Jack lifted the rear end of the outrigger and shoved it forward until the water lifted the prow of the craft. Another hard shove followed by a deft leap settled Jack inside the canoe. It tried to roll, but the outrigger kept it reasonably stable as he lowered himself onto the seat and grabbed a paddle. Then, with long strokes, he propelled the boat across the protected lagoon toward the channel.

○ ● ○

Had it not been for his long familiarity with The Ripper's penchant for survival, the journey between islands in this crudely constructed watercraft would have terrified Khal Teth. Although a member of his race could live indefinitely, that did not mean that they could not die. Yes, it was night, and nightstorms in the island belt were relatively rare, but this last daystorm had left the sea exceptionally rough. Instead of heading toward the nearest of the islands visible on the horizon, Jack had chosen the largest—a reasonable choice given the fact that they needed to find civilization, but the extra distance increased the risk of something going horribly wrong while at sea.

Khal Teth tried to see the possible futures and failed. Just one more frustration of many. The worst of these was how he had been forced to allow Jack's continuous control over his body throughout their extended stay in the wild. Until Khal Teth returned to civilization, such passivity was his only way to survive.

Still, there was no doubt that the vicious training routine that Jack had put Khal Teth's body through was now paying dividends. Jack had paddled almost constantly for most of the night, only stopping for an occasional drink or to swallow some of the fruit he'd collected for this journey. Now, as they approached the island, Jack angled toward a spot where the vegetation came all the way to the water's edge.

Khal Teth didn't know if this island was inhabited. He had seen no boats or aircraft during their lengthy approach, but this was a far larger island than the one they had left. Regardless, they needed to get on shore before the daystorms came. And from the way Jack kept checking the horizon, it was going to be close.

○ ● ○

Jack's arms, back, and abdominal muscles screamed for relief. He ignored them. If the line of clouds growing on the horizon arrived before he reached land, he would lose the boat, along with most of his supplies. Even though he was confident he could swim to shore from here, those losses would be a serious setback, especially if this island proved to be uninhabited.

He began a sprint that significantly increased the speed with which the outrigger cut through the water, but left him gasping for breath. Then, as Dorial's first light painted the eastern horizon bright orange, the nose of the canoe slid beneath the overhanging foliage and struck the muddy bank. Jack leaped from the bow and dragged the canoe out of the water, his bare feet sinking ankle deep in mud that slurped with each backward step.

Satisfied, he retrieved a braided-vine rope from his supplies and secured the outrigger to the trunk of a tree. Then, slinging his bow over his shoulder, Jack grabbed his spear and moved up the adjacent hillside to a point where he could get a better view of his surroundings. Tired as he was, he was happy to be out of the boat and getting his land legs back. From his vantage point atop a cliff against which the ocean waves crashed, he could see that he had reached shore on the point of land that formed the south end of a large sunlit bay.

Situated at the mouth of that bay was a small town of perhaps a hundred wonderfully curved, translucent buildings, their beautiful colors gleaming in distant Dorial's pale morning light. Several water vehicles were moored along a single pier, although Jack couldn't tell how many.

Khal Teth's hiss distracted him. "Yesss!"

Glad as he was to have reached this point, a growing uneasiness troubled Jack. He understood. Once he got out of these woods, Khal Teth would take charge and Jack would be forced back into the role of the rider.

A shadow moved across the bay as a dark cloud blocked Dorial from view, followed by the distant rumble of thunder. For several more seconds Jack watched the sky, then turned and moved back down the hill toward the canoe. He needed to grab his things and seek shelter. The coming daystorm was going to be a bad one.

○ ● ○

Khal Teth walked into town wearing only the animal-skin breechcloth and vest, his bare feet splashing through puddles left by the first of the daystorm squalls. With his bow slung across his body, spear in his left hand, and foot-long ivory knives sheathed at each side, he felt primitive in an oddly satisfying way. His rider's doing.

He didn't know this fishing village, so he reached out with his mind, identifying 1,007 residents, a quarter of them children. All but sixteen of the villagers were of the Khyre race. Having evolved on land, as opposed to having risen from the seas like Khal Teth's amphibian Dhaldric race, these short, gray-skinned beings made up the vast majority of the Altreian population and the bulk of its military. Unlike the Dhaldric, they had developed only limited psionic abilities, able to link their minds with the machine intelligences built into their starships and military craft, but little else.

He touched the minds of those who had taken shelter from the storm in the nearest buildings, extracting the information he wanted as he continued on his way. This village was called Trion, one of hundreds of such in the chain of islands ruled by Lord Reiath, a minor territorial functionary whom Khal Teth had met on two forgettable occasions.

But Reiath did not live in such a rustic place and thus he was not Khal Teth's current target.

Like others of its kind, Trion had no streets and but a single walk-way. The glass-like buildings formed a graceful arc along the eastern end of the bay, their colors shifting from burgundy to the greens and blues of the sea as seen from different angles. Grouped by purpose, those that supported the fishing industry occupied the center of the arc, where the lone pier stretched out into the bay.

The few citizens who were out and about in the storm did not notice Khal Teth, though he walked right past them. All was as he intended. He would allow their minds to observe him when he finished the business at hand.

Walking up a short ramp, he stepped into one of the waiting bub-ble-cars, entered the address of the Hall of Law, then settled back into one of the hovercraft's four seats. The ride was not a long one, but by the time the craft pulled to a stop in front of the single-level blue build-ing, a break in the clouds allowed Dorial's bright light to shine through, casting Khal Teth's shadow out before him as he entered the building.

The unadorned entryway led to a spartan waiting area with three rows of pedestal chairs and a reception station beside a closed portal that provided access to the offices of the local officials. None of the eight who awaited admittance even glanced at Khal Teth as he walked to the reception station. When he came to a stop, the female Khyre reception-ist looked up, her surprise suddenly replaced by a helpful expression as she motioned toward the opening portal.

"Village lord Brensho awaits you, master."

Without acknowledging her words, Khal Teth stepped into the hallway beyond. Of course she did. He had commanded it when first he had touched minds with the female. Brensho stood as he entered the meeting room, not daring to comment on his appearance. She was Dhaldric, but a lesser mind than Khal Teth. Unsurprising. There were no greater minds than his. Now she was his.

Such was the Altreian way. Those with the power to dominate the minds of others did so. The greater their psionic ability, the more minds they could dominate. Once bound to a psionic, an Altreian remained bound, unless released by his master or taken by a more powerful psionic, in which case the bond was merely transferred from one master to another.

There was a hierarchy. A low-level Dhaldric might be able to master a mere handful of Khyre. The more powerful could forge a bond with hundreds or thousands and could even bond other Dhaldric to their service. The elite who rose to the level of the High Council remained unbound.

The bond was not without its limitations, the greatest of these being range. To truly dominate another's mind required that the bonded be in their master's presence. For an elite mind, that presence might extend over an entire island. And numbers mattered. A psionic who could control a thousand Khyre might only be able to manage two hundred low-level Dhaldric or five powerful ones.

But any psionic power that went into maintaining a bond weakened the master, potentially making him a target for a rival. The game underpinned all of Altreian politics.

That did not mean the overlord was the most powerful psionic of all. Any Dhaldric who aspired to that position merely had to gain the support of enough members of the High Council to have a preponderance of psionic power on his or her side, a feat made possible with an alliance consisting of a minority of the most powerful council members. In Khal Teth's case, it would have only taken the support of one other. Parsus. The betrayer.

Khal Teth refocused on Brensho, who stared back at him. She was quite attractive. How long had it been since he'd had such a thought? Dismissing it, he seated himself across from her, motioning for her to do the same.

"My dear Brensho, I will be needing a number of things from you and your village during my brief stay."

For a moment, he felt the slightest hint of a struggle as her mind tested his. He clamped down on her mind softly, saw her eyes widen, then smiled.

"I am sure you will find my desires most agreeable."

○ ● ○

For three orbdays, Jack had looked on as Khal Teth consolidated his hold on the village of Trion. There had been no real reason to delay that long, but Khal Teth seemed to enjoy getting his aristocratic groove back. The act was nothing but a disgusting abuse of power that left Jack seething.

Khal Teth seemed to think it was perfectly fine to take whatever he wanted because he could. Worse, the people he abused seemed to expect such treatment—at the very least, they accepted it as their fate. Having arrayed himself in the finest clothes this town's elite could provide—pants, shirts, and boots that shimmered with the mottled maroon of Altreia itself—Khal Teth availed himself of the three Dhaldric women he found desirable.

Khal Teth even took perverse pleasure in the suppressed rage of their spouses. Since he had bonded each of these Dhaldric people, their inner feelings made no difference. Having seen such behavior during his years in the Middle East, Jack wasn't shocked by the overlord's antics. But that didn't mean he had to like it.

Unable to do anything to interfere with Khal Teth, Jack set about learning as much as he could about how this world's ship of state functioned and how Khal Teth used his abilities to navigate it. One thing became clear quickly: no matter how powerful the psionic was, he couldn't control tens of thousands of Altreians directly. Instead, they set about creating a pyramid structure, or working their way as high up a preexisting structure as their skills allowed. Rather than manage a hundred of their people, it was more efficient to handle five more-powerful individuals, each of whom controlled about twenty others.

An Altreian master didn't directly manipulate those he had bonded unless he wanted to make that person do something specific. Bonding was more like extracting an enhanced pledge of fealty. However, the master would be alerted if any of his bonds were broken. Therefore, the Dhaldric were keen on knowing their limitations, lest one attract the wrong kind of attention.

Khal Teth had just stolen Trion's village leaders from Lord Reiath. Reiath wouldn't necessarily know who had done the deed, but the act was certain to piss him off. Clearly Khal Teth hoped the regional lord would come to personally investigate. What easier way to take over a small region than to bond its leader?

Jack didn't approve of that plan, not that Khal Teth was paying any attention to him. While it might work in this instance, staying in one place as you attracted the attention of more and more powerful people would inevitably lead to disaster. At some point during Khal Teth's climb up the pyramid, the offended lord would respond with military force.

You wouldn't have to personally battle another with your mind if you killed him first. All that was required was to launch a long-distance strike from outside the other's mental range. Problem solved.

Of course, Khal Teth knew this. So what game was he playing?

Jack wanted to find the answer before his host got them into a situation that The Ripper couldn't get them out of.

o ● o

Lord Reiath was nobody's fool. Neither was he overly bold. The fact that someone had just hijacked one of his remote island fishing villages wasn't terribly unusual. That was the way of things. Frequently a talented young Dhaldric would try bonding his way up the hierarchy, rising until someone more powerful bonded him into his proper place. This was the meritocracy that had made the Altreian civilization into a galactic beacon of prosperity.

But occasionally, someone much more dangerous decided to make a calculated power grab. Such moves were frowned upon due to their potential of bringing very powerful high lords into opposition. In such cases, the overlord himself might be forced to intervene, something that could shake the current balance of power on the High Council. Almost certainly, no such forces were in play here. Still, a dose of caution was in order.

Focusing his mind, Reiath contacted three of his five regents, directing them to load a force of one hundred guardsmen on five fast-attack craft and make haste to deal with the Trion situation.

Satisfied, he leaned back on his couch and took a sip from a frosty glass of chosk, enjoying the warm glow it generated on its way to his stomach. Things would soon be restored to their proper order.

○ ● ○

Khal Teth felt the minds of the converging hostile force long before they entered the bay, his thoughts turning to Lord Reiath. The island regent was not such a fool after all. That was good to know. Perhaps Khal Teth could make use of him. But first he would deal with this minor annoyance.

"I hope you're not planning what it seems that you are." Jack's mental voice surprised Khal Teth. He thought he had blocked the human's thoughts. Was he getting stronger?

"Watch and learn."

Jack continued as if he hadn't heard Khal Teth. "Because the full-frontal approach isn't likely to go well."

With a growl, Khal Teth strengthened the block, shutting out the distraction that Jack's thoughts presented. He could still feel the man's anger, but that was just fine.

He had debated sending the whole village out to meet the guardsmen and their police hovercraft but had rejected the ploy in favor of something far more dramatic. He would meet them alone and in person.

Khal Teth stood up and walked out of his new office, down the hall that opened into the reception chamber, then stepped out of the Hall of Law onto the walkway that ran along the beach. He stood alone in the twilit evening, all of the village inhabitants having retreated into their homes or places of work as he had ordered. A deep stillness had descended on the island in response to his will, even the gentle breeze having died out.

The air smelled damp from the last of the daystorms. Altreia's reflection off the bay completed the illusion that the entire brown dwarf rested upon the horizon, the small specks of the distant hovercraft seeming to have been launched from its surface. Tonight Altreia appeared more heavily mottled with black and red as great storms eddied across its surface.

He walked forward, wearing the maroon uniform he had come to favor, with his two ivory knives strapped to his thighs. His long strides carried him down the pier, past the watercraft moored to both sides, all the way to its end. Khal Teth stopped, lean arms crossed over his powerful chest, and filled his lungs with the salty sea air. The physical torture that Jack Gregory had put him through had transformed his body in ways that Khal Teth found both startling and wonderful. A body to match his powerful mind. There would be no mistaking him for Parsus any longer. A new god had arisen from the sea, and he awaited his onrushing deniers with a sense of eagerness.

The three hovercraft grew ever closer, their shimmering black sides reflecting the colorful sky as they approached the pier. Khal Teth entered the minds of the sixty-seven guardsmen and crew members, forcing the latter to bring the craft to a halt just beyond the end of the pier. There was no astonishment on the faces of the male and female Khyre guardsmen, nor for their Dhaldric masters. Instead, they knelt before him, thankful that he did not kill them all then and there.

A strange sense of wrongness wormed its way from Jack's mind into his.

Khal Teth reached out to more thoroughly examine the minds of the group's Dhaldric commander. The thoughts that he found there horrified him. A streak of light appeared from over the horizon, its fiery trail clearly that of an autonomous seeker.

"Shit!" Jack's voice tore its way through Khal Teth's mental block. "If you want to live, give me control right now."

The brightening streak arced toward Trion, freezing Khal Teth in place.

"Listen, you son of a bitch . . ." Jack's voice acquired a razor edge. "You want vengeance? This is who I am. This is what I do."

With a snap Khal Teth retreated to a safer place.

○ ● ○

Jack was back.

He dived from the pier and entered the cool water, his powerful legs driving him down until he found the bottom. Counting off the seconds, he swam away from shore. He reached a deep shelf and plunged into the murky depths, his body automatically maintaining neutral buoyancy as he sought to put as much of the shelf as possible between himself and the impending pressure wave.

A flash of light strobed the depths, followed almost immediately by the wave. The explosion had doubtlessly obliterated the village and all of its occupants, along with the boats full of guardsmen whom Khal Teth had bonded. If the attack had consisted of an underwater burst, the pressure wave would have killed him, despite the distance he had put between himself and the shore. Instead, the blast just left him with bleeding ears and one hell of a headache.

That pissed him off.

What kind of sick bastards were these Dhaldric pricks that they would so casually sacrifice the people they deigned to lead? Heather, Mark, and Jennifer had thought the Kasari were the bad aliens. Now Jack was leaning more to Janet's way of thinking. Apparently absolute power in the hands of a few quasi-immortals wasn't such a good thing. But here he was trying to help one of them climb back to the top of that ladder.

He continued swimming away from the island. Whoever had launched that weapon was bound to send in some force to do a battle damage assessment, and Jack didn't plan on being anywhere close when that happened.

Jack recalled what Khal Teth had gleaned from the mind of the commander just before the missile had appeared. Lord Reiath had sent more than a hundred guardsmen, not the sixty-seven who had shown up in the bay. And there had been five hovercraft instead of three. The smaller part of the group had stayed far from the island, well out of psionic range, even for Khal Teth. And among those Altreians had been the Dhaldric commander of the entire force. Clearly the psionic who had captured Trion was too powerful for Reiath to challenge directly. Thus the kill order had been given and executed.

Good call. It had damn near worked.

But Jack hadn't come here just to be killed. He had never made a habit of letting people who tried to kill him keep on living, and he didn't intend to start now. As he continued swimming, he made a mental note to pay Lord Reiath a visit.

But first he had something far more important to take care of.

:CHAPTER 29

Mark had delayed his return trip to Hanau, sending Aaden back through the gateway while he remained behind with Heather. The nagging worry that she was in trouble had only grown worse since he had last seen her. The white streak in her hairline was confined to a small spot in the center of her forehead, but the sight of it terrified him. He had done his best to mask his reaction, but she had noticed.

Now that Aaden had departed and Robby had closed the Earth gate, he intended to get to the bottom of things.

"Robby," Mark said as the boy climbed out of his seat at the control station, "would you mind giving Heather and me some private time?"

A knowing smirk spread across Robby's face. "Aaden was right. You two really should get a room."

Heather laughed and Mark found himself grinning as well. He had to keep reminding himself that Robby was only nine despite looking like an athletic early teen. God help the girls if he ever got loose in the real world.

"Scat," said Heather.

They stood together watching as Robby exited the lab. Once he was gone, Mark turned to Heather, started to say something, then reconsidered. The large, mostly empty room felt downright wrong for the discussion he wanted to have with her.

"Let's go get a cup of coffee," he said.

Her right eyebrow lifted slightly, but she nodded. Taking his hand, she walked out of the laboratory through the larger equipment room and then into the hallway that led to the break room. But then an obviously angry Janet Price intercepted them.

Despite having not seen Mark in weeks, Janet ignored him, spinning instead on Heather.

"What the hell do you think you're doing?"

Heather took a deep breath, then sighed. "You mean with my dad and the Smythes?"

"Damn right I do."

"Let's step into the break room."

"Why? Do you think a robot will overhear us?"

"Robby might."

That stopped Janet, who frowned but nodded. "Fine."

She touched the wall, the door slid open, and Heather followed her inside. Mark followed the two women in, wondering what had happened to set Janet off. Jack's departure had created underlying chaos, the team's tight-knit universe undone.

Janet and Heather sat opposite one another at a table that seated four. Mark grabbed a chair between the two women, all thoughts of coffee forgotten.

"What makes you think that I need your parents' and in-laws' intervention? My grief is my own, and I'll deal with it."

"I've just been worried about you. I thought a little social interaction might help."

Janet's eyes narrowed. "Look, I'm stuck doing a job that's unnecessary while you try to take on the whole world. Speaking of intervention, have you looked in a mirror lately?"

Heather ignored the question and asked her own. "Unnecessary?"

"You've cloaked this facility and the housing area, and erected stasis fields. I don't think any bad guys are going to fast-rope out of a helicopter and take us by surprise. They could drop a nuke and it wouldn't even give us sunburn."

Despite how he hated to see Heather and Janet at each other's throats, Mark forced himself to shut up and listen. Their conversation held something just beneath the surface. A solution lurked at the edge of his consciousness, a dancing firefly that stayed just beyond his grasp.

"Look," said Heather, "we're both tired."

"No. You're tired. I've been sitting on my ass wishing I had something besides make-work to take my mind off Jack. Family visits aren't going to cut it."

Suddenly everything crystallized in Mark's mind. They had thought that they understood how the Altreian headsets had altered Heather, Mark, Jennifer, and Robby to fulfill the vacant Second Ship crew positions.

But they had been wrong about Heather's role. Her headset hadn't been designed to be worn by a starship captain.

He slapped his hand down on the table, turning two sets of angry eyes on him.

"I know what's wrong here."

Before they could speak, he rose to his feet and leaned down to place both hands on the table as he gathered his thoughts.

"We only thought we knew what the four headsets we found on the Second Ship did to us."

This unexpected statement pulled puzzled expressions onto both Heather's and Janet's faces, but neither of them interrupted him. He focused his gaze on Heather, drinking in her beauty, mind, and soul. So driven.

"It's been gnawing at me for a long time, but it wasn't until just now as I listened to you and Janet that it clicked. You're not supposed to be the commander or the strategic planner. Your special augmentation is mathematical, specifically, short-term probability. Not calculating the future. Trying to apply your talent to planning is what has been draining you. Don't you see?"

Heather frowned, but he continued.

"There was no captain position on the Second Ship. It was a scout ship designed to carry four small crew members. The imagery Robby pulled from the Second Ship's database showed that the *AQ37Z* had four small gray-skinned crew members and one tall fellow with red-and-black-mottled skin and gills on the sides of his neck. That guy was its captain, and he stayed with that ship. I'll bet you anything that he's still on board in one of the suspended animation cylinders . . . unless Jack killed him."

He watched Heather's eyes widen as her probability calculation told her he was correct.

"Of course," she said. "Why didn't I see it?"

The last of the anger melted from Janet's face. "I think there's plenty of blame to go around. I've had my head up my ass. Now that you've finished the mathematical and equipment-design work, your best skills are being wasted here."

"Worse than that," said Mark, "you've been burning yourself out trying to calculate the whole world's future. I need you with me out in the field, seeing what's about to happen in our local operating environment. That's what worked when we took down the Stephenson Gateway, and that's the only way we're going to take out this one."

Heather shook her head. "I can't do that. Somebody needs to do the strategic planning and run our operations from here."

Mark turned and looked at Janet. "Do you really want to get back in the game?"

"Are you offering me command of this operation?"

"You're the most qualified of any of us."

Janet shifted her gaze to Heather. "What about you?"

Heather paused, her eyes going milky white. When they returned to their natural brown, she nodded.

"If you want it, it's yours."

For the first time since the day that Jack had told them about his dream, Mark saw Janet smile, although this one left him cold.

"Okay then. Let's get to work."

○ ● ○

The crackle and pop of the pine logs in the fireplace was drowned out by Heather's rising moans as she moved atop Mark's naked body on the thick rug covering the hardwood floor. Beneath her, his sweat-coated skin felt like a damp satin sheet stretched over rippling muscle. Mark's undulating form writhed in her embrace, his hands grasping her hips so powerfully that she thought he might break her. But as her lips and tongue sought his, she didn't care.

A spasm shook his body, carrying her to a pinnacle of ecstasy higher than she had ever experienced. With all her enhanced senses, Heather tried to stop time but only managed to slow its passage, dragging out the sweet bliss until it seemed that she would burst into millions of glittering crystal shards.

When the moment finally passed, she collapsed limply atop him, his gasping murmurs merely a pleasant buzz in her ear, unintelligible. As the smell of their sex filled her nose, she felt herself relax into his arms beneath the dancing shadows cast by the fire. Then Mark pulled a blanket over them, and Heather, who had not slept in years, let the sandman carry her away.

○ ● ○

U.S. Senator Freddy Hagerman strolled in front of the Jefferson Memorial, his umbrella protecting him from the drizzle. As it often did, bad weather exacerbated the ache that radiated out from the spot where his artificial leg connected to the stump of his left thigh. Right now that weather was exactly what he wanted, driving the vast majority of tourists inside, guaranteeing him the privacy he needed for this call.

Despite how often he swept his Senate office for bugs, he didn't trust it or his Watergate apartment for any truly sensitive discussion. Neither did he trust his phones. But the one in his jacket pocket was different. A button on this phone allowed him to select between its subspace communications or quantum-entangled modes of operation. Although both were absolutely secure and untraceable, the subspace mode gave him access to the network within the secret Smythe facility, while the second connected directly to Heather's cell phone, wherever she was.

Truth be told, he had no idea where the Smythe operation was located, and he liked it that way. As he was well aware, torture could make anyone talk. Well, almost anyone. Eight years ago, the NSA had failed to break Mark, Heather, or Jennifer while they held them in their supermax interrogation facility known as the Ice House. But Freddy had no such faith in his own ability to avoid spilling his guts.

The investigative report that had won Freddy his second Pulitzer had cleared the names of Mark, Heather, and Jennifer, along with those of Jack Gregory and Janet Price. Unfortunately, more-recent events had returned them to the top of the FSS, FBI, and Interpol most-wanted lists.

As the official founder of the nonviolent Safe Earth movement, Freddy himself was under constant suspicion. If not for his public popularity, he probably would have been arrested for suspicion of supporting the Safe Earth resistance, the movement's violent offshoot that Mark and Heather had spawned after they had been forced into hiding.

He stopped beneath a group of Japanese cherry trees and pulled the Smythe phone from his pocket. Although he had had the phone for several months, this would be only the second time he used it. Freddy stared down at the mobile, wondering at his reluctance to press the button that would connect him to Heather Smythe. As much as he liked her and Mark, they were perhaps the most dangerous people on the planet, and any closer association with them would very likely get him killed.

He sighed. *Ah shit!*

This afternoon, two of the finest cyber-warriors in NSA history, Dr. Eileen Wu and Jamal Glover, had hacked their way past Freddy's firewall and left a message on his office computer, one that only he would understand.

Your lucky marble asks . . . want to play a game?

No, he didn't. But the question hadn't been intended for him. Rather, it was directed at the only people who were capable of playing the kind of game that Eileen and Jamal were talking about.

The riddle had two distinct references. The lucky marble told him who the message was from: Jamal and Eileen. After all, he had given them the beautiful iridescent marble he received from Mary Beth Riles, the wife of the deceased NSA director. He had carried the trinket in his pocket for years until Jamal and Eileen had identified it as the holographic data sphere that had gotten several people tortured and killed. Freddy was glad to be rid of it.

The second part of the message was a question that came from an old movie about a computer AI that wanted to play global thermonuclear war. Since all four of the big nuclear superpowers were members of the United Federation of Nation States, such a war wasn't likely to happen. Therefore, the question referred to an even greater potential cataclysm: the activation of the wormhole gate under construction by the UFNS in Germany. The message was a warning, one that required that Freddy put Heather in direct contact with Jamal and Eileen.

Freddy stared through the drizzle at the domed and columned white monument to one of the United States' founders. Then, beneath the weeping cherry trees, he lifted the phone and dialed.

○ ● ○

When Heather opened her eyes, she saw bright morning sunlight streaming through the living room window, amplified by its reflection off a foot of snow that covered the ground beyond the enfolding stasis field. The sounds of rattling pans from the kitchen and the smell of frying bacon told her that Mark was in the midst of preparing breakfast. She yawned, rose, and walked back to the master bedroom to get ready for this new day, feeling a sense of well-being that she couldn't explain.

After all, the world was a screwed-up mess, and they were no closer to stopping an impending alien invasion than they had been yesterday. But somehow, having turned over operational control of the effort to Janet had lifted a load that freed her mind and gave her a renewed sense of optimism. Or maybe it was last night's wild romp. Didn't matter. For the present, life was good and she was determined to enjoy every minute of it.

That good feeling lasted almost until she reached the kitchen table, interrupted by the ringtone from her QE phone. She had embedded sixteen different quantum-entangled switches within its specialized circuitry, the twins of those switches residing in other phones that had been distributed to key players in the Safe Earth movement around the globe. She glanced at the caller ID, which displayed a picture of Freddy Hagerman.

So much for her leisurely, low-key breakfast.

She sat down, pressed a button, and set the phone on the table.

"Hi, Freddy. I'm here with Mark. I have you on speaker."

"I've been contacted by someone you two are going to want to meet."

As Freddy didn't bother with the niceties of an intro, Heather immediately focused her attention. A glance at Mark, settling down beside her, said that he felt the same way.

"Go on," she said.

"You remember Admiral Jonathan Riles, the former NSA director."

"Sure. Jack and Janet worked for him when the whole Rho Project mess began. He was one of the good guys."

"Yeah. That's what got him killed."

Mark broke in. "So what does this have to do with Riles?"

"It's a longer story than I want to stand around in the rain telling. Let's just say that I ended up with a trinket from a box of Admiral Riles's things, given to me by his wife, Mary Beth."

"Didn't she kill herself a few months ago?" Heather asked.

"Yes, but only to avoid being tortured to death by those who were looking for that trinket. The police and the press missed that part of the story. Two others were brutally murdered before her, a top NSA analyst named Levi Elias and an ex-NSA hacker named Carolyn Brown."

Mark whistled softly. "Some trinket."

"It turns out that I was wrong about that. It was actually an exceptionally sophisticated holographic data-storage device designed by a medical-device billionaire named Steve Grange. A dozen years ago, Admiral Riles sent Jack and Janet to retrieve that device. I don't need to tell you that things got bloody, but they retrieved it. The president was so convinced of the danger posed by what it contained that he ordered the device destroyed. But that never happened."

Heather felt a lump form in her throat. "So Janet knows what's on it?"

"You'll have to ask her. I don't want any part of it. But the reason I am calling you is because I gave it to three other former NSA employees, Dr. Eileen Wu, Dr. Denise Jennings, and Jamal Glover. This afternoon, they hacked into my computer and left a message that said they needed you to contact them."

Her perfect memory provided the data on two of the three individuals mentioned. She had never met either of them, but Jamal Glover had been the subject of an extensive article in the *Business Times* last year. One of the finest programmers in the world, his high-speed trading software had made many fortunes for the investors in Jim McPherson's Maximum Capital Appreciation Fund. As for Dr. Eileen Wu, eight years ago, at the age of nineteen, she had been one of the NSA's top computer forensic specialists. That was at a time when Mark, Heather, and Jennifer were being interrogated inside the NSA's secret supermax facility known as the Ice House. The reminder left her cold.

"How do we reach them?" Mark asked.

"The last I heard, they had linked up with the Mexican president, Manuel Suarez."

"Good," said Heather. "He's a reliable Safe Earth member."

"Yes, he is," said Freddy. "I've met him several times. He's a fine man."

Heather glanced at Mark and nodded.

"Okay, then," he said. "We'll sit down with Janet and figure out what we want to do about this. Anything else bothering you?"

"Nothing worth standing here getting soaked," Freddy said. "I don't need to tell you to be careful, but I will."

Heather felt the tension in his voice. "Will do. Now get back to that warm Senate office of yours before you catch a cold."

Freddy harrumphed and hung up.

She caught Mark's eye. "Let's go see Janet."

He shook his head. "It'll wait a few minutes. Let's eat these eggs before they get much colder. It might be the last home-cooked meal either of us gets for a while."

Heather paused, then nodded. She had the feeling that he was right: 96.375 percent probability.

:CHAPTER 30

Dr. Eileen Wu looked up from her workstation as Jamal Glover walked into the newly upgraded computing center that had been set up in the bunker beneath Los Pinos, the fortresslike Mexican presidential residence in the Chapultepec Forest. His footwear, with the black-and-white spats, sounded almost like tap shoes on the panels of the raised flooring that provided access to the cables and wires routed underneath his feet.

Eileen had to admit that Jamal looked fabulous in his 1920s-style suit, his white-banded black fedora pulled low across his brow. She hadn't believed that there was anyone better at hacking than she was, but Jamal might contend for the title.

That thought disconcerted her. At thirty, he was four years her senior, yet she felt like the older one. She knew that it was his razor-sharp wit that made her feel like this, something that had never happened before. She was Hex, the Caltech hacker legend who had become the NSA's top computer scientist at the age of nineteen. Yet, at twenty-six, she somehow felt inferior to this man.

He winked at her as he walked by. "Glad to see you're still here this morning, Hex. I thought you might have defected to a more important project."

"More important than trying to save Earth?"

"Hey, I hear there's an opening for intergalactic savior."

"I'll pass."

"Good to know. It would get awfully lonely down here by myself."

She watched as he doffed his hat, hung it on the edge of a monitor, and sat down. He swiveled his chair away from her to power up his workstation, bringing the semicircle of monitors to life, their glow creating a reflection halo from his shaved scalp. That thought almost pulled a laugh from Eileen. There were many things that Jamal Glover was, but a saint wasn't one of them.

The fact that neither of them had visited the surface in the months since they had arrived here would have horrified anyone except for computer geeks like her and Jamal. Despite comfortable bedrooms, a workout facility, and a computer center, their accommodations were essentially one big isolation chamber that kept them safe from those who relentlessly hunted them.

Their presence here was one of the most closely guarded secrets within the Safe Earth resistance. Until a few days ago, that secret was known only to President Manuel Suarez, his chief of staff, and Freddy Hagerman. A small number of the household staff served the cyberspecialists their meals and provided cleaning and maintenance services, but they had no idea who these important guests might be.

But Jamal's message to Freddy had added a few others to the list of those in the know, namely Mark Smythe, Heather Smythe, and Janet Price. Until now, there had been no need to inform the movement's leaders that two former elite hackers for the NSA had volunteered their services to President Suarez in return for his protection. They had known all along that this kind of protection came with a cost, one far preferable to the kind of death their colleagues had suffered.

Jamal's voice pulled her thoughts back to the present. "Any word on when Janet will be arriving?"

"No. She has managed to stay fully under the radar of any of the UFNS intelligence services."

"Pretty impressive. Sounds a lot like us."

"If we were at the very top of the UFNS most-wanted list," said Eileen.

"Don't worry. We'll get there."

"Ah. Can't wait for that."

Jamal flashed her a smile just as Dr. Denise Jennings walked into the room, her iron-gray hair tied back in its usual tight bun. At seventy, she retained her sharp mind, but the pressure of life on the run had clearly taken a toll on her health, something that betrayed itself in her recent weight loss and the way her hands trembled.

"What can't you wait for?"

Eileen knew that this kind of banter about their situation made Denise uncomfortable, so she shifted to Jamal's original question.

"We were just talking about how Janet Price should be arriving soon."

"I don't know what good that will do." Denise seated herself in a chair across from Jamal's workstation. "I wish I hadn't lived to see these terrible times. And the terrifying truth is that they're about to get much, much worse."

A message-received alert sounded, drawing Eileen's eyes to her workstation. Its contents were exactly what she'd been waiting for.

"Janet has just arrived. President Suarez is bringing her down here."

Jamal stood up. "To the conference room, then?"

Eileen rose to follow him. "Might as well get this over with. Our news isn't going to get better with age."

o ● o

Jamal wasn't a big fan of being kept waiting, even if it was for the Mexican president and Janet Price. When they finally did walk into the conference room forty-seven minutes later, he had to force himself to stand, if only in deference to the man who had given his protection for these last few months and for the operative who, along with Jack Gregory, had saved his life a dozen years ago. But he shook their hands and said his greetings, taking that time to study the leader of the Safe Earth resistance.

Janet caught his gaze, looked deep into his eyes, and smiled. She could see right through him. Twelve years had passed since this tall, athletic woman and Jack Gregory had fought their way through a laboratory to pull Jamal from the sensory-deprivation tank where his brain was being scanned by Steve Grange. He had to admit, she still looked damn good. And she clearly could break his hand if she wanted to.

"Sorry for keeping you waiting," she said, releasing her grip. "President Suarez was kind enough to let me clean up after my journey. Fat suits are a bitch."

Then it hit him. Of course she had been heavily disguised, what with half the world hunting her. Jamal felt his annoyance fade away.

"Understandable."

President Suarez took his seat at the head of the conference-room table, and the others followed suit with Jamal, Eileen, and Denise on his left, and Janet Price on his right. The president leaned back, curiosity painting his handsome face as he looked at Janet.

His English was flawless. "Not that I'm unhappy to see you, but what enticed you to risk yourself by making this journey? And why are you so eager to see my three guests?"

Jamal arched an eyebrow. The fact that he and Eileen had sent the message that had brought Janet here was probably something that they should have informed their host of before now. Uncomfortable, but it was time to confess.

He cleared his throat. "Mr. President, that would be because of a message I sent by way of Senator Hagerman."

"I played a part in this, too," Eileen said.

Denise Jennings pursed her lips but remained silent.

"Wait just a minute," President Suarez said. "You sent an e-mail message from this facility to Senator Hagerman without my knowledge or permission? What exactly were you thinking?"

Jamal clenched his teeth but failed to stifle his retort. "We were thinking that we are the best in the world at what we do. Of course we didn't send an e-mail. We hacked his computer and placed a single line of text there, something that only he would understand. The fact that Janet is here should tell you that we know exactly what we're doing."

To his left, Eileen leaned forward, her black eyes blazing. "And we had a good reason for doing it, as you're about to find out."

Before the red-faced president could respond to these double-barrel outbursts, Janet leaned forward, pulling all eyes to her.

"Mr. President," she said, "rather than argue, I recommend that we listen to what they have to say."

Again Jamal marveled at the power that radiated from this woman. Even President Suarez visibly calmed beneath her gaze. For several seconds, her suggestion hung in the air. Then the president leaned back in his chair.

"Very well," he said, sparing a scowl for Jamal. "I suppose being cooped up in a bunker for several months could make anyone lose their sense of propriety. Janet, since you've made the trip here, perhaps you'd like to guide this discussion."

"Certainly," she said, turning her attention to Jamal. "What does this have to do with the Grange holographic data sphere?"

Jamal shook his head. "Absolutely nothing. I just referred to that to get your attention."

"You have it."

"Alexandr Prokorov appears to be ahead of schedule on constructing his Frankfurt wormhole gateway. He's now targeting early October for portal activation and plans to keep that a secret until after it has been activated to send a friendship message to the Kasari."

Janet arched her left eyebrow. "How confident are you in that?"

"Very," said Eileen. "If I were still at the NSA, I'd be telling Admiral Connie Mosby the same thing."

Janet stared hard at Eileen. "We aren't without resources. Do you mind telling me how you're able to gain access to this information when we haven't?"

"You may have superior tech," said Jamal, "but as I've stated, Eileen and I are the best at what we do, and, as you're aware, we've had lots of experience doing this type of work for the NSA. In this game, that kind of skill counts. We think we would be much more valuable to the Safe Earth resistance if you brought us directly into your operation and gave us access to some of your capabilities."

Jamal watched as Janet paused to consider his idea. The acceptance of their proposal was the main thing he and Eileen had hoped to achieve with this gambit, and they had one major factor working in their favor: Janet knew from personal experience that he wasn't exaggerating their skills.

A glance at Eileen revealed her eagerness; Denise's flat expression revealed she didn't share the sentiment. To Denise, joining the Safe Earth resistance was one more frightening change, just when she was beginning to adjust to her current circumstances.

Jamal extended his hand across the table. "What about it?"

Janet met his gaze and held it for long enough that Jamal began to feel awkward, but he refused to withdraw the offered hand. Not until she said no.

As if reading his thoughts, Janet smiled and then shook his hand, sealing the deal. The fact that President Suarez posed no objection didn't surprise him. Suarez would probably be glad to get rid of them.

The president rose, as did the others.

"Mind telling us where we're headed?" asked Eileen.

Janet smiled again. "I'm afraid you're just going to have to wait and see for yourself."

Something in Janet's tone put butterflies in Jamal's stomach. He had the distinct feeling that his life was about to take a wondrous new turn. And right now, he was ready to embrace it.

:CHAPTER 31

Jennifer barely suppressed the thrill she felt at reestablishing headset contact with Raul but somehow kept that feeling from crossing the boundary from the protected part of her mind to the Kasari-controlled portion. Her plan was working. She had taken advantage of the Kasari group commander's obsession with recapturing the Rho Ship by feeding the hive-mind a protected memory of her headset's ability to form a subspace connection with the vessel.

She had felt the hunger in Commander Shalegha seep through the nanobot communications array embedded in her brain. Jennifer carefully avoided suggesting that Shalegha have her recall Raul and the Rho Ship. Instead, she had waited for the Kasari commander to give her that order. Her wait hadn't been a long one.

Now she followed Shalegha's command to the letter, fooling both Raul and Dgarra into thinking that she was supporting the war effort by arranging for a secure rendezvous. The mental effort required to maintain these multiple levels of deception was placing tremendous strain on Jennifer, but that was just one more thing she could put to good use. She let Shalegha feel her inner tension, knowing that the commander would interpret the emotional response as an impotent struggle against being forced into yet another betrayal of Dgarra.

"Raul, it's me."

"My God, Jen, it's good to hear your voice in my head."

"What," she said, "VJ isn't good enough for you?"

"Actually, that's the kind of thing she would say to me. Maybe my simulation is better than I thought."

Jennifer felt Shalegha query her mind, seeking out her intent. Once again Jennifer let a subtle half-truth slide from her mind into that of the hive, that this banter was absolutely necessary to avoid raising suspicion within the other human.

"You still there?" Raul asked.

"Sorry. You just had me laughing. Where have you been?"

"That little bombing run you had me do didn't turn out so well. We've been working on repairing the ship ever since."

"Well, you sure saved our asses. Thank you."

Raul paused as he took in her unexpected praise. "Glad it worked out so well, then. Am I to understand that you've been kicking Eadric and Kasari ass during my absence?"

"We've been holding our own . . . barely."

"Well, that's better than I expected. On the plus side, VJ and I have come up with a couple of nice upgrades to the Rho Ship that I think you and Dgarra are going to like."

She tried to resist asking but found herself compelled by Shalegha's desire to know.

"Like what?"

"I think you'll need to see for yourself. Have you got a safe place where I can set this ship down to take on supplies? We're getting pretty low on food."

"As a matter of fact, I do. Dgarra was hoping you'd show up sooner or later. Hold on while I transfer the landing cavern's coordinates."

"Are you sure it's safe?"

"It better be. It's deep within the mountains about five miles from the nearest exit to the outside world."

"Okay, then. Send away."

As Jennifer complied, the faintest hint of a smile twitched her lips.

○ ● ○

Group Commander Shalegha found that the Eadric capital city of Orthei was starting to grow on her. She stood still, the toes of her boots extending just beyond the balcony of this tower that she had transformed into Assimilation Command Central. The Eadric people had wasted a huge quantity of resources on turning their cities into architectural marvels. The multicolored glass spires rose into the sky, separated by airways. The widest of these were designated for air vehicles, but the vast majority were reserved for winged flight.

None of these towering edifices had stairways or elevators. Open balconies served as launch and landing platforms for the winged occupants, while the Kasari were forced to use aircars to come and go. A hundred and eighty floors below her feet, the parkways that separated these buildings were testaments to beauty.

Shalegha felt the southwesterly breeze that blew in off the Lillith Sea cool her skin as it passed through Orthei and continued on to the northwest across the mighty Doral Sea. Beyond those waters, the Koranthian Mountains towered above the warren of caverns that formed the subterranean home of the hated species.

As she looked in that direction, she released a small flood of endorphins, savoring the warm feeling of satisfaction it produced. Within the next hour, the hijacked Kasari world ship would shift out of subspace to appear within one of those caverns, a technological feat that came from a synthesis of Altreian and Kasari technologies. How the humans had managed that was mystifying, but as soon as that ship was returned to its rightful owners, the Kasari would learn how this had been accomplished and incorporate that knowledge into the hive-mind.

The world ship's recapture was assured, assuming that General Magtal timed his arrival at that cavern to allow Jennifer Smythe to entice her human counterpart from the vessel. The price Shalegha had negotiated with the Koranthian general had been sufficient to ensure that he would play his part well.

She turned away from the balcony and walked back into her command center, confident that today would see the stolen Kasari world ship in her hands.

○ ● ○

Jennifer knew this was going to be close. She would have one shot at stopping Shalegha from seizing Raul and the Rho Ship. Despite her knowledge of the Kasari plan and General Magtal's complicity in it, she was helpless to alert Dgarra. If not for this chance to make things right, Jennifer's final betrayal of the general, who had defied his emperor in order to place her at his side, would have shredded what remained of her soul.

Now she and Dgarra, along with a half dozen of his engineers and fifty warriors, stood in a side passage that opened into the empty cavern, awaiting the Rho Ship's arrival. Dgarra's lead engineer had activated a portable stasis field generator to seal the opening. It would protect them from the shock wave that the Rho Ship would produce when it shoved aside the air in the cave upon emergence from subspace.

She knew that General Magtal's soldiers, who secretly waited in a side chamber, would have no such protection. The shock wave wouldn't be powerful enough to seriously hurt them, but it might make their ears bleed and give them one hell of a headache. She sure hoped so.

In her left hand, Jennifer clutched the pendant that Dgarra had given her when he made her his ward, as if rubbing the sharp trident-shaped piece of metal could summon an underworld god to release her from this terrible bondage. Since that wasn't likely to happen, she would just have to roll the dice. In her mind she could hear the call of a ghostly croupier.

Everybody place your bets. New shooter coming out.

○ ● ○

Raul, seated in his blue-tinted captain's chair, turned to look at VJ. Her black leather uniform had seemingly gotten even more formfitting since the last time he really studied her. Maybe that was because she had managed to achieve an almost-lifelike opaqueness as opposed to the earlier ghostly transparency. Even her short, spiked-up blond hair looked so natural that he was sure it would feel right if he ran his fingers through it.

Crap. Here he was thinking crazy thoughts again, probably because he was nervous about the maneuvers he and VJ would soon be executing. That and the fact that if they made the slightest mistake, they could materialize inside the cavern with a relative velocity that would send them crashing into solid rock. Or they might miss the cavern altogether.

He just had to keep telling himself that they had done this before. For the Rho Ship's neural net, this was a set of trivial calculations. Yes. That line of thinking was already making him feel better.

VJ studied him. "Are you okay?"

Raul frowned and straightened in his chair. "Of course I am. Why?"

"For a second there, I thought you were going to be sick."

"Just focus on getting us down safely."

She grinned knowingly, then turned back to the semicircle of translucent displays that arced around her.

"The calculations check out. If Jennifer didn't make any mistakes with the coordinates and cavern dimensions that she sent us, we'll be fine."

That comment gave him something new to worry about. Jennifer hadn't taken advantage of her ability to connect to the Rho Ship's neural net to make her calculations. How could he be confident she hadn't made a mistake?

"I want a full worm-fiber scan of that cavern. Verify all the numbers, pick an execution time, and then calculate the velocity vector we will need to match."

"I'm on it."

After a few seconds, VJ turned to look at him. "Jennifer's figures are adequate, but I made some minor improvements. I am prepared to initiate the maneuvers that will produce the velocity vector match in twenty-seven seconds."

"Do it."

Raul settled down in the chair and wrapped himself in a protective stasis field as his mental countdown progressed toward zero. The plan called for a short subspace jump from the back side of the farthest of Scion's moons, followed by a normal-space maneuver, then another subspace jump into the cavern.

He watched as VJ locked in the sequence and then gave him a thumbs-up, a uniquely human gesture that he had never seen Jennifer use. So how had VJ picked it up?

As the last few seconds ticked off via his internal counter, Raul tensed and readied himself, not just for the intricate maneuvers, but for the prospect of seeing the real Jennifer Smythe again. That was something that made all these risks worthwhile.

○ ● ○

When the Rho Ship appeared, Jennifer's enhanced eyesight saw the shock wave propagate outward as a cylindrical-shaped ripple in the air. But with the stasis shield sealing the opening where she and the Koranthians waited, the volume was muted to only the sound transmitted through the rock walls. As soon as it passed, Dgarra signaled his chief engineer to drop the stasis field. Then he and Jennifer entered the cavern together.

Three steps in, the Rho Ship disappeared again, but that was to be expected. Raul had merely activated the cloaking mechanism after having transitioned out of subspace into an area of hostilities.

Jennifer felt her mind reestablish the connection to Raul's neural net.

"You made it," she said.

"You don't sound surprised."

"I had faith in you."

Raul laughed. "That makes one of us. This place must be a mile underground."

"Almost two."

"Stay back. I'm lowering the ramp."

Jennifer placed a hand on Dgarra's arm, and they both came to a halt, staring at apparently empty space in front of them.

After several seconds Raul spoke again. "Okay. I'm coming out."

Jennifer nodded, and Dgarra stepped forward with her. When they stepped through the cloak, the air shimmered as if they had just stepped through a translucent mist, and Raul appeared at the top of the ramp that had dropped from the cigar-shaped starship's midsection.

Jennifer felt her heart climb into her throat as they approached Raul, suddenly aware that Shalegha had just sent General Magtal a message. She didn't have to know the specific wording of that message to understand that Magtal and his warriors were on the move. If she was going to act, the time was now.

Ten feet in front of her, Raul reached the bottom of the ramp. Jennifer felt her foot catch on a broken stalactite that the shock wave had knocked from the ceiling, and tumbled to the ground, the sharp pendant slicing deeply into her left hand as she hit. Before Dgarra could reach out to help her, she scrambled forward, clutching at Raul's extended arm with her bloody hand.

At that moment, she tightened her focus, activating her telepathy, and thrusting the protected part of her mind into Raul's. Knowing that she only had moments until the hive-mind realized what she was doing, she made her message brief.

"Get back in the ship and get out of here. I'm compromised."

Feeling the hive-mind react to shut her down, she passed Raul a vivid image of her pulling the Kasari dart filled with quivering fluid from her neck. Then her consciousness winked out.

○ ● ○

General Dgarra watched Jennifer trip and fall. But when he reached out to help her up, she lunged forward and grabbed Raul's arm with a bloody hand. The move so surprised Dgarra that he stood frozen as a faraway look transformed her face, only to fade as she collapsed to the ground at Raul's feet.

Dgarra regained his senses and kneeled beside her, gently rolling her onto her back as he checked for injuries. What in the name of the dark gods had caused this bizarre behavior? Had she hit her head on a rock when she fell?

When he glanced up at Raul, he received another surprise. The human was running back up the ramp that led into the starship. Dgarra signaled to Captain Jeshen, and his courier lunged after Raul, only to careen off the invisible wall of a stasis shield.

Suddenly a commotion behind him pulled Dgarra back to his feet. He was startled to see General Magtal advancing across the cavern toward him, accompanied by scores of his uniformed warriors, blasters held out at the ready while more of his warriors covered the group from a passage in the south wall. Dgarra's men reacted immediately, forming a protective wall between him and Magtal's warriors, their own blasters out and ready.

Ignoring the ramp that closed behind him, Dgarra stepped out through the holographic curtain of the Rho Ship's cloak. His warriors parted to allow him to pass through them to the spot where General Magtal stood with one of his aides by his side.

"General Dgarra," Magtal said, his loud voice resonating in the cavern for all to hear, "in the name of Emperor Goltat, I place you and your pet human under arrest on the charge of high treason."

Dgarra stopped two paces in front of Magtal and glared at his rival. "What nonsense is this?"

Before Magtal could answer, a thunderous boom shook the cavern. As his and Magtal's warriors dropped to a firing crouch, Dgarra turned, knowing what he would see. Nothing. Only this time he knew that it was not because of the Rho Ship's cloak. The boom had been produced by the ship's transition back into subspace.

When he returned his gaze to General Magtal, Dgarra was pleased to see the look of confusion in the warrior's eyes.

"What was that?" Magtal asked. "Where is the Kasari starship?"

"I do not know what you are referring to. Did you or any of your men observe such a craft when you entered this cavern?"

Magtal scowled. "I received word from one of your people of the starship's presence here as my warriors and I debarked our transport from ArvaiKheer. Captain Jeshen. Step forward."

When his trusted courier left his side and moved to Magtal's, Dgarra felt rage replace his consternation at this turn of events. Seeing his expression, Magtal grinned.

"Do not blame Captain Jeshen. He has proved himself to be a true patriot, placing the good of his empire above loyalty to a traitor who welcomed a Kasari spy into his headquarters, disregarding the advice of others."

Magtal stabbed a finger at the spot where Smythe lay faceup on the cavern floor. "The emperor's personal physician tested the blood on the material that Captain Jeshen retrieved, torn from her pants leg. It was filthy with the Kasari mechanical microbes. There lies the spy who betrayed you, resulting in the deaths of thousands of your warriors. Whether or not you were aware that she is a spy is irrelevant. She played you for a fool. You bear full responsibility for placing your command at risk."

For a moment, the cavernous room seemed to fade as the impact of Magtal's words cut into Dgarra. Could Smythe have deceived him? He had noticed a recent sense of withdrawal in her but had blamed it on the psychological impact of their battle losses. As Dgarra's men shifted uncomfortably behind him, General Magtal took one step forward, his grim stare locking Dgarra's eyes to his.

"So I ask you, General Dgarra, do you surrender of your own accord to the emperor's order, or do you make me enforce it with violent action?"

With the weight of his shame threatening to bow his head, General Dgarra spoke loudly enough for his men to hear.

"I submit myself to the emperor's will."

Magtal gestured, and a female warrior moved to kneel beside Smythe. As Dgarra watched her snap a shock collar in place around Smythe's neck, Captain Jeshen stepped forward and fastened a second around Dgarra's.

When the collar activated, Dgarra managed to remain standing until the punishment stopped, ignoring the blood that seeped from the corner of his left eye. For a moment a hint of awe crept onto his rival's face.

Then, at Magtal's signal, two warriors escorted Dgarra from the cavern to begin the long trip back to ArvaiKheer.

CHAPTER 32

When Jack crawled up onto the island where he had trained this body, he forced himself to rise and move away from the black-pebble beach with its scuttling stoneling predators. He had left his bow, arrows, and spear in Trion, but the two ivory knives were still strapped to his thighs. And as he climbed into the tree house he had built during his extended stay here, he allowed his exhausted muscles to relax. He had lost the boots, but his sleek maroon uniform was in reasonably good shape, and since it had protected him from most of the sea-jelly stings, he decided he would keep it.

"Here?" Khal Teth's angry voice intruded on his thoughts. "Why did you bring us all the way back here?"

Jack had known this question was coming. He was just surprised that it hadn't come before now.

"Because this is where you and I are going to make a deal, whether you like it or not."

Khal Teth laughed. "I can take this body away from you whenever I want."

"Go ahead. I look forward to watching the survival expert in action."

For several moments, there was no response, although Jack could feel Khal Teth's rising frustration.

"If I die, you die."

"Yeah, I get that. But since you've almost gotten us killed twice now, I'd rather go out watching you suffer than let you keep screwing up your inept attempts at a power grab."

"Inept?"

"You heard me."

"And you think you can do better at seizing power over a psionic empire than the most powerful psionic in history?"

"No. But I know we can do a hell of a lot better if we cooperate. You let me handle the strategy and tactics, and you can back me up whenever I need your brand of firepower."

Again there was a pause as Khal Teth considered the gauntlet Jack had just thrown in his face.

"And if I decline your offer?"

"Then you get to try to get yourself off this island and back to civilization."

"You just made the swim. There's no reason I can't do it."

"Knock yourself out."

"You know," replied Khal Teth, "I could agree to your deal and back out once you get us back to civilization."

"Maybe, but I don't think you will. We both want the same thing: to put you back in power so that you can fulfill your part of our bargain and prevent the Altreian planet killer from targeting Earth. And I'm the best there is at this type of work. You know it as well as I do."

Khal Teth asserted himself, briefly taking charge of his body, before fleeing the exhaustion and pain he found there.

As Jack recovered his control, he stretched out on the woven pad on the tree-house floor.

"Tell you what," he mentally replied while yawning, "you think about it while I catch some sleep. You can let me know what you decide upon when I wake up."

Then, without waiting for a response, Jack closed his eyes and released his tenuous grasp on consciousness.

○ ● ○

Wearing his shimmering blue robes of office, Overlord Parsus stood at the top of the magenta, purple, and azure dais that rose from the center of the Parthian's Hall of Lords to tower over the assemblage, Lord Reiath at his side. The midtier lord's face looked frozen with a terror that radiated outward to the thousands of Dhaldric faces that surrounded the dais. He understood the murmurs that echoed throughout the vast hall. There had not been such a public execution for a score of cycles.

Parsus sent out a mental pulse that brought the crowd babble to a sudden halt. When he spoke, his voice was picked up by perfect acoustics and carried clearly to all those present.

"My fellow lords, I stand before you on this day to invoke swift punishment on one who has violated the very foundation upon which our meritocracy rests."

He extended his hand toward the trembling lord who stood beside him, locked within the power of the overlord's mind.

"Lord Reiath is guilty of the cowardly act of destroying one of his own fishing villages, murdering more than a thousand of our citizens. And why did he do this? Because he feared a confrontation with a mind challenger who might have supplanted him. By so doing, he not only revealed himself as a coward, he denied us the opportunity to judge the talent of this unknown newcomer.

"Since I assumed the title of overlord more than three thousand cycles ago, I have sought to cleanse our political elite of the corruption that rises from such cowardice and robs us all of the will of the sacred pyramid."

He spread his hands, raising his voice so that it reverberated through the hall. "What is the central tenet of the pyramid?"

The response of the crowd washed over him. "True power rises."

"And what is the punishment for those who seek to interfere with that tenet?"

"Death!"

The shouted word echoed through the chamber, carrying a sense of anticipation at the spectacle to come. As those echoes died away, the silence that descended was absolute.

Parsus drew a ceremonial blade from a sheath on his left hip, turned, and offered it, hilt first, to Lord Reiath. The condemned man reached out a shaking hand, then pulled the blade flat against his breast as Parsus walked five steps down, leaving Reiath alone atop the dais.

Reiath's entire body quivered and jerked as his mind fought against the will of the overlord, but slowly he raised the inverted blade high above his head, the hilt clasped tightly in a two-handed grip. He tilted his head back until he stared up through the transparent ceiling at the orange plume of the Krell Nebula.

Then the blade plunged down into his throat, burying its tip deep within his chest cavity as a fountain of blood splashed the white tile at his feet. For several moments he continued to stand, his body locked in place by the power of Parsus's mind so that it might leave a lasting impression on all in attendance.

Although the sight gave him no satisfaction, the effect was important. So the overlord once again returned to the top of the dais, letting Reiath's body collapse at his feet.

"Lord Velathian!" Parsus called out.

A striking female in a crimson gown stepped up onto the bottom step of the dais. "Yes, Overlord?"

"I expect you to name Lord Reiath's successor within two orbdays."

She bowed her head. "It shall be done."

Without another word, Parsus turned, descended to the bottom of the dais, and made his way out of the hall as six members of the High Council Guard fell in behind him. In the Hall of Lords, none moved until after he had passed through the nanoparticle door into the hallway that led to his chambers.

○ ● ○

During the twelve orbdays since Khal Teth had finally agreed to Jack's ultimatum, Jack had built himself a new outrigger and found his way to another inhabited island. But this time Jack had retained control, using Khal Teth to mask his presence from the Dhaldric who oversaw the fishing village.

Jack had headed directly for the village pier and climbed aboard the *Dark Promise*, the largest of the fishing vessels docked there. Khal Teth had wanted to bond the crew of six Khyre to him, but Jack had refused, insisting instead that they be freed from their bonds to their current master and allowed to make their own decisions as to whether to accompany him on this journey.

Two had refused, suspecting Jack of being a renegade Dhaldric who was fleeing from the law. He couldn't really blame them for that, given his crudely fashioned sandals and the beating that his maroon clothing had taken since his escape from Trion. But over the subsequent orbdays at sea, the others had come to trust this Dhaldric who had freed them from their mental bonds and asked them to take him to the Khyre homeland of Basrilla, the nearest of the two continents on the far side of Quol.

The crew progressed onward through calm and storm, and with each passing orbday, the mighty magenta orb of Altreia crept lower and lower until it was a maroon sliver on the horizon. For the first time since leaving Earth, Jack experienced a truly dark night. Like most of the Khyre fishing vessels, the *Dark Promise* was capable of moving just above, on, or below the sea surface. For deep fishing, subsurface field netting was the most efficient. But for high-speed travel, either surface or hover mode was preferred.

As Jack stood on the deck, gazing at the bright stars, the ship's captain, Moros, stepped up beside him. The Khyre man's bald head came only to Jack's shoulder, but wiry muscles rippled beneath the gray skin of his bare arms.

"Ripper, you be one strange Dhaldric."

Because he couldn't stand being constantly referred to as Khal Teth and because it wouldn't do to have that name spread around, he had introduced himself to this crew using his human nickname.

Jack nodded. "You have no idea."

"We be a day out of the port city of Kalathian. Me crew would that I ask something of you before we get there."

"Name it."

"We would be bound to you."

Jack turned toward the Khyre man, wondering if the words meant what he thought they did.

"I don't understand. You are all free."

The captain leaned against the rail, looking out over the sea as the hydro-jets propelled the vessel through the waves.

"For now," he said. "The unbonded be never free for long. We would have you bind us to your service."

The implications of what Moros had just told him clenched Jack's gut. Damn it. Enslaving these people wouldn't facilitate the coup he would need to pull off in order to replace Parsus with Khal Teth. He could hear Khal Teth's deep, told-you-so chuckle in the back of his mind.

Then another idea hit him. "Captain Moros, are the Khyre people able to bond others to their service?"

The captain turned to look at him, an inquisitive look on his face. "All have the capability. The strong can bind the weak."

"But you do not?"

Moros frowned. "That be the way of the Dhaldric, not the Khyre."

"But you are capable of binding me to your service?"

The captain laughed. "You would break such a bond with ease."

"Only if I wanted to."

Moros looked confused. "What be the purpose of that?"

Heretofore, Jack had been playing with the idea of building a free rebel army among the enslaved Khyre. Now a new plan crystallized in his head.

"I want no part of being your slave master."

The Khyre sighed in disappointment. "I feared as much."

"But I will make you a counteroffer."

Captain Moros perked up. "What be it?"

"I will bond you, so long as you willingly consent. In return, I will permit you to bond me. Should either of us desire to break free, all bonds shall be broken."

"Such a bonding be no bond at all."

"Untrue. We will be twice bound in a pledge of fealty, one to the other. Should someone try to harm you, I will know of it, as will you should someone attack me. So tell me. Do you find this arrangement to your liking?"

Moros stared up at him, rubbing his pointed chin with his right hand. "I cannot speak for others. But I be willing."

Jack reached out to place a hand on Captain Moros's shoulder and smiled. "Then we have a deal."

A broad grin spread across the captain's face. "Good. Then I shall be first of the Twice Bound."

○ ● ○

At first, Khal Teth considered what Jack was doing to be both naïve and idiotic. After all, he was wasting time gathering willing followers in the homelands of the Khyre when he could have directly bonded them into his service by the thousands. But the numbers of those who called themselves the Twice Bound continued to swell, thanks to the candidate recruitment and screening efforts of Captain Moros as he guided The Ripper along the Basrillan coast and up its many deep fjords. They had visited more than twenty towns and cities, including Far Crossing, a shipbuilding city situated along the jagged rent that formed the Chasm Sea, which separated the Basrillan and Janiyan continents. During that eight-orbday journey, two amazing revelations had revealed themselves to Khal Teth.

Ordinarily, the maximum number of people a psionic could place under his control was determined by the combined powers of their minds. A master required a certain amount of power to bond each psyche, a subtractive process that eventually became dangerous. Bind too many and you could lose a mental battle with a Dhaldric whom you could dominate if at full strength. But because their bonds were made willingly, that didn't happen with the Twice Bound.

The willful bonding was an additive process. Khal Teth had discovered that the mental powers the Twice Bound granted to Jack increased as each new recruit added his or her potential. And because Jack was in charge during the ritual, the Twice Bound were primarily bonded to him. That produced an odd and disturbing side effect. Whenever Jack yielded mastery to Khal Teth, the channeled power of the Twice Bound weakened dramatically.

Even more incredibly, each of the Twice Bound became impervious to the attempts of more-powerful psionics to dominate their minds. The phenomenon made a strange kind of sense once Khal Teth thought about it. Normally a psionic could bond another if his mind had greater power than the opponent. But each of the Twice Bound had also bonded Jack, adding his psionic power to theirs. That meant that the only person capable of bonding any of them was someone who could forcibly bond Jack and, by association, Khal Teth, a feat that was the exclusive domain of the Circle of Twelve.

There were limitations. A weak mind could not channel the power of Khal Teth's brain without destroying itself. But the fact that no one could gain mental dominance of any Twice Bound gave each connected citizen his or her own special brand of power. And though Jack might eventually reach a limit beyond what Khal Teth could handle, he could currently channel the sum of all of their psionic power.

So, for the time being, Khal Teth would continue to honor his most recent bargain with The Ripper, as the man surreptitiously built his army of followers in these cold lands where only the Dhaldric who had the poor fortune of being assigned to these duty stations would choose to live. Until Khal Teth was named overlord, he would continue to let this most dangerous of men do things his way.

CHAPTER 33

"Now that be a mob," said Captain Moros, pointing at the line of Khyre people who were making their way along the steep mountain trail into Jack's remote canyon campsite.

Jack nodded as he shrugged the coat's collar up to keep the sleet pellets from sliding down the back of his neck. This Dhaldric body might be great in the water, but it was ill suited for dealing with the harsh weather on Quol's back side. He'd even draped a thick scarf over his head to keep his ears from freezing off.

Moros watched, a slow grin spreading across his face. "Ripper, you show poor appreciation for my homeland's balmy weather."

Jack ignored the good-natured jab. What he had seen so far of the Basrillan continent reminded him of springtime in Norway, with its deep fjords and high, glacier-capped mountains. But at the lower altitudes, the meadows were filled with waist-high turquoise grass and brilliant orange flowers.

He had chosen this particular spot for encampment because of its sheltered beauty and abundance of fish in the stream that wound its way through the broad meadow. Captain Moros had selected fifty Khyre men and women from among Jack's Twice Bound followers to set up the camp, including the transparent hypertent at its center. It reminded Jack of a megatech version of one of the old-time revival camps that his mom had taken him to see when he was in grade school.

Funny. Despite her best efforts, religion had never stuck to him. Now here he was, offering up his own brand of the gospel, promising to lead these people out of slavery if only they would sneak out of their cities to pledge their lives to him. Hopefully he wouldn't get them all killed for their trouble. But for a chance to save Earth, Jack would risk it.

As the last of the group made their way into the big tent, Jack stood up from the rock he had been sitting on.

"Well, Captain Moros," he said, "it looks like it's time to welcome some brand-new Twice Bound. How many will this make?"

"With this mob of five hundred and seventeen, the Twice Bound be more than three thousand strong."

Jack nodded and began walking from his overlook down to the ceremonial tent. Three thousand was far fewer than he needed, but to avoid concentrating his Twice Bound in any one location, he had traveled from city to city, like a wandering minstrel. And all that travel slowed him down.

Captain Moros had 350 Earth years of experience recruiting his ships' crews, also developing detailed knowledge of the Basrillan coastal towns and cities. Thus he had been instrumental in prescreening and recruiting candidates to join Twice Bound ranks, especially targeting those with exceptional technical or military skills. With Khal Teth's cooperation, Jack searched the mind of each new recruit during the double bonding, and the prescreening cut down on the number of applicant rejections.

As Jack neared the tent, he could feel the minds of those who awaited his arrival. He was getting surprisingly good at accessing the psionic abilities of Khal Teth's brain, most likely the result of closely observing how the Altreian performed each bonding. Thousands of repetitions over the last several orbdays had unlocked an understanding of myriad psionic processes, like how to search another's mind for hints of betrayal and how to shield one's thoughts from other telepaths.

Khal Teth was conditioning his mind, much as Jack had conditioned Khal Teth's body. He was still a neophyte, but repetition worked wonders. As Jack followed Captain Moros into the big tent, the gathered crowd grew silent at the sight of this Dhaldric barbarian who offered them freedom in return for a pledge of fealty.

Then Jack climbed up onto the platform where, one by one, those gathered would step up to become Twice Bound. But in so doing, he sharpened his focus. For the next several hours, as he bonded with these new applicants, he would use this opportunity to enhance his psionic skills.

○ ● ○

Parsus felt the mind of the high lord who approached from the hallway and adjusted the nanoparticle door to allow her entrance to his chambers. If he had ever decided to take a mate, it would have been Shabett, but such a merging would only have weakened him. To rely upon the loyalty of another only provided an opportunity for betrayal, even if she was the civilian head of the Altreian military. He had brought home this lesson to his twin brother.

She stepped into his audience chamber dressed in a flowing chartreuse gown, its narrow straps crossing her upper arms but leaving her shoulders bare. Glittering fire-agates hung in loops from the delicate tips of her swept-back ears, complementing the beauty of her silky-smooth scalp. When her eyes met his, she inclined her head so casually that he almost thought he had imagined it.

"Overlord," she said, her mellifluous voice enhanced by the sending from her powerful mind.

Rumor had it that Shabett could bewitch male or female with but a whisper, yet another reason why Parsus had never let her lips anywhere near his ear.

"Shabett," he responded, "it is a little late for a formal audience, do you not think?"

"I bear disturbing news from Basrilla."

As was standard for all members of the High Council, her mental guard was up, and he could draw no hint of what she was about to reveal. The continent of Basrilla was an unpleasant place for any Dhaldric to be assigned, but it provided the industrial infrastructure and major land-based support facilities for the Altreian space fleet. Basrilla and its sister continent, Janiya, formed Quol's industrial hub and were home to the bulk of the Khyre population.

Thanks to the way the Altreian political system was structured, no trouble worthy of High Council interest had arisen there for thousands of cycles.

"What is it?"

"I have received a series of reports from smaller towns and cities, mostly along the Basrillan coastal region, of growing numbers of our Khyre citizenry being freed from their masters' bonds."

"There is nothing unusual about that. Why isn't this being handled by the Basrillan political hierarchy?"

Shabett seated herself on a comfortable divan that was set at an angle to the chair in which Parsus lounged.

"That would be the usual way of things. But these Khyre subsequently fail to show up at their assigned places of work. And there have been isolated incidents of theft of military property."

"What?" Parsus felt his temples throb. Such a thing was unthinkable. "How many Khyre are we talking about?"

"Because some of their masters are unwilling to reveal such weakness, a precise estimate is unavailable. But it is certainly in the thousands, and, like a sickness, it is spreading."

Unable to remain sitting, Parsus rose and began slowly pacing, his brow wrinkled in thought. Nothing like this had happened since the establishment of the Altreian Empire. He couldn't understand how such an event was even possible.

"Surely we have recaptured and interrogated some of these freed Khyre."

"A small number have been arrested, but the local interrogation efforts have gleaned little in the way of useful information."

"Why not?"

"These Khyre refer to themselves as the Twice Bound and appear to be impervious to all mental probes or to forceful rebonding."

This brought Parsus to a halt. "Have you sent some of our senior inquisitors to take charge of these interrogations?"

"As soon as I learned of it, I dispatched three of my best. They should be arriving at their destinations shortly. In the interim, local officials have requested permission to try some long-banned physical-interrogation techniques."

"No," said Parsus. "Your inquisitors will be there long before any such archaic methods could produce results. You said that we have gained little useful information. What have we learned about these Twice Bound and their leaders?"

"Only that they appear to be structured in small, independent cells. It is unclear how they receive their instructions. There have also been some outlandish thirdhand rumors that appear to be little more than myth."

"Enlighten me."

Shabett crossed one leg over the other and laced her fingers as her eyes found his.

"There have been scattered reports of a wandering Dhaldric vagabond, a madman who patterns himself after Dhaldric warriors of old and calls himself The Ripper. It is ridiculous, but the sightings have some correlation to the rise of the Twice Bound."

"And what does this vagabond reportedly look like?"

"A tall, heavily muscled male wearing ragged clothes and with two ivory knives strapped to his sides."

Parsus felt a wave of relief pull a laugh from his lips. "There is little chance of that being the source of our Basrillan problem."

Shabett rose from the divan and smiled. "Agreed. Now, I must be getting back to my work. I will inform you as soon as my inquisitors have acquired the information we need."

Parsus inclined his head, dismissing Shabett, then watched as she left his chambers, before resuming his seat. For a moment during her rendition of this unusual problem, he had suffered the fear that somehow Khal Teth had survived to plague him. But the description of this Ripper character had eliminated that possibility, remote as it had been.

No, his brother was good and truly dead. And soon, Parsus would have the answers that would enable him to crush this minor insurrection before it could become more than a minor annoyance.

○ ● ○

Lord Inquisitor Grellen stood at the forefront of his two high inquisitors, all dressed in the white robes of office, staring down at the five Khyre who proclaimed themselves Twice Bound. At High Lord Shabett's command, these prisoners had been brought to the port city of Ashelan so that her interrogators could gather the information she required in a single session. The three females and two males were shackled hand and foot to the red prison bench that stretched along the wall. As he paced slowly in front of them, tilting his head to study their faces, each of the five met his gaze. No trace of fear showed in their eyes.

Grellen smiled. That was about to change in ways beyond their comprehension.

At his signal, Inquisitor Trantor seated himself in front of the female prisoner on the far left side of the line while Inquisitor Quoran sat facing the male Khyre farthest to the right. Grellen stepped back to observe the finest of his high inquisitors at work. Less-advanced civilizations interrogated prisoners separately so that they couldn't synchronize their lies, a time-consuming process that had no place in his world. Much better to let those who would be next observe what was happening to their compatriots, building unbearable dread. The mind was a beautiful thing to break.

He inhaled and released a slow breath, drawing the prisoners' eyes to him.

"Do any of you, who call yourselves Twice Bound, care to make a statement that might ease the tribulation that awaits you?"

The heavyset Khyre female on the left spat a wad of phlegm that spattered Inquisitor Trantor's white shoes. Grellen stared at her. Whatever joining the Twice Bound had done, it certainly had not improved this prisoner's manners.

"Anyone else?" he asked.

When none of the others responded, Grellen spread his hands.

"All right, then. Let us begin."

Grellen sensed the powerful mental probes from his two high inquisitors cut into the brains of their subjects to reveal the secrets hidden beneath, feeling no sympathy. These prisoners had already missed their opportunity to cooperate with the authorities and, in so doing, had decided to place themselves at the mercy of the high inquisitors.

When the probes failed to pull screams from their subjects, a frown clouded Grellen's features. At both ends of the bench, the subjects of those probes stared into the faces of their interrogators and smiled. As if on cue, all five spoke in unison.

"We are the Twice Bound. Pledged to The Ripper as he pledged to us. Your fear marks his coming."

Grellen felt his eyes widen in shock. His inquisitors increased their concentration, focusing all their psionic might on piercing the mental barrier that blocked them from the minds of these Khyre. He watched in fascination as his inquisitors switched targets, their jaws clenching with the mental strain. But despite their best efforts, the chant of the Twice Bound continued, unabated.

Taking two strides forward, Grellen halted before the prisoner in the center and gazed deep into her eyes, focusing all the psionic power of a high lord into her mind. The time for half measures was at an end.

○ ● ○

Jack was getting better at manipulating the entanglement of his mind with Khal Teth's. Tonight he and his thirteen Khyre commandos moved through Ashelan's dark alleys on their way toward his chosen target. And as he moved, he hazed the minds of all who would have otherwise observed them.

The port city of Ashelan was Quol's second largest, with a population of just over twenty-three million. Although the Khyre formed the vast majority of its population, the Dhaldric formed its political elite, as they did everywhere on this Altreian home world. Whereas the inland third of Ashelan was as beautiful as anything on Quol, with the exception of the Parthian itself, the city grew steadily more industrial as one progressed toward the port.

The vast dock area reminded Jack of an alien version of the shipping centers of East Asia, albeit with advanced technologies that included a skyport that supplied the spaceports and starships of the Altreian fleet. Still, the locale had that gritty feel that came with heavy industry. The contrast between the shadowy night and the brightly lit work areas almost made him feel at home.

An outbound shuttlecraft lit the sky as it ascended from the distant spaceport, followed several seconds later by the deep rumble of a sonic boom. At street level, there was only pedestrian traffic, but aircars, buses, and transports zipped overhead, landing or taking off vertically from the designated landing pads sprinkled throughout city plazas and rooftops.

Unlike on Earth, where video-monitoring equipment was ubiquitous, there had been no requirement for monitoring the people of Quol since the ascension of the Dhaldric race to power. Once their mental control of the population had been established, crime had all but ceased to exist except for the occasional misuse of power. And when the rare crime did occur, the government inquisitors quickly solved it, eliminating the culprits from the Altreian utopia. Tonight Jack intended to weaken the glue that held their perfect world together.

Jack brought the group to a halt where the alley opened into a broad plaza, its dimly illuminated walkways intended to enhance the view of the night sky. In all the Khyre cities that Jack had visited, they had built these open spaces to celebrate the heavens. On this side of Quol, without the magenta illumination from Altreia, the night appeared even more spectacular. Backdropped by a spray of stars and planets, the lacy orange Krell Nebula and Quol's purple moon took his breath away. But this intentional minimization of light pollution gave Jack what he really wanted: the dark.

Across the plaza from where he crouched, the low facade of the House of Inquisition rose to a squat roofline, atop which the silhouette of several government aircraft sat unlit and unmoving. Jack studied his objective, then issued a mental command that sent all his commandos into their final assault positions. Moros dropped to a knee beside him, his own pulse weapon at the ready.

So far so good. Now they just had to wait for the go signal. There was no chance they would miss it when it appeared.

o ● o

The realization that he could not penetrate any of these Khyre minds staggered the lord inquisitor. What could it mean? Was a member of the

High Council behind this insurrection? There were only a few members of the High Council who had more psionic ability than Lord Grellen: Overlord Parsus and High Lord Shabett the most powerful among them. Clearly the overlord would not incite such insurrection. Shabett or one of the other high lords could have initiated a plan to overthrow Parsus, but Grellen didn't believe it.

That left one, distinctly uncomfortable, possibility. If Khal Teth was not dead . . . well, it was time to find out the truth of that. If mental enticements were not sufficient to extract the information he required, then he would have to fall back on more-primitive means.

Lord Inquisitor Grellen issued his mental orders to the senior officer who waited just outside the door of the interrogation room. Several moments later she stepped through the nanoparticle door, set a black case on the table, and departed.

Grellen touched the magna-clasp and lifted the lid, revealing an assortment of carefully arrayed tools, edged, pointed, and blunt. He lifted them, one after the other, carefully watching the faces of the captives for signs of fear or revulsion that he could not pick up from their minds.

He and the high inquisitors who labored for him had been selected for their positions for a reason. Whereas the more refined high lords regarded some of their work as an unfortunate evil, necessary to keep society safe from those who would otherwise try to tear it apart, the inquisitors had a certain affinity for the suffering of others. To be truly good at any job, one needed to enjoy it.

Even though Lord Grellen would not be able to feel the mental suffering of those he was about to interrogate, he would see and hear it. And he would get answers.

As he considered which of these Khyre would be his first subject, the floor lurched beneath him, the jolt sending Grellen tumbling forward onto his face before he could throw his hands out to catch himself.

Gasping, he rolled onto his side, feeling the blood pour from his mouth and nose. As he struggled to orient himself and rise, the blare of distant disaster warning sirens wormed its way into the building's interior.

Once again the prisoners spoke, their voices a chorus that sent prickles along Lord Inquisitor Grellen's spine.

"The Ripper comes. Flee now or die."

Grellen felt Inquisitor Trantor grab his arm, help him to his feet, then steady him. He glanced down, seeing rivulets of rich red blood stain the front of his white robes, and struggled to clear his head of the dizziness that threatened to drop him back onto the floor.

"What is happening?"

Trantor glanced at the open door. "Lord Quoran has gone to find out."

Just then Quoran reappeared, fear distorting his face. "There have been multiple explosions at the spaceport. The ministry of defense has ordered all officers to respond to the scene. We must get you to the roof and evacuate this building, immediately."

Before Grellen could process this new information, he heard and felt the concussion of another explosion, this one from within the building itself. The screams of the dying in the forward section were accompanied by the distinctive pop and sizzle of firing pulse weapons. Krell's bands! They were close.

"Go," Grellen snapped.

"The prisoners?" asked Trantor.

"No time. Leave them."

Lord Quoran raced from the room, rounded the corner that led to the lifts, and came to a sudden halt. For a moment Quoran stood there, impaled on a white blade that pierced his chest and jutted a hand's width out through his back, the inquisitor's entire body held erect by the powerful hand and arm that gripped the weapon. Then a shove from the blade bearer's other hand sent Quoran's corpse flying into the far wall as he turned to face the lord inquisitor.

To his credit, Trantor rushed forward to place himself between Lord Grellen and the apparition that appeared before him. The powerfully built Dhaldric barbarian tore Trantor's throat out with an effortless slash that Grellen's eyes barely followed, sending the second inquisitor's body tumbling down atop the first.

Without pausing to look at his latest victim, the barbarian stepped forward, backing Grellen into the wall. As their eyes locked, Grellen tried to seize control of his enemy's mind but only managed to elicit a grim stare.

The way the barbarian's eyes danced with an inner fire left Grellen struggling to draw breath. Despite the drastic transformation of the body and its lean, muscular jaws, he recognized those eyes.

"Khal Teth!"

The familiar voice that growled from those lips froze his soul.

"They call me The Ripper."

Then the blood-soaked ivory blade sheathed itself in Grellen's abdomen, spilling his internal organs in a pile at his feet. And as horrified as he was by the sight of his own entrails, it was the smell of them that chased him into the dark.

:CHAPTER 34

Fifty-eight hours had passed since the Rho Ship had made the subspace jump that had taken Raul and VJ to the far side of Scion's orange moon. Having cloaked the vessel and landed in a deep crater, they had so far avoided detection.

Raul looked up at VJ, who had changed into a slinky uniform of shimmering purple, as if that could distract him from the worries clawing at his brain.

"Have you finished the tests on Jennifer's blood?"

He had extracted the sample from the spot on his sleeve where Jen's bloody hand had gripped his arm as she flooded him with her brief vision.

"The analysis confirms that her blood is heavily infused with materials matching the formula for Kasari nanites stored in our ship's database."

"Great," Raul said, slowly shaking his head. "Do you think that puts her under Kasari control?"

"I took the liberty of running a simulation of the Kasari nanite formula being injected into a human body modeled on her scans. You understand that means I tested it on myself, right?"

Her voice was so full of pride that it surprised Raul.

"You injected your virtual body with virtual Kasari nanites?"

"It let me study the probable interactions between Jennifer's body and the nanites."

Raul started to understand where VJ was going with this. "And?"

"The simulated nanites spread throughout her body evenly with one area of exception. A large concentration of nanites assembled themselves into a matrix within the brain. That cortical array appears to have two complementary purposes."

"Which are?"

"To provide a communications link to her brain and to bypass or override her voluntary physical responses."

Raul slumped back in his command chair. Just as Jennifer had feared, being assimilated into the Kasari Collective involved shedding your free will.

"So," Raul began, then paused to consider the possibilities.

"So what?"

"Is there any way to reprogram the nanites to restore free will and prevent the communications link from happening? More importantly, can they be reprogrammed after they're already inside a host?"

VJ cocked her head slightly, and Raul felt her pull on the full processing power of their shared neural net, running a huge number of simultaneous simulations. When she returned her gaze to him, she wasn't smiling.

"The nanites are programmable, but such instructions would normally have to be sent over the communications link to the host's brain."

"You said normally," said Raul. "How else can we do it?"

"I can design a nano-virus that can reprogram the nanites, but it would require someone to inject the nano-virus serum into the host, who, by the way, will certainly resist that."

"Well, since I don't think the Kasari are going to let us hack into their hive-mind communications link, the nano-virus serum looks like our best option."

VJ frowned. "I can design and manufacture the nano-virus serum, but without real test subjects, it could have unanticipated side effects inside a real human body. It could even cause the Kasari nanites to kill their human host."

Raul had already figured that out for himself, but hearing her say it still put a lump in his throat. But with such limited options, he had to go forward and hope for the best.

"Okay, then. Go ahead and make the serum, but also start working on the signal we'll need to send if we can find a way to connect to Jennifer's nanite comm-link."

"Mind if I ask what you're going to be up to while I'm doing all the work?"

There it was again, the not-so-subtle challenge to his command authority. Even if VJ was joking, the tone was irritating. As he quickly glared at her, he saw that little satisfied lift of her right eyebrow.

"I'm going to find out where the Koranthians have taken Jennifer and start working on a plan to get her out of there."

"If my nano-virus doesn't work, you won't want her back aboard this ship."

"I didn't come this far just to leave her there to die. No way I'm letting that happen."

VJ stared at him, her eyes narrowing. "If I were the one who was trapped down there, would you take the same kind of risks to rescue me?"

The intensity of feeling that the question triggered in him surprised Raul. When he spoke, he did so from the heart.

"You can count on it."

As VJ studied him, Raul was aware that she was examining all his vital signs, judging the truth of his statement. The smile that lit her face held a beautiful, childlike innocence.

"Then I guess I better make darn sure my serum works."

○ ● ○

Wearing the rags that were all that remained of her uniform, Jennifer stared at the bowl of slop that had been shoved through the narrow slot at the bottom of the solid-steel door to her dungeon cell. Only her mind's ability to convert reflected sound waves into imagery let her see her surroundings. The echoes of her jailer's heavy footsteps as he walked down the hall and then up the stone steps beyond gave her a clear view of what lay outside her cramped abode.

Although she could see other closed cell doors, her enhanced senses confirmed that she was the only prisoner on this level. When the door at the top of those stairs clanged closed and the sound died away, the blackness of the place was absolute. She began clicking her tongue, the sound enabling her to see her surroundings.

Her cell, in fact the entire dungeon level, had been roughly hewn from solid stone in ages long gone. The water that dripped from the walls and low ceiling had left flowstone deposits that formed the beginnings of limestone stalactites and curtains that felt slick to the touch. The liquid pooled on the floor, eventually draining into the small toilet hole in the back left corner. There was no bed, not even a stone bench. If Jennifer required sleep, she would have had to curl up on the cold stone floor.

She picked up the bowl and sat down cross-legged, leaning back against the wall. She ate quickly, ignoring the smell and rancid fish taste as she scooped the meal into her mouth with her fingers. The important thing was to get something in her stomach that would quiet the nanite-driven cravings that amplified her hunger. She finished by licking the bowl clean and then sliding it back out into the hall. Then, leaning down, she placed her lips into the cold water that puddled on the floor and drank deeply. Aside from the grit, it tasted wonderful.

Since she had been unconscious for an unknown amount of time, Jennifer didn't know precisely how long she had been down here. She wondered if she had already been tried and sentenced to spend the rest of her life alone in this claustrophobic space.

Even her nanobot cortical array had lost its connection to the Kasari hive-mind. Had they judged her situation so compromised that they had disconnected her, or was she so deep underground that their communications network was unreachable? Since they had no trouble controlling her when she fought in the caverns along the Koranthian northern front, she suspected the former.

For the present at least, she had regained her self-control, not that it would do her any good. Any attempt to speak with her guard resulted in the activation of her shock collar. Maybe she would be allowed to speak when judgment was passed on her, but who would believe anything she said? Although she had tried using her empathic powers on her jailer, the Koranthian had an exceedingly low IQ and lacked any spark of kindness that she could amplify. And reading his mind revealed that he knew nothing about political goings-on. Any attempt to use her telepathy in a more direct way would only reveal her abilities to others.

She felt sick. Not from illness, but from the guilt of her betrayal of Dgarra and the crushing weight of her helplessness. No matter how much she told herself that she had had no choice but to destroy the warrior she loved, Jennifer had pulled down House Dgarra.

With a mighty effort, Jennifer shrugged off the lead-weighted cloak of depression that threatened to transform her back into the sniveling child she had been when held captive at the Columbian drug lord's estate in Medellín.

Jack Gregory's words replayed themselves in her head: *And remember this. No victory is certain. No situation is hopeless. When you find yourselves in a hopeless situation, change the rules.*

She'd done that by putting her bloody hand on Raul's arm while delivering her telepathic message. Now she just needed to have faith that he would figure out some way to make this right. In the meantime, her job was to stay ready.

Jennifer drew in a deep breath, held it for five counts, and slowly exhaled. Then she lowered her hands to the floor and kicked up into a handstand. In a steady rhythm, she began doing vertical push-ups, the beginning of a workout that would last for the next six hours.

○ ● ○

General Magtal sat at Emperor Goltat's right hand as General Dgarra was led into the Chamber of Judgment, his hands and feet shackled in chains of triton steel. Stripped of his black and purple, Dgarra wore prison gray. But his eyes showed no sign of the humiliation he had endured since his fall from grace.

All three hundred of the chamber's seats were filled with observers, although none from House Dgarra had been allowed entry to the proceedings. After today, House Dgarra would be no more. Magtal was confident in that.

During the month since Dgarra's arrest, the northern front had been placed under General Magtal's command and the tides of war had turned in the empire's favor, just as he knew they would. Such a turn was all part of the deal he had made with Kasari group commander Shalegha, a deal that ensured Dgarra's disgrace would be followed by Magtal's glorious string of victories. None could doubt that the judgment Emperor Goltat would soon render in these chambers was justified.

Dgarra halted inside a red circle, five steps in front of the emperor. His two guards walked back to posts beside the main door, leaving him alone. He stood there, shackled, radiating more power and authority than the emperor himself. The sight drew awed murmurs from the crowd and pulled grudging admiration from Magtal. This dangerous warrior would soon have his head cut from his shoulders, to be kicked through the streets by Koranthian children.

Emperor Goltat's deep voice drew the crowd's attention away from Dgarra.

"General Dgarra. You stand before me charged with high treason for allowing an alien spy into your inner circle, an act that led to the defeat of your army and the deaths of thousands of our mighty warriors. What say you to these charges?"

All eyes shifted back to Dgarra. When he strode toward the dais where Magtal and the emperor sat, a collective gasp rose from the assemblage. Someone activated Dgarra's shock collar, causing the muscles in his face and neck to crawl beneath his skin, but the general continued forward, coming to a halt directly in front of Emperor Goltat.

To Magtal's utter amazement, Dgarra dropped to one knee but kept his eyes locked on those of the emperor, as if he were about to be awarded the Koranthian Order of Valor.

"My emperor," Dgarra said, "long ago I pledged my life and honor to the empire. My determination to uphold my oath has never wavered in the midst of battle, and it has not been tested elsewhere. If it is your will that I shall die for these alleged offenses, then the empire can take my head. But when death comes for me, it will find me with my honor intact."

The guards, although slow to react, rushed forward to drag Dgarra back to the circle of judgment. But when they touched his arms, the power radiating from the active shock collar knocked them away and left them twitching on the ground.

Magtal found himself reaching for his weapon before he remembered that, by law, he had left it in a locker outside the Chamber of Judgment.

His piece said, Dgarra rose to his feet and took four steps backward until he was once again standing tall in the red circle.

"You have heard my words. Now I await your judgment."

To Magtal, the silence in the chamber acquired a preternatural intensity that seemed capable of stopping the hearts of all present.

For a moment, the emperor bowed his head, but when he lifted his chin, his expression was grave.

"So be it. General Dgarra, I hereby declare you guilty of high treason against the empire. Your house name shall be struck from all public records, and your property will be redistributed as I decide. I sentence you to death by public beheading, the execution to be carried out three days hence in the ArvaiKheer Amphitheater."

Then Emperor Goltat rose to his feet, turned, and walked through the door behind the dais, leaving the stunned audience frozen in place.

General Magtal also rose and signaled to the two guards, who had managed to climb back to their feet.

"Turn off that shock collar, and take this traitor back to his cell."

As they grabbed Dgarra's arms and roughly dragged him away, he met the general's eyes. For that brief moment, Magtal had the feeling that it was he, not Dgarra, who faced violent death.

Then Dgarra was gone, taking with him Magtal's fleeting moment of fear.

:CHAPTER 35

VJ stared at Raul, wondering if he had lost his mind.

"You want to shoot one of our subspace torpedoes into the Koranthian capital city?"

"I need you to redesign it without the explosive payload," he said with a strange look on his face.

"What are you talking about?"

Raul began pacing back and forth, his eyes unfocused, his right hand stroking his chin.

"How good of a pilot are you?"

With every word that left his mouth, Raul added to her confusion. VJ decided to play along and see where he was going.

"I am capable of maneuvering this ship to the limits of its capabilities and, barring some sort of equipment failure, with near perfect accuracy."

He stopped right in front of her, his brown eyes finally meeting hers.

A thought momentarily distracted her. She knew that she really didn't see through these eyes, but she had worked so hard at becoming almost human that VJ felt like she was seeing, hearing, and smelling through her virtual sensory organs. She was still working on touch and taste.

Raul continued. "Good, because I'm going to be inside that torpedo and I really don't want to die when it drops out of subspace inside Jennifer's dungeon."

His plan answered one of her questions. She had once heard him use a description that now seemed applicable. Raul had gone totally bat-shit crazy.

"Say what?"

"According to what I've learned during my worm-fiber hunt for Jennifer, the Koranthian emperor has scheduled General Dgarra's public execution inside the ArvaiKheer Amphitheater for two days from now."

VJ narrowed her eyes, starting to understand where he was going with this.

"You're planning on using the execution as a distraction?"

He smiled and placed both hands on her face. For a moment she thought he might kiss her.

"You better believe it. And you're going to make it all work."

○ ● ○

Raul had no illusions about the dangers involved in the plan he had proposed to VJ. But to her credit, after a lengthy discussion of the options available to them, she had agreed that this provided the best chance to rescue Jennifer. On the other hand, she thought the maneuver provided an even better chance for Raul to get himself killed or captured. He found the worry in her eyes oddly touching.

But he also knew that if his and Jennifer's positions were swapped, Jen would come for him.

Raul was no warrior, but in this case he didn't need to be. He just had to get to the dungeon cell where his worm-fiber search had found

Jennifer and inject her with VJ's freewill nano-virus. If she survived that, he would give her a laser pistol and lead her to the preplanned rendezvous point, where VJ would meet them with the Rho Ship. That assumed VJ met success with her part of the plan.

The modifications to the subspace torpedo had gone faster than predicted thanks to a number of VJ's creative design optimizations. The basic design of the torpedo was largely unchanged. The removal of the warhead hadn't freed nearly enough space to allow his body to be stowed within the torpedo, and thus Raul had thought they would need to redesign the entire thing.

Instead, VJ had replaced the warhead with a miniature stasis field generator. It would create a stasis field bubble on the outside of the torpedo with sufficient room to hold his body, a spare uniform for Jen, weapons, the serum, and enough air to keep him alive until the torpedo arrived at its designated target location. This would, of course, place additional demand on the super-capacitor power supply, but VJ assured him that there was enough power to get him there with a good thirteen seconds to spare. For her, that was practically a lifetime, but to Raul the margin for error still felt small.

He would have preferred to design and manufacture a small shuttle craft to pop down to Scion, load Jennifer aboard, then make the subspace hop back to the Rho Ship. But they lacked time. Instead, he was going to be lashed to the outside of a subspace torpedo and shot through subspace on a terrifying, one-way trip into the heart of an ancient alien dungeon. And then he and Jennifer had to fight their way through a bunch of Koranthians to reach the rendezvous point.

Having followed VJ to the airlock where the subspace torpedo awaited, he tried to swallow but just couldn't work up the spit. If this hadn't been his idea, he would have suspected that VJ was trying to get rid of him. Instead, she nervously flitted around him, dressed in a sheer black-and-purple uniform with a braided purple loop on her left shoulder, double-checking that all the equipment he needed was securely strapped to his body. His and Jennifer's dark uniforms felt like tactical necessities, but VJ's was the most critical to their plan.

Raul took a deep breath and stepped up to the torpedo. He no longer believed in a higher power, but some rosary beads sure would have felt nice right about now.

"Are you sure you want to go through with this?" VJ asked, her eyes wide with concern.

Putting on what he hoped was his brave face, Raul nodded. "Time to work your magic."

As he prepared to lie down atop the torpedo, an image from a classic movie filled his mind: a man, cowboy hat in hand, riding an atomic bomb down toward its target, whooping and hollering right up until detonation. That would be the way to do this with style.

Unfortunately, the neural net relayed that there wasn't enough power to create a stasis bubble big enough to accommodate such antics. So instead Raul lay facedown atop the torpedo, his arms and legs hugging the cylinder to him.

Under VJ's control, the cloaked Rho Ship accelerated, maneuvering so that its velocity vector exactly matched that of the targeted room at the instant the torpedo would emerge from subspace. Beside him, the AI began a ten-second countdown. When the stasis field activated around him, her voice cut off. The airlock opened, and the ship's stasis field thrust him out into the void, then stabilized the subspace torpedo a hundred feet off the Rho Ship's port side.

For five seconds the torpedo coasted beside the Rho Ship, exactly matching the vessel's velocity. Then, as the torpedo transitioned into subspace, the Rho Ship and the surrounding stars winked out of Raul's view.

Raul didn't really want to start a mental countdown, but he couldn't help it. As each second ticked off in his mind, the tension in his body increased until he found himself shaking. Thankfully, this time he didn't wet himself. VJ would be so proud.

The transition out of subspace into an unused section of the dungeon should have set him down softly. To give credit to the precision of VJ's calculations, the velocity vector was perfect. However, the height at which the torpedo materialized above the stone floor wasn't.

The eight-foot fall rattled his teeth and knocked the breath from his body. It also collapsed one of the two landing struts that had been added to the torpedo's underside, causing it to turn over. Raul clenched his teeth, ready to be rolled out flat as cookie dough, but the stasis field lasted until the other strut brought the torpedo to a stop. When the field finally died, he tumbled to the floor and lay there, gasping.

Raul forced himself to stand up. The backpack, though not particularly heavy, threw his balance off. Once he had his feet under him, the weight ceased to matter. He was thankful for his new robo-legs and the cyborg eye that turned shadow into a psychedelic mix of colors, mostly purple and blue.

Even now he could hear the distant echoes the sonic boom produced when the torpedo dropped out of subspace into the warren of connecting passages. Though some distance from Jennifer's cell, he and VJ had selected this particular point because the sound of entry would radiate outward, reflecting off walls and down side passages. Surrounding guards would be unable to tell the origin of the noise.

Now he had to wait for the distraction.

"Raul, can you hear me?" VJ asked.

A fresh flood of adrenaline shot through his veins. His cortical array had reestablished its subspace communications link with the Rho Ship's neural net.

"Bit of a bumpy ride at the end, but I'm fine. How do the worm-fiber scans look?"

"The pressure wave has got the dungeon staff confused. They've sent all but five of the on-duty guards to investigate."

"How many?"

"Seventeen. But none are currently headed in your direction."

Raul concentrated, and the imagery from the active worm-fiber scans formed in his mind, along with a detailed 3-D map of the warren of passages. Jennifer's cell was highlighted in red.

"Are you ready for your part in all of this?" he asked.

"You know I am."

"Okay, babe. Let's do this."

He felt her surprise at the pet name, knowing it was inappropriate. But screw it. He probably wasn't going to live to regret the act.

Then, as he knew it would, his mental link to the Rho Ship died.

Raul removed his laser pistol from its holster pocket and switched its safety selector into the ready position. For more than half a minute he waited, straining to hear. He didn't need to. The rumble he had been listening for vibrated the tunnel walls and put him into action. Reaching into a recessed slot on the side of the subspace torpedo, he engaged the self-destruct timer and moved out, letting his powerful legs propel him forward at a run.

He might not be a warrior, but being a cyborg didn't completely suck.

○ ● ○

The boom that echoed through the dungeon, a distant thrum that brought Jennifer to her feet, lit her surroundings like the midday sun. She recognized that sound. Something had just made the subspace-to-normal-space transition nearby. Her mind worked the problem. It had to be the Rho Ship, but it sounded so far away. The sound had been distorted by a particular echo path. Suddenly a much deeper rumble vibrated the cavern walls.

The heavy footsteps of running guards gradually faded into the distance. Then she heard new footfalls, although these were much lighter than those of the Koranthian guards.

Raul's voice on the far side of the solid-steel door startled her.

"Jennifer, can you hear me?"

"My God, Raul. How did you get here?"

"I'll explain later. Stand back from the door."

She complied, putting her back against the wall to the left. "Ready."

A sizzle and hiss accompanied the thin red glow that began to eat its way through the door hinges. As the last of the hinges became a glowing, molten puddle, the heavy door fell inward.

Raul stepped into her cell, lowering the pistol in his right hand. Then, as Jennifer stepped forward to embrace him, he raised another and fired.

She staggered to a halt, her shocked gaze drawn to the thick dart lodged in the center of her chest.

"What the—?"

The agony that curled her body into a convulsing mass on the floor killed the question.

○ ● ○

General Dgarra, chained hand and foot, stood atop the emperor's dais looking out across the parade grounds where he had led Jennifer and his ten thousand warriors into this very amphitheater in the not-so-distant past. Before him was the notched block where he would soon kneel to rest his neck. There was no basket to catch his head. It would be allowed to tumble down the steps and onto the field below. Then, at the emperor's command, the watching crowd would release their children from the grandstands to kick it around the stadium until the traitorous head was unrecognizable.

To Dgarra's left, Emperor Goltat faced the gathered crowd, his blue robes swirling slightly as he drew the war-blade from its ceremonial sheath on his back and held it high.

The crowd roared its delight and anticipation, a sound that shook the huge stadium. Dgarra looked out at the faces of those who had recently cheered him and understood their hatred. They believed that he had betrayed his own army. Whether his actions were intentional or based on negligence made no difference.

His impending death held no fear for him. But the thought that Jennifer Smythe had somehow deceived him ripped at his soul. How had it happened? He had been so sure that they shared the same feelings. He had staked his life on that trust. Now, appropriately, his uncle would take that life from him. Dgarra welcomed it.

Emperor Goltat lowered the black blade, and complete silence descended on the stadium as the crowd held its collective breath. The emperor turned and motioned Dgarra forward. He complied, stepping forward, then awkwardly knelt. But as he began to lean down, a tremendous blast knocked him flat on his back.

The shock wave left him dizzy, but he rose to see Emperor Goltat lying, unmoving, a body length to one side, his war-blade having tumbled down the steps. The Rho Ship sat directly in front of the dais. As he watched, a ramp lowered from its side and Jennifer Smythe walked out, wearing the black-and-purple uniform of his aide-de-camp, a stern look of disapproval on her delicate features. Her hair was different, light colored and short, as it had been the first time he had seen her.

A group of the emperor's guards, having recovered from the initial pressure wave, raised laser pistols and fired. Although the air around Smythe shimmered, the beams glanced harmlessly away as she continued off the end of the ramp and began calmly climbing the steps toward the top of the dais.

Drawing war-blades, a cohort of more than two dozen warriors charged, but she gestured with a hand and they froze midstride, locked in place as if by magic. As panic spread through the surrounding stadium, the civilians in the crowd surged toward the exits, blocking the path of the warriors who sought to reach the stadium floor. But when the guards did reach the ground level, they found their way forward blocked by an invisible force shield.

Smythe paused just before the top of the dais and gestured toward the black war-blade, levitating it into her right hand. Then, with a quick glance at the unconscious body of Emperor Goltat, she stepped up to Dgarra.

Shaking his head, Dgarra managed the utterance that encapsulated his disbelief. "Smythe!"

She pointed, and his shock collar and chains burst apart, sending the pieces clattering to the dais around him.

"Close enough," she said, giving him a subtle smile. "Time to go."

Another gesture lifted Dgarra and set him on his feet. Then she turned and began walking slowly back down the steps, ignoring the pandemonium that reigned supreme outside the protective shield.

Since there was only one way to get answers to the questions that flooded his head, Dgarra followed her back to the Kasari starship. As he walked up the ramp behind Smythe, Dgarra had no idea what awaited him inside, but apparently this was not his day to die.

○ ● ○

General Magtal watched helplessly as the horrifying scene unfolded before his eyes. Having hammered his hands bloody against the invisible barrier that blocked him from getting at Dgarra and his pet human, he raised his communicator to his mouth and ordered all city guards to make utmost haste to the amphitheater. Maybe if he could bring enough firepower to bear on the shield, he could overload it.

But as he watched, the ship's ramp closed. Feeling the force shield give way, he took two strides forward, but a new sonic boom knocked him backward, though this one was not as intense as the first. The starship had disappeared.

Taking advantage of this new confusion, Magtal rushed to the dais and then, taking the steps three at a time, hurtled to the top. Emperor Goltat lay faceup, eyes closed. Magtal glanced around at the panicked crowd and at the confused warriors moving toward the spot where the starship had just been. Dropping to a knee, he took the emperor's head in his two powerful hands and hammered it into the stone edge of the chopping block, feeling the satisfying crunch all the way up to his elbows.

General Magtal rose to his feet, cupped his hands to his mouth, and yelled, drawing the attention of the warriors below.

"Guards! To me."

Major Groltar was the first of the emperor's elite guards to reach the top of the dais. General Magtal pointed at the spot where blood and brains oozed from the back of the emperor's broken skull.

"Major," he said, noting the shock on the other's face, "the traitor, Dgarra, has murdered our emperor. Have your warriors guard this body. Let no one disturb Emperor Goltat's final rest until the royal honor guard can be assembled to respectfully transport him to the Hall of Valor."

Seeing the fury build in the major's eyes, General Magtal placed a hand on his shoulder and squeezed.

"Do not despair. We shall exact our revenge on the betrayer, Dgarra. And it will not be the quick death that our emperor offered him today. On that, you have my word."

: CHAPTER 36

Jennifer opened her eyes to find Raul bending over her, deep worry lines etched in his forehead. She tried to rise, but she was stopped by the tremors in her limbs. Jesus. What had he done to her? And then she felt it. The mental barrier she had erected was gone. Panic almost overcame her as she thought about what that meant. But something felt different.

She focused, calling upon her neural augmentations, trying to understand precisely what else was missing.

"You're free," Raul said.

Jennifer licked her dry lips as she struggled to find the meaning behind his words. There it was again, that odd yet vaguely familiar feeling. Suddenly everything snapped into place. She wasn't quite sure how she knew, but she did. The Kasari nanobot cortical array was no longer functioning.

She felt her eyes widen in joyful disbelief. "How?"

Raul held out his hand, and she took it, letting him help her to a sitting position.

"We analyzed your blood sample, and VJ designed a freewill nano-virus serum. Sorry about shooting you with it, but I couldn't take the chance that the Kasari might make you kill me."

For the first time in weeks, Jennifer managed a genuine laugh. "Can't say I blame you."

"Look, I don't mean to rush you, but I don't know how long VJ's distraction will keep the Koranthians from sending someone to check on you. We need to be going. Can you stand?"

Jennifer stretched her arms, happy to see that the tremors had stopped. Her strength was returning.

"Let's see."

She managed to get up with barely a wobble. Once she was steady, Raul dug in his backpack and handed her a clean black uniform, a pair of boots, and a laser pistol. Then he turned his back to let her dress. The gesture was unnecessary, but she found it sweet nonetheless. She quickly changed.

"Where to?" she asked.

"I've got the map in my head."

Jennifer concentrated and felt her mind slip into his, making the memory her own. She was ecstatic to be back to her old self. If she only had a war-blade, the transformation would be complete.

As Jennifer started to withdraw from her link with Raul, she felt his mind connect with the Rho Ship's neural net and VJ, followed by the distant rumble of another subspace transition.

"Where are you?" VJ asked.

"Headed for the rendezvous point along with Jennifer," said Raul as Jennifer led the way out of the cell and toward the rendezvous point marked on his mental map.

"Hurry up. I stirred up a hornet's nest when I interrupted Dgarra's execution."

Jennifer felt her heart jump. "Is Dgarra okay?" she asked, interjecting herself into the mental conversation.

"He's standing right here beside me on the command deck, and if I can get you and him to shut up with all the questions, I might be able to help you guys get back here alive."

A relieved sigh escaped Jennifer's lips as she replied. "Okay."

"I'm monitoring all movement in the dungeon tunnel system through the worm-fiber feeds. Calculating the optimal course for you to take now."

Jennifer saw scores of video feeds blossom in the ship's neural net along with a 3-D map corresponding to what she was seeing. The selected path appeared as a green line running down a series of passages to the distant cavern where the Rho Ship had reemerged from another subspace jump. Unfortunately, the path wasn't entirely clear of Koranthian prison guards.

"Ouch," said Raul, having also seen what Jennifer observed.

"Sorry," said VJ, "but we couldn't really expect my diversion to completely empty the prison of its guard force. It's also unsurprising that they heard my arrival. I suppose I should spend some time designing a subspace-transition sound buffer."

"Forget about it," Raul said as he raced along behind Jennifer. "Focus on the task at hand."

Jennifer had to admit that his robo-legs were an impressive improvement.

"Careful," VJ said. "You're coming up on the first group now."

"Got it."

Jennifer slowed to a walk, her laser pistol held in a double-handed shooter's grip as she moved to the next corner, scanning ahead with her own telepathic senses. Four guards were moving down the passage that branched off to her left, coming toward them.

In one quick motion, she spun around the corner, firing a rapid sequence of pulses that dropped the first three guards, but the fourth dived into an open cell before she could target him.

"Damn it. Cover me."

Then she sprinted forward, keeping her pistol leveled at the cell's doorway as she launched herself into a headlong slide on her right side. A laser pulse heated the air above her just as she depressed her own trigger. Her first pulse took off the guard's gun hand. The second hit him in the center of his face, sending the Koranthian's limp body slumping to the floor.

As she climbed to her feet, she saw Raul step up beside her. He looked at the smoking face of the Koranthian and stifled a gag, but didn't puke. Not bad for his first combat action.

"If you hurry," VJ said, "you can beat the rest of the guards who are headed this way."

Jennifer noted the route modifications that came through Raul's mental link and picked up the pace, hearing his footfalls right behind her. Two turns later they entered the large natural cavern where the Rho Ship waited.

As she and Raul sprinted onto the ship's ramp, Jennifer thought it was the finest welcome mat she had ever seen.

○ ● ○

Waiting at the top of the ramp, Dgarra saw the real Jennifer Smythe run toward him. A boiling stew of emotions left him immobilized. Despite how thoroughly the virtual construct who had introduced herself as VJ had explained Smythe's betrayal, he hadn't been able to let it go.

But then Smythe vaulted upward, wrapping her arms around his neck with a strength that belied her delicate frame. She buried her face against his as she gasped out the words that pulled down his barriers.

"I'm sorry I let you down. So . . . so sorry."

His arms reacted of their own accord, squeezing her to him as he tried to sooth the tremors that racked her body. A warm wetness trickled down the side of his neck, and he realized that it leaked from her eyes. A human reaction he had only observed from her once before, during another instance of intense emotion. Right now it did not seem like a bad thing.

"Uh . . . love birds," VJ's voice intruded, "transitioning to subspace in thirty seconds. I suggest you get your asses back to the command bay so I can wrap you up tight before that happens."

Dgarra realized that he had barely been aware of the Koranthian guards whom the stasis field had blocked or of the retracting ramp that had sealed the Rho Ship. He lowered Smythe to the floor, and she stepped back awkwardly, wiping her eyes with the back of her hand.

But she managed a smile and then turned and led the way onto the command deck. They were met by a scowling Raul, who impatiently waved them forward. Then, as Raul settled back in his translucent blue command couch, Dgarra once again felt the stasis field enfold his body as, beside him, Smythe also floated into the air.

"Transition in five seconds," VJ said. "Say your good-byes to Scion."

By all the dark gods, Dgarra didn't like the sound of that. But since there was nothing he could do to change the events that had brought him to this point, he settled back and relaxed, letting the Rho Ship carry him away from the only world he had ever known.

○ ● ○

Kasari group commander Shalegha didn't understand how this could have happened. Jennifer Smythe had been a sacrifice she'd been willing to make in order to help bring General Magtal to power. But from the reports her other Koranthian spies had delivered, the Smythe woman had somehow escaped in the stolen Kasari world ship, taking General Dgarra with her.

The apparent use of subspace technology to cause the starship to materialize in the ArvaiKheer cavern, deep beneath the Koranthian Mountains, was mind bending. But even more disturbingly, Jennifer Smythe had apparently found a way to neutralize the nanobot cortical array linking her brain to the hive-mind, something that, until now, the Kasari had considered impossible.

Still, the bad news was limited to one rogue starship, two rogue humans, and one rogue Koranthian general. And by all indications, they had fled the Scion system. Shalegha's alarm had gone out to the entire Kasari Collective that these dangerous rebels were to be destroyed on sight. As badly as she wanted to capture the stolen ship and investigate the hybrid Kasari-Altreian technologies the humans had created, the ongoing dangers they presented made the risk involved in such an attempt far outweigh potential rewards.

But she had also received much better news. Emperor Goltat had been killed during Dgarra's escape, and General Magtal had been crowned emperor in his place. Shalegha had subsequently pulled back the Kasari support she had provided the attacking Eadric army, gifting Emperor Magtal a series of small victories that had resulted in an armistice between the Kasari and the Koranthians. The war was not over, but the cessation of hostilities fulfilled Shalegha's bargain with Magtal.

More importantly, instead of expending so much effort on battle, the Kasari could now focus on the assimilation of the Eadric, who composed the vast majority of Scion's population and controlled a corresponding percentage of the world's territory. Granting the Koranthians control of their subterranean empire also gave the Kasari Collective power over Scion's surface, the airspace above it, and the space beyond that. All in all, not a bad bargain.

Shalegha leaned back in her chair, surveying her strategic-operations center, and smiled. She had no doubt the Koranthians would violate the armistice sooner or later, but by the time they made that decision, she would be ready to hammer them into extinction. For now, she could afford to be patient.

CHAPTER 37

In the weeks since Janet had escorted Jamal into the New Zealand secret facility, he had remained in a perpetual state of awe. The robotic technologies that Mark and Heather Smythe had created beneath the mountains were incredible. The facility's computing and subspace hacking capabilities were what really triggered Jamal's interests, and he knew that Eileen felt the same way.

Although Denise claimed that all of "this alien-inspired insanity" scared her, she had been one of the true AI pioneers, having created the NSA's massively parallel supercomputer known as Big John. The entity had only one purpose: to mine all available data on selected targets and then cross-correlate that data with all other available information. Big John's tendrils extended into everything.

Nobody comprehended exactly how Big John worked. The scientists who had designed the core network of processors understood the fundamentals: feed in sufficient information to uniquely identify a target, then allow Big John to scan all known information—financial transactions, medical records, jobs, photographs, DNA, fingerprints, known associates, acquaintances, and so on.

But then things shifted into another realm. Using the millions of processors at its disposal, Big John began sifting external information through its nodes, allowing individual neurons to apply weight to data that had no apparent relation to the target, each node making its own relevance and correlation calculations.

No person directed Big John's complicated genetic algorithms that supplied shifting weights to its evolving neural patterns. Given enough time to study a problem, there was no practical limit to what Big John could accomplish. The retired Dr. Denise Jennings's software kernel had been inserted into antivirus programs, protecting millions of computing devices around the world. Although those programs provided state-of-the-art antivirus protection, their main activity was node-data analysis for Big John.

Big John was a bandwidth hog. No matter how big a data-pipe feed, Big John always needed more. Dr. Jennings's software had provided an elegant solution to that problem. Commercial antivirus programs scanned all data on protected devices, passing it through node analysis, adding their own weighting to the monstrous neural net. If some devices were turned off or even destroyed, no matter. If data nodes died, more and better processors constantly replaced them. In a strange way, the entire global network was Big John. Dr. Jennings had come to regard Big John as a specific type of artificial intelligence known as an oracle, whose sole purpose for being was to answer the questions of those who were authorized to ask.

But several months ago, a nine-year-old Robby Gregory had used the alien AI in his head to take down Big John, keeping the oracle from reestablishing its network ever since.

The Smythe operation was as compartmented as any of the programs concocted inside the copper-infused, black-glass Puzzle Palace at Fort Meade, Maryland. Jamal approved of the way the Smythes were careful with their secrets. After all, he, Eileen, and Denise had their own secret, and it slept inside a half-inch holographic data sphere that Senator Freddy Hagerman had once thought of as a lucky marble.

Far from being lucky, that small device had gotten a lot of good people killed, two of whom had been Jamal's former lovers. Even though Jillian McPherson and Carolyn Brown had been slain a dozen years apart, both murders were so clear in his mind's eye that they felt like they happened yesterday. If Jack Gregory and Janet Price hadn't fought their way into Steve Grange's California research facility to rescue him, Jamal would be just as dead as his two girlfriends.

Threatened by the weight of those blood-soaked memories, he shifted his thoughts to the job at hand. He was reminded of his time in the NSA, leading the group of superhackers that Admiral Riles had nicknamed the Dirty Dozen, as they each climbed into their Scorpion full-immersion workstations. The Dirty Trio just didn't have the same ring to it, and the Three Amigos was already taken.

But as cool as the Scorpions had looked, they couldn't compete with the setup Heather had created for the three former NSA superstars. She had made each of them a headset that looked something like a color-shifting Alice headband with small beads at each end designed to be placed over the temples. And once those little beads settled into place, the real mind trip began.

As the headset connected with his mind, the real world dropped away, his senses experiencing the virtual world created through the subspace linkage of his brain to one of the three Smythe supercomputers within this facility. Keyboards? A thing of the past.

Jamal glanced at Eileen, who had just settled into her comfortable couch, one of three that had been placed in a triangle, each facing the center. The setup facilitated discussion whenever they weren't lost in the virtual worlds of their minds. They could still communicate while connected through the headsets, but that was more like invading each other's dreams than popping open a video-chat window.

With Denise catching some sleep, her couch remained empty.

"Better bring your A game, Eileen," he said. "Otherwise you're about to find yourself eating my dust."

"Keep telling yourself that. Maybe someday you'll believe it."

Jamal grinned. Eileen was the second woman he had met who was as confident as he was. He slipped his headset on and performed a rapid diagnostic, knowing Eileen was performing her own system check. As expected, everything was working perfectly.

"Janet, you out there?" he asked.

"I'm here. You ready for action?"

"Donuts and coffee have me all charged up. What did we miss during our break?"

"So far so good in Hanau. According to Robby and Eos, there have been no breaches in Mark and Heather's security. The operation is still a go."

"Okay, then," said Jamal, "Eileen and I will focus on the security perimeter around Prokorov's Frankfurt Gateway, but I don't see how the FSS can pack any more troops and weapons into that area."

"Find me a weakness that Mark and Heather can exploit," Janet said. "I'm counting on you two."

Jamal felt his excitement ebb under the pressure of that last statement. The time had come for the hackers to prove they were as good as Jamal had boasted.

○ ● ○

Forty-eight hours before the scheduled activation of the Frankfurt wormhole gate, Alexandr Prokorov settled into his chair, having just returned to The Hague after an inspection of the site's security forces. Per his instructions, no security personnel were allowed into the man-made cavern where the gateway had been constructed. Earth had already made that mistake at the site of the Stephenson Gateway, something that had resulted in armed conflict with the lead elements of the aliens whom Dr. Stephenson had meant to welcome to the planet.

If not for the threat posed by the Safe Earth resistance, he wouldn't have allowed the military or police anywhere near the gateway cavern located sixteen miles northeast of Frankfurt. Prokorov knew that the Smythes would try to stop the scheduled activation of the device. In fact, he was counting on it.

He was surprised they had managed to remain hidden for so long, despite the assets that Prokorov had pressed into service in an attempt to find them. But if he couldn't find their hiding place, he would pull them to him.

Since he had insisted on extreme precautions to prevent the possibility of the Smythes hacking into the gateway remotely, they would have to try a physical assault on the facility. The air and ground forces the Germans had put in place were ready to take out the Smythes and their allies. And if the Smythes didn't attempt such an attack, Earth would make contact with its alien benefactors. Either way, a big win for the UFNS and for humanity as a whole.

What high-tech tricks would the Smythes pull from their bag of treats? He looked forward to finding out.

○ ● ○

Heather answered the call on the second ring.

"Hello, Aaden. What have you got for me?"

"It's an abandoned construction site seven miles south of the UFNS wormhole gateway. The upper part of the structure is incomplete, but the underground parking garage is adequate for our purposes and the range to the target meets your criteria. Best of all, it's isolated from other structures by a half mile of woods."

"Good. That gives us our final staging area."

"A team of my people will keep the perimeter secured until you get here. I'll text you the coordinates as soon as I hang up."

"Okay," Heather said. "Time of execution is still midnight."

She switched off the phone and turned to Mark. "We've got three hours."

"More than enough to get these last few trucks dispersed," he said.

She turned to look at the row of self-driving big rigs still waiting to be deployed from the warehouse compound, each with a logo from a different shipping firm, none of which was Hanau Trans-Shipping. They had been preloaded inside the main warehouse with combat robots, just as the trucks sent out at varying intervals throughout the day had been. Some of those vehicles had been driving for hours along routes that would bring each to its unique destination in time to release its bots. The supporting drones would be automatically released from special launching rails mounted inside other trucks.

The storm of death she and Mark were about to unleash on the outskirts of one of Europe's major population centers horrified her as much as the memory of the nuclear detonations they had triggered to destroy the Stephenson Gateway.

She felt herself momentarily swept into a vision of soldiers fighting and dying before swarms of enemies unlike any they had ever faced, EMP-hardened machines that had been designed for one purpose: to kill humans. Even worse, the kill decisions would be left up to these robot swarms, allowing them to continually optimize the paths to achieving their designated objectives. And, unlike humans, they would make those calculations without emotion, on a nanosecond timescale.

Part of this was being done to provide a diversion for the act that only she could perform, but that Mark had refused to let her do alone—an action very likely to get them both killed.

○ ● ○

Private Lance Falk had been a member of the German army for less than a year, but these last four weeks had felt like four months. His unit had been stuck in the most boring place possible, assigned to guard a portion of the perimeter around the world's favorite new science project. Day and night he had watched construction equipment and busloads of scientists and engineers come and go without incident, knowing that the Frankfurt nightlife was a mere sixteen miles from the farmer's field where he was stuck.

If he had been part of the rapid-reaction force stationed closer to the site where the Frankfurt Gateway was being built, he would have at least been sleeping inside a real building instead of catching catnaps in a tent between his six-hour shifts walking the triple-strand razor wire that formed the outer perimeter. Those KSK guys got all the fat duty. He spat into the dirt. Kommando Spezialkräfte—bah. Lance could have qualified for the special forces if he had wanted to. He was sure of that.

This time of night was the worst, especially with the evening fog that had become a consistent companion since the beginning of October. Visibility was so poor that he and his squad mates had to be careful to avoid wandering into the concertina wire. Even the standard-issue night-vision goggles were of little use in the swirling soup.

His left foot caught on an unseen stone, and he stumbled forward, barely managing to avoid falling. Lance cursed under his breath but continued on, glad he hadn't heard any laughter, as that would mean the other members of his patrol had seen his clumsiness. A sound to his left brought him to a halt.

Lance cocked his head and stilled his breathing. At first he only heard movement from the other members of his squad, but then he heard the sound again—a staccato crunch of metal on stone and soil, coming from well outside the perimeter. It was getting closer.

"*Achtung!*" he yelled, dropping to a knee and raising his assault rifle. As he flipped the selector from safe to automatic, he heard something hit the wire, accompanied by the loud twang of strands giving way.

The laser that cut his left arm off at the shoulder continued its arc through his upper torso. As automatic weapons chattered all around him, Lance never managed to scream.

○ ● ○

Janet stood in the Smythe operational control room, watching the bank of monitors that covered the far wall. She could have worn a headset like Robby, Jamal, and Eileen, but she couldn't stand the hated things. She would continue to rely on the information her own five senses delivered instead of the hallucinations the headsets piped into their brains.

The conditions around the Frankfurt Gateway project were both good and bad for the robotic attack that had begun. The fog vastly reduced the visibility and range of infrared targeting and surveillance systems, allowing the robotic attackers to get close to their enemies before being engaged. But it also limited the information available from the Smythes' drone aircraft.

For now, she relied on drone telemetry relayed through subspace links back to New Zealand. So far the attack was progressing better than expected, although she knew that wasn't likely to last. The robotic force had attacked the Frankfurt Gateway's outer perimeter from six directions, taking minimal losses in penetrating the outer line of defense. Once through the razor wire, each of these six swarms had unleashed the dog-shaped fast-attack bots, sending them bounding forward across the relatively flat terrain at speeds up to fifty miles per hour, to probe for weak spots.

These penetrating attacks achieved a number of simultaneous objectives, creating confusion and producing friendly-fire casualties as German and supporting UFNS forces were caught in each other's crossfire. Because the bots were aware of each other's positions, they were able to build a rapid map of engagements, allowing them to flow around strong points in the defense toward weak areas.

Unfortunately, those weak areas would become much harder to find as the fighting progressed toward the elite forces guarding the inner facilities that gave access to the wormhole-gateway cavern.

Staying below radar and with the fog making their air surveillance ineffective, the small drones were reduced to providing communications relays among the ground swarms. But when the time came, they would crash themselves into assigned targets, detonating their internal bombs. All of it was controlled by the logic of the swarm to which they were assigned.

Her thoughts shifted to Heather and Mark, who had positioned themselves inside an abandoned industrial construction project halfway between Hanau and the Frankfurt Gateway cavern. Despite keeping a small number of combat robots and a contingent of Aaden Bauer's Safe Earth resistance forces with them, their position left them exposed in a way Janet didn't like.

If Heather could implement her work from New Zealand, they would be safely operating from here. Unfortunately, such a feat wasn't possible. The micro-bots were too small to have subspace-communications capability, and the latency induced by relaying the signals was unacceptable. Heather's savant brain would have to absorb everything they would be sensing so that she could manipulate the bots as if they were extensions of her own body.

There was no getting around the requirement for her to be there, so there was no possibility of keeping Mark away. Janet understood that feeling. It was the way she and Jack had been before he—

She angrily shoved the thought away. The operation was still in its initial stages. Very soon now, the elite German forces closer to the Frankfurt Gateway would join the fray. Things were bound to get interesting.

○ ● ○

Robby had used Eos to distribute the mission objectives to each of the swarms now attacking the Frankfurt Gateway. And he would keep Eos focused on the ongoing battle as long as it lasted. As he had already experienced, these much larger swarms could operate autonomously, having placed themselves in a mode that disabled instructions potentially overridden by external hackers.

The Smythes and Robby had debated eliminating this measure but had instead opted for better defining the target objectives in a way that Heather believed provided the lowest probability of generating extensive collateral damage. Nonetheless, there would still be collateral damage. But with the fate of mankind hanging in the balance, certain risks had to be accepted.

What Robby couldn't accept were the risks Heather and Mark were taking by assigning too small a force of robots for their own personal defense. Despite Heather's attempts to reassure him that she had selected the optimum course of action, neither Robby nor Eos agreed with her probability calculations.

So he had made a small addition to the instructions Eos had passed to the robotic swarms. *Destroy any force that moves to attack Heather or Mark Smythe.*

The simple instruction would only be triggered if that one condition was met. And since the loss of Heather would cause their entire plan to fail, the addition was logical. He knew he should have asked Janet's approval before implementing the change, but he hadn't.

He took a breath and refocused his thoughts on the here and now and things he could control.

:CHAPTER 38

Having been the recipient of the latest formulation of the Rho Project nanites, Alexandr Prokorov no longer had any need for sleep. Thus he was at his desk when the call came in that propelled him down the hall to the FSS strategic-operations center.

He entered the room's upper tier and was met by General Dimitri Zherdev, the chief of FSS military operations.

"Minister," Zherdev said, "the Frankfurt Gateway compound came under attack a little over five minutes ago."

Prokorov walked forward to the curved glass wall that gave him a clear view out over the operations center and the twenty-foot-tall wall that formed a massive view-screen. The room below bustled with an energy indicative of the combat action displayed on the far wall.

"Talk me through it."

"If you take a look at the map on the upper left corner, you'll see that the outer perimeter has been breached in six locations by attacks that appear to be entirely robotic."

Prokorov frowned. Knowing the ruthlessness and utter disregard for public safety that the Smythes had previously demonstrated, this could be very bad indeed.

Zherdev continued. "The outer perimeter is designed to be a trip wire that is six miles outside the inner fortifications. The robots aren't bothering to widen the breaches, just pouring through the punctures at top speed. The lead elements are acting like a cavalry covering force, charging forward to give the follow-on elements a clear picture of our inner defenses."

"Have we engaged them from the air?"

"Not with any kind of precision. The fog is severely limiting our airborne surveillance assets' capabilities. We are picking them up on ground-surveillance radar, but that's only useful for artillery targeting. The tanks and precision-guided munitions rely on visual or LIDAR targeting, both of which are impacted by the fog."

"Engage with artillery."

"The civilians—"

"We're talking about a few farmers versus humanity. The Smythes won't hesitate to kill civilians, and neither will I. Give the order."

"Yes, sir."

As the general picked up the phone to give that order, Prokorov stared at the updating displays. What he wouldn't give to be rid of the Smythes once and for all. Assuming Galina wasn't dead, she remained his best option.

○ ● ○

Nikina Gailan walked alongside Aaden Bauer as he made his circuit through the partially completed, multistory concrete-and-steel structure, hearing the distant rumble of what could only be artillery fire. When was the last time the heart of Germany had experienced the rumble of that metallic wall of death? The 1940s. The decade that had laid the egg that hatched this one.

Craziness.

The Smythes were a significant part of that craziness, as was Aaden, as was she. On these rare nights when death hung in the air like fog itself, she felt totally alive.

Mark and Heather had staked out a secluded spot in the underground parking garage to set up their sophisticated communications gear. Although they hadn't bothered to brief her or Aaden on its purpose, she gathered that this location was critically important to controlling some of the robots in the attacking force. Once Heather took over that part of the operation, she was not to be disturbed for any reason.

Movement to Nikina's right drew her attention, and she shifted the muzzle of the assault rifle in that direction only to see a group of three robots patrolling the perimeter. Two were bipedal models standing just over eight feet tall, with a turret containing a high-powered laser and a sensor array in place of a head. The third was the size of a large dog but with the capability of continuously standing erect or running forward on all fours. The dog-bot's feet could transform into hands by way of extended grasping digits.

But the robots that freaked her out were the crab-like bombs that skittered around or over obstacles with remarkable agility. When they folded themselves up, they were no bigger than softballs and capable of magnetically attaching themselves by scores to the outside of the larger robots, giving their bigger cousins a lumpy appearance. The thought of trying to defend a position while those things swarmed you left her cold.

While the bots' movements weren't exactly quiet, the electric motors that powered them were remarkably so. The technology that allowed them to store that much electrical energy was far better than anything Nikina had ever heard of and would be worth a fortune on the commercial or military markets.

As Aaden completed his inspection of the Safe Earth resistance fighters he had positioned around the skeletal structure, he stopped beside the two dozen black motorcycles that had brought them here to stare through the fog toward the distant sounds of battle. Nikina stopped beside him. She couldn't hear the screams of those that fought and died in this shrouded night, but she sensed them.

If all went well, their sacrifice would be worth it.

○ ● ○

Mark watched Heather closely in the underground parking structure. She sat cross-legged on the dirty concrete floor, using a specially designed headset that lacked the subspace-communications aptitude that allowed her to link with the New Zealand supercomputers. This headset linked with the small rack of communications equipment in front of her to receive sensor and telemetry data from thousands of micro-bots, giving her the ability to control their actions. She also controlled the crawling carrier bots worming their way through the narrow ductwork that provided pathways for the gateway cavern's wiring and plumbing.

The big robots had already accomplished the main goal of their attack. Having reached the maintenance building that provided access to the underground ductwork that carried the wiring and plumbing to the cavern, they had released the crawler bots into the tight space. From this point on, the larger robots would continue to fight to provide distraction.

With the micro-bot swarm still within the bodies of the crawlers, the number of bots Heather had to control simultaneously was only in the dozens for now. But when the crawlers arrived at the release point and discharged the flea-sized micro-bots, the mental stress on her mind would rise exponentially. The tiny bots had to reach and get inside the gateway system without being observed, and so she would have to direct the swarm over a much greater distance than they were normally expected to travel.

She had factored in the potential for significant losses along the way, but the smaller the number of micro-bots that successfully penetrated the machinery, the longer it would take to complete the rewiring of the circuit boards. Since they needed the diversion from the assault by the combat robots to continue throughout the process, any delays could endanger the mission.

The crawler bots were at least fifteen minutes from reaching the spot where they would release the micro-bots.

In the meantime, Mark would continue to use his subspace headset to monitor the status of the battle being waged outside the gateway cavern. Beyond that, the only thing he could do to help his wife through a task that would push her fabulous mind to its limits was to stand watch.

○ ● ○

The worry in Eileen's voice over the room's speakers pulled Janet's attention from the maps displaying the progress of the attack.

"We've got a problem."

"What's wrong?"

"Jamal and I have intercepted FSS communications with a convoy of armored vehicles that are currently headed north from Hanau on Highway 45 to reinforce the troops defending the Frankfurt Gateway. That route is going to take them very close to the spot where Heather and Mark are located."

Janet felt the tension creep into her shoulders and consciously relaxed. "So long as Aaden's people don't get trigger happy, that shouldn't be a problem. In the fog, the convoy won't even know they are there."

"Okay. Just letting you know."

"Thanks."

Janet studied the digital displays showing the positions and status of their robots. The attacks from the south and southeast had faltered, failing to penetrate the heavily armored defenses in those areas, but three other swarms had punctured the second of three defensive rings, extending tendrils that reached within two miles of the gateway cavern. But as she watched, her eyes were drawn back to the three southern swarms.

They hadn't just halted their advance—they were in all-out retreat.

She pressed a button and spoke. "Robby. What's going on with the southern swarms?"

"Uh . . . I'm not sure."

"Not sure, or don't know? If you have any idea what's happening, now would be a good time to tell me."

When no immediate response was forthcoming, Janet felt her jaws clench. "Robby?"

"Eos thinks their drones have detected the convoy approaching from the south and the swarms are moving to intercept it."

"Did you command that?"

"No. I couldn't if I wanted to. The swarms are making the tactical decisions they believe give them the best chance of accomplishing their mission."

"Their mission is to attack and destroy the wormhole gateway."

She heard him clear his throat. "And to destroy anything that threatens Mark or Heather."

Janet glanced back at the big map, finally understanding what she was seeing.

"Oh shit."

:CHAPTER 39

At first Prokorov had thought the news from the defensive forces on the south side of the Frankfurt Gateway complex was good. Reports indicated that the robots had pulled back after meeting stiff resistance before going into high-speed retreat. What confused him was how those actions differed from the way the swarms of robots were throwing themselves into the German defenders north of the gateway.

"Our German armor convoy reports enemy contact north of Hanau," said General Zherdev.

"Losses?"

"Two Leopard tanks and four armored personnel carriers. The robots were on them before they could tactically deploy into battle formations."

Prokorov cursed. "What about air support?"

"The forces are intermingled in the fog. Our air power would certainly hit our own troops along with the enemy."

"Show me on the map."

The general signaled to one of the captains sitting at a console, and the map zoomed out so that it showed not only the ongoing engagements at the Frankfurt Gateway, but also those north of Hanau.

Prokorov studied the display, feeling a renewed sense of optimism. Maybe this was for the best. By turning to attack the convoy, almost half of the attacking swarms had pulled themselves away from the gateway cavern, allowing the defenders there to concentrate their fire against the reduced swarms. Thus the robotic advance of two of the three swarms had slowed to a crawl and the defending troops were able to counterattack the left flank of the third swarm.

Then he noticed something else. "Zoom in on the action north of Hanau."

The map display shifted to show the actively engaged military units as a series of blinking icons. The emerging pattern formed a thirty-degree arc that bowed around a central point.

"Do you see that?" Prokorov asked, pointing at the computer monitor at the captain's workstation.

General Zherdev leaned forward. "It looks like they're defending something."

"That's a pretty big area. Show me some daylight satellite imagery, and keep the combat icons overlaid on the image."

The area had a number of farms and villages, some industrial facilities, and an abandoned construction site. The deploying tanks and infantry were engaged in a desperate fight that stretched almost three miles wide.

"It's going to be pretty hard to pin down what they're defending," Zherdev said. "Do you want me to call in an airstrike?"

Prokorov considered the question. "No. If they are defending something, then it must be a high-value target. What special-alert forces are ready for immediate deployment?"

"We have the U.S. Third Ranger Battalion on alert at Ramstein Air Base. They are currently assigned to support FSS military operations."

"Get them in the air. I want them to sweep that whole area and find out what's there."

Watching General Zherdev turn to issue the orders, Prokorov smiled. The Smythes had just made their first big mistake.

○ ● ○

Robby felt sick to his stomach. The fact that his mom hadn't torn into him for modifying the robots' mission statement only made him feel worse. Now he had to find a way to fix the mission before Mark and Heather were killed.

He felt Eos scan the data being provided by the robots in the southern swarms, looking for a new way to bypass the protection protocols preventing any changes to the locked-in mission. Eos wasn't finding squat.

"What about feeding them bad sensor data, making them think that the Smythes are located inside the gateway cavern? Maybe that would cause them to go back to where they're supposed to be."

"Negative. After I was able to hack the robot sensors in the capture-the-flag trial run, I created an upgrade that prevents that from happening. And since they calculate their positions within the swarm without reliance on GPS, I can't get in that way either."

Robby bit his lip. *Damn it! Think, Robby. Think.*

The status of the robots fighting the enemy armored convoy just north of Hanau didn't look good. Despite creating heavy casualties in the opposing force, the robots were vastly outnumbered and their losses were mounting.

Suddenly one of the swarms shifted strategy, abandoning the fight and sprinting cross-country toward the outskirts of Hanau, with enemy heavy armor in hot pursuit.

"Eos, what's happening?"

"Checking."

"Can you show me what the leading robots are seeing and doing?"

"Passive viewing isn't a problem. Establishing a link now."

The vision that was piped into his mind startled Robby so badly that his body jerked in his chair. He felt like he had been transported inside the running robot's body as it crashed through a section of woods only to rush into a neighborhood of two- and three-story half-timbered homes.

Other robots broke from the woods on his left and right, the swarm sharing a vision of where its functional members were, optimizing the path of each to achieve what the swarm had determined was its optimal course of action: to create a diversion that their human foes could not ignore. If it could not defeat the massed enemy tanks, the swarm would attack their civilians, many of whom would be military family members.

Robby watched in horror as the robot crashed through the door of the nearest apartment building, racing room to room, ripping apart the people it found there or burning them down with laser fire. In the final seconds before leaving the apartment house, the robot ripped out the gas line, igniting the gas with a laser blast before rushing back out into the street.

"No!" Robby screamed. "Eos, please stop this!"

"I am working on the problem."

As Robby watched the metallic body race toward its next assigned target, German screams of terror filled the night. All around him houses burst into flames, painting the river of fog that flowed between them bright orange. On his left, a burning girl ran out through an open door only to be crushed beneath the feet of another metal monster.

"Kill the link," Robby gasped. "I can't watch anymore."

As the link dissolved, Robby gagged and vomited in his lap. The whole operation had been transformed into a chaotic maelstrom of violence against innocent men, women, and children. The robots didn't care who they killed so long as the action scored higher on their mission-accomplishment value scale. And they would adjust their destructive path toward Frankfurt, one of the most densely populated cities in Europe.

The headset allowed the supercomputer to project him into the scene representing that scenario's most likely outcome. The destruction that even a handful of these metal monsters could inflict on the city would make human terrorist attacks pale in comparison. And the bots would attempt to optimize the problem, maximizing the impact of their attacks. The supercomputer projected those targets: hospitals, nursing homes, apartment buildings—any place where people congregated would fit the swarm's killing agenda.

Robby pulled off his headset, his hands shaking so badly from the visions that he dropped it on the floor.

"What have I done?"

○ ● ○

Colonel Herzog, the commander of Task Force Bayern, looked at the aerial imagery his intelligence officer had just transferred to the command vehicle. He shook his head in disbelief. Just when he had thought he could transition his armored force into a mop-up mission, a swarm of robots had broken off from direct combat and had raced into Hanau's northern outskirts. Despite the limitations imposed by the fog, this imagery confirmed the reports he had received of the ongoing destruction the monsters were inflicting on the city's civilian population.

His fury threatened to consume him. This was exactly the kind of bullshit that had led to a worldwide ban on autonomous combat robots. From what he could tell, the Smythes had unleashed robots that were making their own kill decisions without any human involvement.

If Colonel Herzog hesitated to act, the robot swarm would continue their Hanau rampage unopposed. No police could contain what was spreading through the city, and the massacre would likely spread from Hanau into Frankfurt. Right now, unless the warning sirens had awakened them, his wife and four kids were sleeping inside his house in the Hanau suburb of Klein-Auheim. He'd be damned before he let these abominations continue their atrocities.

In quick, clipped tones, he spoke the orders that would send the bulk of his task force hurtling back south along Highway 45, leaving two companies to fight a rearguard action. Herzog would have to get ahead of the swarm. Then he would hunt down and destroy every single robot. If luck was with him, God would deliver the Smythes into his hands before this night ended. He prayed that would happen. Court-martial or no, his Heckler & Koch had two bullets with their names on them.

:CHAPTER 40

"We have micro-bot release."

Mark heard Heather's excited announcement and then saw her eyes go milky white, knowing that she had gone deep in order to control the thousands of flea-sized bots that would scurry along the conduits, electrical lines, and support structures toward the wormhole gateway. From this point forward the tiny swarm would all be directed by Heather.

The bots' small size had placed severe limitations on their communications and computing capabilities, which was why Heather needed to set up within a fifty-thousand-nanosecond communication radius of her army. Since this abandoned structure was slightly over eight and a half miles from the Frankfurt Gateway cavern, the round-trip communication latency of ninety microseconds met that requirement.

Mark watched her for several seconds as he continued to receive status updates through his SRT headset. He hadn't told her of all the things that had gone wrong with the ongoing combat operation. She needed to focus on the daunting task that faced her.

Three of the combat-robot swarms that had been ordered to attack the Frankfurt Gateway had gone off mission to attack a convoy of reinforcements. Then, in an apparent attempt to draw off the enemy, the bots had rampaged into Hanau, killing civilians by the thousands and setting the northern part of the city ablaze. Mark felt his teeth grind thinking of the surrounding death caused by machine minds failing to understand their creators' intentions.

Now Janet had just informed him that a fleet of helicopters was dropping U.S. Army Rangers across a wide zone. Jamal and Eileen had also intercepted communications that indicated that the mission of these Ranger units was wide-area reconnaissance.

There was little doubt what they were searching for: Mark and Heather. And if they found this hideout before Heather finished her task, despite the thirty combat robots and Aaden Bauer's twenty-two Safe Earth resistance fighters, the two would be in deep trouble.

Hefting his SCAR-L assault rifle, he turned and made his way toward the stairwell that would take him to ground level. Now that Heather had gone deep, his immediate presence would serve no purpose, but up there he might be able to buy her extra time.

○ ● ○

Thousands upon thousands of images blossomed in Heather's head, threatening to knock her out of the trance into which she had descended. But she let it wash over her, allowing her mind to process the legion of perspective microviews into one coherent vision.

She willed the bots forward and, when some branches reached dead ends or encountered pathways that led away from their objective, redirected them along different paths. As the swarm advanced, a detailed 3-D map formed in her mind.

The first group entered the gateway cavern through a ceiling vent, followed almost immediately by another branch of the swarm entering through electrical outlets along the north wall. A rapidly expanding view of the cavern opened up before her. The size of three football fields, the monstrous equipment that formed the matter disrupter filled the western half of the facility. Thick supercooled power cables snaked through a latticework support structure toward the inverted horseshoe that formed the wormhole gate, while others were routed to what could only be the stasis field generator that Heather had seen when scanning the facility blueprints Nikina had provided.

But the focus of her attention was the extensive banks of equipment that formed the wormhole-gateway controller. Despite what she had seen and read in the design documents, the view startled her. Instead of gazing upon a futuristic layout, she was looking into the distant past.

Whereas, eight years ago, the Stephenson Gateway controller had been a hive of state-of-the-art computers, this was a monstrosity consisting of racks of wires and switches around which hundreds of scientists and technicians scurried, working through the checklists that would ensure everything was a go for the scheduled activation. The scene reminded Heather of the photographs she had seen of the crowd of old-school telephone operators, back when every call had to be manually switched.

A new vision formed in her mind of what the activation sequence would look like, dozens of scientists sitting in front of a long line of racks, each plugging the correctly colored cables into sockets whenever the LEDs beneath each of those sockets changed color. Toward those racks she sent her swarm, adjusting many paths so as to keep the scurrying micro-bots from attracting workers' attention.

She updated her estimate on how long it would take for a critical mass of micro-bots to reach the racks she was targeting. Thirteen minutes. Then another twenty-two to make the circuit modifications—if nothing went wrong. Heather started to slip into one of her near-future visions but forcibly extracted herself. The micro-bots needed all her attention.

Tonight the future would have to fend for itself.

○ ● ○

Mark walked up to the spot where Aaden and Nikina stood in conversation by the motorcycles, his eyes making out their shrouded forms backlit by the orange glow the fires of Hanau gave to the fog-shrouded sky. They turned to meet him, and he saw that, unlike him, they both wore IR night-vision goggles.

"How's the perimeter looking?"

"No problem so far."

"I've got bad news. Prokorov has dropped in several companies from the Third Ranger Battalion to perform area reconnaissance. They'll be widely spread out, hunting us in relatively small patrols in order to cover as much area as possible."

Aaden cursed, but Nikina retained her stoicism.

"How much longer is Heather going to need?" Aaden asked.

"Maybe forty-five minutes."

"Do you mind telling me what she's doing down there?"

"Screwing with the Frankfurt Gateway's control system."

Mark was grateful when the crackle of distant gunfire interrupted the conversation. He trusted Aaden, and Nikina had proved herself to be valuable, but the fewer people who knew the specifics of what Heather was doing the better. When the gunfire was answered by a much closer burst, Mark's gratitude faded.

Without a word, Aaden broke into a run through the skeletal structure, Mark and Nikina following. To his right, Mark could see one of the doglike robots bolt into the darkness, followed by six of its larger bipedal cousins.

Aaden brought them to a halt at the southeastern corner outpost. "Who was firing?" he yelled at the four men who crouched behind a low concrete wall.

"None of us," came the answer from the man in the center. "I think one of the robot patrols must have run into some bad guys."

As if to confirm his statement, a new round of firing erupted from the east, accompanied by the thump of grenades and an explosion that must have come from a shoulder-fired antitank weapon. That firing was answered by the glow of laser fire slicing through the fog. The distant yells of hard-fighting men and the screams of the dying echoed through the night.

One of the Ranger patrols had indeed stumbled onto some of the combat robots. And even though a single patrol wouldn't threaten this position, Mark knew that one or more of those Rangers was already reporting the engagement.

Mark focused on his SRT headset, sending the details of what was happening to Janet, who had no doubt already been informed by Robby what the telemetry from the engaged robots was telling him.

She didn't directly respond, but there was a sudden rush of movement as a half-dozen robots raced toward the fighting. Mark understood what she had just ordered: an attack to kill this patrol and then confront their inbound reinforcements before they could get closer to the Smythes.

"Spread out in groups of two!" Mark yelled, moving to a covered firing position several yards from the others.

He heard Nikina's distinctive Latvian accent as she settled in on the other side of the abutment where he lay prone.

"I think we're about to become very popular."

Mark didn't respond. His mental countdown told him the bad news. They had to hold here for at least another half hour. He let the stock of his SCAR-L settle into a firm cheek weld as his mind converted the battle echoes into imagery that penetrated the swirling fog far better than his enhanced eyesight could.

Then he felt the breeze out of the northwest, and his heart froze. A stiff wind was the death of fog. Not a sign of good things to come.

He took a deep breath and pulled forward the perfect memory of a favorite meditation, instantly acquiring the calm that dropped his heart rate to forty beats per minute.

Easy, Mark. We're not dead yet.

○ ● ○

Robby felt his desperation rising with every failed attempt by Eos to hack into the robots she had hardened against just such an intrusion. When his mom appeared through a virtual chat session, he jumped.

"Any progress with Eos?"

"None," he said, trying to give a calmness to his voice that he didn't feel.

"Mark says they've just come in contact with a Ranger patrol. The weather update says the freshening breeze will cause the fog to dissipate in the Hanau area within the next thirty minutes. We're out of time."

Great. What else could go wrong?

"We're doing our best," he said. "If Mark and Heather are in trouble, why haven't the robots turned around to go help them?"

"All of the robots are too far away to get back in time to make a difference," said Janet. "I want you and Eos to abandon the hack-a-robot attempt. Are there any attack aircraft in the area that you can take over?"

"There are, but they are disconnected from any military data links that might be hackable and are taking care not to send telemetry that could give us accurate positional information. Without precise coordinates, Eos can't target them with a subspace hack. Heather could probably do it, but she's not available to us."

"What about ground-based artillery systems?"

Robby could have kicked himself for not thinking of this. After all, the defenders had fired artillery at the robots during the early phase of the assault on the Frankfurt Gateway.

"Checking now," he said.

Eos shifted her attention from the robots to the defenses around the gateway, rapidly scanning the electronic systems arrayed around the gateway cavern. Robby felt her come alert as she zeroed in on a particular set of coordinates.

He felt his excitement rise as Eos identified the target.

"We've located a GPS-guided multiple-launch-rocket-system cluster on the southeastern edge of the Frankfurt Gateway compound. The three launchers can each blanket a square mile with almost eight thousand M77 submunitions in under forty seconds."

"Can Eos hack those fire-control systems?" asked Janet.

"I'll tell you in a second," Robby said, shifting his focus. "Eos, please tell me you can do this."

"They're emplaced and aren't moving. I have good coordinate locks. Taking charge of the fire control won't be a problem."

"How long will it take you?" Robby asked.

"Approximately three minutes fourteen seconds," said Eos.

Janet interrupted. "As soon as you've got all those MLRS launchers, I want the three grid squares, for which I'm sending you the coordinates, blanketed in steel. Mark and company will have to fend off the Rangers that are already too close, but we can put a hurt on any reinforcements from the east."

A new worry struck Robby. "Once we expend the missiles on those launchers, the crews won't reload them. And they'll try to manually cut the power to stop the volley of rockets once we start firing."

"It's why we'll only get one chance at this. Now get started."

"Already on it."

Robby felt Janet drop the link and shifted his attention to the work Eos was doing. In a few minutes he would be killing a bunch of

America's finest, all in the hopes of giving Mark and Heather a chance to finish and get out of there alive.

○ ● ○

Janet felt herself pulled into a memory of other times she had helped Heather kill American special operatives who were just doing their jobs. The first had been eight years ago at Jack's Bolivian hacienda when they had killed a platoon from SEAL Team 10. Less than a year ago, Robby and Heather had used another aircraft to kill three dozen Delta Force operators. Now she was using her son to kill Army Rangers. She was practically swimming in the blood of innocents and of those tasked with protecting them. And she didn't even have Jack at her side to reassure her that the ends justified such indiscriminate violence.

Janet inhaled deeply, then forced her thoughts back to the situation at hand. The time for recriminations would come. Now was the time to finish the acts that would make regret inevitable.

○ ● ○

Deep inside the Frankfurt Gateway cavern, the swarms of micro-bots moved with the speed of ants toward their targets, all directed by the power of Heather's mind. And as they spread out and began converging on the top and rear of the extensive collection of rack-mounted equipment that composed the gateway controller, her view of the system of electronics began to fill in.

A technician moving along a catwalk on the south side of the cavern caught the toe of his shoe on the steel grating and tumbled outward, barely managing to catch the railing as he flipped over. His feet scrabbled desperately for a foothold, kicking a bundle of cables beneath the walkway, dislodging the hundreds of micro-bots that moved along it, sending them sifting downward like a thin curtain of dust toward the cavern floor forty feet below.

Heather shifted her focus, issuing the terminate command to all those that fell, causing each of those tiny bots to curl inward and switch itself off so that they were almost indistinguishable from fine sand or dirt. The workers who looked up in horror at the technician who struggled to regain the catwalk blinked and stepped back from the falling dust as they tried to keep their eyes focused on the struggling man above.

As the technician's hand began to slip, another worker reached him, grasped his arm and lab coat, and hoisted him back up. A loud cheer went up from those who had seen the nearly fatal fall. The handful who had been almost directly below him wiped away the dust that the faller had sent sifting down onto their heads and shoulders, then patted each other on the backs and went back to their own tasks.

The small disaster added to Heather's workload when she was already almost at her maximum, the net effect leaving her dazed and exhausted. She bore down, restoring her focus on getting as many of the micro-bots as possible into the inner workings of the gateway control system. As the machines spread throughout the interior of the equipment, she was relieved to see that, although there were minor variances from the design diagrams, she would not have to make extensive changes to the electrical modifications.

Distantly she felt her body shake as tremors shook the parking structure in which she sat. But she shunted that aside and went to work, sending the micro-bots scurrying to rewire key circuits within the stasis field generator. They cut through certain electrical traces and then linked together to form new conductive paths, thereby changing the way the circuits functioned. The intention wasn't to disable the machine, but to make it appear fully functional, capable of passing all diagnostic tests. In the process, she even corrected preexisting errors in the circuitry that would have resulted in test failure and circuit-card replacement.

As Heather finished with each section of equipment, she sent miscellaneous micro-bots to create new circuits to the floor beneath the racks, where they curled into dust particles and shut themselves down.

Just as she was finishing the last trace, she felt a powerful hand on her shoulder and heard Mark's loud voice in her ear.

"Time's up. Gotta go now!"

Although his meaning registered, she shook off his hand and spent an additional thirty-seven seconds finishing up and shutting down the remaining micro-bots.

The cacophony of nearby explosions, mixed with the screams of dying men and women, finally pulled her from her trance.

○　●　○

Mark lifted Heather to her feet as her eyes shifted back to their natural deep brown. But when he released her, she staggered and would have fallen had he not reached out.

"We've got to go now!" he yelled over the sound of combat just outside the stairway that led up to ground level.

When she drew her Glock and ran for the stairwell, Mark breathed a sigh of relief, pulled the safety pin, and set a thermite grenade atop the specialized communications gear. Then he raced after her. Reaching the top of the stairs, he leveled his SCAR-L and followed it around the corner to the covered position beside the parked motorcycles where Aaden, Nikina, and Heather knelt. Behind an adjacent pile of concrete blocks, a group of five of the dog-bots, each with a full load of the crab bombs attached to their bodies, stood waiting to be deployed.

"Aaden. Status?" Mark yelled.

"I have three men penned down inside that far corner of the building. We still have a handful of robots fighting out beyond the compound walls, but they won't be able to hold off the Rangers for much longer. It's now or never."

Heather looked at the dog-bots. "And those?"

"They're going to punch a hole for you two to get out. Nikina will accompany you."

"What about you?" Nikina asked.

"I'm going for my men. We'll be right behind you . . . or we won't."

Mark glanced around the corner and could see the muzzle flashes from a heavy automatic weapon, sending tracers streaking through the dissipating fog.

"Okay," he said, motioning toward the cycles. "Let us get mounted up and then let the robots run."

Mark, Heather, and Nikina each climbed onto motorcycles and switched them on, the thrum of their idling engines echoing through the concrete shell of the building. The flash of a nearby explosion illuminated the left side of Aaden's face, which was covered in blood.

"Who let the dogs out?" The big German grinned. "That would be me."

He spoke into a small device, and the five robots burst into action, exiting the building and then spreading out as they raced southeast toward the nearest machine-gun positions. A shoulder-fired rocket streaked toward the middle dog-bot as it released its magnetically attached crab bombs, sending them scuttling forward even as it exploded into chunks of flying shrapnel.

Then the other dogs reached the forward Ranger positions and loosed their crab bombs to seek and destroy while they raced on toward other targets. Mark's heart pounded in his chest as adrenaline brought his senses to crystal clarity.

"Follow me!" Heather yelled, sliding her SRT headset over her temples.

As the wheels of her cycle left a smoking trail of rubber on the concrete floor, that's exactly what Mark did, with Nikina's bike screeching out behind him. He again placed his faith in the abilities of this exceptional woman to lead him through the chaos of the night.

○ ● ○

Janet stared at the situational-awareness display and activated the virtual chat session, connecting her to Robby, Jamal, and Eileen.

"Mark and Heather are on the move. Now I need some of that hacker magic you guys brag about to help get them back to our Earth gate."

"We can't give you control of the robots," Robby said.

"I don't care what it is; I need something."

Jamal Glover's voice carried its usual cocky undertone. "How about a self-driving-car demolition derby?"

The image those words put into Janet's mind brought a smile to her lips. "Focus on unoccupied vehicles."

"Got it," Jamal said. "Won't matter if they're awaiting fares or just parked; Eileen and I can send them anywhere and at whatever speed we want."

"Heather is wearing her headset, so you can use that to track her location. I want anybody chasing them intercepted right now."

"Okay, Jamal," Eileen said, "prepare to watch and learn."

"Funny," he replied.

"Robby," said Janet, "I need you and Eos to redirect every available satellite feed of the Hanau area to my situation room. Make the satellites go dark for everyone else. Can you do that?"

"No problem," he said, sounding happy to have another opportunity to redeem himself.

As the group moved into their cyber-warfare mode, Janet withdrew from the chat session and returned to the map that provided her real-time situational overview. The graphic included imagery from the few surviving robots and drones, but with any luck, the map would soon come alive with satellite feeds hijacked from the four UFNS member nations.

Fortunately, the robots that continued to rampage through the city of Hanau, battling police and the German military, would avoid the Smythe facility there. And since the Earth gate had its own cold-fusion power supply, the widespread power outages would have no impact on its operation. With Heather about ten minutes out from the Hanau Trans-Shipping warehouse where the Earth gate waited, the sooner Janet's team of elite hackers got their act in gear, the happier she would be.

○ ● ○

As Mark banked hard onto the southbound lane of German Highway 45 headed toward Hanau, he watched in amazement as hundreds of cars and trucks headed directly toward them, filling both the north and southbound lanes.

But Heather refused to throttle down, and he and Nikina maintained the pace. As they raced toward the wall of death metal approaching from the south, Mark envisioned a giant game of chicken—three birds on one side and five hundred on the other—and felt himself grinning wildly. His savant was a serious badass. When the vehicles headed north parted to allow them passage, it barely surprised him.

Black magic.

○ ● ○

Alexandr Prokorov stared at the video wall in disbelief.

"Where did my satellite imagery go?"

General Zherdev picked up the phone, his square face having acquired the countenance of an angry bear. By the time he ended the conversation and hung up, his apparent mood hadn't improved.

"It's not just these. Hackers have just taken down all satellite feeds of the Frankfurt and Hanau area. And I mean for every satellite that could provide video or still imagery."

Prokorov cursed, tempted to kick over a chair. "The Smythes!"

The phone's ringtone sounded, and General Zherdev punched a button to put it on speaker.

"What now?"

The voice of the military intelligence captain sounded rattled.

"Sir, we've just received a report of hundreds of vehicles charging into the military and police vehicles in pursuit of the three motorcycles that escaped through the Ranger lines."

"What do you mean, 'charging into'?" asked Prokorov.

"I mean they are intentionally crashing into or blocking the path of the pursuing vehicles. What's more, these vehicles all appear to be unoccupied."

"What about aerial pursuit?"

"A Black Hawk helicopter with thirteen Rangers aboard followed them to an industrial complex on the north side of Hanau. The three cycles disappeared into one of the warehouses."

Prokorov terminated the call and turned to face Zherdev. "General, have the Rangers on that chopper secure that industrial park. I want those three individuals captured alive."

"Yes, sir."

"And get some reinforcements headed that way. Now that we've got them cornered, I don't want to lose them again."

As the general picked up the phone to issue his orders, Prokorov looked at the blank screens on the situation wall.

Not this time, Smythes, he thought. *Tonight you are mine.*

○ ● ○

Heather skidded to a stop inside the warehouse, twelve yards in front of the inactive Earth gate, Mark and Nikina screeching to a halt beside her. The whoop of the circling helicopter lent wings to Heather's feet as she sprinted toward the switches that would power up the cold-fusion reactor and send a subspace signal to New Zealand, requesting remote gateway activation.

Janet had already informed her that Robby was standing by in the master control station for the primary Earth gate, ready to initiate its sequence as soon as Heather initialized the one on this end.

She heard the squeal of metal as Mark triggered the app on his cell phone to close the warehouse door through which they just entered. Reaching the control station, she initiated the power-up sequence to bring the cold-fusion reactor to full power. The process would take just over two minutes. Unfortunately, the helicopter overhead sounded like a Black Hawk, and that meant it was carrying a cargo load of pissed-off Army Rangers who were most likely fast-roping down right now.

Mark and Nikina took up covering positions behind a nearby fork-lift. Heather focused her attention on the gradually rising power levels. If the Rangers came a-knocking before the gateway activated, her team's only chance would be the trapdoor covering the bolt-hole leading down to the half-mile-long escape tunnel. But then the Rangers would be right behind. Even if the Smythes and Nikina managed to reach the far end of the tunnel, by that time, choppers would be swarming the skies, watching for them to reemerge.

Not a scenario Heather wanted to try out.

○ ● ○

"Screw it," Janet said, sliding into the cursed SRT headset and the mind trip it generated.

She had only tried using the headset on one previous occasion, and it had scared her more than an acid trip. Having vivid, waking dreams pumped into her head threatened to produce an addiction. The effect was enhanced by her thoughts dictating the scenario: one second she could be standing at the top of Mount Kilimanjaro, and the next she could be in a running gun battle through the streets of Cairo. Even though she didn't really move while using the headset, the link between the computer and sensation centers in her brain were superb, with almost no discernible difference between the virtual world and reality. For God's sake, she could be with Jack again anytime she wanted. Delving into her memories, the computer would fill in the details of whatever scenario she desired.

The loss of Jack had robbed Janet of the self-discipline she had spent a lifetime honing. Right now she really needed it back.

So she focused on the enhanced satellite feed of the ongoing activity within the Hanau Trans-Shipping industrial park. As a door gunner provided cover, a dozen U.S. Army Rangers fast-lined to the ground and then raced to surround the vast central warehouse.

That was good news since it meant their orders were to secure the perimeter and prevent the three warehouse occupants from escaping, without immediately moving in for an assault. But that also meant more help was inbound.

She shifted her focus, mentally scanning all the satellite video feeds. Sure enough, three more Black Hawks were rapidly closing on the compound. And these guys would be the assault team. Worse, they were less than a minute out.

"Eileen," Janet said, having to focus on speaking mentally.

"Yes?"

"I need you to buy Heather some time. We still have three trucks in the Hanau Trans-Shipping compound. Get them moving, and throw in any other distraction you two can come up with."

"We're on it."

Janet turned her attention to the power readout being transmitted from the remote Earth gate. Fifty-seven percent.

"Come on, Mr. Fusion," she breathed. "Get your ass in gear."

○ ● ○

Ranger lieutenant Kurt Landow prepared to lead his platoon's assault on the warehouse, watching through NVGs as Staff Sergeant Vasquez placed the explosive charge on the locked office door. As soon as Vasquez backed off and blew the door, Kurt would lead second squad in an assault through the opening while first and third squads provided cover.

But as Vasquez ran to a covered position, Kurt heard a big diesel engine rumble to life.

"What the hell?"

As if in answer, an eighteen-wheeler squealed around the corner of a distant warehouse and accelerated directly toward the troops.

Kurt spoke two words into his jawbone mike: "Kill it."

From his left, he heard the whoosh from the recoilless rifle as a high explosive, dual-purpose round left the barrel of the antitank weapon. The shot streaked seventy yards and impacted the truck's grill, obliterating the engine and cab and sending the trailer careening into the wall of an adjacent building. Smoke from the explosion chased spinning chunks of metal into the firelit sky.

Suddenly every light in the industrial park turned on, erasing the predawn darkness and washing out Kurt's view through the NVGs. As he tried to come to grips with how this was happening despite the city-wide power outage, fire alarms blared from every building in the park. The racket augmented the sensory storm that assaulted his Ranger platoon, masking the sound of the semi that crashed through the remnants of the destroyed rig and hurtled directly toward his position.

"Shit!"

As gunfire crackled through the night, his men scrambled to get clear of this new truck's path. Lieutenant Landow grabbed the arm of the corporal to his left and pulled him into a run, just as the truck swerved so hard that it rolled over onto its side, plowing through the place where, only seconds before, second squad had been set for assault.

With the roar of another truck sounding in the distance, Kurt muttered, "Screw this," and issued the order he came here to give.

"Vasquez, blow the door. We're going in."

○ ● ○

The rumble of explosions, gunfire, and crashing trucks was almost drowned out by the blaring horn of the warehouse alarm.

Mark yelled at Heather. "Power level?"

"Ninety-three percent."

"Close enough."

"No," she said. "Any less than ninety-seven and the gate could fail and kill us all. We're twenty seconds out."

An explosion from within the office put him in motion. He climbed onto the forklift and started driving it toward the office door.

"Nikina, cover me."

The operative dropped to a knee and began riddling the inner door with bullets, pausing only to swap magazines. Mark raised the forklift's twin prongs, bringing the vehicle to a halt with the prongs up against the door, holding it closed.

Then he leaped off and sprinted back toward Heather as the Earth gate activated.

"Let's go!" yelled Heather, who began firing her Glock at the closed office door.

The trio sprinted out of Hanau and into the New Zealand Earth-gate laboratory.

Sliding to a stop beside Janet, Mark yelled at Robby. "Blow the far gate!"

When nothing happened, Mark rushed to where Robby sat. "Detonate it! We can't just deactivate the gate and let them capture it."

"I'm trying," said Robby. "The self-destruct isn't working."

Mark grabbed his last thermite grenade from his utility vest and turned toward the still-open portal. But before he could begin his run, Nikina grabbed his arm.

"Give it to me. I'll do it."

"No."

"Don't be stupid. You're too important to the movement. I'll get out through the bolt-hole."

"She's right," said Janet. "Give it to her."

Another loud explosion echoed into the lab from the Hanau warehouse. With a curse, Mark handed Nikina the grenade and his quantum-entangled phone.

"Put it on top of the Earth-gate controller," said Heather.

Nikina nodded and sprinted back through the gateway to disappear from view around its right side. Then, with a loud crackle and pop, the remote Earth gate winked out.

Mark continued to stare at the bare wall where the Hanau warehouse had been only a moment before. The sense of loss hit him. Aaden gone. Nikina gone. The German Safe Earth resistance decimated. Untold thousands of German civilians dead. And they didn't know if the modifications Heather had made to the Frankfurt Gateway would destroy the portal.

His memory pulled him back to a time before he had become a killer. Using their unnatural muscle control to put disguising age lines on their faces, he and Heather had climbed into the car that would take them in search of Jennifer. On the radio, a British singer had crooned "Maggie May." When he'd reached the verse about the morning sun really showing her age, Mark and Heather had broken into laughter that brought tears to their eyes.

Mark blinked away that memory of one of their last moments of innocence. Suddenly he felt Heather's arm slip through his so that she could grasp his hand with hers. For several minutes the two of them stood side by side. At some point during their silent memorial, Janet and Robby left them alone in the big room. When Mark finally turned to look down at Heather's tear-streaked face, he saw an exhaustion that went far beyond the physical.

"Ah, my love," he said, drawing her eyes to his, "tell me it's all going to be worth it."

The ghost of a smile tried to lift the corners of her lips and failed. Mark leaned down and gently kissed them. Then they turned away and slowly walked back into their own secret world.

○ ● ○

Inside the Hanau warehouse, Nikina lifted the trapdoor as the thermite grenade hissed and crackled as it ate its way through the Earth-gate power supply. From across the warehouse, the sound of running feet was accompanied by a yell.

"Freeze!"

Nikina froze, letting her H&K fall from her fingers to clatter on the concrete floor. Strong hands grabbed her roughly from behind and slammed her facedown on the floor. In seconds her hands were zip-cuffed tightly behind her back. She knew that these were professional grade, immune to the zip-tie-breaking and picking tricks that charlatans pitched to the public in their paid personal-combat courses.

After being thoroughly frisked and having all weapons and other possessions removed and bagged, she was hauled to her feet and half carried between two Rangers as another followed with a gun leveled at her back. She wasn't certain, but she had a pretty good idea where they were taking her. This was just the beginning of what had already become a very long day.

Nothing new about that.

○ ● ○

Prokorov stepped into the interrogation room and motioned for the guards to leave.

"I want to talk to this prisoner alone."

They nodded and walked out, closing the door behind them.

Prokorov glanced around. As he had instructed, the prisoner had been brought to a room that wasn't monitored. Here there was no one-way mirror with observers on the far side, and there were no microphones or recording devices. His people had swept the area to make sure. There was only a metal table with two metal chairs on opposite sides. He seated himself across from the prisoner, her hands manacled to a belt chain.

Galina had disappointed him. The Rangers had reported seeing her run out of the Smythe gateway from a large room on the far side. Prokorov met the gaze of her ice-gray eyes. She stared back at him.

"Hello, Galina," said Prokorov, keeping his face impassive.

"Alexandr," she replied.

"Last night," Prokorov said, letting accusation creep into his tone, "you were inside the Smythe facility with a chance to remain there, and you failed to seize the opportunity to remain there. Why?"

"Overeagerness breeds distrust. By taking the actions I took, I demonstrated loyalty to the Smythes and to the Safe Earth resistance, and I salvaged some important technology for you."

Prokorov paused to consider this. As much as he hungered to know the location of the Smythes' secret compound, Galina had a point. Patience was the key to penetrating the Smythes' inner circle.

"You damaged the Smythes' Hanau gateway."

"No. The Smythe Earth gate is in fully functional condition. I merely destroyed its power supply instead of the gateway controller as the Smythes wanted me to do. It uses something they call a subspace receiver-transmitter to communicate with the master gateway. Even though the wormhole can only be initiated by the master station inside the Smythe facility, your people should be able to glean some of its secrets."

"We'll see." Prokorov leaned forward to rest his elbows on the small table. "The cell phone the Rangers took from you has some modifications that our people haven't figured out."

"It's quantum entangled with one of the Smythe phones."

"What can you tell me about the Smythe facility?"

"Not much. I went through the gateway into a big room that had obviously been excavated from solid rock. It had a larger version of the gateway, but I didn't have much of a chance to look over the rest of the equipment. Once I escape from your custody, I'll have the credibility to find out more."

Prokorov glanced down at her shackles. "That will happen tonight, while you are being transported to another secure facility. I'll start making the arrangements."

"How many guards will I have to kill?"

"I'll provide you the details later today. In the meantime, try to get some rest. I'll have you put into an isolation cell until you can be transported."

"Sounds lovely."

Prokorov stood and walked to the door, rapping on it smartly with his knuckles. When the door opened, he turned to the German army captain in charge.

"I want this prisoner transferred to an isolation cell. No one is to speak with her without my direct authorization. Is that clear?"

"Yes, sir."

"Good."

Prokorov walked out of the building and stepped into his waiting sedan. He had finally put a chink in the Smythe armor. And when Galina was free once again, she would make sure to render their defenses useless.

: CHAPTER 41

Jack stood at the prow of the fishing vessel, *Dark Promise*, with Captain Moros at his side, staring across the undulating sea toward the band of islands silhouetted against Altreia's magenta orb.

He wore a black uniform of his own design. Fashioned after a typical biker's outfit on Earth, the outfit had calf-high boots with square toes, black pants, shirt, and jacket of the same material, but without a Hell's Angels logo emblazoned on the back. The carbon nano-fiber weave was supple, but with far greater tensile strength than Kevlar. The fabric revealed the muscles that rippled beneath with every movement. The overall effect was enhanced by the twin ivory blades strapped to both thighs and the pulse blaster holstered on his left side. Jack liked the look.

His thoughts turned to Janet and Robby and all the light-years that separated him from his family. If the coup that he was about to attempt was successful, he would soon be holding them in his human arms. That thought sent a pulse of longing up his spine before he pushed it back into his subconscious. He couldn't afford to think of them. Not until he had accomplished the task he had set for himself and his followers, the Twice Bound.

As the *Dark Promise* shifted beneath his feet, he returned his gaze to the sea. With the hull tank full of freshly caught fish, the boat peeled off from the fishing fleet to embark on the last leg of its merchant voyage. The Parthian's thousands of occupants loved their fresh seafood, and over the cycles that he had been doing this, Moros and his crew made this run hundreds of times. But today they would be delivering something extra: The Ripper. And this time Jack wouldn't let Khal Teth interfere.

The ongoing distractions created by the Twice Bound resistance movement on the Basrillan continent had drawn the focus of the Altreian military. But none of the trouble had spread to the band of islands that formed Quol's prime meridian, or anywhere near the Parthian. Events were unfolding just as Jack intended.

"You want to enter the Parthian alone?" Moros asked. "That be a terrible idea."

Jack looked down at the smaller Altreian and nodded. "It's my way. Besides, I need you and your men to be ready to execute your part of this mission."

"You be too muscular, and in that uniform, you no longer look like Dhaldric."

"To them I will."

Moros stepped back, studying him skeptically, and Jack performed one of the mind tricks he had absorbed during the weeks that he'd shared Khal Teth's mind.

Captain Moros's eyes widened in disbelief.

"I'm not at all myself today, now am I?" asked Jack.

"Hand me a deck broom and call me squab," said Moros.

Letting the illusion drop from Moros's mind, Jack grinned and placed a hand on his friend's shoulder.

"Never fear, my good captain. A new day is coming for this world."

Moros shook his head slowly and turned away, his final words following him back onto the bridge.

"There be no doubt of that. Whether you or I be there to see it? That be the question."

As Jack turned his gaze back to the beautiful horizon, he couldn't blame his small friend for asking.

○ ● ○

Parsus left the meeting of the High Council and returned to his chambers, dissatisfied. He might be the overlord, but that didn't mean he got to dictate government action. In the past, he had never had a problem recruiting enough of the high lords to form a sufficient power bloc to make policy. But the rise of the Twice Bound resistance and the subsequent string of sabotage attacks on government facilities had produced dissension on the High Council. They felt threatened, and blamed him for failure to put an end to these activities.

What concerned Parsus the most was the correlation between the rise of the Twice Bound and Khal Teth's return from his mind prison. Despite reassuring himself again and again that Khal Teth could not possibly have survived the explosion at sea and that the barbarian leader of the Twice Bound was nothing like his twin brother, his growing dread persisted.

Now there were reports that some of the Dhaldric had become Twice Bound. Again he struggled to understand how this could be happening on the Altreian Empire's home world. The phenomenon reminded Parsus of religious movements that swept primitive societies, as if a messiah had arrived to free his people. But if the leader of the Twice Bound was a god, he was the god of war. No, not a description that applied to Khal Teth in any way.

Fortunately, the empire had managed to turn a few of the Twice Bound into double agents. The Twice Bound's strength was also its weakness. As the dual bonding was truly voluntary, each new member added their strength to the power of the group. But since the bonding was based on free will, they had no mental minders watching the thoughts of each member. And any such organization had weak links who could be tempted or threatened into cooperation once their identity had been discovered.

Still, concern remained, thus why Parsus had judiciously sprinkled the Parthian with seekers. These rare Dhaldric had only minor psionic power, but they had developed an unusual mutation: they could see through the mind shrouding of any psionic who invaded their personal space, which extended for roughly a body's length around each seeker. The power of the other psionic made no difference.

Seekers could not determine the other's identity if they didn't know that person, but illusions would nonetheless slip away. And since this was a passive ability, other psionics were completely unaware that they had passed through a seeker's personal space. The mutation had arisen during the thousands of cycles after Khal Teth had been imprisoned.

But why should that matter? Khal Teth was dead.

Parsus shifted his thoughts, manipulating the controls that adjusted his outer-wall and ceiling transparency, making them completely disappear. Clasping his hands behind his back, he strode to the center of the gentle curve that faced the mighty orb of Altreia, resting on the star-filled horizon. The view was the reason he left the wall completely unadorned. Its peace filled his spirit, leaching away dull, aching dread.

Khal Teth's escape had been an ill omen. Surely it was no more than that.

○ ● ○

Captain Moros expertly guided the *Dark Promise* into the dock, watching as the magnetic tethers secured the boat in place, giving it the freedom to rise and fall with the swells but keeping the hull a near-constant distance from the hard surface. He didn't know why The Ripper's plan left him so uneasy. Over and over again, the Twice Bound leader had proved his power and loyalty.

Maybe Moros felt uneasy because the plan relied on so many moving parts working in perfect synchronicity. At The Ripper's signal, Moros would make the radio call, which would set the fishing fleet into motion, sending hundreds of distant vessels racing toward the Parthian. They wouldn't have to travel far. Just get close enough to bring the minds of the Twice Bound they carried within range of The Ripper's, suddenly adding their strength to his.

In the meantime, Moros just had to go about his merchant duties, selling his holdful of fish to the highest bidder among the fishmongers who roamed these docks.

Through the bridge's transparent walls, he looked at The Ripper, who appeared to be the uniformed port official who had come aboard the *Dark Promise* to perform an inspection of its cargo. That port official now lay bound and unconscious belowdecks. The Dhaldric's death would have been felt by his bond master, so he had to remain alive.

Moros walked down the gangplank and onto the dock, glancing up at the monstrous bulk of the Parthian, beneath which this dock lay. To think of The Ripper walking alone into that den of sea snakes sent a shiver up his back. Yelling instructions to his crew, Moros turned and followed his leader off the dock. There he paused to watch as The Ripper disappeared into the milling crowd, hoping with all his might that this would not be the last he would ever see of this being who had allowed Captain Moros to taste the pride that only freedom could deliver.

○ ● ○

During the long months since Khal Teth had allowed himself to be subjugated in his own body, he had felt his frustration gathering like a tropical storm. In the half orbday that remained before Dorial once again poked its fiery head above the horizon, his situation would change once and for all. The deal that he had made with Jack Gregory would send this human mind back to its own body for good.

Khal Teth could take his body back whenever he wanted. But Jack Gregory had been the one to bond with all those who called themselves the Twice Bound, and during those brief intervals when Jack had returned primary control to Khal Teth, the power of that bond weakened greatly. So Khal Teth had been forced to cooperate with Jack's attempts to access the psionic powers of his Dhaldric brain.

The Ripper learned fast. And even though he was nowhere close to attaining the mastery that Khal Teth enjoyed, Jack's skill represented a rapidly rising threat. If his learning continued in such a fashion, there might come a point where Khal Teth could no longer take charge of his own body unless Jack allowed it.

So, as he watched Jack move through the crowd, adopting the appearance of whomever he wanted while shielding his mind from probes by others, Khal Teth forced himself to be patient. His chance was coming.

○ ● ○

Jack stepped into the turbo-lift, using a subtle mental push to make others wait, allowing him to enter and depart alone. He used the ride upward to scan the Parthian for the location of two specific Altreians: Parsus and High Lord Shabett. The second he merely wanted to avoid running into along his path to his primary target.

When he stepped out of the lift on the top level, he did so cloaked in the sultry image of Shabett. To the eyes of the Khyre workers and Dhaldric officials that he passed, he wore the sexy chartreuse gown that she favored.

As he turned into the inner hallway that would eventually take him to the swooping perimeter hallway, a lower-level Dhaldric official performed a double take. High Lord Shabett loved to create such an effect, but for some reason the reaction bothered Jack. But the official had disappeared around the corner without taking further notice, so Jack shrugged off the feeling. He was working hard enough to maintain the illusion and his mental shield while monitoring Parsus and the real Shabett that he couldn't spare the extra energy to delve deeply into the minds of all those he passed. At least not while almost all of his Twice Bound remained beyond his psionic range.

The more Twice Bound that were within his psionic range, the more the increased power they provided extended that range. At present, Captain Moros and his crew were the only Twice Bound available to Jack. At his signal, Moros would call in allies, but that sudden movement of the fishing fleet would draw the attention of the senior officers in the Parthian's military-operations center. And they would alert Parsus and the other members of the High Council.

So Jack needed to wait until the timing was just right. First he wanted to pay his respects to Overlord Parsus.

○ ● ○

The message from one of his seekers brought Parsus to high alert. The Dhaldric barbarian whom the Twice Bound called The Ripper had been spotted on this level of the Parthian in the guise of High Lord Shabett. Slick. The intruder took on a guise that would have succeeded in deceiving Parsus into allowing The Ripper into his presence. From the behaviors the barbarian had previously displayed, violence would have ensued.

Parsus issued a number of mental commands, then leaned back into the comfortable couch that occupied the elevated portion of his audience chamber.

The Twice Bound movement was about to meet its end.

○ ● ○

The *Dark Promise*'s engineer, Drogo, retrieved his bag from beneath his bunk, reached inside, and extracted a rectangular hand-sized device that he tucked inside his tunic. Then, with a quick look outside the crewmen's berth, he made his way to the stairs that led down to the ship's engine room.

As he entered the machine-filled space, ship's crewman Koloth looked up to meet him, her wide eyes questioning.

"Is this not your break?" she asked.

"I ate. Take your turn."

Crewman Koloth acquiesced and set the tool she had been using down atop the leftmost of the hydro-jet engines. Before Drogo could change his mind, she made her way out of the engine room.

Drogo watched her climb the steps that led to the next deck, then made his way to the aft, where the jet nozzles exited the compartment.

As he knelt to place the device between those nozzles, he hesitated. Could he really betray his captain? Betray his people? He looked down at his hands and willed them to stop shaking.

Those Dhaldric demons had taken his wife and three children. This was the act that would save them, even if it meant they and the other Twice Bound would go back to the way things had been before the coming of The Ripper. But had that been so bad? No. He had been stupid to think that the Twice Bound could make a difference.

With a deep breath, Drogo flicked on the switch that electromagnetically attached the device to the hull. Then he reached for the button that would snuff out his worthless life and rob the Twice Bound of their vengeance.

○ ● ○

Having finished making the deal that would result in the off-loading of his hold and a nice deposit into his merchant account, Moros headed back toward the dock, where his boat awaited its captain. Right now all he needed to do was to return to the *Dark Promise* and await The Ripper's order to send the communication that would summon the distant fishing fleet.

But as he stepped onto the dock, an explosive shock wave dropped him on his back. He looked up to see a cloud of smoke from which the flying chunks of debris that had been the *Dark Promise* hurtled forth. All along the dock, the torn bodies of the dead lay scattered among the writhing, screaming forms of the wounded.

A warm wetness ran down the left side of his face, blurring his vision. When he attempted to rise, a wave of dizziness assailed him, accompanied by a wave of sorrow. Worse than the loss of his beloved *Dark Promise* was the knowledge that he would fail The Ripper. Without the communications gear on his vessel, he could not relay the message to the fishing fleet.

Finally, managing to rise, he was almost knocked back down by one of the emergency personnel who rushed onto the dock. As sirens echoed through the hovercraft bay, Captain Moros lifted his eyes to the massive edifice that formed the roof above him. Somewhere up there, the leader of the Twice Bound moved among their enemies.

As of a few moments ago, The Ripper was truly on his own.

○ ● ○

As he walked along the beautiful arc of the Parthian's outer walkway, Jack felt the loss of all but one of the Twice Bound crew of the *Dark Promise*, followed by the rumble of a distant explosion. Almost immediately, alarm Klaxons sounded throughout the Parthian. Coming to a stop as panicked Altreians raced past him, he turned to look out through the transparent wall at the expanse of sea. Since the docks were beneath the Parthian, the *Dark Promise* wasn't visible to his eyes, but when his mind reached out to Moros, he could see the devastation through those of the captain.

Moros was injured and disoriented, so Jack sent him a soothing thought. "Captain Moros. Get yourself some medical attention, and don't worry about me."

"But the fleet—"

"The fleet was always a fallback plan. I'll be fine without it."

Refocusing his attention on the critical task that lay just ahead, Jack dropped his mental link with Moros. He squeezed his fists so tight that his knuckles popped, and he resumed his path toward the overlord's chambers. The Ripper would have to do this the old-fashioned way after all.

○ ● ○

Parsus could not sense the mind of the one called The Ripper, but his seekers informed him of the barbarian's progress toward his chambers, still draped in the illusion of High Lord Shabett. So intensely were the overlord's eyes focused on his door that he barely noticed the low rumble and slight tremor that vibrated up through the floor and into his feet. The alarm Klaxon and the accompanying mental update from the military operations center changed that.

Sabotage had finally reared its ugly head in the very bowels of the Parthian.

The explosive hadn't been a big one, just enough to destroy a single fishing boat without producing significant damage to the hovercraft bay. The vessel had to have been small not to have triggered the detectors that scanned all inbound and outbound craft. The fact that this distraction had happened even as The Ripper strode these halls could be no coincidence.

The Ripper was not the only one with the power to hide minds from outside scrutiny. And now he was about to come up against the best that the Altreian Empire had to offer. Parsus was more than ready for him.

○ ● ○

As he stumbled along with the crowd of the dazed and confused walking wounded, Moros thought about what The Ripper had told him. *Take care of yourself . . . Don't worry about me . . . I'm fine*, or words to that effect. In all the cycles he had been captain of the *Dark Promise*, he had learned that if something looked like fish dung and smelled like fish dung, you didn't need to taste it to be certain. And even though he couldn't see it, The Ripper's reassurance smelled like fish dung.

He stopped, turned around, and began moving against the flow of people leaving the docks. He didn't head for the dock where the *Dark Promise* had blown up, but toward the second one to its right. Along the way he was stopped twice by well-meaning officials who attempted to direct him toward medical assistance. But when he showed his identity badge, informing them that he was the captain of the *Green Fin*, a fishing vessel that was docked there, and explained that ship's procedure after any serious incident was for all hands to assemble on deck, he was allowed to continue. The well-established practice that enabled a captain to account for every member of his crew proved invaluable.

But instead of the fishing boats, Moros headed for the small seaguard hovercraft that had been dry-docked for maintenance. Since all of the maintenance personnel had been evacuated from the docks, nobody was near the vessel. With a quick glance around, Captain Moros hopped aboard and ducked into the bridge.

Biometric recognition was normally required in order to power up the hovercraft's systems. But this boat was in maintenance mode, which allowed those working on the vessel to power up to perform tests and make repairs. He couldn't start the engines, but engaging the engines in dry dock was rarely a good idea. Luckily he was after something else.

Moros switched on the power for the subspace radio, surprised to see how his hands shook as he adjusted the settings and tuned in to the desired channel. He glanced down. Where had all that blood come from? Then he remembered his head wound, and that thought unleashed a wave of dizziness that narrowed his vision. Shock.

He gritted his teeth and continued, desperately aware of the passage of time. If one person of authority passed by and glanced into the hovercraft, the game would come to a rapid end. If this had been one of the fancy starships, its AI would have linked with the captain's mind and helped him. Instead, Moros somehow had to gather the focus to do something he used to know but now couldn't quite recall.

But then his fog cleared long enough for him to lock in the final settings, and he gasped with relief as the video connection happened.

The man at the far end looked as frazzled as he felt.

"Moros? What happen to you?" asked Captain Jantho.

"Sabotage. Best guess, a crew-member betrayal."

Jantho issued a string of curses.

Moros interrupted him. "Time to move the fleet closer."

The darkness in Jantho's look increased the tightness in Captain Moros's chest.

"Would that I could. We have a traitor of our own. The sea slime sent a message to military command and we be attacked from the air. A third of the fleet lost before the remainder could submerge and disperse."

The news robbed Moros of his breath. "Can you get nobody to come?"

There was a brief silence on the line as Captain Jantho rubbed his chin. "I come. Maybe others, though I know not how many."

With growing despair clouding his vision, Moros wiped the blood from his eyes. "Gather those who be able, and make haste. The balance be weighted against us."

Jantho inclined his head, and then the connection died.

As he powered down the equipment, a new voice snapped his head around.

"Who are you and what are you doing on my boat?"

If he had any luck at all, Moros would have now faced a returning member of the maintenance crew. Instead, he now found himself facing a Dhaldric sea-guard captain and his ensign, both of whom held pulse blasters leveled at the captain's chest. Before he could answer, Moros's tenuous grasp on consciousness faded away. He never felt himself hit the deck.

○ ● ○

Jack felt the group of guards approaching from ahead before they rounded the gentle curve to become visible. He considered killing them, but that would lead to a violent confrontation with Parsus. And he couldn't afford to kill Parsus. Not yet. Not until he extracted what he needed from within the overlord's mind. But these men and women were definitely aware of his disguise and were advancing toward him with bad intent, weapons drawn. And without the presence of the Twice Bound, he wouldn't be able to overcome the psionic help Parsus could give them.

As much as he hated to do this, he had to turn the situation over to the only one who could.

○ ● ○

At last.

Khal Teth felt the thought try to growl its way out of his throat but stifled the impulse. Instead, he swatted the gnats who swarmed toward him.

As the twenty-three guards slumped unconscious to the floor, he dropped the Shabett illusion and stepped across their bodies, reveling in the barbarian appearance that The Ripper had adopted. He found his reaction strange, considering the disdain for physical prowess that the

Dhaldric race had long maintained. But because this fit body seemed to sharpen his mental powers, looking like a barbarian worked for him.

With a massive psionic sending, he amplified the fear that the explosion and the alarms had triggered in the occupants of the level he was on, sending them scurrying into whatever corners or cubbyholes they could find. Anything to get away from Khal Teth.

So intense was his concentration that he could feel the presence of four members of the High Council that Parsus had summoned to his chambers, despite their attempts to jointly mask their minds from his. His mind touched that of Parsus, finding a boldness equal to his own. Unsurprising. In fact, he was counting on such arrogance. Parsus was, after all, Khal Teth's identical twin. Feeling his muscles ripple with each stride, he grinned.

He and Parsus were no longer identical. And while The Ripper had been learning Khal Teth's psionic techniques, Khal Teth had been absorbing The Ripper's combat skills and tactics. Once he dealt with Parsus and his cronies on the High Council, that new knowledge would come in very handy for the new rule Khal Teth would put into place.

Up ahead, the entry to the overlord's chamber came into view. Its nanoparticle door was closed solid, but Khal Teth could feel the eagerness in Parsus's mind. Parsus would welcome in the brother he had yet to recognize, thanks to his appearance and the more powerful mental block that Khal Teth maintained.

Yes. This was going to be well beyond sweet.

○ ● ○

Parsus had summoned the other eleven members of the Circle of Twelve so that they could all be in close enough proximity to link their minds as one. But the disarray that had resulted from the sabotage in the hovercraft bay had delayed several of the high lords. Not that it would matter.

Though impressive, The Ripper had relied on his ability to physically shock and intimidate his foes to achieve success. And Parsus had taken steps to make sure that no such tactics would be employed within this chamber.

The battle would come down to a contest of minds. Parsus wouldn't require the help of the other high lords to emerge victorious, yet it never hurt to be prudent.

Sensing The Ripper pause outside his door, Parsus issued the thought command that dissolved the portal into a thin curtain of translucent mist. And through that curtain, The Ripper stepped into his chambers.

As the barbarian passed through, Parsus issued a mental command for the door to resolidify, something that should have sliced his nemesis's body into two nearly equal halves, leaving an unsightly mess on his lovely floor and in the hallway beyond. At least he tried to issue the command. Parsus was so startled when The Ripper blocked the thought that he sprang from his chair. Across the room, The Ripper gripped one hand with the other and squeezed, producing a cracking sound from his knuckles.

The sight of that muscled body, wrapped in a savage black uniform with ivory blades strapped to each thigh, prickled the overlord's scalp. But it was the red glint in those dark orbs that robbed Parsus of breath.

"Hello, my brother," said Khal Teth. "It is good to see you, too."

○ ● ○

Khal Teth felt the other minds in the room coalesce and blocked them even as the twins stood frozen in concentration. And though Parsus's mind was powerful, Khal Teth wrapped it in crushing bonds that dropped the overlord to his knees. Then Jack's thoughts intruded on Khal Teth's with a clarity that startled him.

"You need what Parsus knows."

Even though the thought intrusion angered Khal Teth, The Ripper was right. Parsus had millennia of knowledge that his brother had not been privy to but would need in order to establish a ruling coalition.

Khal Teth walked forward, coming to a stop directly in front of where Parsus struggled to make his trembling body rise. Placing his right hand in the center of Parsus's high forehead, Khal Teth thrust his mind across that boundary, his pent-up fury letting him shrug aside his twin's futile resistance to the mental violation. For several moments, Khal Teth's mind became one with that of his brother, absorbing even the most intimate of memories.

Only when he withdrew did he realize his mistake. The melding of minds had tired him far beyond what he would have expected, enough so that the four assembled high lords and Parsus began to chip away at the mental blocks he had placed upon them. Khal Teth felt the mental strain clench the muscles in his jaw.

Had The Ripper sensed that this would happen and enticed him into this trap? That made no sense. If Khal Teth died, so would Jack, and so would his beloved Earth.

Then things got worse. Two more high lords entered the chamber, one of them High Lord Shabett, and Khal Teth felt the power of their minds join that of the group. Parsus swatted away Khal Teth's hand and struggled back to his feet, shaking with the effort.

What only moments before had offered Khal Teth a clear path to victory had turned into a mental stalemate. Yet Khal Teth felt his strength gradually returning. The others felt it, too. He could sense the fear building in their minds. Fear mixed with hope. Hope of what?

The answer entered through the portal: three more members of the High Council. Two short of forming the Circle of Twelve.

This time it was Khal Teth who felt fear knot his stomach. For The Ripper to have come all this way only to rob Khal Teth of his victory was madness. Why had he done it?

The answer that came was one he understood all too well.

○ ● ○

Jack felt Khal Teth falter. He had known the danger involved in nudging the former overlord to merge his mind with that of Parsus but, if what he planned was to have any chance of success, he had to take the risk. Now the strange intuition that had saved his life and almost gotten him killed hundreds of times was forcing him to take another.

Steeling his will, Jack took advantage of Khal Teth's outward focus and, with an effort greater than any he had yet attempted, retook control of the Altreian body. For the briefest of moments, the shock of the withdrawal of Khal Teth's mind from the fight threw the assembled high lords into confusion. And in that moment, the ivory blades of The Ripper flashed out with such violence that they almost severed Parsus's head from his body.

Amid a fountain of blood, Jack's momentum carried him into Shabett. His foot-long blades impaled her a second before Jack hurled her dying body into two other high lords, sending them tumbling over a small table on their way to the floor. As he continued toward his next victims, one of their minds found his, latching on with such strength that it stalled his attack.

Jack grunted with the effort of raising a mental block, drew his pulse blaster, and fired, burning a hole through the middle of the attacking female's head. As she slumped to the floor, Jack stepped across the body, ignoring its death spasms. Blood soaked and dripping, he stood before the cowering survivors of the High Council as they huddled together like frightened children.

"Listen carefully," Jack said, his voice low and calm. "If anyone tries something that makes me angry, I will cut you into pieces your friends and family won't recognize. Any questions?"

There weren't.

Just then, Jack felt the power of the Twice Bound funnel into his mind. As the first boatload of his allies entered psionic range, their added power extended his range, bringing about a reinforcing cascade that made his head throb. As he studied the terrified faces of the surviving high lords, letting them feel the awesome power of his mind, a slow grin creased the corners of his mouth.

Better late than never.

Then, with a mental pulse that radiated outward in all directions, Jack freed every non–Twice Bound mind in the Parthian.

CHAPTER 42

Thirty-six hours after the disappearance of the Smythes, Prokorov watched the live streams of the countdown to activation of the Frankfurt wormhole gateway on the big screens inside the FSS military-operations center. Unlike the dog-and-pony show that accompanied the activation of the Stephenson Gateway eight years ago, there were no reporters, no military, and no onlookers allowed inside the cavern. Everyone had been cleared out, with the exception of the scientific and technical staff who would handle the banks of switches that would manage gateway activation and shutdown.

Today's action was barely newsworthy. The goal would be to briefly activate the gateway in the general vicinity of the same Kasari staging planet that the Stephenson Gateway had linked with, broadcasting a multimedia message explaining and apologizing for the disaster of first contact. The message would also provide the coordinates and codes to enable the Kasari to establish a link from their gateway to Earth's, should the aliens decide to grant the human race another chance. Since the Kasari would certainly disallow any direct connection to their gateway, the entreaty was the best that humanity could hope for during this attempt at second contact.

The unanchored wormhole would, of course, waggle through space within a few million miles of its target, but since humanity merely wanted to broadcast a message through it, that shouldn't matter.

On another screen, Dr. Guo, the lead scientist for the Friendship Gate, and Dr. Lana Fitzpatrick, the U.S. undersecretary for science and energy, would observe the proceedings from the secret North Korean site. If all went well, their phase of the operation would soon be given the green light. If not . . .

Prokorov inhaled deeply and shoved the negative thought aside. One foot in front of the other, one step at a time. That's all most people could do. Others, like him, learned to work in parallel.

The voice on the speaker began counting down from one minute. The activity along the line of switchboard technicians increased as glittering LEDs illuminated and hands moved to plug the matching colored cords into the illuminated sockets. A low hum rose as the stasis field generator powered up, followed by the gateway itself.

At ten seconds out, all activity stopped.

Only a single technician held a red cable, his hand trembling as he waited to insert it into the last socket.

Three.

Two.

One.

The hand moved. The plug penetrated the socket. The gateway churned and shimmered into swirling beauty.

A view of an alien star field spun and then shifted as the message broadcast began.

"What . . . ?" The panic in Dr. Guo's voice brought Prokorov to peak alertness.

The star field beyond the gateway shifted again, looking somehow off-center within the gateway. Then Prokorov saw that it wasn't the gateway that was the problem—the stasis field that sealed it from the void of outer space seemed to be shimmering.

"Shut it down!" Guo yelled.

But before his words could register with the technicians, the stasis field failed, unleashing a hurricane as the cavern decompressed, sucking scientists, technicians, and equipment through the gateway. While Prokorov stared at the display in shock, the destruction escalated as machinery was hurled into surrounding gear, knocked loose to be thrust into space. Then, as suddenly as it began, every audiovisual stream from within the Frankfurt Gateway cavern simply ceased.

A dull knife of dread speared Prokorov in the chest as he stared at the blank screens that tiled the far wall.

He barely heard the words of the scientist whose distraught face filled the upper left window on the big screen. Dr. Lana Fitzpatrick put her face in her hands in the adjacent display. Prokorov knew with certainty what this meant.

The Frankfurt Gateway was gone. And it had taken a good chunk of the world's top scientists and technicians along with it.

:CHAPTER 43

Senator Freddy Hagerman jogged along the Washington Mall, his breath puffing out in small clouds. Today he felt an unusual hitch in his stride that meant he might need to get his running prosthesis tuned up. For now, though, he intended to ignore it.

Up ahead on his left, the white spire of the Washington Monument rose up to touch the sky, a symbol of the American greatness that President Benton and his cronies had ceded to the UFNS. Fortunately, there were still those willing to stand up and fight for liberty, even though that fight carried a cost. And the cost of last week's battle outside Frankfurt had been horrible to behold.

At the time, Freddy had thought that the Smythes had been unsuccessful in their attempts to destroy the Frankfurt wormhole gateway, a failure that the worldwide press had loudly heralded. But less than two days later, when the UFNS had activated the gateway, the brilliance of the Smythe plan had become clear for all to see. They had somehow sabotaged the gateway so that it would destroy itself. Their actions had elevated the rewards being offered for information leading to the capture or death of the Smythes to more than $1 billion each.

In a move to protect its peaceful political activities, the Safe Earth movement had disavowed any association with the Smythes and their outlawed Safe Earth resistance. Freddy and the other leaders of the Safe Earth movement had firmly denounced the robotic attack that had killed so many German civilians. Despite these efforts, Freddy knew that only the SEM's millions of nonviolent members worldwide prevented the UFNS and its member nations from outlawing that organization as well. There may come a time when that would happen, but not today.

Freddy harbored no illusions that the Smythe victory would stop Prokorov and the rest of the UFNS from again trying to welcome the Kasari Collective to Earth, but that was a battle for another day. Right now, he planned on enjoying the rest of his run among the glorious monuments to past greatness.

CHAPTER 44

Jennifer Smythe sat in the conference room created from one of the configurable quarters amidships, leaning back in her chair as she watched the others make their way in. Captain Raul, as General Dgarra had insisted that everyone call him, took his place at the head of the table that was capable of seating six. This ship had a crew of four, assuming she could come to grips with VJ being one of them. But the others had accepted VJ's status as a virtual person, so Jennifer would just have to get over her mental prejudice.

As if she had read Jennifer's thoughts, VJ took the seat directly opposite her, wearing an utterly inappropriate copy of the uniform General Dgarra had created for Jennifer. Not her aide-de-camp uniform, but the slinky black-and-purple number that Jennifer had worn the day she marched into the ArvaiKheer Amphitheater at the head of Dgarra's ten thousand warriors. Refusing to be baited, Jennifer decided to ignore the outfit.

Dgarra seated himself to Jennifer's left, at the end of the table opposite Raul. Although the military hierarchy that Dgarra expected clearly still made Raul uncomfortable, he was doing his best to act the role of ship's captain. As such, he opened the meeting for which Dgarra had created the agenda.

He cleared his throat. "Uh-hmm. This being our first official meeting of the crew, I would like to place a few things into the ship's log as a matter of record."

Ship's log? Jennifer thought. *Good lord. Was she the only one at this table who recognized how cheesy that sounded?*

But when she glanced at the others, she decided that the answer to her question was yes, so she kept her comment to herself.

"General Dgarra," Raul continued, "has requested that items be put before the crew for agreement. Therefore, I'll turn the proceedings over to him."

Dgarra picked up as if he had just been introduced to a group of his subordinate commanders. He leaned forward, his large arms braced on the table.

"First of all, it has come to my attention that this starship is named after an Earth project that was responsible for welcoming the Kasari. Therefore, I propose changing its name to something more appropriate."

Jennifer realized that although she hadn't consciously thought about it, she had never liked the name. She nodded.

Hearing no objections, Dgarra continued. "VJ has given me a suggestion that I find most appealing. The tallest of the Koranthian Mountains, in fact the tallest mountain on all of Scion, is known as Mount Meridian. Scaling its peak is the first of the Koranthian rites of passage out of adolescence and into adulthood. Therefore, I propose that this ship be renamed the *Meridian Ascent*."

"I second the motion," said VJ, clearly pleased.

Despite her irritation at VJ's phrasing, Jennifer had to admit that the *Meridian Ascent* had a pleasant ring to it.

"I like it," she said. "What about you, Captain?"

Raul pursed his lips, most likely to suppress a grin at her calling him captain rather than because he was mulling the name over.

"Agreed," he said.

As if his motion had been a foregone conclusion, Dgarra nodded and continued, his face taking on a grim cast.

"Next, we must turn our attention to the tasks that lie before us."

Jennifer tensed. She braced herself for the topic they had all rigorously avoided in the days since they had fled Scion and made the wormhole transit that had taken them twenty-three light-years away. That had been the first trip she ever made through a wormhole that hadn't felt like being put through a blender. But they were still all wanted, dead or alive, by multiple alien empires, one of which spanned a considerable part of the galaxy.

"At the top of our list," Dgarra said, "we are short on food."

VJ lost focus on behaving human and floated up into the air, drawing all eyes to her eager face.

"I believe I have a solution to that problem," she said. "I've been experimenting with the matter disrupter-synthesizer and have been able to create a number of complex proteins, including amino acids. Given time, I see no reason why I couldn't build a version of the MDS capable of duplicating foods such as the Scion eels that we have on ice."

"I can't wait to taste that," said Raul, bringing a chuckle to Jennifer's lips.

"Regardless," said Dgarra, restoring a serious tone to the meeting, "I propose that we return to Scion."

"I don't like that idea," said Raul. "Our recent endeavors there didn't turn out so well, and it's not like your own people would welcome you back into the fold. We're public enemies one, two, and three."

"Don't forget about me," VJ said, scowling down at them.

Jennifer took a deep breath, not liking that she was going against Dgarra. "Personally, I would like to return to Earth. Maybe we can make a difference there that we weren't able to do on Scion."

"The fact that we weren't successful doesn't mean that we can't be," said Dgarra. "We just need to come up with a better plan."

Jennifer smiled, placed her small hand atop his, and squeezed. "What do you say if we let VJ try to solve our food dilemma while we think this over? In the meantime, if you can come up with a plan that gives us a reasonable chance of changing things on Scion, we'll give it full consideration."

Dgarra looked at her, and she saw his face soften ever so slightly. "Fair enough."

Raul leaned forward, his face taking on a serious expression.

"Since that's settled, I want to make a few comments. We've all been through a lot since this starship left Earth to come to the Scion system. In different ways, the *Meridian Ascent* has become our new world. General Dgarra has been betrayed and denied his rightful role as Koranthian emperor. Jennifer and I have both lost our home world because it may have been either destroyed or assimilated by the Kasari. But even if Earth survived intact, due to a time dilation induced on our trip here, more than eight years have passed since we departed. And we have been changed by the events that have unfolded."

Raul shifted his gaze to VJ, who had settled back into her chair.

"I also want to acknowledge the valuable contributions that VJ has made. Without her, I would not have been able to survive to rescue the rest of you."

Jennifer saw VJ blink and smile, but she said nothing.

"So," Raul continued, "the *Meridian Ascent* has not only become our home; we have become her crew. As captain, I believe each of you forms a natural fit for a crew position. Jennifer, you will be my first officer, and, given your unique abilities, you will also serve as my communications officer."

Jennifer knew that it was foolish to feel a flush of pride that Raul had selected her as his second in command, but she did. Her mind detected no hint of disapproval from Dgarra, and VJ made no objection.

"General Dgarra will fill the role of tactical officer and be third in the chain of command. VJ will be my science officer."

Raul leaned back. "I want to thank General Dgarra, who advised me strongly in this matter. For this to work, I need all of you to buy in on major decisions. If there is disagreement, then I will make the call, but only after having listened to all of your arguments. If anyone has an objection to what I've just laid on the table, now is the time to let me know about it."

Jennifer looked at the others gathered around the table. There were no objections.

"Okay, then," said Raul, "our first decision will set our course, be it for Scion or for Earth. General Dgarra will inform me when he is ready to make his argument for Scion. Until then, this meeting is adjourned."

They rose from the table, with Jennifer and Dgarra the last to exit the room.

As an electric thrill worked its way up her arm, she noticed that he still held on to her hand.

:CHAPTER 45

Heather strolled outside the holographic illusion of the cloaking field, well beyond the inner bubble of protection that the stasis field generators provided for their New Zealand facility, enjoying the feel of the November sunshine on her face. She stopped to listen to the gurgle of the fish-filled stream that wound its way through the flowering meadow. Throughout the long winter months of June, July, and August, she'd spent almost all her time belowground, expanding their facility and designing the tech they'd used to attack the Frankfurt Gateway. Now, with Mark at her side holding her hand, she almost remembered what it felt like to be ordinary.

Ordinary had gone out the window on that Los Alamos summer day when she, Mark, and Jennifer had stumbled upon the crashed Altreian starship and had been remade. The day had been very much like this one. A sudden breeze swept down from the beautiful, snow-capped peaks, bathing her in a river of cold air that raised goose bumps on her arms. Where had that youthful innocence gone?

"Memories?" asked Mark, squeezing her hand.

"Memories," she confirmed.

"We stopped it, you know."

His words pulled another vivid memory from her mind. Although it had been nearly midday in Germany when Prokorov's scientists had activated the gateway, it had been nighttime in New Zealand. Robby and Eos, working alongside Jamal and Eileen, had hacked their way into the audiovisual feeds from the Frankfurt cavern, and the entire population of the Smythes' Tasman Mining Corporation compound had gathered to watch the related visuals on the big screens in the operations center.

When the gateway had stabilized, the stasis field generator took longer to fail than Heather had deduced. The delay had curled knuckles of dread around her throat. When the generator finally did die, unleashing a vortex of annihilation within the Frankfurt Gateway cavern, the onlookers cheered, including Heather. But their cheering was short-lived, and Heather's elation had quickly turned into disgust as she watched more people being slaughtered by her actions. As was the case with almost everything else she had done, she had known this would happen. And no matter how she had tried to spin the story, to convince herself that innocents died in every war, she still felt sick.

The vision cleared, and her eyes met Mark's.

"Did we?" she asked. "Or are we just spitting into the wind? Somehow everything we touch turns to blood. And then, before we know it, the wheel turns and brings us right back to the same mess we were trying to prevent."

Mark draped his right arm around her shoulder, and she leaned into him, feeling his surprising warmth. Mark gently lifted her chin and kissed her. When it ended, the feel of his lips lingered on hers. Heather looked into his eyes and could detect only happiness.

"Right now is all we've got," he said.

She gazed up at him, so handsome with the breeze ruffling his brown hair, and remembered that there were some things she still liked about the present. She liked looking at him, liked the way he looked at her, loved the way he held her. She had her family here, and Mark's family. She had Janet, Robby, and Yachay, the Quechua woman who had delivered Robby and been his lifelong nanny and protector. Even though Janet clearly longed for Jack, she still had Robby. And the banter between Jamal and Eileen was nothing short of hilarious. Even the sometimes-morose Dr. Denise Jennings was a nice person to be around.

Unfortunately, this peaceful isolation wouldn't last. They had been fortunate that nobody had yet violated the corporate "No Trespassing" signs, locked gates, and remotely monitored electric fencing that surrounded the 172 square miles of their remote Tasman Mining Corporation property.

But as she looked into those deep-brown eyes that showed no trace of loathing, she breathed in the crisp spring air, letting it cleanse her cluttered mind. Lowering herself into the soft grass, Heather tugged Mark down with her.

"Then we better make the most of it."

CHAPTER 46

Silhouetted by Altreia's magenta orb, The Ripper, wearing the black carbon nano-fiber uniform that had become his standard, stood at the top of the dais that rose from the center of the Parthian's Hall of Lords, with Captain Moros at his side. A long line of Altreians, both Khyre and Dhaldric, snaked up the dais to become Twice Bound. Since the decision was voluntary, many in the Parthian did not elect to become Twice Bound, but those who did numbered in the thousands.

Through Jack's eyes, Khal Teth watched the ceremony, which had become a nightly occurrence, and marveled. Like a house that had its foundation ripped from beneath it, the Altreian government had collapsed upon itself. The coup threatened to spawn a civil war, but since the Altreian fleet's rank and file were mostly of the Khyre race, the would-be Dhaldric rebels found themselves vastly overmatched. Thus, most of the Dhaldric were falling all over themselves to join the Twice Bound rather than face the same fate The Ripper had doled out to Parsus.

As much as Khal Teth needed The Ripper to consolidate his hold on the government, the power that the Twice Bound had granted him now presented a serious problem. Without Jack's consent, Khal Teth could not regain control of his body. And unless he did something about that before Jack got too comfortable in his new role as overlord, Khal Teth's situation might very well become permanent.

That was why, at the end of tonight's bonding ceremony, he would complete the bargain he had made with Jack and send his mind back to his Earthly body. Even that involved risk. For the process to work, Khal Teth would have to wholly accept the bonds to the Twice Bound in the same way that Jack had accepted them, making them his own. The only reason the ex-overlord had waited this long was his need to learn precisely how Jack was doing so, ensuring a seamless transition of minds.

For a time, Khal Teth would have to become The Ripper. He was certain he could deceive all but one of the Twice Bound. Captain Moros would have to be killed, but he would die defending The Ripper from a rebel assassination attempt. Then the Twice Bound would build a statue of Moros inside the Parthian, and Khal Teth's deception would be complete.

Khal Teth felt a warm glow of anticipation fill him. Yes, it was high time to send The Ripper back to his lovely wife and young son.

○ ● ○

The ceremony lasted almost a quarter of the night. So many Altreians wanted to share the bond that Jack could never get to them all. His psionic range now extended throughout Quol, as if the Twice Bound formed some sort of psychic circuit, granting him more power than even Khal Teth's brain could safely channel.

Dismissing Captain Moros, Jack had just reentered his chambers when Khal Teth planted the vision in his mind that swept him out of this reality and into Janet's arms. He felt her body pressed against him as her soft lips met his, felt the heat rise up to consume him.

Then the scene shifted. He stood across from Robby on a rubber mat, both wearing loose-fitting white karate uniforms. When Jack had moved into an attack, Robby executed a perfect counter, sweeping Jack's legs from beneath him and throwing him onto his back hard enough to pull a grunt from his lips. When Jack had rolled back to his feet, he saw a look of pure joy shining in Robby's young face. And Jack felt that same joy spread to him.

The vision faded, and Jack found himself standing at the transparent outer wall of his chambers, staring out into the alien night. Gone was Janet's heat. Gone was Robby's warmth. He was alone. He swallowed, unable to make these eyes shed a tear.

He knew the vision's purpose. It was time to decide. Stay here and fulfill his commitment to the Twice Bound, or reenter the chrysalis cylinder and allow Khal Teth to return Jack's mind to his original body beneath the Kalasasaya Temple.

Surely he had done enough. He'd given the Twice Bound a chance at freedom. Turning them over to Khal Teth wouldn't break the bonds. And Khal Teth would find the power provided by the Twice Bound too addicting to sacrifice. That would impose limitations on Khal Teth's abuse of power, lest the Twice Bound release their bonds. Over time, Moros would recognize the change but would probably come to believe that it was caused by The Ripper's ascension to overlord.

Jack repeated the thought again and again, all the way to the chamber where the chrysalis cylinder awaited.

The nanoparticle door dissolved at his mental instruction, and he stepped into the room that had but a single chrysalis cylinder, the one into which Parsus had entered the specialized command sequence that banished Khal Teth's mind from his body, imprisoning it in the interdimensional void where he could sense multiple futures, but feel nothing.

Khal Teth had found partial release from that by discovering that when a human lingered on the life-death boundary, he could form a mental bond and deliver the adrenaline kick that would push him or her back to life. The feat only worked if the host agreed to the bond and only if that person wasn't beyond the possibility of natural recovery. Jack was intimately familiar with the symbiotic relationship.

As he stood beside the horizontally mounted chrysalis cylinder, staring down, the worry about the fate of Captain Moros and the Twice Bound who had placed their faith in him returned with a vengeance. His intuition told him . . . something felt wrong.

And there was another problem with returning to his Earthly body. Could he trust Khal Teth not to send the planet killer should the UFNS welcome the Kasari Collective through a stable wormhole gateway?

Jack cursed himself, gritted his teeth, and handed control of this body to Khal Teth.

○ ● ○

Khal Teth gazed down at the hated chrysalis cylinder that had imprisoned him for all those thousands of cycles and smiled. Finally, he had arrived at the endgame. Only one sequence of moves remained to be played, a progression that would set him free from this most disturbing of humans—the one host whom Khal Teth had been unable to break to his will.

Khal Teth reached into the memories he had stolen from Parsus and retrieved the code sequence that would cancel the cylinder's original program, the one that had separated Khal Teth's mind from his body and cast it into an interdimensional prison. For the briefest of moments, a wave of vertigo assaulted him, but he gritted his teeth and blinked it away. Then Khal Teth climbed into the cylinder.

He lay back and entered the command that would close and activate the cylinder. As the lid slid shut, a familiar thrum pulsed through his mind. He felt the same ripping sensation he had experienced millennia ago. He searched for the presence that was Jack Gregory and, when he failed to sense the human's mind, experienced a thrill that he would savor until the end of time. Having his mind linked to the human had been an exciting ride, but he was happy to let go. Finally, he was free to fulfill his ultimate destiny.

But as Khal Teth tried to lift his hand to reopen the cylinder, a sense of wrongness engulfed him. He could not feel his arms or legs. He could not feel his body at all. A wave of panic flooded his mind, and as that mind struggled to understand what was happening, he saw multiple futures stretch out before him. Along one of these blood-soaked paths, he strode Earth, once again the rider in another human's body, hunting The Ripper's wife and son.

No!

This could not be happening to him.

Not again.

Khal Teth tried to scream, but no sound issued forth from the mouth he could no longer feel.

Desperately attempting to calm himself, Khal Teth searched for answers. He still had his memories. This time they had not been stripped from him before his mind was cast from his body. But how had this happened? He had entered the codes that should have canceled the chrysalis cylinder's original imprisonment program. Had he not? He remembered reaching for the control pad. But then the wave of dizziness had taken him and he had climbed into the cylinder.

As he examined that memory, he recalled another presence there with him in that moment, distracting him.

The Ripper!

A fresh wave of despair filled Khal Teth's mind as he tried again to feel something—anything but betrayal. This was not the end. Not for him.

Khal Teth felt his hatred coalesce into the one thing that could sustain him. As he had done before, Khal Teth would find a way back. And when he did, The Ripper would pay for this betrayal.

:EPILOGUE

With his arms folded over his powerful chest, Jack Gregory, in Khal Teth's black-uniformed body, stood at the transparent wall in the overlord's chambers, an ivory blade strapped to each thigh. Far beyond that wall, the magnificent magenta orb of Altreia hung on the horizon, dark storms swirling across the brown dwarf star's surface. Higher in the twilight sky, bright stars bejeweled the Krell Nebula's orange lace. A gorgeous sky to be sure; it just wasn't his sky. Somewhere out there, Earth hurtled around its sun, carrying the woman and child he loved. The thought filled Jack with an unbearable longing.

He had tricked Khal Teth into activating the chrysalis cylinder without canceling its prior programming. His plan had worked, but at a hellish cost—it had sent Khal Teth back to his mind prison but had also trapped Jack here.

Technically, Jack wasn't stuck here. All he had to do was walk back to that room, climb into the chrysalis cylinder, and enter the code sequence that would synchronize it with the cylinder on the Altreian research vessel buried beneath the Kalasasaya Temple. Then he would wake up in his own body and return to Janet and Robby.

But if he did that, the Twice Bound would once again find themselves at the mercy of their Dhaldric masters, and the old order would return under a new overlord. Painfully, Jack had made his choice. Now he would have to make the best of it.

Unfortunately, another complication plagued him. Although the chrysalis cylinder had been programmed to block Khal Teth's mind from returning to his body, the cylinder held no such power once Jack climbed out. Even now he could feel the tendrils of Khal Teth's mind seeking a way past the mental blocks that Jack had erected to keep the Altreian from returning. If not for the power of the Twice Bound, Jack was certain those blocks would have already failed.

Jack turned and made his way to the elaborate throne that faced away from the star field. He sat down, took a deep breath, and prepared himself for those who would soon enter this audience chamber seeking to manipulate their new overlord for personal benefit.

He absolutely hated politics. But just maybe, if he worked at it hard enough, Jack would find a way to build a government that was stable and trustworthy enough for him to go home.

In the meantime, he would have to live with a mental itch that he just couldn't scratch.

:ACKNOWLEDGMENTS

I would like to thank Alan Werner for the hours he spent working with me on the story. Thank you to my editor, Clarence Haynes, for his wonderful help in fine-tuning the end product, along with the outstanding editorial and production staff at 47North. I also want to thank my agent, Paul Lucas, for the work he has done to bring my novels to a wider audience. Finally, my biggest thanks go to my lovely wife, Carol, for supporting me and for being my sounding board throughout the writing of all of my novels.

:ABOUT THE AUTHOR

Richard Phillips was born in Roswell, New Mexico, in 1956. He graduated from the United States Military Academy at West Point in 1979 and qualified as an Army Ranger, going on to serve as an officer in the U.S. Army. He earned a master's degree in physics from the Naval Postgraduate School in 1989, completing his thesis work at Los Alamos National Laboratory. After working as a research associate at Lawrence Livermore National Laboratory, he returned to the army to complete his tour of duty. Today he lives with his wife, Carol, in Phoenix, where he writes science-fiction thrillers—including the Rho Agenda series (*The Second Ship*, *Immune*, and *Wormhole*), the Rho Agenda Inception series (*Once Dead*, *Dead Wrong*, and *Dead Shift*), and the Rho Agenda Assimilation series (*The Kasari Nexus*, *The Altreian Enigma*, and *The Meridian Ascent*).

6924